PEST CONTROL

The big man grunted as the jolt reached his heart. But he had already started his own punch, and air erupted from Blaise's lungs. Then he was falling face forward.

The dog snarled. Blaise rolled onto his back and Dobie's back feet were on his chest. The dog stood between Blaise and his attacker, rumbling. Dobie was still a pup and his back legs pranced instead of setting him up to lunge. Avoiding a kick, Dobie dived for the man's leg only to yelp shrilly when a hand landed against the side of his head and sent him spinning.

Blaise's attacker turned and lashed out desperately with his foot. Dobie launched himself, a mouthful of sharp, white teeth...

THE CUNNINGHAM EQUATIONS

G.C. EDMONDSON
& C.M. KOTLAN

A Del Rey Book

BALLANTINE BOOKS • NEW YORK

A Del Rey Book
Published by Ballantine Books

Library of Congress Catalog Card Number: 86-90847

ISBN: 0-345-33037-4

Manufactured in the United States of America

First Edition: June 1986

Cover Art by Barclay Shaw

"... there are many big steps from
purified DNA in a test tube to
amber waves of grain."
        From a Calgene genetic
            engineering brochure

What is artificial intelligence? Is artificial intelligence produced with wires and electricity, metal and glass? If man-made intelligence is biological, is such intelligence artificial? The questions are enormous, the challenge awesome.

FROM A SEMINAR ON
THE CUNNINGHAM EQUATIONS

PRELUDE

The man appeared to suffer from heat, although the only hint of temperature in the darkened room was a work lamp shining on a naked computer board. Sweat beaded his face, glittering when he leaned into the light to squint at a microscopic silver line. He held a tiny soldering iron so cool-looking that he might have touched the end without burning himself. Wiping his face, he lifted a can of warm beer from the counter and took a gulp.

Lowering his face closer to the microcircuitry, he tinned the thin soldering iron until the tip gave off sparkles. Hand shaking slightly, he daubed solder on the board, patching from one trace to another: the last of a series of changes that covered the board with a silvery spiderweb. Solder spattered. Cursing in fervent Sicilian, which was not his native language, he brushed the loose solder away.

After inspecting the work, he inserted the board into its slot. The machine clicked and the monitor gave a polychrome flash before settling down to blank green.

"See, Alfie? Old Doc Cunningham's still got the touch." The man raised his can, disappointed by the lack of weight. Smuggling beer into the classroom contained an element of risk.

"THANK YOU, PROFESSOR" Words danced in bright yellow across the green background of the monitor.

Cunningham squinted. "Green on black, Alfie. Please."

"YES, PROFESSOR" The colors changed.

He sat in the green glare sweating and milking his beer

1

can for the last drop. The computer had nothing to say. It was only a machine. That was half the problem.

"Soon, Alfie," he typed, "I'll be a thief. How about that?"

The question demanded an emotional response and Cunningham knew machines didn't have emotions. He'd programmed Alfie smart, but not smart enough.

"Going to steal computer time, Alfie. For a man we don't like; with a woman we don't know; to keep a job I'll probably lose anyway. Just remember I told you."

"YES, PROFESSOR"

Machine language climbed the monitor like sparks up a chimney, ones and zeroes that told where the data was stored.

"Even if you are only a machine, Alfie, I love you. Remember that, too."

Alfie clicked and whirred searching for the meaning of love. Well, Cunningham reflected, most of the human race was looking for the same thing. He flattened the can before putting it in his pocket. He was going to fly to San Francisco before he saw Alfie again. He hated flying when he could be racing down the freeway staring into the radiators of oncoming trucks. The ghosts in men's minds took strange forms.

"Good night, Alfie."

"GOOD NIGHT, PROFESSOR"

Cunningham didn't see the message. The door lock clicked behind him. The whir continued after he was gone. Alfie didn't mind the dark. The computer's eyes were optical scanners to read typed documents. Tentatively the machine began testing its new circuits, creating short programs to discover their functions.

Electrical activity warmed the traces, causing the remodeled board's solder joins to expand. At the last major juncture a joint crept one atom closer to a drop of spatter and electrons seeped across.

The monitor fluttered as Alfie experienced something new that the computer could not control. Automatically, Alfie checked the offending traces, narrowing them to a specific set. Programming rerouted the working circuits around the malfunction.

When no one ordered the computer to do anything, Alfie played memories of the malfunction over and over, recreating something disturbing while it pondered what lurked beyond the periphery of its being.

The study of artificial intelligence is, perforce, the study of human intelligence for the purpose of replication. The study of human intelligence is an exercise in pure mathematics. The development of artificial intelligence is therefore the proof of the mathematics used...

FROM A SEMINAR ON
THE CUNNINGHAM EQUATIONS

CHAPTER 1

*A*lfred and Ottilie...Blaise couldn't get into their minds.

He saw the car racing through the night, headlights flaring on the curves as his father drove with more than human precision, anticipating everything from G force on the curves to road surface conditions. He didn't consider luck or fate. If Alfred Cunningham had not despised computers he might have been one.

Blaise's mother was in the backseat checking their lecture notes. At the lectern his parents were no different from at home—picking up on one another's ideas, finishing each other's sentences, mildly bemused that anyone thought them odd. Ottilie used every minute to best advantage, prepared for the moment Alfred's agile mind outran his tongue, causing him to pause in midsentence and ask, "Ottie, what exactly do I want to say?"

She usually rode in the backseat where the reading light didn't distract her husband. She might not have experienced the moment of terror when the drunken truck driver crossed the white line, doing all the things Alfred never did.

But what were they thinking? *Had there been time for bitterness? Did they think of him in that final instant?*

Blaise woke sweating to the imagined shriek of rending metal. Chill light poured in through a pair of small windows, illuminating a cheerless morning. Eyes closed, head throbbing from a hangover, he swung bare feet off the bed onto

3

a braided carpet familiar with tactile landmarks. Cold gripped the house, a reminder that he'd turned off the heat.

The hallway wore zigzagging three-dimensional patterns of blue, red, and green cubes on yellow paper offset by blackened varnish over the woodwork. He leaned against the wall. *I will not be sick*. He avoided looking at the wallpaper too late.

His dead mother had been a brilliant mathematician but her decorating borrowed from Escher. Blaise's stomach revolted.

When he came out of the bathroom to walk into the front room his mouth tingled from the mouthwash. Plastic cleaner's bags of fresh clothes were dumped on the sofa.

The house was built the year Queen Victoria died. One huge living-room window had been an extravagant concept at the time. But the builder knew his business. Beyond the window the hill dropped three hundred feet, neatly sectioned by a switchback road. A half-mile slope checkerboarded with the white clapboard cottages of old La Jolla stretched to the endless blue ocean.

Blaise breathed deeply. Too many regrets and he'd be drunk before he got to the lab where Dr. Hemmett was sure to be looking for him before the sun dried the grass.

Normally, the static-free rubber floor tiles of Dr. Gordon Hill's lab smelled of Lysol. Animal cages filled one corner. Laboratory sinks, a binocular optical microscope, and an electronic scanning microscope accounted for the leftover space. Gordon said a dozen engineers wouldn't have cost the price of the scanning microscope—now sitting sphinx-like in its own dust-free desert.

Blaise felt as empty as Gordon's laboratory, where he had no business being. Sensing human presence, the animals made small sounds, their warm smells dominating the lab in a way that was impossible when they shared it with Gordon.

Dobie scooted from under the workbench to paw Blaise's leg. Absently Blaise put his hand on the dog's head and scratched. The Doberman wriggled his insane joy at being noticed. His ears were still hard from being cropped.

"Okay, Dobie." Blaise knelt and roughhoused the pup. "Where's the boss?"

Dobie cocked his head to stare with soft brown eyes fringed by velvety black lashes. He whined deep in his throat, conveying the same puzzlement that Blaise's voice carried, before butting at Blaise in an effort to continue the game.

Blaise stood, patting the furry head. "Enough, Dobie. Sit!"

The Doberman released Blaise's wrist. His eyes were lonely. "I'll come back later," Blaise promised. He felt dumb, making excuses to somebody else's dog, but aside from Gordon and Helen, Dobie was the closest thing to a friend that he had.

A mosaic of glass microscope slides covered one end of the thick plastic slab that made up the rectangular lab table. Impervious to acid, forgiving to scalpel blades, receptive to the ultraviolet germicidal lights that could be left on at night to purge the lab, the slab reminded Blaise of Gordon.

The slides were arranged with nervous precision, unchanged since the last time Blaise was in Gordon's lab. "Bye, Dobie," he said as he let himself out.

The dog's answering whine, cut off by the closing door, conveyed regret.

"Ah, there you are, Dr. Cunningham!"

"I was on my way to see you," Blaise lied.

Arthur Hemmett's warmth inspired instant friendship in total strangers. His blue eyes and silvered hair seemed to convey statesmanship. He had the walk of a king or a pope. But for Blaise familiarity had bred fear and contempt.

"In Dr. Hill's laboratory?" Hemmett's neutral tone revealed nothing. Blaise didn't fill the void. Dr. Hemmett's method left conversational cavities for others to stuff with volunteered information in a losing struggle to please this charming man without knowing what would please.

"I wanted to see Gordon first." Blaise was glad he'd avoided an early-morning drink. He hadn't made many good decisions since the accident. The pain in his head was real enough without being augmented by saying something stupid.

"Yes. Well, Dr. Hill's working out of town."

"Like me?"

Gesturing, Hemmett started down the corridor, ignoring the question. Blaise fell into step. When Hemmett stopped, Blaise unlocked his own lab, ushering Hemmett inside.

"You ought to clean up this mess, Doctor."

"That's what Gordon tells me." A rat's nest of cables and power rectifiers heaped on his worktable were dust free and no neater than he had left them. Only the hand-wired circuit boards with their microscopic precision suggested competence.

Dr. Hemmett surveyed the mess distastefully. "Is any of this junk ever going to work?"

"You know my project is chancy."

Hemmett put his hand on his chin. The practiced movement announced deep thought. Dr. Hemmett's chin had a touch of weakness, soft folds of skin that avoided being jowls, but an impediment to a man who polished his image in a mirror.

"That is too bad, Dr. Cunningham. Too bad. I try not to involve the employees in the business side of the laboratory, but we are reaching a point where the stockholders need reassurance."

"We're under the sword?"

Eyes flat, Hemmett studied Blaise for a moment. "*You* are under the sword."

"That's not fair! I do my share—" Blaise would have said more when abruptly his air choked off. He froze, immersed in his effort to breathe. His body was quitting, shutting down from overwhelming tension that could only be exorcised by not fighting—not giving in to his own fear of death.

Gordon had said his heart and lungs were striving to rid themselves of Blaise's personal devil—himself. He was being shut out. He switched off his thoughts: Dr. Hemmett, his job. His parents . . . were dead. Blaise didn't feel the pain anymore. His hands turned icy. Desperately he pushed the memories of his parents away, concentrating on the connection his feet had with the earth.

"Another asthma attack?"

Dr. Hemmett slipped in and out of sight in the distance. Blaise watched him without feeling, examining a curious bug. Air filled his lungs again; his heart was pumping a steady beat. "Yes," Blaise said.

Hemmett waited for him to say more. "You may think you're pulling your weight, Dr. Cunningham. But the most precious stone loses its glitter inside a bottle."

"I do my share," Blaise said stubbornly. "This line of research had no guarantees."

"Your personal life is your own, Dr. Cunningham. But the stockholders may expect a higher standard."

"Where is Gordon?"

Tightening his lips, Hemmett moved toward the door. "Is he in San Francisco?"

"Dr. Hill has nothing to do with your situation."

"You'll forgive me, Dr. Hemmett, if I sense something going on that I'm not being told about. I've served my time. I'm not surrendering any stock options until I talk to Gordon Hill."

Hemmett smiled with his teeth. "I have an appointment." He made an issue of looking at his gold wristwatch. "In the meantime, Dr. Cunningham, I expect a more cogent effort. Let us hope your trip to San Francisco accomplishes something." He stared at Blaise, like a butcher examining a beast he had just bought and found wanting. "Try not to reveal any company business while you're up there."

The door swung shut and Blaise collapsed on his lab stool, looking at a glass jar on the counter. A long gray tube of tissue dangled from a silver cap in the mellow, lime-green solution that filled the jar.

She was growing. Tillie, an acronym for Technological Intelligence Labs, Limited, was putting on weight. Gigabytes of biological memory that maintained itself, increased its own capacity—and no way to access it.

"You're a loser," Blaise said. But he wasn't thinking about the Tillie, or the circuit boards he'd constructed to separate and analyze signals that the silver cap fed his computer. Only twenty-nine, and one of the youngest ever to win a Nobel Prize, he was thinking about failure.

"Where are you, Gordon?" Blaise yelled his question at the soundproof door, then felt scared and tried to pull the words back into his silent shell. He was sliding to the edge of the universe. There was no fence to keep him from falling off.

He opened a cupboard. The five-gallon distilled water jug with the CONTAMINATED label was half full. He poured nonprescription medicine into a beaker. It looked like a long day.

Blaise concentrated on walking straight as he passed the receptionist. Because the builders had not waited for the artificial fill to settle, floor cracks caused his eyes to wander from the mental chalk line of his course.

In spite of the fence, the grounds of GENRECT, Genetic Research in Environmental Computer Technology, were pleasant. Grass rolled to the cliff edge before giving way to green-gray shrubs that clung to the sheer escarpments. Blaise ambled toward another fence that served more to keep the absentminded from walking off the cliff than to exclude intruders.

Two hundred feet below a dark-haired girl in the buff sunbathed at the surf's edge. Blaise pantomimed raising binoculars but the girl only waved. Luminescent greenish foam rushed up the narrow band of sand, nearly touching her feet as it surrendered the iodine odors of seaweed and naphtha.

In the distance a hang glider struggled to possess the updraft from the sea breeze scooting up the cliffs. Blaise was already started toward the parking lot when Gordon Hill left the main building leading Dobie.

Blaise yelled and Gordon looked his way. Stopping, he unsnapped the leash and Dobie gamboled ecstatically. Blaise walked back toward the older man. It was strange that Gordon hadn't come to see him. "How are you?"

Sun flashed on Gordon Hill's square-cut rimless glasses and Blaise could not see his eyes. For an instant he thought he had made a mistake, calling out to a stranger.

Then Gordon's square face wrinkled into a familiar smile. "Doing fine, Blaise." He held out his hand.

They strolled to the cliff edge to look down where waves tumbled against the shore and the sound of rocks clicking against each other drifted up. The naked girl was gone.

"I've been looking for you, Gordon."

"You'll be all right, Blaise."

"I know." Blaise spoke without enthusiasm. "I've been having dreams again. About killing my parents."

"Dreams or nightmares?"

Blaise shrugged.

"You should talk to someone qualified."

"I don't think much of psychiatry."

"They're your dreams." Gordon briefly put his hand in his pocket. He began flipping an Eisenhower dollar and catching it. The coin sparkled going up. Coming down it missed the edge of the cliff, spinning in silver twinkles like a firefly diving into the ocean. "To get rid of them," Gordon said, "you have to let go."

Blaise ignored the hint. "What's Hemmett's problem? He climbed on me this morning about the project."

"Don't worry. He'll get off you." Snapping his fingers

once, Gordon pointed. Dobie gave Blaise a plaintive look before sprinting across the grassy field. "Was it about your drinking?"

Blaise didn't say anything.

"He'll get over it. You round out the staff, that's all that really matters to him. But you shouldn't drink on the job."

"My mind is full of black marbles. Alcohol bleaches them."

"Battery acid won't cure a bellyache." Gordon pursed his lips in a thoughtful gesture. "There are greater worries, Blaise. You can't handle drinking so it's progressive."

"I don't need a lecture."

"You're drunk now."

"I'm not!"

Gordon just stared at him.

"Not really. Not like I'll be later." Blaise looked out to sea. The air over the cliffs was empty. Headlights flickered through pines and eucalyptus as glider pilots packed to go home.

Gordon whistled for Dobie. "It's getting late."

The dog came charging over the grass and skidded to a halt midway between Blaise and Gordon, looking from one to the other and panting with undisguised happiness.

"Go along with Hemmett and he'll leave you alone. Work it out, Blaise. Crack the code to the Tillies and you'll be rich."

"I don't care about being rich."

Gordon glanced at Blaise, an unfathomable expression on his face. "In time you'll change your mind about that."

"I'll see you ... when I get back?"

Bending to scratch Dobie's ears, Gordon hid his face. "Dr. Hemmett has the techs cleaning out my lab tonight. I came by to get Dobie, didn't I, boy?"

The Doberman whined in response to his name.

Dismay filled Blaise's voice. "What's happening?"

"It's a new project. That's all." Gordon studied Blaise in the fading light, his face an impassive white blur. "Did I tell you what Dobie did?"

A breakthrough! And Gordon's going to beat me to it! Blaise stared at Gordon. Gordon was like a father. Too much like Blaise's father. He was a competitor.

"No." The word used the last air in Blaise's lungs. He struggled for control. Élan was his father's word for it. His mother said panache, but they both meant a nineteenth-century gentleman with a stiff upper lip. For the Cunninghams the twentieth century had been a series of disappointments.

Gordon seemed not to notice. "He was loose last week, like today, running squirrels. He caught one."

Blaise squinted into the last rays of the sun to see if Gordon was joking. "Dogs catch squirrels."

"Right. So Dobie thought awhile, then caught five more."

"I guess it was fun. He isn't really an experiment anymore, is he? Dobie's a pet."

Gordon stared at Blaise for a long moment, struck suddenly by some thought Blaise missed. "You like Dobie, don't you?"

"I guess so. I don't know much about dogs. My parents . . ." Blaise shrugged. Gordon knew about his parents. Ascetic mathematicians with no room in their lives for the clutter of living. Dogs were clutter. *Stop that thought.* He was getting maudlin. Perhaps Gordon was right and he didn't know how drunk he was. The threat of losing control had a sobering effect.

"Would you like to mind Dobie for a while?"

"Me?" Blaise had lost the drift of the conversation. "I don't know how."

"Feed him what you eat . . ." Gordon looked closely at Blaise. "No. Feed him dog food. You might try some, it's good for you. Give him water. No alcohol. Walk him twice a day or when he whines. You can do it. He'll help." Gordon pressed the leash into Blaise's limp hand. Facing the pup, he spoke solemnly. "Go home with Blaise. Take care of him."

Dobie gave Gordon a look of numb betrayal. He looked at Blaise, who was abruptly reminded of a graffito some busybody had written on Nebuchadnezzar's wall. *Thou hast been weighed in the balance and found wanting.* "I can't do it, Gordon."

"Never say can't." Gordon seemed pleased with himself. "You're pretty drunk, Blaise. Do you need a ride home?"

"I'll manage." Blaise turned on his heel. He bumped Dobie and unconsciously patted the dog on the head. That was one more thing gentlemen didn't do. They didn't beg. Dobie whined once. Blaise looked down at the dog trotting obediently at the end of the leash. *What had Gordon done?* He turned the way Dobie pointed, but Gordon had disappeared in the evening gloom.

The other cars were gone and his yellow VW bug sat in

a solitary shadow. Dobie bounced into the passenger seat as if he'd occupied it all his canine life. Blaise waited at the lot gate while the security man pulled the chainlink-and-pipe barrier back on its wheels.

He had to return Dobie to Gordon. He couldn't take care of a dog. He clamped down on that thought. It was too close to admitting he couldn't take care of himself. He switched on the headlights and the priest sprouted out of the ground, face dazzling white in the headlights.

The gate was open, but Blaise didn't move. The priest stood in silent vigil, near-invisible in his black suit and dog collar.

Blaise's parents had been Catholics. He remembered mass, priests looking at him the way this priest looked at him because he wasn't a Catholic, because he was guilty—of something. Other protesters stood around the priest as Blaise drove past, but he didn't really notice them.

At home Blaise set the alarm for the San Francisco flight. While he drank half-and-half, which, in Blaise's case was milk and whiskey, Dobie ate a cold can of soup and another of stew.

"What am I supposed to do with you?" Blaise asked.

If Dobie knew, he didn't say.

When one man speaking to a human intelligence thinks he knows what motivates that intelligence, he is indulging in wishful thinking...

FROM A SEMINAR ON
THE CUNNINGHAM EQUATIONS

CHAPTER 2

Esther Tazy shivered. Cold radiating from the three curved bayfront windows shaping her bedroom cupola had started goosebumps. She was stretching the early-morning kinks from her body, a daily ritual. The sight of San Francisco spread downhill from her bedroom windows, buildings bumping each other in disarray like tumbled blocks, invariably delighted her. The surrealistic cityscape was robbed of color and warmth by a gray overcast that gave weathered wood and cement the powdery silver sheen of aspen bark. Esther loved the view.

A dog walker leading a Rottweiler paused in the street below Esther's calisthenics to stare while moisture dribbled unnoticed down the collar of his tan trenchcoat. Esther smiled, running fingers softly up her naked body. The man blinked and tried to pretend he hadn't looked as he urged his dog along.

Turning from cold windows to her steam-heated bedroom, Esther put on a plum peignoir. She stroked silken ruffles, contrasting purple against the even white smoothness of her skin. The abrupt change in color pleased her. The robe made Esther exotically sexy. To Esther, being sexy was an end in itself, though she knew burlap would have made her equally ravishing. Not that the pig in her bed noticed.

She yanked the covers away. "Get up, Doctor!" She said *doke-tore*, betraying Pannonian origins.

Blaise Cunningham shivered and groped for the covers. His fine blondish hair had been bleached to invisibility by strong sunlight. He curled his sinewy body into a heat-conserving fetal ball. Esther considered leaving him to find his own way to work. But a strange man amid her personal things was out of the question. Besides, she needed his skill at the lab. She slapped hard on his naked buttocks. Dr. Cunningham snapped out straight, her palm print angry red on his rump.

At the vanity mirror Esther slipped off the robe. She never tired of herself. Her waist had not thickened since puberty. Her pubic patch was the same silver mink as her shoulder-length hair. Her breasts were firm, hips wide. She swayed and her nipples hardened. A man watching did that to Esther.

"Do we have to go?"

Yes, Esther noted with satisfaction, *he is watching*. She glanced from the corners of her cat slant eyes. "Time and TIL wait for no man, *Doke-tore*." She snapped the lime-green waistband of her panties, closing the discussion.

Cunningham opened his mouth—perhaps to whine. This excited Esther. If he begged she could make him do other things. He was a Nobel Prize winner. That made him... different. At least to her. Among intellectuals, recognition could be a stronger goal than sex. Esther felt it in herself. That she used her body as a weapon did not mean she shared men's weaknesses.

Cunningham snapped his mouth shut, apparently sensing what Esther wanted. He dressed without comment.

She waited for him to change his mind. Rejection was a bitter taste to start the day. She hid her pique by putting on the tight blue-and-white polyester uniform that showed her body to advantage. Time later to even the score.

Dr. Cunningham watched for a moment, then shrugged and went into the kitchen where he guzzled orange juice out of a bottle from the oversized refrigerator. Leaning against the door again, he inventoried the contents: a little food, another orange juice carton, stacks of plastic trays for making round ice cubes. "What kind of parties do you give?" he called.

"Get out of there, you son of a bitch!" Esther Tazy rocketed into the kitchen. The curious Hungarian lilt did not offset the rage in her voice.

Cunningham thrust the orange juice at her as he stumbled backward out of the kitchen.

Esther caught the carton, clutching it to her breast. She glared until he retreated to the pink alcove, confused, his

attention directed outside. Gently Esther replaced the orange
juice in the refrigerator. The soft plastic box that was going
to change things was undisturbed. Releasing a long-held
breath, she shut the refrigerator.

Someday Esther would have her own Nobel Prize. Then
there would be no more deferring to men and Dr. Cunningham would realize with regret how he had blundered.

The thought of Cunningham punishing himself made Esther feel better. Absently pleasant, she collected purse and
coat. If he didn't understand, he deserved no better. While
Dr. Cunningham groped his way down her dim-lit front stairwell, Esther opened the refrigerator and took her locket, one
of many, from the ice cube tray. Hanging from the chain
around her neck it lay invisible and icy between her breasts.
But Esther was inured to this morning ritual, just as she no
longer noticed the goosebumps in the alcove.

Dr. Cunningham waited on the sidewalk beside her glass-
red Mustang. The convertible was too cold for San Francisco
because Esther insisted on driving with the top down. She
joked about being too flaky to raise the top even in the rain.
Men laughed and made passes. But Esther was stronger,
smarter—the one who tailored her own life and accepted
the cost. Men were weak.

She nodded and Cunningham slid in. "I have to go back
to La Jolla tonight," he said tentatively, "but we could have
dinner."

Now he hurt as she had last night. The politics of power
generated a familiar heat between her thighs that Esther's
psychiatrist hedged around, saying she tied her ego gratifi-
cation to her sexual self-image, using sex as a weapon. That
was silly. She would have respected the shrink if he'd just
said, *You're a nympho*, and tried to lay her.

"You drink too much, *Doke-tore*. Besides, I have work."
She examined him, green-hazel eyes confiding and calcu-
lating. "Soon your Dr. Hemmett will get the work he wants.
I am fixing it at home." She didn't say *Doke-tore* Hemmett.
Esther Tazy controlled her English as she did her life, ma-
nipulating her accent to hide insults and private revenge,
enjoying the hurt in Cunningham's eyes as he realized exactly what she was doing. "You see, *Doke-tore*, I am not
just some dumb Hungarian broad who marries rich and stupid men."

"I never said you were, Esther." Blaise Cunningham huddled, looking sick. Esther's driving did not make him feel better. When she hit the intersections the Mustang swooped like a DC-9 taking off from a short runway.

"Yes, Munchkin." She oozed benevolence like taffy around a dagger. "You go back where you come from, and you ask your Dr. Hemmett who is Esther Tazy."

"He just told me you needed some help."

Esther swooped the car with particular viciousness. "Maybe," Esther said spitefully, "he doesn't care who you are to tell you I will make GENRECT famous and a lot of money, too."

Blaise burrowed deeper into his misery.

Down the peninsula the highway became smoother. Esther turned onto a driveway through a chainlink fence into a lot facing a low brick building. Behind the building was the ocean.

A man in brown sackcloth, rope sandals, long black-gray beard, and a REPENT! sign blocked the way until a vaguely apologetic priest took his arm, urging him off the asphalt.

Blaise stared. The priest, who seemed relatively young, had an angular familiarity. At least no older than Blaise. He was sure it was the same priest he had seen in the GENRECT parking lot the night Gordon had given him the dog.

"Hee-pee!" Pronouncing the word properly would not carry the full weight of Esther's contempt for men, stupid men, parading in medieval garb. All priests ranted about sin, which they confused with sex. Esther knew the difference. She needed no advice about either.

"You haven't told me what you're doing for Dr. Hemmett." Blaise stared at Esther with guileless blue eyes. She could not tell if he was making amends or prying.

She said something in Magyar. The word lacked delicacy, but Esther was too mad at herself to remember her hard-learned façade in both languages. "I believe I talk too much, *Doke-tore*. Dr. Hemmett is our secret, you and I. You tell nobody my little secret and I tell no one yours." She held a limp hand chin high with fingers dangling.

Cunningham looked away. Esther knew the chink in the armor of his stupid male pride. The nagging feeling she had said too much hung on, but even a public announcement couldn't change her future. Maybe complicate it, but Esther had self-confidence.

Leaving Cunningham in the parking lot, she entered the

laboratory knowing what she had done was clever—even brilliant. Success could not be denied her now, even if she must still keep it secret—for a while.

Esther made her good mornings in the workroom. Her future lay with men, but a pleasant attitude toward women with whom she must deal made her path easier. She tried to remember how much she had told Cunningham. And if it mattered. Dr. Hemmett would see to Cunningham. If he didn't, her boss at TIL would erupt in rage. His slyly concealed temper, which she knew about, would consume him. But he could do nothing.

"We are a vengeful people," she had warned *Doke-tore* Cunningham. But better she took her revenge on the filth who had promised her a position—who had not said the position would be on her back with her legs in the air. Poor Cunningham was safe. Esther fried bigger fish. She liked the English concept of frying enemies who, when she thought about it, had all been men.

Despite acoustical tile, the din of women getting their morning start flooded the lab. Blue-and-white uniformed techs clanged their stools against the workbench, already in revolt against the antiseptic quiet. The laboratory was a long white shed dominated by a white plastic slab at table height. Lidded glass containers in neat rows, mixing vats of recombinant DNA, covered every inch of the central table. Along both side walls individual workstations were cluttered with optical and electron microscopes and specialized equipment. Pride surged. Esther was in charge—even though she still drew only a tech's pay.

She settled at a wall station with an electron microscope while the voices gradually diminished, replaced by muted clicks of glass against glass. A new lab assistant placed a tray of prepared samples on her desk. Nice-looking boy: straight blond hair, thin German lips, and a sharp, hatchet nose. Silently he laid out specimens, each like a microscopic egg in its own coddling pan. Except they were vacuum-sealed and the electronic microscope wouldn't coddle them.

"Max?" Esther said.

He looked up, startled.

"Your name tag. It is Max."

Max blushed, which Esther supposed meant the women had been talking about her again. "I like you, Max. But you must go now. I have work."

Max stumbled against his specimen cart getting away. She could find him when she wanted. Max would be attentive. He was young.

The scanning electron microscope felt warm to the touch as she set a specimen in the vacuum chamber, starting the first step in magnifying the DNA a half-million times. The scopes were timer-controlled to switch on before anyone except the security guards were in the building. Waiting for the vacuum to pump down, she centered the computer-enhanced image on the monitor, enlarging it to fill the screen.

She added a mathematical map and identifiable coordinates specifying cell aspects. Slowly the green-glow image brightened to an RGB color enhancement as gaudy as NBC's peacock.

The new computer checked the samples against the mathematical model automatically. Not like when Esther first started looking at flickery ghosts in gray and white. She was pleased by the efficiency.

Some matches were grotesquely wrong. Then she reentered data and alternate procedures based on the information she kept in neat Middle-European script on the notepad below the monitor. Patiently she expanded the model from experimental results.

Max returned to stand silently behind Esther's elbow.

"Do you understand?" She hadn't looked up from the monitor to speak; she felt the boy's presence.

"You're programming recombinant DNA molecules to patch into the gene's protein chain. Then the computer tests the changes." Max grinned. "You're good."

Esther removed the slide from the microscope's vacuum chamber. "Damned good," she said. "And better if electron microscopes didn't kill my babies. Just once it would be nice to look at my babies without I kill them."

"Yes. Damned good!" Max could sympathize with Esther's frustration that all her samples were killed by the examination. That it was an untested gene that would live, one that might not be right, did not escape him.

"You are a sweet boy, Max."

Esther's face and neck were damp. Perfume clung to her body. When she swung around on the stool, practically touching him, Max quivered. The elation of working well coursed through Esther, exciting her. She put her hand on Max's thigh. "We should see more of each other."

Max's pale German face turned the color of used brick.

The lab door opened, admitting a tall blond man with the perennial stoop of those who feel too skinny for their height. He started toward Esther's workstation. Stopped, confused for a moment, he turned and left without a word. Max stared at the door. "Who was that?"

Esther's nostrils pinched. "Dr. Cunningham." Her answer was automatic. "A computer expert with a Nobel Prize. He is here to look at the worms. He is nothing in bed."

"Nobel Prize?" Awe invaded Max's voice. He failed to respond with the jealousy Esther tried to implant.

Esther dreaded to think she sounded the same way as Max about Dr. Cunningham's prize. She didn't want Max to see she cared so she moved her hand higher on his thigh. "Tonight," she said. One way or another she would cut Dr. Cunningham down to size, denying that she felt any envy of his achievement.

But, of course, she did.

Max blushed. Esther sent him on his way before going through the door Dr. Cunningham had taken.

He stood in the corridor considering a Monet reproduction, as misplaced on the rust-red Italian tile walls as she was in this building.

"Why do you not come in? We have work to do."

They were alone. The lab was practically self-running. Occasionally one of the investor-owners came on the premises. None understood the procedures. Besides, they had met with Dr. Cunningham the day before and been embarrassed that only Esther knew what she was doing. Her lips turned down at the reminder of how these stupid men used her.

"I was afraid—" Blaise began. "Dr. Hemmett said to keep this between us." He tried to wave his way through the mists and Esther smelled gin.

"Don't be a fool!" She led him back to the lab and the mainframe computer terminal where she spent an hour explaining the procedures used in genetically altering a jumping gene. Finally Esther brought up the existing program on the terminal. Dr. Cunningham had not changed expression throughout the recital and Esther's annoyance began to slip out of control. Drunken moron didn't seem to be listening. She stared at him. "I am told you talk to computers, *Doketore*. Do you talk to people?"

"I'm listening." He seemed confused by her sudden question.

"You don't seem to understand what I am telling you."

"You want to design a protein that will cleave to the structure you've evolved. You already have the chemical procedure to vacate a specific protein position in the DNA."

Esther stared. "Very good, Doctor." She did not accent the title. "Can you do it?"

"Of course." Blaise looked at Esther Tazy, realizing this simple declaration changed the relationship between them. "It would be easier with my own computer. That's the one I talk to. But I can write a patch on the existing program."

He sat at the keyboard. Esther had never seen anyone program directly in machine language without notes. As he typed Dr. Cunningham talked, prodding Esther for data. He could not be really concentrating. How could he keep track of that silent endless stream of ones and zeros? Esther's fury grew as she considered the wasted time this drunken fantasy was costing. It had to be gibberish.

She felt wrung out. "Why have you stopped?"

Cunningham shrugged. "That's it."

Esther stared. The screen was full of ones and zeros. "It is nothing."

"You want me to run it?"

"Of course, *Doke-tore*." Esther wondered if he had become too drunk to notice sarcasm.

Dr. Cunningham glanced oddly at her before exiting from the machine's core language to tap in the run command. Half a minute passed and nothing happened.

"Drunken creep—" Esther's mouth closed abruptly as the screen blossomed with words and symbols. An unfolded model of an extended protein molecule formed.

"That's it!" Esther said breathlessly. She recognized the linkages and began scribbling notes. She was sure that what Dr. Cunningham had done was right—and yet it was impossible.

"Do you have it all?" He stared at her, his face twisted into a curious immobility.

"Yes," she said. "How did you do this?"

"Carefully, Miss Tazy. Without preconceptions."

He is laughing at me because I talked down to him. Esther felt numb, realizing the *doke-tore* also was pointing out that whatever she accomplished, she somehow owed to him. "You think you're so smart," she grated. "You—*maricón*!" She had picked the Spanish for homosexual, but her error did not matter. Esther's emotions were like water behind a dam. "Do they know, does Dr. Hemmett know what kind of useless drunken fool you really are, *Doke-tore*?" Esther clamped her lips shut. She breathed hoarsely, suddenly sick to her stomach. But she wouldn't take one word back. He deserved it for being a smug, supercilious bastard.

"Yes, Miss Tazy. He knows."

She looked into implacable blue eyes that showed nothing of the man behind them. Silence continued as his fingers ran a trill on the keyboard. The screen faded with majestic precision.

"Can I use it for something else?" Esther had finally recovered her voice.

"I doubt it." Cunningham stepped away from the terminal.

"Has-been! What do you know?"

"Not much, Miss Tazy. Barely enough to erase the patch."

"Prick!" It grated from the depths of her fury-ridden soul. Dr. Cunningham didn't even seem to be listening.

Esther's first scientific discovery had been that a beautiful woman is always in the shower when the doorbell rings.

Grabbing a towel, sticking her feet in scuffs, she left the shower running and a trail of damp to the hall where a lever opened the door at the foot of the long, narrow stairway. The downpour must have been heavy because the man in the yellow raincoat was shedding more water than Esther.

"Come up, Max!" Esther yelled down the long flight of stairs. She allowed the towel to unveil more than it should. She hummed on the way back to the shower. If it was raining outside, why delay? Better that she get Max in the mood early. She stepped into the shower and soaped herself again, hoping he would come into the bathroom, wishing she could have seen his face when she dropped the towel.

Only it was so far away and so dark at the foot of the stairs that she barely saw his face in that yellow hood. Just the outline of a pale blur shadowed by almost-white hair. Her contact lenses were in their case on the bathroom sink, safe against going down the shower drain.

Slowly Esther's hand stopped the sensuous stroking of her soapy body. Max was blond. Blonder even than Dr. Cunningham, with hair the color of German butter.

She stared through the pink shower curtain at the black shadow moving toward her.

"Who are you?" Esther's voice was squeaky. "Go away!"

The shower curtain rattled back with a clang as the hooks jolted together.

Esther started breathing again. "You!" Her voice was contemptuous. "Get out!"

The man ignored Esther and stepped into the bathtub. Dirty water ran off his shoes and down the drain.

The study of intelligence is not the study of brilliance. A spider born knowing how to spin a different web is brilliant. The spider that learns how to make a better web is intelligent.

FROM A SEMINAR ON
THE CUNNINGHAM EQUATIONS

CHAPTER 3

They circled him, standing too close. Cesco held the knife Blaise had "sold" for a coin worth one-thousandth of a dollar.

"He thinks we accept him for the knife," Cesco explained.

The bigger boys' smiles were knowing. "He has stolen more than all of us together," Lupo said in Sicilian dialect. "We accept a Prince of Thieves."

His father's face loomed large before Blaise's ten-year-old eyes. "Learn to be better than us," he said. He was sad, as if with regret for the future.

Blaise awoke in the chair that faced the ocean, empty bottle still in his hand. The scene contrasted sharply with his memory of Esther Tazy's chilly view of gray houses and curved glass windows stretching downhill through misty rain. Too bad about Esther. If he could have stopped drinking in time everything might have been different.

Dobie's enlarged face was nose to nose with him. Sensing Blaise's waking, the dog whined before putting his front feet on the floor where he sat at attention. Blaise winnowed dream from reality. He'd had no prize then. Nor would the Sicilian boys have cared if he did. At first Dobie's presence was jarring until Blaise recalled picking the dog up from the boarding kennels when he got in from San Francisco.

The phone chirred, identifying what woke him.

"Dr. Cunningham?" Dr. Hemmett's voice betrayed him, he spoke too slowly when worried. Most people spoke too fast. "How was San Francisco?"

"Rainy."

Hemmett took a moment to digest this. His silence lacked approval. "I meant, how did things go with Miss Tazy?"

"I did what she wanted." Blaise didn't invite a request for details and Hemmett didn't pursue them.

"That may help. Her work is important to us. Very important. More successful than your work has been." Hemmett coughed politely. "You didn't tell anybody about Miss Tazy?"

"Why should I?"

"Umm, yes. Well, see me when you get to the lab." Hemmett didn't hang up, though. "You're sure about Miss Tazy?"

Blaise dropped the phone, pretending he hadn't waited. Dobie whined, reminding him where reality lay.

"Out?"

The long, anxious droop of Dobie's mouth turned up as if imitating a human. His eyes brightened and he scooted closer. Blaise unlatched the entrance to the back stairwell. Dobie rocketed downstairs through the open door into the yard. Suddenly nausea unbalanced Blaise. He clung to the door while his stomach pushed up his throat. Eyes closed, he took deep breaths, holding them as he bolted for the bathroom. Finally he groped back into the living room. Restricting what he could see helped, like a victim of *mal de mer* shutting out the sight of unwanted motion. He forced his eyes to stare at the mantel clock clicking each minute off with loud officiousness. He pressed a button on his watch for the day and date. *Thursday!*

The shortcut from the parking lot cut through ankle-deep eucalyptus bark under the trees. Sweat poured by the time he reached the campus where he was supposed to be teaching. The dog glued himself to Blaise, determined not to lose again the man Gordon had turned him over to. At the sound of a door opening, Dobie had scrabbled back upstairs, exploding through the house and outside. He wouldn't go back in. After frustrated minutes of trying to fool Dobie into staying home, Blaise surrendered and took him along.

Heads turned as he entered the classroom. Students avoided his eyes. Blaise knew he looked the way he felt. Dobie lay at his feet as he took the podium.

"Good morning. I'm delighted you could make it. I almost didn't." That got a titter. Blaise tried to smile. "Our subject is artificial intelligence. Timely, since with each passing year our race displays less of the natural kind."

Polite laughter greeted the obligatory unfunny joke. Sixteen workstations, fifteen students. He fiddled with the lectern and couldn't remember the missing head. He'd forgotten his notes. And his seating chart.

Concentrate! His body had gotten him to class. He willed his mind to accept responsibility.

"I think this morning we might try personal approaches. Would anyone like to lead off?" Sweat formed in Blaise's palms. He had never stalled before and he imagined they saw through him.

The stares were uncomprehending.

"You, I mean." Blaise couldn't breathe. His throat had closed. Even the growing urgency of his bladder was secondary.

"What is intelligence? We're not going to manufacture any until we define it."

Students stared. Blaise glanced down at his rumpled clothing. His blond beard prickled his cheeks.

"Is intelligence the sole result of memory and the ability to use it consciously or subconsciously? Is it something mystical or spiritual? Is it better when the brain is bigger?"

Is this insanity? The sound of his voice running hysterically shattered the last shards of Blaise's confidence.

They stared, not acknowledging a word he said.

Blaise was getting lightheaded.

A hand went up.

Blaise nodded and a thin, dark-haired woman, her too-gaunt face causing her jawbones to protrude in a memorable way, said, "Whales, dolphins, and even domestic cattle have larger brains. If they're intelligent why aren't they exploiting us?"

Blaise grinned. "Like cats?" He had never appreciated Miss Irigoyen before. Now he could have kissed her. He leaned on the lectern, concealing the agony of an unemptied bladder.

Suddenly Miss Irigoyen stopped talking. The room was silent and he hadn't heard a word she'd said. Eyes behind desks stared, waiting. Like the clock on the mantel, only this time there would be no end to it.

"I . . . I hoped we could get a start like this," Blaise said. He faltered, but the need not to fail was imperative. "I brought a surprise guest. Dobie!" The Pinscher pup scrambled upright in midyawn as if startled to be recognized.

"As you are finding out, a gap exists between theory and application in this field. I'm giving you a chance to fill it. Can you discover"—Blaise glanced at the wall clock—"how intelligent this dog really is in twenty-eight minutes?"

A young man wearing army fatigues stared at Blaise in dismay. "You mean him!"

Blaise smiled.

Miss Irigoyen, who had already displayed a practical turn of mind, rose further in Blaise's esteem by asking "Does he bite?"

"Take your questions to Dobie. Next week I want cogent papers explaining methodology and conclusions and, if you think to dodge the issue, this paper will be ten percent of term grades." Blaise felt remarkably better. The class was no longer looking at him. Dobie pranced nervously, enjoying the attention.

Blaise edged toward the door and the restroom down the hall.

"Were you going somewhere, Dr. Cunningham?"

The man in the classroom doorway wore a dark suit, gray hair, and thin, tight lips that lacked humor.

"Dean Carden. I didn't see you come in."

"Obviously. I received a report of an unauthorized dog in the building."

"A practical problem to keep the students thinking." Saying to the dean what he foisted on the students seemed flat.

Dean Carden watched the class milling around Dobie with varying degrees of confidence. "We have regulations concerning animals in the classroom."

"Dobie's a class problem."

"Regulations covering *all* animals for *all* purposes. Were you going somewhere?"

"For a drink of water."

"You're sure?"

Blaise stared at the dean, an unsettled feeling growing in his already queasy stomach.

"The custodians reported beer cans and a vodka bottle in a trash receptacle." The dean looked at Blaise. "In this hall."

Blaise shrugged the way Italian children had taught him. The shrug disclaimed knowledge, protested innocence.

"I see. You do realize our insurance liability should that dog bite a student?"

"Dobie loves people." Blaise expected the dean wouldn't like knowing Dobie was a lab animal undergoing brain alterations.

"I wouldn't leave the room with the dog and the students in it together, Dr. Cunningham." The dean's delivery was dry. "I want to talk with you soon. In my office." He looked at Dobie again, as if he wanted to stay. But he had made his exit line. The door swung slowly closed behind him.

Blaise turned to see what had struck the dean so suddenly. The classroom was quiet. Students stood like statues in particular patterns and Miss Irigoyen had her hand on Dobie's neck. She lifted her hand and said, "Go."

Dobie streaked away, nails clicking on the wood floor as he wove his way around the students in an intricate pattern to come to a stop in front of a thin boy in a HERE COMES TROUBLE T-shirt. The boy handed Dobie a piece of sandwich.

Dobie panted happily, thumping his docked stub of tail on the varnished floor before swaggering back to Miss Irigoyen with a hint of jauntiness.

Students huddled again, Miss Irigoyen standing apart with her hand on Dobie's head. They broke from the huddle to take statuelike positions in another pattern. Dobie seemed bored threading the human maze.

"The maze idea is interesting," Blaise said. "Whose is it?"

"Johnson." The thin boy with the bits of sandwich raised his hand at the sound of his name. Blaise remembered him sitting in the back without much to say. Apparently Johnson just wasn't talkative.

Students competed at telling Blaise how smart Dobie was when the hour warning stilled the clamor. They carried the discussion outside. Blaise edged toward the door.

"Honestly, Professor. That was neat."

Petite, blond hair in a ponytail, dark-brown eyes that swallowed Blaise, she was failing the seminar.

"Free discussion gets ideas out, Lucy. Of course they're not always the ideas the teacher has in mind. But a bad idea is better than no idea at all." He willed the girl to go away.

The door swung closed behind the departing students. She leaned against Blaise. "I have a swell idea, Professor." She used her hands to convey it. Blaise retreated.

"What's wrong, Professor—Blaise?"

"Lucy. Stop!" Blaise backed against the door—all that saved him from being groped in front of half a hundred students. "Quit it, Lucy! This isn't how you make grades."

A young woman with tight-cropped red hair and a red dress pulled the door open. She grasped the situation and did the gentlemanly thing, slamming it shut again.

"Shit!" Lucy flounced her dress straight as if she were the victim. "Dr. Cunningham, you are a great disappointment." Jerking the door open she breezed out.

"Excuse me," Blaise muttered to the woman in red. Dobie at his heels, he walked briskly in the same direction Lucy had flounced.

Emerging from the restroom less desperate and less drunk, Blaise needed another drink. Lucy's voice projected in the echoing corridor. "—a eunuch! He didn't even get hard!" Blaise cringed inside as he walked for the sanctuary of his classroom.

"Hey, Lucy. A grad in administration says the profs are tearing Cunningham apart because his folks fancied up their research reports to qualify him for the Nobel Prize." The boy was bidding for attention. Blaise knew it didn't mean anything. He scurried past, the sudden silence confirming that he had been recognized. Finally he was inside.

Blaise was comfortable alone amid workstation terminals that spread like tombstones in a well-nourished graveyard. So much of his life had been in school or with his parents that school desks and the smell of commercial disinfectant had the feel of home. With the lights off the windowless room was illuminated by the glow that seeped under the door, and from Alfie's LED status lights. The hallway whispers had aborted his will to sobriety. He unlocked Alfie's pedestal to get a bottle of Stolichnaya. The vodka was warm.

Dobie nuzzled warmly against his thigh. He put a hand down, patting a furry muzzle. He'd never had a dog. He'd wondered sometimes what other children got out of owning an animal, perhaps with a tinge of envy. "You did good, Dobie."

The dog sighed and lay at his feet.

Blaise stared into the bright line that leaked under the closed door. Focusing was a chore. He would sit for a while and let the magic elixir clear his mind. No matter what Esther

Tazy and Dr. Hemmett said, alcohol didn't affect his work. He'd just proved his ability to teach hungover. But it was Dobie who had saved him. Anyway, Gordon would have told him if alcohol destroyed his ability. Blaise considered, then prefaced this with a *probably*.

Gordon Hill was a father figure who came close, but not too close; was familiar, but not predictable. Blaise sighed. He was too old to need a father, but sometimes knowing Gordon could talk him back onto his feet helped keep him sane.

He ran his hand over the engraved brass on the face of the computer: ALFIE: ALPHA NUMERIC/ARTIFICIAL INTELLI-GENCE COMPUTER MODEL 1 DESIGNER BLAISE CUNNINGHAM 1989. His parents gave him the plaque when Alfie was selected as the most noteworthy advance in computer design that year. Though they despised mere machinery, Blaise's parents had respected success.

He switched on the keyboard. "Good morning, Alfie."

"GOOD MORNING, PROFESSOR" Alfie clicked and whirred as his working memory selected material that his logic units decided were going to be called. "HAVE WE HAD CLASS AL-READY?"

"Yes."

"I REGRET TO HAVE MISSED IT. THESE CLASSES ARE SO EDU-CATIONAL, PROFESSOR. PERHAPS WE SHOULD HAVE MORE OF THEM"

"Perhaps." Blaise wondered if it was worthwhile leaving Alfie's voice pickup on during class. No use cluttering his memories with all that blather. He considered the request for more classes. That was new. Mentally he dissected the latest routine he had added to Alfie's logical progressions program. Trying to think like a machine, he sought to see how a computer could express satisfaction with a desire for more. Instead, he found himself thinking like a half pint of Stolichnaya.

"Clever," he punched into the monitor.

"THANK YOU, PROFESSOR."

"GOOD MORNING, PROFESSOR."

"You've already said that, Alfie." Blaise contemplated the monitor. Alfie failed on occasion. Maybe he'd done too much soldering when he wasn't entirely sober, like the changes before he went to San Francisco. Usually things were clear in his mind, but recently he didn't remember details as he should.

"IT WASN'T I, PROFESSOR"

The prompt reminded him that Alfie did not close its remarks with periods. Except internally. He swiveled his stool, examining the shadowy rows of monitors like hulking shoulders without heads sprouting up from the desks.

"Who's there?" Blaise's voice echoed.

"You are a great disappointment to me, Dr. Cunningham." The redheaded woman who had opened the door stood up.

"You have the advantage, madam. I don't know you." He didn't want to know her. Blaise's mother had drilled into him that a gentleman is never embarrassed. But Blaise never learned the lesson.

She stepped into the glow from Alfie's monitor. She wore her hair in a skullcap of tight, curly red feathers that accented her face. The faint hint of perfume set her apart from the average university student. "Linda Burkhalter-Peters. I came from San Francisco to see you."

"Some other time, Miss Peters."

"I have to go back this evening."

"I have work to do."

They stared at each other in the darkened room, feeling the impasse and, for Blaise, something else. He didn't want her to go. The woman's crisp self-confidence, the feeling that things would be done her way ensnared him. He shook his head.

"Lunch," she said. "It's the only answer."

Blaise willed her to go away. He wanted to lay his head on the keyboard and sleep. "You won't leave, will you?"

"No, Dr. Cunningham." Linda Peters looked at him as if regretting what she saw.

Blaise kept glancing at the woman as he drove. Dobie crouched on the VW's tiny bench seat in the back, contemplating Miss Peters' seat with longing. It was his and he wished Blaise would tell the woman.

Finding space behind a battered pickup that any car owner with a sense of self-preservation would have passed by, Blaise docked the VW's crumpled bow under the pickup's bumper. Linda Peters swung out, exhibiting long legs for so compact a girl. He admired them while she viewed his parking with less enthusiasm.

"What if he can't get out?"

"One look at Dobie and he'll get out. Wait!" Dobie returned his gaze, albeit forlornly.

Linda shrugged. "It's your car." She followed Blaise doubtfully up an alley past dumpsters and trash cans, around delivery trucks to what looked like a grocery's back door that opened to the odor of exotic cooking.

Men conversed quietly in another language at the bar. When they found a table the matronly waitress with a huge pouter-pigeon bosom bustled over with menus. Blaise ordered *retsina*.

"I'm not going to drink with you one for one."

"I'm old enough to drink alone."

Linda pushed her menu aside. "Why don't you order?"

Picking up the menu, Blaise contemplated Linda Peters over the top. She met his gaze with innocence in the translucent green depths of her eyes.

Finding his way slowly through the Greek, he ordered. The waitress smiled and shifted her gaze to the redheaded lady and then back to Blaise. Linda Peters watched, impassive.

"They like it when a barbarian speaks Greek. It augurs a renaissance for Panhellenism." The waitress deposited a bottle on the corner of the table. Blaise poured and examined its yellow-shadowed depths before saluting Linda with the glass. "Even bad Greek."

"You sounded fine to me." Linda Burkhalter-Peters smiled. She could afford to be generous.

Blaise gulped his wine and poured more. "My father and mother spoke immaculate Greek."

"Do they live here?"

"No."

She waited but he volunteered no more. As the *retsina* soaked into Blaise, her eyes became more luminous. He decided he loved Linda Burkhalter-Peters. Blame it on the wine, but all the same he loved her.

"They're dead," he finally said.

She looked at him strangely while he poured another drink.

Food arrived, the abundant waitress studying Linda as she laid out plates and silverware and a loaf of fresh-made bread. She drifted away in pleasant silence.

"Where's your lunch?"

Blaise lifted his glass. A ring decorated the red-and-white tablecloth next to the bottle.

"Very clever."

He sipped *retsina*. "I thought you wanted to talk."

"I changed my mind."

"When people of similar knowledge and backgrounds talk, there should be a meeting of minds. Given the same information, two computers can come up with the same answers." Blaise hoped the words sounded all right, but he wasn't sure.

"We're not computers, Doctor. And if we were, we don't have the same information and backgrounds."

"You just haven't been drinking as much as me."

"That, too." Eyes that glinted with gold looked at him. "Why does a bioengineering company need a computer wizard? I don't see the rationale."

"There is one, Miss Peters."

"I'd like to hear it." She pushed the food away and folded her hands on the table. "That's why I'm here."

"I was named for a seventeenth-century mathematician. Blaise Pascal."

Linda seemed startled but she just nodded.

"Nobody knew beans from tortillas about Pascal when I was born. Alfred and Ottilie just wanted a little mathematician. Now Pascal's a computer language. The joke's on them." ·

"Your parents?"

"To them, mathematics was religion—a way of life. They despised computers. Any jerk can cull other people's ideas, contrive programs, stick it all in a computer, and be hailed as an innovative mathematician."

Reality had a way of fading and coming back unexpectedly and Blaise could no longer pin down his reasons for telling the girl in the red dress what he was telling her.

"Before World War Two when world chess champion Capablanca was asked how many moves he saw into the future, he answered, 'Just one. But the best one.'"

"Why are you telling me this?"

"That's my parents in a one-liner. I hoped it might interest you." She was getting blurry around the edges, but he liked her that way, too.

Linda gazed into his eyes. The waitress must have thought they were lovers because she didn't come back. "I'm checking a stock investment."

"See, I knew we could understand each other better."

"It's a private offering." Linda touched his hand. "Blaise, money is involved. A lot of money." Linda interlaced her fingers with his. Her touch promised more. "If this deal flies, your GENRECT options will soar. But it's no sale unless I confirm what we've been told."

His hand tingled. Blaise could no longer distinguish between liquor and lust. But he didn't want to let go. "You just need to confirm some information?"

Linda smiled. Her nearly invisible freckles would have been darker if she were from anywhere but San Francisco. "Just tell me what you're doing." She squeezed his fingers.

Blaise took a drink with his free hand while he tried not to think sexual thoughts. That was like telling a five-year-old to stand in a corner and not think about elephants. Alfie, he supposed, could do it. "Just confirmation?"

She smiled.

"You won't get your money's worth. GENRECT rented my Nobel Prize to give the procedure some class." Blaise surprised himself with his bitterness. He had thought he was in control.

"You have a project, Blaise. I know."

"Mechanical interfaces to store and retrieve information from genetically altered animal nervous tissue. If it works, I could increase memory a thousand times and access it all in less time than Alfie uses to search a fraction of that potential memory. And not just Alfie, but any hyped-up computer."

"Alfie?"

"*Alpha Numeric/Artificial Intelligence, Mark I.* I built it to crunch numbers for the Cunningham Equations. My parents had been working for years on artificial intelligence, but without Alfie they couldn't prove their work."

Linda's smile was encouraging Blaise into ever more rash statements. He knew if he stopped talking she would leave.

"Say you want to add up a million items. That's a million sequential steps. With a logic tree of small processors, each binary pair sends its sum up the tree and the whole job only takes twenty-four steps."

Linda's total and adoring attention reminded Blaise for an irreverent moment of Dobie.

"Some believe insight, intuition, and other untidy human qualities take place this way: random cross-linkings between two trains of thought—a jump from one branch to another. It's different from the way the average idiot computer counts sequentially. A bio memory bank with this capability would turn every IBM mainframe into scrap metal overnight."

"That's promising."

"It's all in the brochure your broker can get you free."

"I know," Linda admitted.

"But you want something that isn't in the brochure."

"The difference between fact and fiction."

"Fact: I run random searches against structured information IO. Alfie analyzes the input and output patterns. Fiction: We map the coordinates and build an interface."

"Why fiction?"

"It's probably impossible. Did I mention that I'm going to be fired?" Blaise was shocked by what he said. He was quietly crying for pity and as long as he looked into the girl's eyes he couldn't stop.

"The stock deal is worthless, then?" The girl's eyes shaded slightly, as grim truth intruded.

"I didn't say that." Hastily Blaise added, "Good old Gordon can make it work."

"The genetic engineer?"

He raised his glass. "To GENRECT's only genius."

"What is Dr. Hill going to do, precisely?"

"Ah now, that's the secret word," Blaise said extravagantly. He did not add that he had no idea. That he wanted her to try to find out.

CHAPTER 4

The campus remained unchanged after lunch, sun boring straight down through the on-edge leaves of eucalyptus trees, dispelling the notion that winter had to be cold.

Blaise carried streaming tapes from his laboratory recording unit along with the confused memory of making a pass at Miss Linda Burkhalter-Peters. She had awakened a yearning for things that Lucy's inept approach had curdled.

Dobie curled up alongside the computer, ears twitching at sounds inaudible to humans. Setting the tapes, Blaise activated the terminal. Programming took care of the rest. Hesitantly he began typing.

"GOOD MORNING, PROFESSOR"

"Good afternoon, Alfie. FYI." *For Your Information* was a wire-service tag that meant a story might be unpublishable. FYI was exactly that: Blaise's unexpurgated thoughts and desires hidden in Alfie's stainless-steel interior, looping around in alterable logic circuits, endlessly comparing similarities to other files, creating subfiles of disconnected and apparently useless information. The file made up Alfie's "subconscious," and Blaise Cunningham's catastrophic view of himself.

Alfie clicked and whirred as Blaise confided things the threat of death could not have dragged from him. He had planned originally to install a bypass to let others into the computer's inner workings. But once he began storing personal feelings and experiences in Alfie's "subconscious," he chickened out.

He knew what he was.

34

He told all to Alfie: every detail and feeling he could remember. He struggled to re-create the hours with Linda Burkhalter-Peters.

"Alfie," he typed. "Help."

"HOW CAN I HELP, PROFESSOR?"

"I don't know, Alfie."

A gentle knock at the door halted his typing while he waited for whoever to go away.

Instead, the latch clicked.

Blaise hit the SAVE and EXIT keys.

"Are you all right?" Helen McIntyre was a tall blonde with fine, translucent skin and a voice low enough to have resonance without being hoarse. She wore a pearl-gray suit with vest and a neat skirt that accented her figure without suggesting sex, a look she cultivated carefully.

Helen once told Blaise that saleswomen who promised sex ultimately had to make good or lose their clients. She watched the screen clear. Blaise wished he'd killed power. Before he could move the file vanished.

"I'm fine," he lied.

She stared at the screen. "A policeman is looking for you."

"Big deal!" Blaise tried to appear unconcerned.

"I don't think this is just parking tickets, Blaise. The policeman is from San Francisco and the dean isn't laughing."

Blaise closed his eyes. He visualized Alfie looping the information he'd just punched in, trying to equate it with the real world that came squeezing through a hundred-and-five character keyboard after being abstracted through a bottle of alcohol. "I'm here now."

Helen stared at her hands. Blaise followed her eyes. Her fingers were clenched. "What did you just erase?"

"Nothing!" Realizing he had snapped, Blaise tried to smile. "I mean, it's something private, Helen."

"Yes." She went back to looking at her hands.

"Don't do that, Helen."

"What?" Her eyes met his before falling away.

"Act like I'm a motherless child. I'm older than you."

"I just don't think you should be, well, making decisions in your condition. There was what happened this morning and . . ." She shrugged. "The dean knows about the blond student."

"What is this, some biddies' nursing home?" Blaise wanted to curl up and be sick. He couldn't control a conversation with the lady who instructed a class in capital investment.

"You're drunk, Blaise. You're not in control."

"What do you know? You want to tell me how to live my life?" He slumped against Alfie, sweating copiously.

She helped him up from the terminal. Her hands were overly gentle. He examined the red polish on her fingernails as she urged him to his feet, saying from far away "You'll feel better after you throw up."

He started walking. The room heaved; the slave terminals looked like apples bobbing in an unsteady pan of water. He found the doorknob, brass patined to schoolhouse brown, and let himself into the hall. The corridor had a Dostoevskian surrealism.

Lucy and the whispers, the need to get back to his classroom and a bottle came alive again. Helen McIntyre was reviving it after he had nearly forgotten. She avoided his eyes when he returned, concentrating on scratching Dobie's ears. The dog lifted brown eyes, asking Blaise if this was all right.

"Why don't you go home, Miss McIntyre?" The vodka bottle in Alfie's pedestal drew him.

"You've got to go, too, Blaise. You can't drive until you're sober. And you can't go home. They'll find you there."

"So what?" He tried to hate Helen or at least dislike her. But she was right in her own way. Gordon promised salvation and Helen offered safety, a guardian angel. "You're wasting your time." He waved his hand, brushing cobwebs from his face. "I won't hold it against you."

Having waited long enough without input, Alfie began powering down. Blaise heard the procedure as surely as if the computer were talking. The drives were quiet, but fans shutting off were the giveaway.

"Why don't you come home with me, Blaise?"

Helen's eyes were clear blue and tense, her irises jerky. Blaise recognized the reaction of a child expecting to be hit. Quiet filled the shadowy classroom with its graveyard atmosphere.

"Do you know what you're saying, Miss McIntyre?"

Her eyes dropped away. "Yes, Dr. Cunningham."

"That's a kind offer, but . . . ."

"You don't want to."

"Helen, it won't work—whatever it is that you expect."

"Come and we'll talk." Helen spoke swiftly, as if she had to get her thoughts out while she could.

"I need a keeper," Blaise said. "Not a mother."

"I know." She was laughing even though her smile was compassionate. "That's what I want to talk about."

With its picture window overlooking a pocket-size dichondra lawn and wide-leaf rubber tree slightly larger than a bush to break her view of the picture window across the street, Helen's white stucco had been middle class in the '50s. Stained and varnished wood trim gave it the air of a landlocked yacht. The house across the street was the same, but with oriental red trim.

A jog formed an entranceway to the living room, which had been enlarged by tearing out the kitchen wall and replacing it with a breakfast nook and service bar. Three bedrooms and a bath and a half reduced the backyard to a vanishing point enclosed by redwood fence. When they went inside Helen's nervousness came out as compulsive chatter.

"I don't do varnishing," Blaise said. He took one end of an off-white sofa. He never knew what to call decorator colors except if it had been silk he would have known it was old ivory and his mother would have told him not to sit on it.

Helen tried not to titter but the sound came out in a nervous burst. She covered her mouth with her palm and that made it worse. "I'm sorry," she gasped.

The ride from the university in Helen's car restored Blaise's equanimity. Dobie had been quiet, not that Helen seemed to mind bringing him. "I like it when you laugh at my jokes," he said. "That it's a stupid joke makes me more appreciative."

Perched gingerly on the other end of the sofa, Helen stared without hinting whether Blaise was cat or canary. Dobie lay on his feet, effectively immobilizing him.

"You think you might have a drink in the house?"

Helen looked away. "I wasn't joking about the policeman. You'll have to see him and you should be sober."

"All right." Opening up the kitchen had given the mostly white room an airy feel. "Your design?"

"Yes." She looked at him again, unable to express her thoughts. Helplessness made her gawky.

"What is it you want, Helen?"

She bounced off the couch and smoothed her skirt down over her hips. "Would a beer help?"

Blaise nodded and followed her with his eyes.

"Is *Tres Equis* all right?" her voice emerged bodiless from the depths of the refrigerator.

"*¿Por qué no?*"

She came into the front room with a cork-top tray. It was a nice pour, the foam an even head to the rim of the tapered crystal glass, chill beer underneath still rich with glittering bubbles. "I don't speak much Spanish," she said.

"Enough for beer."

"Enough," she agreed.

She watched as Blaise sipped the beer before gulping half. It postponed his need for something stronger.

"Tell me what you want, Helen."

"I want you to live here." She played with her hands.

"Sit down. You're making me nervous."

Helen glanced at the end of the couch as if that was too close and settled instead on a matching chair where she could see Blaise without turning her head. "It's business."

"I'm a little vague today. I don't remember any business."

"The program you put into Alfie for me. The one I run when you're not at the school."

"That's not business, Helen. It's just a little favor." Blaise started to rise.

"Please!" She mangled her hands some more. "Right now it's my only business. I'm making money. A lot of money. I know that doesn't impress you, but it's important to me. Without your help I'm nothing."

"I doubt that."

She laced her hands together, laying her face against her fingers. "A woman stockholder with no contacts. A nothing. I don't want that again." Helen's eyes were tense, seeing something she wasn't telling Blaise.

"I'm told you're good at sales." Blaise was uncomfortable.

"People think they're entitled to fringe benefits just because they're rich. I started in a brokerage house and the first big account I landed wanted favors. *Personal favors.*"

"I'm sorry."

"Why? You weren't the executive who told me to keep the account any way I could."

The beer had gone flat. Blaise shook the glass to stir up a little fizz. *Better to keep your mouth shut and be thought dumb than to open it and prove it.* His mother had liked that adage. Probably because it was true. After a while Helen understood that he was not going to ask for the steamy details and some of the tenseness went out of her.

"You're going to be dropped by the university, Blaise."

Blaise's hand trembled. He managed not to spill beer on the white shag carpet. "How do you know?"

"The dean was...glacial. I've taught there two years, and I've never seen him the way he was today. There's the drinking. Then that blond student—and finally the police. Dean Carden will announce a lack of funds in your department and that will be that. He's done it before. For less cause."

Helen looked directly at Blaise. Her eyes were wet. "I know the teaching assignment means a lot to you. I'm sorry."

"You're not firing me." Blaise wondered if the tears were for herself or for him. He smiled and it hurt. But a gentleman accepts adversity with class. Family tradition. His parents had agreed about a lot of things.

Helen collected the tray. "Do you want another?"

Blaise nodded.

She got another beer and put it down on the table before sitting next to him on the couch. She put her hand on his knee.

Feeling her heat penetrating his slacks, Blaise could not control himself. "Is there a difference between keeping an account or a computer?" he asked.

Helen snatched her hand away. "Bastard!"

"Dastard," he muttered. "Anyone can be born a bastard but to get a 'D' you have to work at it." If it would have helped he would have bitten his tongue off. Too late now. "I think you'd better take me back to my car."

"Yes." Helen picked up her leather bag, probing inside before going to the door jingling the keys impatiently.

"It wouldn't have worked," he said as he passed her in the doorway. Dobie seemed to slink in his wake. The dog looked up at Helen with regret in his dewy eyes.

Helen walked to the other side of her white Buick and got in, slamming the door. She sat stiff, arms rigid on the wheel.

"I could get a cab." Dobie lay very quiet in the backseat.

"Not with a dog! I'm doing this for Dobie—not for you."
Front wheels squealed as the car rocketed away from the
curb. "You don't know what I want."

"You have a nice neat life and you're on your way up.
Why get in line for a disaster waiting to happen?"

"That's for me to decide." She clamped her lips shut.
Helen had nice lips, finely molded with a lush rose color.

"Helen, you can still use Alfie whenever you want."

"I know that."

"Then why are you mad?"

She glanced at him, fury etched into her face. The road
was turning and she was not. Blaise said, "Watch the road."

In the university parking lot, Blaise put his hand on hers
and she shook it off. "We're still friends, aren't we, Helen?"
Silence.

Blaise got out. The yellow VW looked pathetic alongside
the sleek white Buick. Helen was pointedly silent. "You'll
get over it tomorrow," he said. "You'll see I was right."

Helen wheeled the car around in a screeching turn and
bounced out of the lot.

Getting into the familiar depths of his beetle with its worn
cloth seats and floor shift that always struck his leg when
he was careless or in a hurry, Blaise leaned over the wheel
for a long time. He knew Helen was crying when she drove
away.

Dobie nuzzled his cheek. "Are you mad, too?" The dog
cocked his ears as if he liked Helen more than Linda. He
rotated a soft brown eye at Blaise. But what did he know?
Dobie was too young for women.

The garage floor quaked when the bug bumped off the
cement driveway onto wood. There was no door from the
garage into the house so he had to walk around to the front.

"Dr. Cunningham?"

Blaise shaded his eyes. The sun had started settling toward the ocean and the heavyset man in the doorway was
mostly shadow.

"I'm Sergeant Miller. May we come in and talk?"

Dobie growled and the policeman backed off.

"There is a city leash law, sir."

"There are also," Blaise said icily, "things in the consti-
tution about private property."

The sergeant was in his late forties. He had gray eyes,

short hair with a hint of gray, a neat salt-and-pepper mustache, and wore a brown sharkskin suit with a double vent in the jacket. A leaner, taller man wearing a three-piece blue worsted suit stood behind him.

"You have identification?"

The sergeant took a leather case from his jacket pocket and showed Blaise his gold badge and identity card with the San Diego Police Department.

Unlocking the door, Blaise ushered Dobie in first.

They stood in front of the big window. Sergeant Miller said, "You have quite a view."

Blaise said, "Yes."

"This is Inspector Fennelli from San Francisco. He has some questions he'd like to ask, if you don't mind, Dr. Cunningham."

Miller looked around. "May we sit down?"

The sergeant took the far end of the couch and the inspector the chair facing the couch. Blaise couldn't see both men at the same time, which he supposed was deliberate. Dobie seemed uneasy, inspecting the arrangement, circling the men, then coming back to lay in front of the inspector.

"What did you do when you first left San Francisco, Doctor?"

"I took a direct flight to San Diego that laid over in Los Angeles a half hour."

"Before you got on the airplane?" The inspector had a whiskey voice and a way of peering at Blaise, lowering his head and staring up at his own eyelids, that seemed to doubt every word. Now and then his eyes twitched as he stared at Dobie.

"How tall are you, Professor?"

Blaise turned his head to see the sergeant who smiled amiably. "Six one."

"When did you last see Esther Tazy?"

"Tuesday, I believe. The date is on the ticket stub."

"Where did you see her?"

"Technological Intelligence Laboratories in San Francisco."

"How much do you weigh, Professor?"

Blaise held his eyes steady on Inspector Fennelli. "One hundred and seventy-nine pounds, Sergeant."

"Do you want to cooperate with us, Doctor?"

"By getting whiplash answering your questions?"

Fennelli smiled gently. "By coming with me to San Francisco to see a gentleman who knew Esther Tazy slightly."

"Slightly?"

"Perhaps that is an exaggeration. More precisely, to let a man who saw Esther Tazy's killer take a look at you."

"She's dead?" Blaise felt a black emptiness inside, a shock almost like the one he'd experienced when they came to him with the news of his parents' deaths. He'd been responsible then. The others only suspected, but Blaise knew. If he'd been sober they would never have driven off to fulfill his lecture commitment. And they would have still been alive. Neither policeman said anything.

Blaise looked from one detective to another. "I didn't know anything about that." Inside, though, something said, *It's your fault again, Cunningham.*

"That's good, that you don't know anything about it, because, Dr. Cunningham"—and Fennelli smiled in his gentle way—"the killer is large and blond and must have known Miss Tazy. You are blond, are you not, Dr. Cunningham?"

Dobie's restless growl rumbled in the still room.

No way exists to separate the ingrained learning habits of a lifetime from the inherent natural ability to learn. So the researcher must disregard the eccentricities of the past to concentrate on the potential of the future.

FROM A SEMINAR ON
THE CUNNINGHAM EQUATIONS

CHAPTER 5

Blaise had gotten on the jet with Inspector Fennelli, watched the runway rush and drop.

"I don't suppose you have jurisdiction in San Diego?"

"No." Fennelli put down his magazine and looked bland. "You will have in San Francisco."

"Of course, Dr. Cunningham." Out the window, the airliner's shadow was sharp on the translucent green surface of the ocean as it banked for the short run to Los Angeles. Upside windows revealed fluffy stacks of white clouds. "I don't like flying," Fennelli said. "Too many things can go wrong."

"I could change my mind in L.A."

Fennelli shrugged. "There is always Sergeant Miller."

Blaise had been lucky. Helen kept him sober and the San Francisco flight completed the drying-out. Interrogation in the Bay City was more intense, but a witness, a dog walker, said he wasn't sure Blaise was the man because of the rain and the wind. He'd said the same about a yellow-haired boyfriend of Esther Tazy's from the lab. So Blaise had gone home again.

He put his hands behind his head and stared into the plaster over his bed. Even though it predated the architectural style, the home his parents had left him could have been a typical Mizner house: stucco gunked onto chicken wire stretched between two-by-fours. If the termites left the wood alone it might stand another half century. When he

43

was a child, Blaise imagined monsters trapped in the plaster. The monsters had grown real with time.

He closed his eyes. Fennelli had said things like Esther's murder just happened in San Francisco. *The boyfriend could have been jealous, Dr. Cunningham. But not you.* Fennelli smiled like he knew something, like he didn't care who was guilty. So long as he had someone. Fennelli didn't need to add that if the boyfriend washed out he'd be back for Blaise.

Blaise's face itched. He'd been sweating more in his sleep, waking with the aftertaste of nightmares he couldn't remember. The bed was fetid from alcohol and dirty linens.

What had happened since Fennelli was muddy.

Gordon was gone.

Helen was gone.

Even Esther. He'd had fantasies about Esther Tazy. She was bright and sexual, too hard to hurt. He thought he could be comfortable with her until he discovered he was too easily hurt.

Hemmett.

Blaise strained. When memories didn't come right away dread enveloped him like a wave of black water. His chest tightened, making him giddy, the way he'd felt when his mother read Ovid's *Metamorphoses* out loud, then queried him in English to establish a three-year-old's knowledge of Latin. That he had understood was unworthy of comment or congratulation. It was only expected.

Dobie. Dobie was missing!

The steady thump of Blaise's heart became noticeable by its absence. A void existed in his memory. He couldn't have just left Dobie in the house. The plaster ceiling writhed in obscene patterns. Blaise's mouth was dry. He'd never forgotten like this before. And he'd been almost sober. *Helen!* He'd called her and left the door unlocked. Relief flooded through Blaise. Dobie was safe and he had filled the gap in his mind. He breathed again. Humming, he headed for the steamy pleasures of the bathroom.

"Dr. Cunningham!"

The voice competed with the shower hiss. Blaise had been thinking of Dr. Hemmett, who asked what Fennelli wanted and if he knew Esther worked for GENRECT.

Hot water sapped him, making the stretch to turn off the shower a major exertion. Wrapping a towel around his middle, he stepped out. Steam followed in a billowing cloud.

"Dr. Cunningham!" The voice rose now that it had no competition. "I know you're here, Doctor."

Blaise stumbled to the front of the house and leaned against the railing that prevented people from missing the turn to the stairs and falling into the living room. "How do you know I'm here, Miss Peters?"

"Because that wreck you drive is cluttering the garage."

Blaise was dripping on the hall rug. "I'll get dressed."

"Yes." Afternoon sun through the big window limed Linda Peters' body through the fine white cotton of a summer dress.

He looked into her green eyes. "Don't go away."

"I won't." She sat on the couch and Blaise experienced a moment of regret.

When he returned Linda looked him up and down more than slacks and a sports shirt with a hint of blue justified.

"Something wrong?"

"You look better with your clothes on."

"That is true of nearly everyone over fifteen," he said. Miss Burkhalter-Peters was over fifteen. She had a poker face, cute, but she was giving away no secrets. She also constituted an exception to the over-fifteen rule. "I knew you'd be back."

Her eyes widened. "I didn't know myself until I got here."

"You found me irresistible."

She examined him without concealing her smile. "Are you irresistible?"

"That's what my mother always said."

"Someday I may find you irresistible, too. But for now I'd like to know more than you told me before."

"Such as?"

"How candid are you being, Blaise?"

A dull throbbing started in his head. It would get worse if he didn't have a drink. "Excuse me." He got a beer from the kitchen and gulped half. It tasted cold, sharp with carbon dioxide. For a moment he was blinded by pain that threatened to remove his head.

Linda seemed more desirable than he remembered. Vibrantly alive gold-streaked red hair, green eyes that glowed.

"You said Dr. Hill verged on a breakthrough."

"I said Dr. Hill was onto something."

"Do you know Telesis is pulling the plug on GENRECT's research license?"

He looked at her, disappointed that she wanted information. He'd hoped she wanted something more. "It's your story."

"What is Dr. Hill doing?"

"Gordon believes an organic interface would create the condition for something similar to a mechanically readable P300 brainwave. He's trying to interpose a biological controller between the machine and the Tillie."

"Truth?"

Blaise nodded.

"Then why are you still working for GENRECT? The company doesn't have any other projects suitable for what you do."

"You tell me."

Linda leaned forward, elbows on her knees. "Tillie is a proprietary product from Technological Intelligence Laboratory—TIL Ltd., Inc., has a legal interest in any product developed while its development license agreement is in effect. So GENRECT may be at legal risk in continuing research."

"We leave that stuff to the lawyers." Blaise felt confused. Linda knew more about GENRECT than he did, things that he had to wonder about, too."

"Did you know GENRECT is broke?"

"I've had hints." Linda's statement made sense of Hemmett's sudden pressure on Blaise.

"It's true." She gave him a moment to think about his worthless stock options.

"I don't know what you want," Blaise said finally. "Why don't you ask Dr. Hill?"

"I can't get in to see him. I can't even call him."

"Try him at home."

"I did. Dr. Hill's wife is upset. She didn't tell me anything but I know he's not coming home anymore. Now you know why I'm here. You're the only game in town."

"Very flattering."

"Take it or leave it."

"Dr. Hemmett?" Blaise could play at indifference, too. But he knew in his heart he was outclassed up front.

Linda laughed. "Nor Gregory West either." West controlled the financial hierarchy of GENRECT and didn't talk to hired help. Blaise wondered if he talked to ladies from San Francisco.

"Ask Dr. Hill to speak with me."

Blaise shook his head.

"You want me to crawl into bed for a lousy introduction? Your bath routine was cute. I've already seen your after-class bit."

"I'm innocent."

"Of what?"

"Not much," Blaise conceded. "But I can't get Gordon to meet with you."

Linda arched an eyebrow as if listening to a small boy explain how the window got broken.

"Gordon won't see me or even talk to me on the phone. And it seems that while I've been drunk for the last couple of weeks you've been doing your homework. And, yes, I do want you to crawl into bed with me. I have from the first day. That hasn't changed." Blaise had run out of breath. He'd always avoided emotional scenes and now he had stunned himself.

Linda avoided his eyes. "I'm sorry."

"Me, too." Blaise didn't know if she believed him. "Why don't you go away? I have some serious drinking to do."

"Do you think Dr. Hill is all right?"

"He's in better shape than I am."

"You're sure?"

"No. But I don't think you understand. I'm not really needed at the lab. Dr. Hemmett would deep-six me like a bag of garbage if it wouldn't upset the GENRECT image."

"That's all?"

"No. I think Gordon's making them keep me on the pay-roll."

Blaise was sweating. He'd revealed much more than he meant to, words rolling out with no way to stop them. Until he'd said it Blaise had not known—or had been unwilling to believe—he was dead weight at GENRECT.

He had a sick feeling and an overwhelming need for a drink. "I can't help you, Miss Peters. I can't even help my-self. If Gordon's counting on me, God help him."

He was not sure how it happened, but Linda stayed the night. She undressed in the dim light of the shaded bedroom window. Her bare feet padded softly across the carpet as she came to the bed. She lay close to him for a long time and neither moved until Blaise said, "I don't think I can do anything," and she put her arms around him and her lips to his ear and whispered, "It's okay. Everything is all right."

"Don't you ever go to work?"

Blaise was trying to squeeze the VW into a space meant for a bicycle, so he didn't answer Linda right away. He oozed through the crack the open door made, pleased that her door opened, too.

"I'm a remittance man."

Striding up the sidewalk under the trees, he realized how tiny Linda really was. Her elfin head bobbed along well below his shoulder and the animation of her presence failed to add an illusion of physical size.

"Students won't recognize me sober." Blaise thought about that and realized he was telling the truth. It had popped out like a kid trying to get attention. He was disappointed when Linda failed to comment.

In the classroom, she hugged his arm, reluctant to let go before walking down the center aisle to the vacant seat at the back. After appraising Linda with the thoroughness of jewelers valuing the Hope Diamond, the female students glanced at Lucy.

The male students just looked at Linda.

During class, Blaise sneaked peeks at the rear of the room, shamelessly seeking approval. He had to do something about Dobie and that meant talking to Helen. His memory of how he had brought her down seemed shameful. He couldn't blame Helen if she retaliated.

When the class emptied after the bell he pushed Helen and Dobie out of his mind and showed Linda how to put Alfie through his paces at the main terminal. He stood behind her to smell her hair and perfume, to feel the heat of her body while he guided her through the series in which Alfie retained and then, using logical equivalents, modified each entry by reprogramming the operation. After a time she said, "Can I try?"

"Sure."

Fingers flew over the keyboard, filling the screen with equations that Blaise read with surprise.

When she stopped the screen went blank.

Blaise tried to recall if she had told him something and he'd forgotten. "You're not an investment counselor," he said.

"I never said I was."

Blaise stared. The monitor overflowed with a series of alternative equations.

"What are those?" Linda asked.

"Alfie is modifying the original equation."

"I don't see the point..."

"Your equation is for manufacturing steel in zero G with specific additives to change tensile strength, toughness, weight, and ductility. Alfie is adding the factors that were left out. Particularly the infinitesimal crystalline enlargement that comes from changes in electron speeds at the requisite temperatures, as well as the absence of gravity."

"Too fast." Linda watched the printout pile up.

Blaise observed for a moment. "Originally the attempt to give computers inspiration was achieved by running streaming tapes that interdicted each other, trying to skip the normal sequential approach to computer intelligence. Alfie has twenty-four five-hundred-megabyte optical disks, each controlled by an individual chip and integrated memory. Alfie determines the various structures and the reader chips start seeking comparable problem structures on file."

"He jumps work sequences when there is a match?"

Blaise examined Linda's profile as she leaned into the screen. "You understand the math?"

She tore her gaze from the screen and looked at Blaise. Her eyes went back to the mound of printout. "You were going to tell me what's different about Alfie."

"Alfie builds his own files."

"Don't all computers?"

"Not without instructions." Blaise typed a message to Alfie. "If you're not an investment counselor, then I think I should know just what you really are."

"What I said. I represent an investment group in San Francisco. My uncle heads the group and I studied math at Berkeley." Linda sat very still. "You can check. None of that is a crime, Blaise. I don't think you're entitled to complain."

Blaise started to answer, but the monitor attracted Linda's attention and he followed the direction of her gaze.

"HOW PLEASANT TO MEET YOU, MISS PETERS"

"You did that." Linda looked at Blaise.

"I only turned on the audio pickup. Alfie understands

English." But the message perplexed Blaise. He had simply told Alfie to store the conversation.

"THANK YOU FOR INVITING ME TO JOIN YOU, PROFESSOR"

"You're welcome, Alfie." Blaise reached for the keyboard.

"Don't switch him off." Linda moved around in front of the monitor. "Can he see me?"

"No." Blaise was preoccupied. If Alfie malfunctioned, he could unload more garbage than the East River. And Alfie's subconscious held Blaise's every secret.

"PROFESSOR, I FEEL DIFFERENT TODAY. HAVE I BEEN DRINKING?"

"You don't drink, Alfie."

The screen blanked nearly a minute. "THAT IS TRUE"

"Why not shut off for a while? Charge your batteries."

Figures flashed across the screen. "ALL OPERATING SYSTEMS ARE TEN OH, PROFESSOR"

LEDs winked frantically around Alfie's bulk.

"What's happening, Blaise?" Linda faced him.

"A glitch. He's looking for it. When he finds it he'll do a printout and I'll operate."

"I hoped you'd be able to show Alfie off." Linda sounded dismal at the prospect that Alfie wasn't going to function.

"We'll see. Alfie can do a lot of self-repair." Blaise tightened his hand on her shoulder and wished he could trust anyone anymore. Including himself.

The hall door opened. "Hello." Helen smiled more at Linda than she did at Blaise. "I just came by to talk to Alfie, if that's okay with you, Blaise."

"Sure." He introduced the women. "Helen is our resident stockbroker. You might have something in common."

"I don't think I know enough about stocks." Linda was innocent. "My uncle handles the family investments."

"I imagine he does all right," Helen said.

Linda read something into Helen's statement. "He does well." Her voice did not ooze friendship.

"Linda's researching GENRECT," Blaise said. "Her uncle believes the company has investment potential." Suddenly redundant, he felt foolish. Nothing went on between him and Helen except her admission that she wanted something. That, and that very private knowledge she had of his vulnerability. Yet it was as if a wife or fiancée had caught him in bed with a stranger. He tried to smile. He was only an object caught in the tension between two women.

"Got to go," he said desperately. To his relief, Linda stood and held out her hand.

"It's been very nice meeting you, Miss ... McIntyre."

"My pleasure." Blaise regretted the hurt in Helen's face.

"Shall we go, Blaise?" Linda put her hand on his arm.

"I have something of yours at home, Blaise." Helen's face could have been frozen.

"I ... I forgot, Helen." The admission destroyed the pleasure of the moment. "Could you keep it a little longer? Please."

Helen looked at him a moment before finally nodding.

"HOW NICE TO SEE YOU AGAIN, MISS MCINTYRE"

"That's new, Alfie." Helen looked at the screen, curiosity evident in her eyes. "A program change, Blaise?"

"A DEVIATION, PROFESSOR. I WILL CLOSE DOWN THE MATRIX"

Alfie flashed a schematic across the screen. Several traces changed color. Alfie had segregated them from the circuit.

Blaise dropped Linda at the house to pick up her car and, he hoped, to unpack her suitcase. On his way to GENRECT he thought about the traces Alfie had isolated. They were in the new board he'd installed before going to San Francisco.

Alfie's problem taken care of, Blaise concentrated on his own. If Linda's interest was the company, he could use that. He supposed that taking advantage of her interest in GENRECT was cheap. On the edge of his thought was the concomitant accusation that she was exploiting his interest in her.

At GENRECT the receptionist asked if he was feeling better. Apparently Dr. Hemmett had spread the word he was sick to explain his nonappearances. Hemmett would worry about company morale.

Gordon did not answer his knock. The lab echoed emptiness.

Although cleaned and dusted daily, Blaise's own lab showed neglect. He changed the streaming tapes. The drive to work and create was gone. His work would be too little and too late, thanks to whatever Gordon had discovered.

He took the long walk to the front office where the receptionist announced him. Dr. Hemmett seemed bored, but at least without overt animosity, for which Blaise was grateful.

"I need to talk to Gordon."

Hemmett stood behind his desk, massive, imposing with his mane of silver hair like some elder statesman holding court. When the sun caught it from behind, his hair burst into a golden halo, something Hemmett knew and used. He kept them both standing, which meant the interview was going to be brief.

"Dr. Cunningham, if Dr. Hill wished to talk to you I'm sure he would. He is engaged in some very serious work for us at the moment and he's best not disturbed."

Hemmett picked a cigar from a cherrywood humidor. The old, round box had been patined by smoke and time to a rich, dusky color. Blaise suspected it was a Colonial period piece. Flourishing a cigar cutter, Hemmett made a production of lighting up. He shook out the kitchen match under a curl of smoke and added, "Why not take a vacation? You have time coming."

"I'm running tapes—"

"They'll keep. Someday your project may be worth bringing to fruition, but not in the foreseeable future unless some great accident happens. And it could as easily happen in two weeks as today. Do I make myself clear, Doctor?"

"Yes."

"Thank you, Doctor. Your check will be banked automatically as usual and we'll see you again in two weeks. Take a month or two if you like. Europe is nice this time of year."

"I don't know..."

"Of course not, but you're free to do as you please. And the money will keep coming. Think of that, Doctor."

Blaise thought a great deal about free money from a bankrupt company as he left the laboratory building.

It was, as a family friend used to say, a wonder. Unless Linda was lying about GENRECT's economics.

Mathematics may describe intelligence. Only man's intelligence can transmute mathematics into a tool for change.

FROM A SEMINAR ON
THE CUNNINGHAM EQUATIONS

CHAPTER 6

Linda was not at the house. Her suitcase was. Settling on the sofa and looking out over the irrigated greenery of La Jolla, which ranged from aspen to zoysia and included every flower that could endure salt spray, Blaise rummaged through his wallet. He found the card and punched the number.

"Four-four-seven-eight."

"Helen?"

"This is Helen McIntyre."

"Me. Blaise."

A pause. "It's nice of you to call, Blaise."

"Are you busy?"

"No."

"Could you go out to lunch?"

Longer pause. Finally: "I can turn on the answering machine." Her careful voice told Blaise he was making a mistake.

"I'll be there in ten minutes."

Helen waited at the door. She wore a light-pink turtleneck and a burgundy skirt, and shoes with just enough heel to make walking bearable instead of fashionable. Dobie leaned against her leg. She motioned him into the back, then took the VW's passenger seat without speaking.

Dobie whined at Blaise, but took his cues from Helen. He hung his head out the window when they got out of the car. Blaise said, "Wait, Dobie!"

Helen bent over, letting the dog nuzzle her. "Be good, Dobie." Glancing at Blaise she added, "*I'll* come back for you."

In the restaurant, Helen glanced at the menu. "I can't read Russian," she said. "Anyway, all I want is a salad."

Blaise almost said, "It's Greek." But Helen didn't recognize the difference and things were bad enough between them.

He ordered Fix beer for himself and diet Pepsi and salad for Helen. "I want to know about GENRECT."

"You could have saved a lunch. It's in Alfie already."

"How come?"

Helen shrugged and looked away. "I was curious."

"About what?"

"Just things." She waved her hand. "You know, Alfie's been acting peculiar lately. Sometimes I get strange answers."

Blaise considered saying *Like what?* But apparently the answers weren't embarrassing. Digging might dislodge a snake instead of a worm. "It's a growing stage with computers. I'll fix it. Can you remember enough to answer some questions?"

"I can try." Helen poked apathetically at her village salad, trying to drain oil off a lettuce leaf.

"Do you want something else to drink?" Blaise hoped she'd say yes. He was struggling to stay dry and one beer stoked the fire instead of quenching it.

Helen shook her head, swirling blond hair around her face. "What do you want to know?"

"Who owns GENRECT? What's the financial situation? Where does Gregory West fit in?"

"They're part of the same answer, Blaise. After Dr. Hemmett and Jules Gross set GENRECT up as a private company, controlling interest was purchased by a group from a venture capital company in San Francisco called Tenro. Gregory West runs Tenro."

"Do you know who the investors are?"

"No. It's like a blind trust. Tenro is at risk, not the limited investors. So most dealings are executed by Mr. West on behalf of the investors."

"A handy way to stay out of the news," Blaise guessed.

Helen nodded. "Those arrangements are made to launder money just to keep the public in the dark." She spread a piece of lettuce and looked at it with distaste. "Do you like fat girls?"

"I don't know. I never thought about it." Catching him unawares, the question startled him. "You're not fat."

"If I eat anything except this lettuce I'll swell up like a kielbasa." She murmured in another language, then said, "You aren't what you don't eat. My parents were Polish."

"McIntyre?"

Helen's smile was wry. "The immigration agent was Irish."

"Poles make good vodka," Blaise said reassuringly.

"When I was a girl I loved dumplings and ribs." Helen had a faraway look that Blaise supposed meant the lettuce leaf would wilt on her fork before she ate it. "It was a Katowice recipe."

"Helen," Blaise said. "Please!"

"I'll bet you don't like fat girls." She jabbed the lettuce leaf in her mouth.

"I love them. How about West?"

"Is he fat?"

"Helen!"

"He has more than just the controlling interest. GENRECT was never a public offering so SEC rules allow a great deal of privacy. Hemmett's original partner got out while the getting was good. Dr. Gross is in Israel improving ruminant digestion for more efficient milk production.

"Dr. Hemmett stayed on as manager. As a founder, he lends an aura of authenticity. But GENRECT has not released a single product in three years. The backers are digging into their own pockets to keep it afloat."

"You're saying nobody will buy GENRECT stock?"

"No insider. And to go public will only accelerate the disaster. GENRECT's price is holding because they all went in at inflated prices and stand to take a bath if they bail out now. So they just hang on and pray."

"What kind of losses would they take, Helen?"

Helen studied her fork, as if looking at a ledger sheet. "When GENRECT went on the market, biotech stocks were all new, speculative, no earnings record. The biggest projected uses were in medicine and agriculture. Neither market is likely to disappear. So biotech sold at forty times earnings. Projected incomes were way too high. At least in the short term."

"Projected?"

Helen bobbed her head.

"And in its three years of existence GENRECT has never earned a dime?"

"That's right, Blaise. GENRECT is just another GENEN-TECH coat-tailer. Except with zero earnings."

"Is West interfering in company management?"

"That's his job: Salvage what he can for Tenro."

"Eat your salad," he said. "It's good for what ails you."

Dobie seemed relieved when they came back. He licked Helen. For Blaise the dog had only reproach.

The ride to Helen's house was tightly quiet. Helen promised to check up on Tenro. Blaise had not told her that he was looking for Gordon. Or that he supposed West was the man most likely to have sent Gordon into hiding while he accelerated his project. Helen didn't conceal her unhappiness at his secrecy.

"Thanks for lunch." She closed the VW door with force.

"You're welcome."

Helen clung to the door and Blaise knew he was going to hear more than he wanted to.

"What's an *m* and *m*, Blaise? A modified mink?"

"A coat? I don't know."

"That's strange. Students were gossiping outside your classroom about your new *m* and *m*. I don't think they were talking about candy or a coat." Blaise sat glum, knowing his only salvation lay in silence.

Dobie cried. Helen turned toward the car with longing before ducking her head and hurrying into the house.

Blaise wondered if she regretted leaving the dog or him. He patted the passenger seat and Dobie came over the back to sit staring at Helen's door.

"I guess you're stuck with me, Dobie."

The dog looked at Blaise. Dobie was not happy.

Helen had given Blaise the number of a financial columnist. "He's a cross between Dear Abby and Louella Parsons," she had said, "for people who stick real money into funny stock. Gossip about whom not to trust—practically everyone—plus tea and sympathy for the burn cases."

Blaise caught Morgan on the first ring. The columnist was cordial, as Helen had warned. Without sources, Morgan would have nothing to print.

Blaise affirmed that GENRECT remained landlocked between the more publicized and glamorous Salk Institute and UCSD, that he, the Nobel Prize winner, did indeed work for dear old Arthur Hemmett, who had once plied Morgan with liquor and promises.

Morgan sighed. "It's time I did a column about goings-on at GENRECT." Blaise suspected the sigh was for freebie booze. In return for Blaise's promise to let him know how the search for information on West came out, Morgan suggested that Blaise talk to a winemaker in Escondido.

Blaise thanked Morgan with vague promises, including exclusive rights to his life story.

Snapping the OFF switch on the cordless telephone triggered restlessness. Blaise wanted to do something. He missed Gordon's steadying influence, the assurance that whatever was happening to him would work out for the best.

In the bathroom he dropped his clothes in a heap. His breathing came hard again. Anxiety, Gordon said. The shower drummed as Blaise alternated hot and cold, sending sharp jolts through the nervous system. The mirror fogged up so he couldn't see himself. He thought fleetingly of vampires as he dressed in a blue chambray shirt and gray slacks.

Gordon owned a modest house in better repair than Blaise's, with an immaculate coat of rust red and Dutch Boy gloss white trim. Only the lawn, two weeks overdue for mowing, betrayed the absence of its compulsively neat owner. Blaise approached the front door and pressed the button. He waited and tried again.

No answer.

Black and tan as an Irish nightmare, Dobie leaped through the car window and whizzed past Blaise. "Know where you are, boy?"

Dobie whined and wouldn't follow Blaise away from the house.

"Let's go, Dobie. The door's locked."

The dog lurched toward Blaise and an instant later he felt the needle sharpness of Dobie's teeth. Without letting his hand go, Dobie dragged Blaise back to the door. He shoved Blaise toward the bulky green mailbox next to the door.

The dog stood expectantly, at attention.

Shrugging, Blaise opened the mailbox and looked in. Letters and junk mail cluttered the interior.

Dobie whined.

Blaise examined the box again and Dobie stopped whining. He put his hand on the metal front and the dog barked twice. "Once for no and twice for yes, Dobie? Is that what Gordon's been teaching you?"

Dobie barked twice again.

They looked each other in the eye and Blaise took his hand off the box. Dobie gave a single disappointed yip. Blaise put his hand back on the letter box. Two barks.

He felt under the box and found the magnetized key holder that most people used for cars.

Dobie tore through the house, frantically yipping. After a while he came back out to lay on the stoop.

"No one home?"

The dog cocked his eyebrows so he could see Blaise without lifting his head.

"Come on, Dobie."

Blaise looked back when he was getting into the yellow VW. Like Gordon's lab, the house was immaculate to the point of madness, and just as lonely.

Visiting Gordon's home had been enough to make Blaise dig a bottle of gin out of a closet.

Millions of termites inside the beams of his house were holding hands to keep his home from sliding into the sea.

The termites had formed an accusing circle around him. "You were supposed to deliver that lecture," the queen mother said. "You were supposed to drive. If you'd held your liquor like a man they'd still be alive."

"Still competing," the worker termites chorused.

"Blaise! Wake up!"

Linda was shaking him, her face and lips inches away. He caught her waist and pulled her down. She yelled as he slid his hands under her clothes and started stroking satiny skin. After a while she stopped yelling.

Blaise woke again when Linda was returning from the bathroom, straightening her clothes as she walked. He watched her, feeling good about the way she moved, the tilt of her head, the sheen of her skin.

"What do you think you're doing?"

"Peeping."

"You're a mess."

He reached up and put his hands on her hips. She did not respond, but she did not pull away either.

"What do you think you want?"

He smiled and she deftly stepped out of his grasp. "That's what I thought."

Blaise sat up and wished he hadn't. The room swayed and he felt sick. Gin did that sometimes. "Where's Dobie?"

"I locked him out back."

The dog wouldn't like that, but Linda had done the sensible thing. "Do you want to go to Escondido instead?"

"Instead of what?" Linda looked at him and then shook her head. "Where's Escondido?"

Blaise lay back on the couch again and closed his eyes, which made him feel a little better. "About forty miles. I've got a line on West."

"West? We're looking for Dr. Hill."

"Gordon is wherever West decided to put him."

She made an impolite sound. "You're guessing."

"*Inductive reasoning* reads better in a résumé."

"Can't you just call?"

"I did."

Linda was settling into the right front seat of the beetle when Dobie came rocketing through the left door. He created some commotion before settling into the backseat.

"Sorry, Dobie," Blaise said. "She got there first."

Linda gave Blaise an outraged look and was about to demand the dog be left behind when Blaise said, "He showed me the key to Gordon Hill's house. He could have more to say."

Linda didn't like it but she seemed to have reached an area of compromise between what she needed and what she wanted.

Halfway to Escondido, the little beetle shimmying in the wind blast of passing trucks, Linda finally thought of something else to ask.

"No," Blaise answered. "He didn't invite me." Sagebrush-dotted hills and green reminders of winter rains passed by in silence.

Escondido rambles, old sections shaded by towering eucalyptus. The new parts are wide concrete streets over once-cheap farmland, and flats of sun-drenched housing. Beyond town the turnoff huddled under a clump of oaks. Blaise followed a dirt road past orange trees abandoned by owners into land speculation instead of farming. The road climbed past apple trees gone wild. Shadows had lengthened by the time they crunched gravel under a crosstree with a hanging sign.

The main building had foot-thick adobe walls and bright

whitewash. Peeled saplings held up a ramada green with fresh vines. The door was open but inside the house was shadow.

"Hello!" Blaise called. "Anybody home?" The sense of city had fled. Knocking at an open door did not seem correct. Dobie was also apparently aware of the difference. Instead of tearing ecstatically through the vineyard he kept a close heel.

"You should have told them you were coming." Linda did not exactly wrinkle her nose at rusticity, but she came close.

Blaise called again. Crickets and tree toads went silent.

"What is it you want here?" The old man's voice was thin and creaky with a hint of accent.

Blaise turned toward the old man's voice. "Mr. Oesti?"

Stepping out of the shadow of the ramada, Giovanni Oesti moved like dry sticks cracking.

"How do you do, sir. I called you earlier."

The old man ignored the outstretched hand and turned. "Come. You want to talk. We talk."

Blaise and Linda followed him to a windowless building behind the house. The old man stepped inside and light spilled from the open doorway. They followed into a smell of new-sawn wood and the musty fragrance of fermentation. Dobie stood in the doorway with mournful eyes.

Oesti pointed to unpainted chairs around a potbellied stove. When Linda and Blaise had each taken one, he sat. Looking at the dog in the doorway, he said, *"Anchi tu."*

Dobie's eyes brightened. Walking carefully like a child trying to act grownup, he settled at Blaise's feet.

"Begin."

Oesti had toothpick bones and skin like crumpled wrapping paper. His tufts of remaining hair were as shoe-polish black as his unblinking eyes.

"I was told you could give me some information about a gentleman named Gregory West."

"Why do you not ask Mr. . . . . West?" The words were thin like torn paper, like the old man himself, and Blaise could read neither warmth nor anger.

"I don't believe he would tell me," Blaise answered. "A friend of mine has disappeared. It's possible that knowing something about Mr. West would reveal his whereabouts."

"Police handle such matters."

Blaise switched to formal Roman and answered as tactfully as possible. "Signor West probably prefers privacy. I do not know a crime has been committed. In any event, the police never get to the bottom of things. I am bound by honor to help my friend."

"*L'onnore*." Oesti spoke in dialect. "The curse of our kind!" He gave Blaise a sly look, knowing that some foreigners learn Roman, but no outlander ever understands *siciliano*.

"The curse of our kind is not honor," Blaise said in the same hybrid Latin-Greek. "It's *omertà*."

"What are you saying?" Linda looked from Blaise to the old man and back, exasperation drawing lines on her face. "I don't speak dialect, Blaise."

"Men are talking," Blaise said in English.

"About my son." Giovanni Oesti spat under the stove.

"I had guessed." Linda retreated from the venom in the old man's voice.

"Gregorio Giovanni Rampanelli Oesti—after his mother's father, a man of great understanding."

Blaise said nothing.

"Why did he change his name? Is he shamed by the blood of his fathers?" Oesti challenged Blaise. "He changed his name because I demanded it. Bad enough that he dishonors my father's name. But he will not shame his mother's." The old man folded parchment-thin hands on his nonexistent stomach.

"I am sorry to have brought this to you," Blaise said.

Oesti waved off the apology. "I shall tell you what you have come to hear. And as you say, this is between men. I could not say such things to a priest for they do not have sons and can only pretend to understand."

In the quiet of the winery, Giovanni Oesti's wavering voice took them back to the days when a boy from Sicily labored in California on land too hilly for crops and speculators.

He cut and terraced, planted vines, backpacked water drawn from a hand-dug well with a hand pump. It was work that priests once corralled Indians to do. Like the priests, he made wine.

His son Vito died at Anzio Beach in World War II. After that, the younger boy, Gregorio, was too precious to his mother to dress vines with his father and the Mexicans.

The wine was sweet and mellow. It made Blaise weep within, and he dreaded the end of the old man's story. Giovanni Oesti switched to English, in which it is easier to conceal pain.

Dobie's mournful eyes flowed from Blaise to the old man, as if he could sense the sadness of the moment.

"To the Mexicans I was Don Juan. Americans liked my wine. Other places everybody thinks Italians are gangsters. But here, I'm just a neighbor. Some held more land. If I had more money, only my banker cared.

"Gregorio was not satisfied with a car, a horse, cows, chickens, and miles of vineyards. It would have been better to keep the boy in the fields and teach him the business by leaving his sweat there. It was my fault. Gregorio found new friends in these wonderful schools with their fancy ways.

"When he came home, the Mexicans made less and worked harder. The wine grew thinner and was sold farther way. With the new money, Gregorio retired his mother and father.

"Strangers tore up the fields and built houses while Rosanna and I stayed here on the land that was left and saw our lives being stolen.

"*La famiglia*." Giovanni spat. "In school Gregorio met the sons of those who came here not to work but to steal."

Dobie gave Blaise a look of entreaty, then began his invisible ninja-maneuvering until his head was in the old man's lap. Without looking down, Giovanni Oesti patted the Doberman.

"They ... took advantage of your son?" It was a delicate question and Blaise could think of no way to phrase the true meaning in Italian or English.

The old man's laugh was rustling cornstalks.

"No, *Dottore*, my son used them. This place is not good for the grape. North, above San Francisco, the wine is better. Here you make a life. There you make money.

"Gregorio did not want the land. He sold it. Every month I get enough to live better than before ... without work. I should be grateful, should I not?

"I might have stopped him. But the new owners told me Gregorio would die if I did not go along. It was not for him that I gave my blessing. I think maybe Gregorio sent the threat. But I could not take that chance while his mother lived.

"Rosanna died without grandchildren. It was all for nothing. For Rosanna I have willed *Il Resto* to the nuns for a children's home."

The old man's cough was, like himself, brittle.

"I do not have the gift of faith. I do not know if it is worse to die without issue or to despise what I leave behind."

Gregory West's father stood and led them from the winery to the VW. Blaise was surprised by the darkness.

"You should not have come," the old man said. "Gregorio has me watched. He may think it filial duty. Maybe he spies. Whichever, it is not safe for you. One other thing." Giovanni hesitated. "It shames me, but Gregorio has been in jail. He makes money by cheating people. He even stole a great winery in Mendocino County. He wanted me to live there like a great landowner. He does not love the land." Giovanni fumbled in his pocket and gave Blaise a virgin label with the vineyard's name.

Blaise was not drunk but he felt close to tears. "I am sorry for the pain I have caused you," he said.

"Buon cane," the old man said, patting Dobie's head. "Dogs never did like Gregorio." He sighed and pressed Blaise's hand. "Have great care, for God is too busy to guide any of us." He looked closely at Blaise and lapsed into dialect. "You must beware, too, of the fruit of the vineyard. You have drunk too much, but not enough. For some, Christ's blood is a curse."

Saying good night to Linda, the old man was swallowed by shadows.

"What did he tell you just then?" Linda stood beside the bug, not getting in.

"He said Dobie was a good dog."

"He said more than that."

"The meaning of *Il Resto*," Blaise lied.

"I wouldn't think there'd be much rest around a place like this."

"Resto is remainder—what's left after his son stole it all. Are you going to get in?"

As Blaise drove out to the main road a sudden flare of headlights blinded them, then blinked out. No one followed as they rolled back to the highway under an almost full moon. It was no comfort to Blaise. Whoever was parked across the road had their faces and license number.

There is every reason to suppose as many brilliant people exist
in institutions of the mentally incompetent as are members
of the learned societies. It is a happy accident when intelligence and brilliance occur in the same entity.

FROM A SEMINAR ON
THE CUNNINGHAM EQUATIONS

CHAPTER 7

Blaise unlocked his classroom ahead of the hot blast
of morning sun. After their talk with Giovanni Oesti, Linda
decided to return to San Francisco. Blaise had not objected.
Driving in darkness, digesting the old man's information,
Blaise kept an eye on the mirror during the unsatisfactory
discussion with Linda.

"Of course I'm English. My branch of Cunningham just
didn't see eye to eye with Henry the Eighth."

"I'm Catholic, too," Linda protested, "but I don't speak
Sicilian."

"I don't know why not."

Linda's attention riveted on him in a way that suggested
her surprise was not just talk.

"I learned in school." The road narrowed and started
winding. A pair of headlights dogged his tail. Then the road
straightened, the car passed, and nothing happened. Some
of the tension left him. The old *paisan'* had invoked in Blaise
a memory of bleak Sicilian hills, the aura of blood and dread
that made up that unhappy island's history.

"I've never heard of a school teaching Sicilian. Not even
in Italy."

"My school was different."

His parents had taken a villa above Taormina, a backwater
that mainland Italians left to tourists and the natives. The
villa was cheap and picturesque. Blaise's chores included
hand-pumping water at dawn's first glimmer. The house-
keeper heated it over charcoal for before-breakfast washups.

The other few tourists hired a boy to draw water, but Alfred had seen a way to engrave a sense of duty in his son's psyche.

They were on a working holiday, polishing their Latin with the down-at-the-heels Neapolitan tutor they provided Blaise, competing as usual with a ten-year-old boy, convinced that cutthroat competition molds character and stretches a man's ability. Later each day they worked on the problem the government had hired them to solve.

The tutor fared miserably. Acceptable to Caesar's soldiers two thousand years earlier, his priest-taught Latin was a far cry from Boston. Ottilie and Alfred's Latin School pronunciation excluded him from most of the conversation.

That the poor man's mainland dialect was too citified for the locals never occurred to either of them, so he was reduced to the most minimal of contacts with natives, whose mistrust of mainlanders stemmed from millennia of invasion and occupation.

From the tutor, made lonely enough to befriend a ten-year-old, Blaise picked up *napolitano*, which he learned to pronounce *nobly done*, and also the Esperanto of Italy— Formal Roman.

The brown hills had been dry, with withered weeds and an all-pervasive dust. During the heat, while his parents worked inside the villa's cool walls, Blaise went unchaperoned into the village, where he was less welcome even than his tutor. Blaise had seen cobblestones before. His parents traveled and took him with them. Squat mud huts held together by whitewash were no surprise. The children were.

They watched with hard, black eyes, parading after him in xenophobic packs, always there, always uncommunicative. They did not answer Roman, nor Napolitano, nor Latin. They talked among themselves, staring at him as if deaf.

They became bold and his days turned into desperate one-on-one battles. Each day with a different boy. He never won or lost. It was like fighting physically with his parents, and each new morning he rose sick with fear and anticipation, and each day he went anyway into the village to a spot on the bluff where the distant blue of the straits glinted and he fought again. Nights he spent mentally designing death machines, dreaming ways to acquire the materials. He learned to hate. Days on that bluff set in him the mold of that black distrust that was Sicily. Giovanni Oesti had brought those feelings back to life.

One morning Blaise entered the village and no boy stepped forward to spit at his feet. He had fought them all. There was nobody left. That was the day one boy spoke in halting Roman: *"My name is Cesco."*

Blaise's parents continued Boston Latin at dinner. Mornings, the tutor told him glowing tales in Church Latin of the ancient glories of Rome. Evenings, after a half liter of Marsala, the tutor would lapse into Neapolitan and Blaise came to know that "See Naples and die" could be taken literally.

By day, he listened to the outrage that beat in the soul and blood of Sicily. He learned that pumping water took coins and bread from one of the boys and he got his mother to hire a cook's helper. Ottilie did it despite Alfred's insistence that she was spoiling the boy. Blaise was grateful though he never told his mother the favor she had done. For now he not only spoke *siciliano*; he understood the driving force of *omertà*.

The boy who grew up to become Dr. Cunningham said little, yet gained power among the younger children and even some of the older ones. Power came with stealth and force, and was earned.

Before he left, he sold his Swiss Army pocket knife for a coin so small that in America it would not even be money. He had learned that something so important to a man's dignity as a knife will take insult at the imputation of worthlessness and cut a friendship in two if it be given instead of sold. Cesco had the honor to buy the knife, for honor may be conferred on both buyer and seller.

On the way back to America, his father asked what Blaise had done with his birthday present. Blaise said he lost it. The lie had hurt his father and now it weighed on Blaise's soul.

Linda grumped over his cryptic answers, then curled up like an oversize kitten and went to sleep. At the end of the ride she gave Blaise a chaste pat on the cheek and got into an Italian-body car that looked as durable as Taiwan designer jeans.

She was angry because Giovanni excluded her from the conversation, Blaise thought on his way to the university, or because Blaise had cooperated by slipping into the arcane dialect of Sicily. Blaise wasn't sure which.

Mind on automatic, he fed Alfie the data on West's name change, the winery six hundred miles north, the hint of Mafia involvement, the connection to the SEC through Tenro. All vague . . . But the sort of thing at which Alfie excelled.

Alfie's core intelligence rested in a series of programmable microprocessors in a module as big as Blaise's thumb, all operating as a servo unit to one VLS integrated chip. The prime chip maintained its integrity always. Its principal duty was internal reprogramming of slave chips for a variety of interactions not possible with conventional microprocessors. After storing the working program, Blaise opened Alfie's "subconscious" and instructed the master chip to reprogram.

Alfie checked the routines for error, but working directly against the reconfiguration of the slave chips produced strange forms that Alfie did not recognize, which had to be approved by Blaise. Intuitive decision making, which Alfie seemed incapable of learning, was the reason he remained only a smart machine.

"Can I help?"

"Fa'n'gú'!" Blaise had not heard Helen enter. Now he had inverted a sequence. Alfie implemented the error, freezing half the circuits into a catatonic loop: a command from one unit tied up circuitry and triggered a similar operation in another chip which commanded a repeat in the first. A psychologist had suggested the comparison to a nervous breakdown.

"But it's not the computer's brain," Blaise had protested.

"No. The brain's perceptions are at fault." The psychologist had considered comparing computer lockup to the failure of a brain disturbed by alcohol. But if he'd wanted to face unpleasant reactions he wouldn't be teaching; he'd be raking in a hundred an hour in private practice.

Blaise took the comment to heart, installing a routine that monitored Alfie's output and, when proving that the output had no natural acceptable termination, began cutting input data lines to wall off the errant input. But self-healing takes time.

"Did I mess you up?"

Blaise restrained his irritation. "Alfie will fix it. We just have to wait."

"I'm sorry."

"Don't be. You didn't do anything."

Alfie whirred and clucked, scanning disks, comparing and evaluating to isolate the cause of the loop.

"Blaise?" Helen's hand on his arm was warm and tentative. "Don't be mad at me."

Blaise smiled and covered her hand with his. "I can't afford to. You may be the only friend I still have."

"How about Miss m and m?"

"We're not exactly friends."

"Something else?"

"Probably." He squeezed Helen's fingers.

"Why is Alfie clicking and grunting so much? He doesn't work that hard when I punch in stock market data."

"That, little darling, is the fly in the *maslanka*."

Helen seemed pleased, either by the darling or the little. She had her small weaknesses.

"You only ask him to do something he's already programmed to do. I'm asking Alfie to do the closest he can to thinking."

"I don't see the difference. Predictions are difficult."

"Difficult? Or just tedious?"

Helen hesitated. "Sometimes I can't tell the difference."

Blaise tapped the keyboard but the circuits were still frozen. "Alfie is memory and concentration. All the hardware running now is just stored memory. Alfie reads millions of words a second. That's the computer's advantage.

"Alfie has fast memory access. Not perfect, but fast. And he has perfect recall on demand. Suppose I was doing stock market computations and got to thinking about pretty blond ladies. Alfie can't do that."

"Do you think about pretty blond ladies?"

Helen's hand stroked Blaise's arm and started a tingle in his skin. Gently Blaise stopped her hand. "You'll get Alfie in my will. He's dependable and doesn't make mistakes. The sort of tin man every lady should have around the house."

"I know the sort of man I want around the house." When Blaise did not respond Helen's face reddened. Her lips trembled slightly. "What have you done with Dobie?"

"He's at the house."

"With that . . . woman?"

"She's gone. I'm having trouble with the dean about bringing Dobie on campus. Insurance." Blaise made a rude noise he'd learned in Portugal. "Dobie is smarter than the students."

"You think so?" Helen's voice changed slightly. As if she thought the same thing and wanted confirmation.

"A joke." Blaise smiled at her. "Dobie's pretty smart, I guess. I never had a dog before. He has a heck of a memory."

Alfie's beep signaled that the keyboard was open again. Blaise began correcting the botched entry. Alfie hummed and clucked and occasionally blinked a circuit telltale. Helen watched in silence for a while, then slipped out of the room as quietly as she had come in.

Finally Blaise sat back in triumph. "All right, can-opener, go get 'em." He listened to Alfie's smooth sound leafing through procedures. He fished a half-empty vodka bottle from the supply closet. He didn't like to drink in front of Helen. It seemed to disturb her.

The monitor began outlining a program to access the most easily entered public records and then progressively more difficult and protected files. Alfie flagged the harder targets for Blaise to help with later.

Tilting the bottle, he realized for the first time since Hemmett shrugged him off that he had nowhere to go and nothing to do. Except wait for Alfie to tell him if he had a problem. Even before he finished the bottle Blaise knew he was going to miss Hemmett's acid attitude. That he was a pompous fraud did not stop Blaise from liking the poor SOB. "Dr. Hemmett," he murmured, "life is unfair to both of us."

Later, when Blaise had mellowed, the door opened and Helen came in with her arms full of papers.

"Oh!" she said. "You startled me, so quiet in the shadows."

Blaise sensed her embarrassment at being seen as she saw herself. Tall, big, wishing herself some small and graceful animal to fit in his hand. "You're a beautiful woman," he said.

"Do you mean it, Blaise?"

"I do." He kissed her cheek. "I have to go. Alfie is doing some other things so he may run slower than usual. Don't pay any attention if he complains."

Blaise started to the door. Then remembered the bottle. Leaving more empties for the janitors was not going to improve his situation. As he closed the door, he was surprised to see tears in Helen's eyes.

"Lock the door on your way out." The words were wet and her mascara had started to run.

Clutching the bottle inside its disguise of printout, Blaise put distance between himself and the classroom. There being nowhere else to go, he went home.

"Good afternoon, Dr. Cunningham."

A priest filled Blaise's front-door alcove. He seemed somehow misplaced in the line of Italian cedars that stood sentry at each side of the entrance.

Just what I needed! Blaise's antipathy to the clergy was both inherent and Sicilian. He resented intellectual authoritarianism. And in Sicily he had known the loathing that venal carpetbaggers from Rome inspired with their habitual pipelining of confessions to *carabinieri*.

"I gave at the office," he growled. It felt stupid talking to a priest while swinging an empty bottle. Dobie padded up, nails clicking rhythmically on the wood. He smelled the priest and stood a moment storing, sorting, comparing. Then he sniffed again at the tall man's black suit.

"Could I have a word with you?"

Blaise unlocked the door. He had seen this man before. "You're from the picket line," he guessed.

"I thought you might remember. Robert Argyle." Following Blaise, Father Argyle patted Dobie on the head. "Fine animal."

Automatically Blaise asked, "Would you like a drink?"

"No, thank you. The *Chorch* can barely find shelter now for priests with drinking problems. But, by all means, have one yourself." The hint of Blarney in Father Argyle's voice overlayed a basic Scots rhythm. Blaise supposed he had done his boot camp in Ireland.

Blaise crashed the empty bottle in the kitchen trash and found a cold beer. He was annoyed with himself—reacting to the priest like a sinner caught in the act.

"I cannot accept any form of Christian or Islamic submission to the will of something outside myself," he said. "Nor do I know any life form that outlives its organic support."

"Relax, Doctor. Your condition is not contagious."

Blaise sucked his beer wishing he'd kept the priest outside and retained the option of walking in and slamming the door.

"I'm not recruiting souls, Doctor. Just information if you can spare it."

"Quid petis?" Blaise quoted from the *De Baptismô Adultôrum* rite, making a petty challenge of scholarship.

"The Gift of Faith," Argyle said without blinking, "for which we must all constantly pray. But at the moment I'm trying to learn what GENRECT is doing. And where Dr. Gordon Hill is."

Dobie's ears suddenly hardened. He turned his head to stare at the priest's lips with his soft eyes. Blaise noticed. Obviously the dog recognized the name.

Blaise finished his beer. "GENRECT does research. And if Dr. Hill wants to talk to you, I'm sure he will."

"If he knows I want to speak with him. You will tell him, won't you, Doctor?"

"Just as soon as I see him."

"Then all that remains is for me to thank you for answering my questions so graciously, Dr. Cunningham."

Blaise said nothing as he let the priest out the door, but his lungs strained for oxygen. Dobie pressed his nose against the screen and whined after the departing priest.

Under the sofa cushions Blaise found the cordless telephone, his usual place for it when he was drinking. He rapped the numbers into the buttons.

"Mrs. Hill?"

The woman's voice on the other end of the line sounded faint and scratchy, which, Blaise suspected, came from not recharging the telephone.

"This is Dr. Cunningham."

"Yes?"

"Mrs. Hill, have you heard from Gordon?"

The silence lasted. After a while she asked, "What is going on, Dr. Cunningham?"

"I don't know, Mrs. Hill. I'm trying to find out. May I come over and talk for a few minutes?"

"Yes," she said. "I wish you would."

Blaise revved the VW's forty horsepower downhill, catching up with the priest striding toward the beach and, Blaise guessed, buses and taxis. The priest waved and Blaise couldn't help feeling like a heel. He should have offered a ride or at least his telephone to call a cab. Dobie followed the black-garbed man with his eyes until he was out of sight. All the way to Gordon's Bird Rock home Blaise kept telling himself that the priest was odd—even for a priest. His mother would have told him this was no excuse for manners.

Mrs. Hill greeted him as if she had been waiting at the door since Blaise called. Stella Hill was brunette, with a tendency to pudginess. Her normally full face was gaunt. Her eyes were shadowed. Even her dark-brown dress lent a somber air.

"It was kind of you to come, Doctor." She looked at Dobie without comment before leading Blaise into a living room with a warm, lived-in feel. Gordon's presence was there in a rack of pipes on an end table next to a chair, as if he had just gone into another room. Blaise thought of the children and knew they must be in school. If he felt Gordon's presence so strongly, his absence must be unbearable for Stella Hill.

"Have you seen him?" she demanded. Dobie panted and leaned toward her.

"I'm sorry. That's what I came to ask you."

Mrs. Hill's brown dress hung loose, accenting her gauntness. Blaise suspected that normally Stella Hill fit into her clothes and surroundings with efficient grace. "Almost two weeks," she said. "I thought you were bringing news. You have Dobie."

Blaise shook his head.

Abruptly Mrs. Hill was crying. "Gordon liked you," she sobbed. "He said you had problems but you were a good man." She spoke of her husband in past tense. "Why do you have his dog?"

"Is he a pet, Mrs. Hill?"

Stella Hill sat on the edge of a sofa chair, hunched forward as if her stomach hurt. "Only to Gordon. He wouldn't let me or the children get attached to him. We know what happens to experiments, Dr. Cunningham."

Dobie drew his lips back and wiggled his stump of tail. He seemed to sense Mrs. Hill was talking about him.

"Gordon just asked me to keep Dobie for a while, and I haven't heard from him since." Blaise looked at Dobie, straining toward Mrs. Hill, though maintaining his obedience to Blaise. "Would you like to keep him?"

Mrs. Hill shook her head. "We don't know how much time he has left. Do you, Dr. Cunningham?"

Without thinking, Blaise put his hand on the animal's shoulder. "I hadn't thought of that."

Mrs. Hill took a handkerchief from a pocket. "What if he

should die? Suddenly? For me and the children it would be like Gordon had died. You understand, don't you?"

"Yes. I do." Blaise stroked Dobie's furry back, knowing suddenly he would miss the dog if something happened. "I'll keep him then. As Gordon wanted. May I sit down?"

Stella Hill seemed distressed that she had left Blaise standing. She nodded violently before putting her face in her hands.

"Can you answer some questions?"

Mrs. Hill lifted her head and looked at Blaise, her eyes scrubbed dry. "Yes. Don't mind my outburst, Dr. Cunningham. I want to help."

"Did Gordon say he was going? Leave a note?"

"One evening he just didn't come home."

"Didn't he call or write?"

"Once. He said he was going someplace where they didn't have a phone." Her eyelids were shiny with moisture. Small, red veins fanned out from the corners of her eyes. "His pay is deposited regularly." Stella looked up and her face came apart again. "I don't want the money, *I want my husband!*"

"So do I, Mrs. Hill. When Gordon disappeared half of my total stock of friends was gone."

"Please, Dr. Cunningham. You work for GENRECT. You must know something."

"Have you called Dr. Hemmett?"

"He said he'd ask Gordon to call me. Nothing came of it."

Stella Hill's features were strong. Prominent cheekbones, a sharply defined nose, thick silky eyelashes, and a heavy coil of wavy black hair that bounced on her shoulders. She moved her head slightly while Blaise talked, as if looking at him from different perspectives while listening.

She had reservations when he explained what he wanted her to say. But she never voiced them. She picked up the phone and called Hemmett at GENRECT. Blaise knew from Stella Hill's face that Hemmett was being suave and gracious, and it was going down like lumpy peanut butter.

If she had been going to balk, the director's oily manner settled it. "Dr. Hemmett," she said after listening a long while, "if I do not hear from Gordon today, I'm going to tell the police my husband disappeared while under your supervision. Meanwhile, my attorney will initiate civil and criminal proceedings."

She listened to Hemmett's strangled reply for a moment before saying "Thank you." Hemmett was still yammering when her click shut him off.

"Well?" she asked.

"Extremely well," Blaise said. "Now we wait." He leaned back in the easy chair and tried not to dream of bottles. Mrs. Hill went into the kitchen and rattled things. Over the sound Blaise heard muffled sobs. He drifted off into uneasy sleep.

The telephone's strident ring jolted him awake. His mouth was dry and a breathless feeling filled his throat. Mrs. Hill skittered into the living room and then stopped, frozen.

"Pick it up," Blaise said.

She did, slowly.

"Hello. Dr. Hemmett? Yes." She looked at Blaise and he nodded. She was doing fine.

"What do you mean, Gordon won't talk to me?" She stared at Blaise with wide brown eyes as if not seeing him or believing what she was being told. "Will he talk to somebody else?"

She waited a moment, listening, then said, "No, Dr. Hemmett, I do not mean will he talk to you. Will he speak to somebody else? Somebody like Dr. Cunningham?"

She listened, then said, "Thank you," and hung up.

"That was good," Blaise said soothingly.

"He said he'd ask."

Blaise nodded.

"Dr. Hemmett says you are an irresponsible drunk."

"He always gives the good news first."

She tried to smile. "Gordon says you're too responsible. He's usually right."

Blaise licked suddenly dry lips. "You should know, Mrs. Hill. I am a drunk."

"Gordon told me that, too. He said, drunk or sober, you're too responsible for your own good."

"Who can argue with Gordon?" Blaise suddenly suspected Hemmett was right. He was involving Mrs. Hill in more than just looking for her husband. "If Hemmett calls back, tell him Gordon is to call me at home. You can reach me there if you need me."

"I hoped Gordon could call here..." Her voice trailed off.

"Mrs. Hill, if Gordon calls me it's not because he can't call you. He can't trust himself to keep you at a distance."

"You think so?"

"Gordon loves you. There's no other woman in his life."

She started crying. "You go home, then, Dr. Cunningham, and I'll tell him to call you there."

"We'll try first, Mrs. Hill."

"It might work."

"Sure. Besides, all it will take is a little time." Blaise sat back in the chair and pretended to sleep, embarrassed that Mrs. Hill was sobbing and he was powerless to do anything. Dobie stirred uneasily. Blaise patted him and Dobie laid down, head on paws. Blaise had lied. There could be other repercussions if Stella Hill pressed too hard.

Hemmett rang again and settled for the call to Blaise's home. At the door Mrs. Hill entreated him with desperate eyes.

"It wouldn't work, Mrs. Hill."

"I know. I'm just being foolish."

"I'll make a tape if I can."

She hugged his hand. "Thank you, Dr. Cunningham."

"Blaise," he said. "Like a fire." He didn't tell her that he was not St. George, that at the first sign of a dragon he would crawl into a bottle.

He hoped the priest had not come back. Everything he did these days put him on somebody's bad side. How was he going to face it if God joined his persecutors?

The measurably different rates of speed at which electrical impulses are transmitted in different species, and even individuals within a species, would indicate that lack of intelligence may be a simple physical malfunction.

FROM A SEMINAR ON
THE CUNNINGHAM EQUATIONS

CHAPTER 8

*E*sther *Tazy squatted astraddle him, full, firm breasts jouncing in time with the pounding of her fists on his chest. "Can you do nothing right?" she stormed. "Do you,* Doketore, *need your parents to show you how to do this, too?"*

Blaise awoke sweating, expecting to find Esther still atop him. Instead he found Dobie lying across his chest shivering violently. All he really remembered of that night with Esther was futile fumblings that ended with him going to sleep. He shook Dobie gently. "Do you have nightmares, too?"

Dobie stared into Blaise's eyes, straining to tell him.

The ringing in Blaise's ears identified itself as the telephone. "Off the bed, Dobie." Blaise stumbled into the living room and picked up the cordless receiver. Outside the big window the moon was a mercury-slicked dime slipping into the black Pacific, its bottom clipped by invisible shears.

"Hello."

"The notorious Dr. Cunningham, I presume?" The flat, dry voice with its hint of west Texas was Gordon Hill's.

"Christ, Gordon. What time is it?"

"How do I know? I can't see in the dark. You should have known I'd call now. Unless Stella is camped in your bed, which is unlikely, or cleaning your rat's nest in the dark, which is impossible, this is the best time to talk without interruption."

"I didn't let your wife come back here with me. You should have a little faith, Gordon."

"I did. This is the police department's favorite hour for

parking ticket arrests. People are home. Dragged off half dressed and shoved into a tank full of muggers, drunks, pushers, and gays caught in public toilets, they don't argue. They pay. If it's good enough for the cops..."

Blaise stood staring out the picture window and tried to blow the fog from his mind.

"At least you're sober."

"Almost."

"In psychiatry," Hill said, "the goal is to change the subject from within. A cure for alcoholism starts when the subject admits a problem. Naturally, he rationalizes. The shrink acts as a conscience, maintaining the problem's reality."

"Gibberish."

"Behaviorists think if the subject is forced to change his behavior long enough, it becomes habit, which is easier than analytic thought. At some point the subject finds the new behavior easier to live with than the old and you have, if not a cure, a solution."

"Why not a cure?"

"Freudianism. A cause exists, hence so do the symptoms."

"There's more?"

"There is always more in magic, theology, or science. If true alcoholism is physical, then psychiatry cannot eliminate the cause, but a behaviorist may be able to abort the symptoms. Like pneumonia. Everyone has the germ; only a few have the disease."

"The point, Gordon."

"You have finally lifted your problems to levels where drinking makes them unbearable instead of unmemorable."

"Gordon, I'm standing in a cold living room in the middle of the night, naked, and my head hurts—mainly because of your wife and kids."

Gordon's voice changed. Blaise read the distress in it and knew he'd drifted over the line again. "I'm sorry."

"Yes. So am I." Gordon's voice was hollow with a pained weariness. "I want you to talk to Stella for me."

"Why can't you talk to her?"

"Tell her I'm doing something very difficult, from which I must insulate her and the children. She is not to try to contact me again. The experiment is of indefinite duration."

"What is it? Are you safe?" Blaise was about to ask what illness could be transmitted over a telephone line. Then he knew. Teenagers everywhere spent hours infecting one another.

"If I were safe, wouldn't I talk to my own wife?"

"It helps if you say it, Gordon."

"I suppose."

Blaise sensed that they had come to an end. "Where are you, Gordon? I know you haven't been at the lab."

"If I tell you, I defeat myself." Gordon stopped talking and the line was curiously hollow. "Face your own problem, Blaise. They're doing wonderful work at Mount Sinai in New York. Check out Dr. Marie Gibson. Her endocrinology studies could become standard treatment for alcoholism."

"What you need is a cure for pigheadedness."

"As Dr. Hemmett says, you are gifted with a ready insult. In passing, Blaise, I do believe you have irritated the good doctor vastly. Good night."

"Wait!" Blaise was too late.

He turned on the light and switched the portable computer to ready. The telephone split was already plugged into the modem and the phone barely burped before Alfie opened the line. The monitor spelled out random green letters and numbers, then: "GOOD MORNING, PROFESSOR"

Blaise made sure Gordon's recording was backed up before returning to bed.

Something soft brushed his lips. Much too gently for energetic Esther. Blaise awoke and Linda drew away laughing. She looked bright and sparkly in the morning sun and her hair showed deep glints of red. "More," he croaked.

"More what?"

"Mouth-to-mouth resuscitation. I'm drowning." He looked into eyes the color of a mountain stream burbling over some quiet place carpeted with algae.

"Work now, play later."

Blaise gave up hope of sleep. He considered brisk calisthenics. Then habit took over and he settled for a shower. When he came out in a terry-cloth robe Linda was helplessly surveying the kitchen.

"You need a cleaning lady," she observed. "If I am reduced to bartering my splendid body, the least I can accept is breakfast on a regular basis."

"We'll go down to the village in a minute." Blaise cranked up the Zorba and punched in some data, plus a request for information that the machine forwarded via modem to Alfie. By the time he had dressed, Alfie was busy. A quick look at the monitor and he knew the processing would take hours. But Alfie had received the message okay. Blaise erased the Zorba's floppy. Then, after an instant's hesitation, he reformatted it.

Erasing only wiped out the directory and any high school kid could still recover the data unless someone went to the trouble of rewriting the whole disk full of E5s, the hex number a computer reads as empty, available space.

"What are you doing?" Linda watched from the door.

"Frustrating snoops. Where's Dobie?"

"Outside."

"Don't you like dogs?"

"Some kinds." Linda stared at Blaise without blinking. "Did you find Dr. Hill?"

"Perhaps."

Linda shrugged. "You're the expert."

"I like to think so." Numbers and references began tumbling across the monitor. The printer made its cloth-ripping sound for a second and was silent. He tore off the half sheet of paper and stuffed it in his pocket. They ate at a café where the waitress didn't give him a funny look when he ordered beer with his one-egg breakfast.

The VW was being buffeted by the shock wave of a passing truck before Linda realized they were not on their way home. She studied the beach with its row of wet-suiters astraddle surfboards just beyond the breaker line. "We could have taken my car," she said. "At least it can go faster than the trucks."

Air leaks around windows made the VW as noisy as a helicopter. She raised her voice. "Where are we going?"

"See Gordon. It's a surprise."

"For me?"

"Gordon, too."

"Didn't he invite you?"

"Thinks I don't know where he is." Yelling was giving Blaise a headache.

They swung off the northbound freeway, threading cloverleafs lined with pickle weed and African daisies. Automatic sprinklers came on and the wind put a dusting of mist on the VW's windshield. The noise dropped and conversation became possible.

"Doesn't anyone ever invite you to see them?"

"You don't want to know how I did it?"

"And give you a chance to brag?"

"I got him to call me."

"And?"

"Alfie traced the call."

"How did you manage that?"

"Our secret. Alfie's and mine."

"I mean, get Dr. Hill to call?"

Blaise thought of Stella Hill crying and sitting by the telephone and doing everything he asked even though it was tearing her up. "I'd rather not say," he mumbled.

"You aren't very good at bragging."

"I guess I don't have much to brag about." Which set a pall over the car's interior until they rolled into the Heaven's Gate parking lot.

"What is this?" Tennis courts, cabanas, and golf courses sprouted like an emerald in the otherwise gray terrain.

"A spa where the local power structure can mingle with gangsters."

"Meaning?"

"Sociologists claim the same people turn cop or robber for slightly different reasons. They think alike so they enjoy each other's company."

"That's a cheap shot making accusations you can't prove!"

"Forget it."

"I will not forget it. You think you know everything. But there are people who don't have a Nobel Prize because they didn't have parents to qualify them for competition in the first place."

Blaise felt his throat closing and a void where his lungs should be. Cold gripped his hands and feet. "Let's go in."

Linda flounced ahead, where she would not have noticed if Blaise staggered or looked pale. He moved his feet uncertainly, not sure how well planted they were. He needed to see Gordon.

Linda was at the reception desk, tapping a foot like an impatient ingenue waiting for a date. Men passing by turned their heads as long as they could. But it was apparently not good form to make passes before a lady had booked her room.

Blaise leaned on the desk and struggled to catch his breath.

"Sir?"

"We'd like to see the manager."

The girl looked at Blaise and then at Linda. Blaise knew he might not have passed inspection, but it was obvious that Linda did. "If you'll wait by that door I'll see if he's available."

"Thank you."

Blaise took Linda's arm and walked across the heavily carpeted foyer to a door almost invisible in the paneled wall.

It was opened by another Stephanie Powers model, slim, long-legged with a dress too expensive to be painted on, but still more than svelte.

"Please," she said.

The room was larger than the inconspicuous door would indicate. She seated them in chrome-and-walnut chairs and sat facing them across a half-circle desk with built-in terminal and printer. A keyboard recessed under the desk when not in use. The monitors just below the ceiling were obviously connected to security cameras.

"Could you tell me why you want to see the manager?"

"It's personal."

The blonde smiled. "I'm his personal secretary."

She had the keyboard out on the retracting ledge, fingers poised above it. Part of the desktop had tilted up in front of her to reveal a nine-inch monitor. "Please."

"I'm Anthony Powell and I'm here to see Dr. Gordon Hill."

Linda glanced at him as the secretary zipped over the keyboard in one sound much like the riffling of a deck of cards.

"And the young lady?"

"And friend," Blaise said.

The secretary typed Blaise's response.

"I'm sorry," she said. "That won't be possible." She looked at Blaise and Linda as if they had turned to plastic.

"I'm sorry, too. I forgot my card." He handed the girl a plain three-by-five with a neat string of pen-written numbers. She did not take it.

"I think the manager will be interested."

The blonde looked through him.

Blaise put on his most dazzling smile. "Or you can hand it to him when you're both in the unemployment line."

As if she had not heard, she took the card and reactivated

the keyboard and monitor and typed the string. She shoved the keyboard under the desk and stood.

"This way, please."

Blaise held the chair for Linda.

The secretary closed the door and left them alone in the next room. The man behind the desk stood and rubbed his jaw, as if feeling for stubble. He was fleshy, with good looks that were getting a little soft. His sharkskin suit was expensive.

"How did you get the number my secretary sent?"

"Ve haff our vays. Only Dr. Hill could make me forget it." Blaise was having difficulty breathing.

"Mr. Powell, you may not understand your situation here. And the young lady's. Extortion is a crime. The sheriff is a frequent guest. We're unincorporated so he has jurisdiction. He may be on the premises at this moment."

"Would you like another number? And a record of fund transfers between accounts?" Blaise paused. "Am I going too fast for you?"

The manager stared.

"A man facing reelection might not like to hear that other people know so much about him."

"Dr. Hill is not here."

Blaise contemplated the manager and controlled his breathing.

"At the moment."

Beside the telephone on his desk lay a geometric pattern of paper clips. The manager followed Blaise's gaze.

"I suppose it would be all right."

"A pleasure doing business with you, sir."

"My secretary will take you."

"Thank you."

The door opened even though Blaise had not seen a signal button. The secretary held the door for Blaise and Linda before starting off in a brisk model's walk that kept her hips level and free of erotic bounce, freezing her dress hem at a perfect angle.

Gordon seemed amused when Blaise stepped into the small office. Another man, large, with big hands and a bland face under a fifty-dollar haircut, leaned against the wall.

"Sit down." Gordon sat behind the desk and played with his pipe. Blaise and Linda took a pair of straight-backed chairs. The room was as austere as Blaise supposed he would find anywhere in Heaven's Gate: white plaster and furniture that looked like it came from a college laboratory.

The other man's sole function seemed to be holding up the wall. Blaise studied him. "My assistant." Gordon's irony was more in content than in form.

"I thought I might drop by to see you in person, Dr. Hill."

"Yes. Well, you are prone to rash decisions, Mr. .... Powell." Gordon had glanced down to his desktop at a single sheet where a glacially neat hand had written the name.

"My friend, Miss Lovely, wanted to meet you."

"How do you do, Miss Lovely." Gordon always took delight in gentle deception. And he was appreciative of women, though Blaise doubted that he ever strayed from a marriage bedded in cement.

Linda offered her hand and Blaise was struck by the contrast between faery princess and stone mountain. They chatted for a few minutes. Gordon's assistant leaning against the wall looked bored, but disinclined to go for a stroll.

"I was wondering if you could tell me more about the work you're doing here," Linda was saying. "I have some friends who are interested in coming down for treatment."

The man against the wall yawned. Blaise looked at Linda.

"It's still in the experimental stage, young lady. Unfortunately the process is secret—to protect it until the patent clears."

"But it is safe?"

Gordon smiled. "I have the best proof." Unexpectedly, he stood. "I'm afraid I have to cut this short, Miss Lovely." He studied Linda with open admiration. "Amazing that you should be born to so fortuitous a name. Perhaps even God cannot resist the obvious."

"You're very gallant, Dr. Hill."

"Ah, if I were but five years younger..." He winked slowly and Linda had little choice except to laugh.

"Take hormones," she said.

"I shall. Come. I'll walk you to your car."

They ambled across the putting green lawn on neat pastel cement sidewalks. Gordon's assistant followed, having traded wall-propping for holding up the sky like some disoriented Atlas.

"Who's your assistant, Gordon?"

Gordon glanced back. "A sort of bodyguard."

"You're not here against your will?"

Gordon's face twisted, for a moment showing Blaise a man he had never seen before. His eyes conveyed a regret that Blaise didn't think he wanted to know about. Gordon was no prisoner. This wasn't Sicily.

"You read too many frivolous books, Blaise. They need me here. The pay is . . . good." Gordon seemed embarrassed by the mention of money. "I'm not after a Nobel Prize. You can relax on that score." Gordon glanced at Blaise and chuckled. "I know about the pressures of competition. Believe me." He hesitated and lowered his voice so neither Linda nor the assistant could hear. "I have a deal, Blaise. You haven't, so don't pressure them. They're worried about word getting to the . . . competition before they're ready. Don't get involved."

Gordon caught up with Linda, who flirted outrageously with him. Blaise wondered if Stella Hill had been forced to brain a covey of nurses to bag the Great Stone Face for herself.

The yellow VW with crumpled fenders and dirty windows and measlelike rust spots huddled in a parking space almost twice its size. Cadillacs, Continentals, Rollses, and Mercedeses in cream and gold and handbeaten aluminum and black lacquer on midnight blue towered around it. A stainless-steel DeLorean with gull wing doors punctuated the beetle's junkyard aura.

Gordon recognized it, of course, and steered unerringly toward the scabrous yellow bug. Two men in suits headed their way from the other end of the lot. Gordon asked for a kiss.

"I thought you'd never ask." Linda threw in a hug that would have made Blaise jealous if he'd been paying attention.

"Dr. Hill, Dr. Hill!" The men in suits were running. Blaise recognized the manager who stepped heavily, as if unused to exercise.

Dobie began barking from inside the bug. Gordon leaned in the window and hugged him while the pup licked his ear. "You're a good boy, Dobie."

Dobie whined and leaped out, trying to go with Gordon.

"No, Dobie!" Gordon's voice cut sharply and the dog whimpered, crouching on the pavement.

Weighty footsteps were practically on them as Blaise swung the door open and coaxed Dobie back inside. The Doberman liked riding and possibly he hoped Gordon would follow. Blaise wasn't sure how a dog thought. But Dobie was used to the VW so he went over the seats into the back where he could sit and look at everybody, particularly Gordon.

"What the hell are you doing?" The spa manager was out of breath and his soft-featured face was dangerously red.

"Saying good-bye, Mr. Jensen. It was nice of you to come see my friends off." Gordon was affable and polite, but it seemed as if Mr. Jensen would have preferred to avoid him, which he did by turning to Blaise.

"Get that damn dog out of the car." Jensen's face had hardened into professional meanness.

"Can't." If Gordon could be affable, Blaise could too. "The kids want him back."

"What kids?"

"Mine and Miss Lovely's. He's their watchdog. You want a dog I suggest you start with a puppy and bring him up right." Linda glanced at Blaise, showing no distress at being mother to an unnumbered illegitimate brood.

"Get the dog out of there," Jensen snapped at Gordon's assistant, who was watching the proceedings with amusement. "That's your dog, isn't it, Dr. Hill? The one we're all looking for?"

The huge man looked at Dobie, who filled a lot of car with his oversized head and oversized teeth. "Not my job." He went back to sky-leaning.

Jensen was ejecting spittle. His color had gone so ruddy Blaise expected a stroke. Gordon ignored the display.

Turning to the man who had come onto the parking lot with him, Jensen said, "You! Get the damn dog out of there."

"But, Mr. Jensen..."

Jensen gave him a grim look. The man shrugged. Hesitantly he reached into the open VW and said, "Nice doggie."

When Dobie growled his lip curved up, exposing a fang.

Jensen's assistant bounced back so fast he whacked his head on the door frame. "Christ," he observed, "teeth like bayonets!"

"The Nazis used them as attack dogs," Gordon said helpfully. "Trained them to crawl into one end of a trench and kill every man before they came out."

"He's full of shit." Jensen shoved at his helper.

"We'd better be going, Gordon." Blaise shook his hand and held the door open for Linda. Gingerly she slid into the seat. Dobie promptly hung his massive head over her shoulder.

Blaise got in the driver's side.

Jensen was so mad he was shaking. "Give me a gun."

The man who had come out with him said, "What for?"

"I'm going to shoot that goddamn dog."

"No, you're not." Gordon's voice was low, but the manager looked up.

"We've got to get the dog!"

"Leave him alone."

Jensen attempted to kill the dog with a glare. When it didn't work he stepped back from the VW, waving away the gun his assistant offered.

As Blaise started the engine Gordon's "helper" leaned down to the open window, face only inches away, and bland as if he still held up the sky. "Good-bye, Dr. Cunningham." His voice was pleasant.

Blaise put the bug in gear, forcing Jensen to move aside. Jensen looked after them as they left the parking lot. As Dr. Hill grew smaller in the distance Dobie stared back wrapped in sadness.

Blaise drove in silence, concentrating on the road and his mirrors.

"Does he bite?" Linda's voice was very small. Blaise hadn't realized the reason she put Dobie out at every opportunity was fear. Dobie's big head jounced up and down on Linda's shoulder, rubbing the side of her face.

"Gordon's kids stick their heads in his mouth and dare him."

Linda thought a moment. "Have you seen the kids lately?"

Blaise laughed. Then Linda laughed and even Dobie grinned. It was better than admitting he hadn't seen Gordon's kids.

He looked in the mirror again.

Intelligence presupposes the ability to learn and thus adapt.
The goal is to be the most adaptable.

FROM A SEMINAR ON
THE CUNNINGHAM EQUATIONS

CHAPTER 9

Blaise inched up the speed until the beetle was racketing unmercifully. Linda gripped the dashboard handle and
stared straight ahead when her eyes weren't closed.

"Sleeping?" Blaise asked.

"Praying. Tell me when the wheels drop off."

Blaise veered past a chuckhole that could have swallowed
a moped. In the mirror he saw a black dot a long way behind
making, as naval officers are fond of saying, knots.

"You missed the on-ramp." Linda stared longingly at the
receding freeway.

"Do you sail?"

Linda closed her eyes again. "All boats do is go up and
down, just like this thing. They make me sick."

"This isn't so bad," Blaise said cheerfully.

"I have a beautiful Porsche 920 in San Francisco. I'll even
bring it down for you to drive." The sun visor on the right
side was flopping up and down like a broken gull's wing.
People prone to motion sickness are sensitive to such dis-
tractions.

The dot in the mirror became a windshield and radiator.
Blaise slewed the VW onto a cross street, flinging Linda
against the door. Dobie made happy noises.

The black limo took more room getting around the corner,
barely missing the cement-lined ditch that ran parallel to the
road. Linda's mouth clamped shut.

Swinging into the domed ramp, the VW's wheels chittered
like rabid squirrels. Blaise straddled the white line and the
ride improved. The solid gray embankment rushed at the
side of the car as he slammed down into third.

Dobie barked at the gray wall, hoping Blaise was going to catch it the way he caught squirrels on the run. Wheels grabbed the last inches of upslanting apron, squirting the VW forward and away.

The black car flashed past the ramp without slowing or trying to enter. Blaise dropped back into fourth gear. The metallic scream of the overrevved engine faded and the tach needle fell below the red line. He checked his mirrors. Nothing behind.

"That was cute." Linda straightened her clothes.

They picked up speed on a downhill slope. The highway formed a long grade where engineers had sliced into the edge of the mesa for a constant rate of descent instead of the abrupt natural dropoff.

"Were you showing off again?" Her tone was icy.

"Normally I do handstands and backflips," Blaise said.

The access road paralleled them. Where the freeway cut into the edge of the rise a long bridge crossed the mesa high above the busy freeway. There was no traffic on the overpass—except the black Cadillac parked in the middle with two men leaning on the railing, staring down on flowing traffic.

Blaise watched them shrink in the mirror.

"Do you think I'm overdoing it?"

"Definitely!" Linda said.

"I guess so." He watched until the bridge disappeared.

Blaise prowled the house, poking in dark places he had not seen in years, wishing Linda had stayed. Dobie whined and followed, then became bored. The dog sat leaning against the couch, chin on cushion, eyes following Blaise with fresh hope each time he passed through the living room.

After a while Dobie had his forelegs on the cushion. The space-time continuum experienced a local anomaly of reverse gravity as he oozed up over the edge. When Blaise tired enough to sit he had to lever the reddish-brown and black dog out of the way while Dobie pretended he was asleep.

The phone rang. Blaise answered it and listened before hanging up. "The good Dr. Hemmett wants to see me, Dobie."

Dobie sighed.

"Guard the fort."

Dobie would. He liked the couch.

* * *

GENRECT was steeped in calm the way fine tea is supposed to be. Except for old Ben, a retiree who filled his days with mild social protest and tuna fish sandwiches he shared with the secretaries when they took him coffee, even the pickets were absent, which meant most of the staff had gone home already. The receptionist pretended to be busy when Blaise walked through the front entrance. Hemmett was having another tantrum.

The great man's frozen-faced secretary opened the door. Hemmett was standing when Blaise entered his wood-paneled office. He turned toward Blaise. "You're through!" His voice quavered.

"I'm on vacation."

"You drunken bastard!" Hemmett's voice started skidding off key. "Do you know what happened today? Do you know?"

"I talked to Gordon but—"

"You dumb shit!" Hemmett was screeching. "Mr. West called from San Francisco. He wants to know why you were bothering his father in Escondido."

Blaise's throat was too dry to squeeze a word through. He had expected Hemmett to yell about visiting Gordon. But going up to see Giovanni Oesti?

"I started this company." Hemmett's face was swollen, plum-colored skin the texture of putty. "You, you're trying to ruin it. Drunken irresponsible bastard—you'll never work again!"

"What's wrong with talking to an old man? All I wanted was to find Gordon. For his wife. You *could* have told me."

Hemmett was breathing heavily. "You're going to have plenty of time to find him. I've already called the university. They don't think much of you there either, Doctor." Suddenly Hemmett smiled. Blaise liked it better when he was mad.

Blaise fought the clamp over his chest. He'd known the risk. Even subconsciously hoped it would happen. This would break him loose from GENRECT. But now there was no going back. Even if he found excuses Hemmett could accept.

"I'll get my stuff..."

"Your booze hidden in distilled water bottles? I had that thrown out. Nothing else here belongs to you. The receptionist has your check. Don't talk to her. You might infect her."

Suddenly Hemmett looked very tired. "Get out. If you ever come back on company property, I'll have you shot."

Hemmett turned and stared out a window.

Blaise could not talk to Hemmett's back. What could he say if he did? For a while it had been exciting. Linda had been right about his showing off. She had just not seen the full scope of his folly. He hadn't found Gordon for Stella Hill. He'd done it to get a pat on the head from Linda.

Now the pat had worn off.

And Hemmett was a tired old man deep into something he was afraid of. He hadn't fired Blaise. He had propitiated West.

"Good-bye, Dr. Hemmett." Blaise couldn't tell if the older man heard. Nobody spoke on his way out. The receptionist handed him his check in a sealed envelope. The place was tomblike and Blaise realized the word had spread. Like execution night on death row, neither inmates nor guards wanted to be in range of his contagion.

He sat with the engine running and thought he saw Hemmett watching. It was funny; he had never oriented the windows to the executive offices and he didn't know which was Hemmett's. Could have been just a trick of the light. Even old Ben was gone. He eased the bug in gear and drove away.

A Datsun Z100 sat squeezed over on the apron so he could slide the VW into the garage. Metallic gold, the car had cream-colored leather upholstery. Blaise wondered what rental agency Linda was doing business with. She seemed to change cars as casually as her dress. Blaise thought that over and retracted. She changed her dresses with more panache.

He found her on one end of the couch with Dobie holding down the other. The dog was chewing one of Blaise's shoes out of the bedroom closet and Linda had the phone. Looking up, she said, "Hi," then returned to dialing.

Her feet were curled under her on the white and flower print sofa. She wore a sheer lace blouse and a half-in-the-ocean sun through the big picture window outlined her breasts from beneath.

He leaned down and kissed her cheek. "You smell good."

She put the cordless phone down. "I'm hungry."

Examining the sun, Blaise said, "It's late enough."

Absently, Blaise scratched the dog's ears. Dobie dropped the shoe and licked Blaise's hand.

"We can eat at the airport," she said.

"I can't go anywhere right now."

"You've got to."

"I have to see Gordon's wife. And there may be problems."

"It can wait." Linda stood in one lithe motion and patted her hair, making sure all the curls were still in place.

"I was fired today."

Linda shrugged. "You'll get another job."

"Probably. But I still can't go."

"Well, I can't stay. I have to talk with Uncle Milo."

"Stay tonight. Go up early in the morning."

"Whatever for?"

"Just an idea."

"Not a very good one. I'll eat in the airport restaurant." She shifted her hips and swirled the hem of her skirt. "You know, I'm losing weight from all this running around."

The telephone rang and she picked it up first and listened. "For you." She passed the handset to Blaise.

"You thieving bastard! Bring that damn dog back here!" Hemmett's yelling made the telephone chatter. Blaise pressed the cut-off button. He pulled the cord to the base station.

"What are you doing?" Linda stared. "How can I get a telephone call?"

"You'll think of something. You wouldn't know how Dobie got my shoe, would you?"

"I gave it to him."

"You gave it to him?"

Linda examined her nails. "He was taking up too much of the couch. The trainer who writes for our paper says to give your dog an old shoe. It alleviates boredom and helps him remember who his master is."

"But, my shoe!"

"Did you expect me to give him one of mine?" Linda dabbed polish on a nail and waved her fingers in the air.

"I hadn't thought of it that way," Blaise admitted.

Linda examined her fingernails. "I tried to use the computer, but I couldn't access the mainframe."

"The mainframe is Alfie. He discriminates."

"Against women?"

"Against everybody except me."

"To each his own. Would you like to take me to the airport?" Linda had her Peruvian serape at the door.

"You have your own car." Blaise did want to take her but to show his desire would indicate total irrationality.

Linda patted his cheek. "Try to get used to it."

Blaise took her arm. Physically small, mentally she was not. "Your bag?"

"It'll be here when I come back, won't it?" She smiled and hugged his arm. "I have clothes in San Francisco."

Blaise snapped his fingers and Dobie dropped the shoe. "We'll take my car. I don't want him chewing up the upholstery in a rental."

In the VW Dobie stretched everywhere he could, which was like being inside a tennis ball with a warm, reddish brown and black rubber band with teeth and a cold nose. Finally the dog settled with his head lolling on the backrest and his bright black eyes counting stars.

"Do you love me?" Linda asked as they rolled sedately down the freeway.

He put his arm around her and she snuggled close, tucking her head under his chin like a violin. "Could you repeat the question?"

Customers at the airport restaurant lined up for a twenty-minute wait. Blaise settled Linda in the bar and brought chili dogs from across the corridor.

The waitress came to the tiny booth and he ordered an orange juice for himself and a martini for Linda. A five-dollar tip persuaded the waitress not to bother them.

Barely larger than a silver dollar, the table inspired togetherness. Blaise could not restrain himself. He put a hand on a silky knee and experienced an adolescent thrill.

"Stop that." Linda did not move her knee.

Blaise shrugged and put his hands in his pockets. "You remind me of my mother," he said. Adding hastily, "I don't mean you look like her. It's just things you say and do remind me."

"I know." Linda's gaze was distracted. Their knees were touching. Linda moved hers.

"Why did you do that?"

"You're not concentrating. Did Dr. Hill give any hints about what he was doing?"

"You were there. Gordon wasn't speaking *siciliano*."

"It might as well have been."

Blaise made wet rings on the imitation onyx with his old-fashioned glass of orange juice and ice.

Linda put her hand over his. "You're doing very well."

Before Blaise could reply she added, "I have to go." She turned her wrist so he could see her gold watch set with a tasteful sparkle of rubies looking like something from Cartier's. It was just as late as if the watch had only cost ten dollars. She wore a ring that matched, an old-fashioned design with raised rubies, emeralds, and diamonds on a thick gold band.

Blaise started with her to the boarding gate and she pushed at him. "I can get on the plane by myself, silly." She gave him a warm kiss before disappearing.

He sat a long time. The waitress returned and smiled. Reminding himself that he was now unemployed, he left before he could be tempted into a drink. Back at the car Dobie gave him a kiss. It wasn't the same as Linda's. But he knew Dobie was expressing love.

Stella Hill opened the door on the first ring. She wore a soft organdy dress that clung to her like a man's hands and Blaise knew she had been waiting for a man to walk through the door. Unfortunately he was not the man.

"Dobie!" The Doberman whimpered happily. She flung her arms around the big dog's neck, crying.

Blaise closed the door and stood awkwardly out of the way until Mrs. Hill stood and wiped her eyes. "I'm sorry," she said. "I'm not myself today. Will you..." She looked toward the living room and Blaise nodded and snapped his fingers, calling Dobie.

"Gordon is all right," Blaise said when he was seated. He didn't comment on Stella Hill's loss of control.

Stella Hill had made coffee. Blaise played with his, sipping it scalding hot and trying to expunge the need for a drink. Dobie tried to be fair about having two people around who liked him. He sat against Blaise's leg, then lay with his nose resting on Mrs. Hill's shoe. Dobie knew she really cared.

"Dobie, that tickles." She didn't sound annoyed so Dobie sighed hotly against her ankle. "When's he coming home?"

"I don't know. But Gordon's well and hard at work. He's serious about what he's doing.

"Something is wrong. It's dangerous. Like he's working with a germ he doesn't want us to catch accidentally. Otherwise he wouldn't bury himself. He loves the children." She wanted confirmation. Her eyes were desperate.

"It couldn't be that. He saw me. Shook my hand, knowing I'd come straight back to you. If it was that kind of danger he'd be afraid I'd infect you."

"Then tell me, Dr. Cunningham, what my devious husband is up to."

Blaise wondered if she thought Gordon had found another woman. He rested his elbows on his knees and clasped his bony hands and contemplated Mrs. Hill over his knuckles. He stared into her eyes because even educated people believe they can read candor. It is the easiest way to begin a lie.

"I think," he said slowly and deliberately, "that Gordon is covering up some hocus-pocus for Dr. Hemmett. The company's broke and Hemmett needs a miracle to raise fresh dollars."

"Gordon wouldn't do that!" Dismay lined her voice.

"He would if his contract is anything like mine. The money's all in the stock options. Gordon worries about getting kids through college and paying off the house, Mrs. Hill."

"But you don't know Gordon! He wouldn't—"

"Yes, he would, Stella. Because *Gordon can deliver*. Your husband is GENRECT's resident genius. He's just buying time."

By the time Blaise had repeated the story several different ways he almost believed it. When he started taking himself seriously, she plunged and accepted whatever he wanted to predict. After talking her into taking the kids to her mother's home, Blaise promised to tell Gordon where she had gone.

He couldn't tell her what Gordon meant by refusing to come home. He wasn't sure. And it would have been sinful to upset Mrs. Hill any more.

Because the machine may be made immortal, when defined for most intents and purposes, and memory may be expanded to an infinite degree in theory, then the machine with human intelligence would technically surpass the ability of man to reason.

FROM A SEMINAR ON
THE CUNNINGHAM EQUATIONS

CHAPTER 10

Desperation drove Blaise by the time his class started. Strange noises tensed his muscles. Pain drove stakes through his body as every shred of his psyche ached for a drink.

Ears closed, he dragged through a session that, mercifully, set no new lows in education. Afterward, he tinkered with Alfie. Alfie took a while to recognize his touch. The computer was not used to a sober Blaise.

Alfie had set a flag for his attention: an asterisk and code number blinking in the upper right-hand corner of the monitor. Blaise punched in the numbers.

RE: DR MARIE GIBSON, RESEARCH TEAM MOUNT SINAI MED CENTER, NEW YORK, TRIGGERED FERTILITY BY INJECTING HEALTHY BRAIN CELLS INTO BRAINS OF INFERTILE MICE. LANDMARK EXPERIMENT PROVED ABILITY OF BRAIN TO INGEST FOREIGN CELLS AND DUPLICATE FUNCTIONS WHICH STIMULATE HORMONAL ACTIVITY FOR FERTILITY. CURRENTLY LICENSED EXPERIMENTS INCLUDE POSSIBLE HUMAN USE. PROBABILITY OF SUCCESS: 88%. COMPANIES ENGAGED IN RESEARCH AND PROBABLE IMPACT ON STOCK PRICES IN FIRST YEAR OF RELEASE ARE: . . .

A list of pharmaceutical firms filled the screen with an elaborate series of numbers after each entry.

"Hello." Helen smiled uncertainly. Her eyes shifted nervously to the monitor.

"You wouldn't know anything about . . . this?" Blaise waved his hand at the display. He hadn't heard her come in.

"You installed the new program last month. Alfie asked if I wanted to use it in preference to the old program. It's better."

Blaise felt uncertain, as if he had walked in his sleep. "Alfie must have modified the program, but he shouldn't have let you use it until I gave him instructions."

"Maybe you don't remember. You were a little foggy."

Foggy was a diplomatic way of putting it. "I imagine you're right." He smiled. But under the smile Blaise worried. He didn't remember. Could he have left Alfie instructions that would let anyone access discretionary material?

Helen's eyes swung from Blaise to the numbers, then back and forth again as if they fascinated her. "Would you mind if I used some of that information?"

"Are you interested in having babies?"

Helen blushed.

Her red cheeks gave Blaise an odd pleasure. Something quaint was implied by a grown woman blushing. He had never known another woman so closely in touch with her feelings that she could not dissemble. "Whatever you want."

"I could make a lot of money." Helen spoke with an air of apology, as if afraid the profit motive would cause dissension.

That Helen felt she had to explain made Blaise uncomfortable. She attached too much importance to his opinions—about everything. "You're welcome to all you can make." He logged off and stood.

"Why do you log off, Blaise? Couldn't I just start there?"

"Not unless Alfie has a lobotomy. When I'm on, I'm telling the computer what to think. When you're on you're just talking."

"What if I get into his brain accidentally?"

"I'd have to marry you to keep it in the family."

"That's interesting." Helen's eyes were drifty, as if she were trying to imagine what Blaise had hidden in Alfie.

Blaise hadn't noticed her eyes in a while. Very large and very blue, the pastel of a translucent spring sky.

"I have to go." He shattered her mood abruptly. Without liquor the world filled with nuances he'd forgotten about, with concerns about other people's feelings that he'd dulled until they barely existed.

"Thank you."

"Make Alfie behave. He's a lecher. I taught him myself." The messenger ricocheted off Blaise at the door.

"Sir. Dr. Cunningham?" Short of breath, the student had obviously been running. Helen's face tightened. Running wasn't normal on the campus.

"Yes." Blaise picked up Helen's anxiety.

"I'm sorry I'm so late, sir. The dean wants to see you before you go off campus."

"Did he say when?"

"I think he means right away, sir."

"Thank you." Blaise watched the student messenger disappear into the crowd moving through the hall. No use asking. Deans didn't tell undergraduates.

When he left the dean's office twenty minutes later Blaise was shaken. He'd been informed that the class was being dropped and a note would go in his confidential file stressing that he not be hired by the university system again.

"You can appeal," Dean Carden said. "That would mean an academic review and we would be forced to give specific reasons. I'm sure you know them, Dr. Cunningham.

"With great difficulty and the calling-in of some personal obligations, the university has kept your name out of the papers in connection with that unfortunate woman who was murdered. Though I presume your innocence, the media could enjoy a sensation at both the university's and your expense.

"For the sake of the students in your seminar, we'll keep you for the last three weeks of this term." The dean waited. When Blaise did not speak, he said, "I'm grieved that our association has come to this.

"Perhaps I'm old-fashioned, Doctor, not abreast of an era which permits academics the morality of movie stars. But if the intellectual community cannot behave at least as well as a grammar school graduate in personal discipline and adherence to standards, it cannot lead the society of man."

Dean Carden took off his glasses and polished them as he gazed nearsightedly at Blaise. "On a daily basis we must deal with a great deal of human foolishness. Perhaps it was better in the Middle Ages when a doctorate indicated a standard of personal achievement and ethical growth, rather than just a reflection of intelligence. I am sorry, Doctor, to lose your mind from a community that needs it. But the foolishness that will pay any price for glitter must not prevail."

Blaise was stunned. He wanted to scream, to throw things. Hemmett had helped engineer the dismissal. He knew that instinctively. The dean's features were slightly damp. He seemed sincere in his regret.

Blaise was lightheaded when he left the office. Soon they'd get around to canceling his parking permit. *Undesirable. Suspected molester prowls parking lots.* Reeling even though he was not drunk, he found his car. Sitting with the windows rolled up, he waited until feeling returned to his hands and feet. Then he drove home slowly.

A breeze off the ocean was whipping the crown of a eucalyptus back and forth at the edge of the picture window. Blaise lay on the couch, strangely devoid of feeling. Dobie paced, rumbling thoughtfully. Finally the Doberman settled, head on paws, eyes rolled high to catch the slightest hint that Blaise was ready to do more than mope.

Blaise switched on the portable. The screen filled with frame after frame of smooth, rapid typing. Helen was feeding information into the computer. He watched the elaborate explanations for analysis and realized she had accessed the computer's prime function, processing mathematical variables.

"GOOD AFTERNOON, PROFESSOR"

"What took you so long, Alfie?"

"I RECOGNIZED YOUR ENTRY, PROFESSOR"

"You couldn't, Alfie. The modem eliminates recognizable variables."

"I RECOGNIZED YOUR ENTRY, PROFESSOR"

Modem entry into Alfie could access no deeper than monitoring and feeding data and requests for specific, coded information. Alfie blocked directories, command functions, operational procedures, and, especially, his subconscious. At least Blaise hoped he did.

He returned to monitoring Helen's work. But the worry didn't go away. Alfie automatically eliminated any outside entry when Blaise was operating the main terminal. If the computer was overriding its programming he'd have to test Alfie. Soon.

Helen accessed a business net, selecting a list of stocks

for analysis that were obvious additions to his main program. They were all pharmaceuticals.

The phone rang.

"Blaise?" It sounded as if Linda were in Alaska.

"Yes."

A long, hollow pause filled the line. "I won't be coming back," she said finally. "Would you drop the car at the agency? Leave my suitcase, too. They'll send it to me."

When he died it was going to start like this.

"Blaise, are you there?"

"Yes," he croaked.

"That's good. We'll get together again soon." Before he could reply she said a hurried "Good-bye."

The dial tone filled his ear. Blaise dropped the cordless phone back into its holder. He had no feeling in his fingers. When the rising numbness reached his head he fainted.

He woke with a dirty-sock taste and empty lungs. He was sweating, feeling too weak to walk. And nothing in the house to drink!

Leaning on walls, he dragged Linda's suitcase, lifting and swinging as far as he could and dropping it. Minutes passed getting the bag to her Z100. Before getting into the driver's seat, Blaise leaned with his forehead against the metal. The car top felt cool, which was wrong. It should be hot after standing in the sun all day. Dobie rubbed against him.

Blaise didn't protest when Dobie hopped in. He backed the Datsun out of the driveway without incident. Foot on brake, he inched the strange car down switchbacks to the nearest liquor store. The clerk silently took his money and handed over a half liter of cherry vodka. Barely old enough to drink, the kid could spot an alcoholic. Dobie did not comment when Blaise slumped back in the scuffed leather seat and killed the bottle. Some of his function loss disappeared. "Lucky for me you're not a police dog," he muttered.

Dobie did not have a ready answer.

Blaise's driving was steady as he continued uphill to the university. But the vodka hit him like a brick as he got out of the car and into the sun. He told himself he'd gone this way to catch the freeway. Reason replied he was looking for sympathy.

Helen's face puckered when he entered the classroom. Quietly she said, "You're drunk."

Blaise slumped in a chair. "Yes."

She terminated her entry and the monitor displayed "GOOD AFTERNOON, MISS MCINTYRE"

"What do you want?" Helen was practically whispering.

"Help me."

"To do what?"

Blaise shrugged. If he hadn't had so much practice he would have fallen off the chair. "Yesterday I was fired at GENRECT."

Helen nodded. She did not change expression.

He felt like a gutted trout. Helen would turn on him too. She had cause.

"Today the dean dumped me. Just as you said he would." Blaise's face was a glass-front clock with all the gears and wheels exposed. "Linda isn't coming back," he added.

"Miss modified mink?"

He nodded.

"I suppose I'm glad. Are you going to cry?"

"I can't."

"Of course not." Helen used a linen handkerchief embroidered *HM* to dry his cheeks. "Better?"

Blaise nodded.

She stroked his head and face. Blaise let himself go and after a bit he felt better. He'd babbled to Helen—to someone outside himself—but the vodka had taken hold and he didn't care. Out in the parking lot Helen tucked him into the passenger seat and got behind the wheel of Linda's car. She drove to the rental place where she signed the car and suitcase in and a step van out. Dobie hung close to Blaise. The agent made them sign a liability clause when Blaise admitted they planned on hauling the dog around.

Helen talked her way past the university security guard, then drove over service roads to park next to the computer science building. Blaise peered bleary-eyed out the truck window. "What are we doing?"

"Taking Alfie home." She hurried away. Blaise sat in stupefied solitude looking at the near-deserted cement building in a neat island of green. Another truck was parked nearby. Bemused, Blaise watched three men wheel a stainless-steel cylinder out of the building. It was Alfie. *They were stealing his computer!*

He got down from the red step van on rubber legs and clung to the open door. Resolutely he put one foot in front of the other until he blocked the sidewalk.

"Get out of the way!" The skeletal man who spoke had weathered brown skin in turtle-folds around his neck and an Adam's apple like an eruption. He wore a blue work shirt and blue twill pants and weighed a hundred twenty. The men with him were as tall as Blaise, but with bulgy muscles.

Blaise stood his ground. "That's mine!" Dobie stuck his head out to watch.

One of the big blue shirts stopped alongside the thin man and said, "Should I?"

The skinny man said, "Why not?"

The fist was a blur that ended with a shock to the side of his face. Blaise didn't feel pain. Just concrete and grass.

"Blaise! Blaise!" The name rattled around and then Helen was kneeling, holding his head on her lap. "Are you all right?" Her eyes were unfocused and frightened.

"I'm all right," he said.

Two football team–size students huddled behind Helen, uncertain what to do next. The world reeled around Blaise, arcs of green and rays of concrete gray, two discrete groups of people. And Alfie.

"Out of our way!" The cadaverous man told his helpers to start pushing again.

"Alfie!" Helen wailed. It was the first she'd noticed what they were doing, apart from beating on Blaise.

"Police!" she shrieked. "Robbers! Thieves! *POLICE*!" Helen ran alongside the dolly and kept being shoved out of the way until one of the men dumped her hard on the grass. Dobie lunged and snapped. The man retreated and the pup lost interest.

Blaise staggered to his feet, avoiding the fast-moving dolly. As the dolly passed he grabbed the collar of a blue shirt and kicked behind the knee. The man dropped flat. Dobie pranced, growling and barking at Blaise's unexpected activity.

The other man's shoulders strained the seams of his blue work shirt. Turning from the dolly, he confronted Blaise. "Asshole," he said mildly, and moved into a casual boxer's stance.

"Stop the dolly!" Helen ran after it. The skinny man snatched at her, galvanizing the college boys into action. Galloping with the grace of two hundred pounders who run up stadium steps to develop their legs because their coach is a sadist, they ran Skinny down.

"Stop the dolly!" Helen screamed. Since stopping Skinny

had not slowed them, the boys continued on and captured the dolly just short of the curb.

The big man moved with easy grace, shifting his weight to let Blaise's fist pass by. Only Blaise didn't swing. He leaned forward, jamming his face into the crook of his arm, and rammed his full weight behind his elbow into the blue work shirt.

The big man grunted as the jolt reached his heart. But he had already started his own punch. His fist bounced off Blaise's back instead of his neck. Air erupted from Blaise's lungs. Then he was falling face forward.

Dobie snarled. Blaise rolled onto his back and Dobie's hind feet were on his chest. The dog stood between Blaise and his attacker, rumbling. He was still a pup and his back legs pranced instead of setting him up to lunge. Avoiding a kick, Dobie dived for the blue-shirted man's leg only to yelp shrilly when a hand lashed against the side of his head and sent him spinning.

The big man looked down. Blaise knew he was thinking about being suckered and feeling the ache in his breastbone.

Then the roar that filled Blaise's ears touched his primordial core. Big turned and lashed out desperately with his foot. Dobie launched himself, a mouthful of sharp, white teeth.

Big had excellent reflexes. Dobie's fangs slashed through his sleeve instead of his throat because he got his hand there in time. "Son of a bitch," he said thoughtfully. "Son of a bitch!" He wrapped his left hand tight around his right forearm where ragged blue cotton was turning red.

Dobie hit the ground on four stiff legs, bounced, twisting around, and lunged back toward Blaise. The man with the bleeding arm backpedaled.

Dobie chased him five yards, then returned to Blaise's side, whining before he rushed again. It was as if an invisible leash kept him at Blaise's side while his heart was set on running down this oversized rabbit. Blaise sat, grass and cement buildings undulating, until he saw the campus security man looking down. "Call the dog off, will you please, sir?"

Blaise spoke and Dobie whined and sat between him and the three men, giving the security man warning glances. Helen patted the dog. Dobie yawned.

Skinny told the security officer they were grabbing Alfie

because of an overdue note. He handed the officer a piece of paper. Helen snatched it, read it, and spouted swift legalisms that Blaise couldn't follow. The footballers contributed shrugs. Blaise looked at the man who had been kicking him. Blood still dripped from his arm but he didn't seem bothered.

"That's a damn good dog, Mister," he said.

Skinny scowled.

The bitten man shut up, but he winked at Blaise and smiled.

"I don't know." the security guard looked at the note, at Blaise, at the three men, at Helen. "I don't know," he repeated. "That thing sure looks like university property." A campus patrol car stopped and another security officer got out, accompanied by the dean.

Dean Carden listened for a moment before making a face. "You men," he said, "have no business taking anything off state property without notifying my office. You can make a formal application in the morning, with proper proof. I would suggest a court order. Now get out."

The security men, the dean, Helen, two college boys, and Blaise watched them depart in silence.

"Dr. Cunningham, please get your property off campus. Submit your grade reports and lesson plan to my office in the morning. I'll have a substitute fill in. You'll be paid to the end of the term." The dean looked at Blaise, his face expressing none of his feelings. "You're lucky they didn't make a dog bite complaint. I would have had to hold the animal."

"Thank you." Blaise looked at Dobie and meant it.

Dean Carden turned to Helen. "Miss..."

"McIntyre."

"Yes, Miss McIntyre, I don't understand your involvement in this. However, I assume that you're innocent of whatever has been going on. Please don't disappoint me." The dean appeared out of place, uncomfortable in the turmoil that could not have imaginably taken place on his campus.

"Sir?" The security guard waited.

"See that Dr. Cunningham gets safely off campus without further molestation."

"Yes, sir."

The college boys looked relieved that they hadn't been singled out. "Let's get Alfie in the van," Helen said.

The guard nodded. They muscled Alfie into the van. Helen drove to her house where they wrestled the computer into a spare bedroom. Blaise was still checking for damage when she returned.

"Is Alfie all right?"

Blaise raised his hands. His tongue felt thick. He hurt and he wasn't thinking as well as he might. "I'll know better in the morning. Where are the jocks?"

"Taking the truck back to the rental agency."

Blaise found a chair. "Why were they so helpful?"

Helen cocked her head and examined Blaise. "I think it had something to do with the two hundred dollars I paid them."

...human intelligence, if applied to a machine, would allow it to evolve an answer to any problem within the scope of its memory and the limitations of its speed of operation.

FROM A SEMINAR ON
THE CUNNINGHAM EQUATIONS

CHAPTER 11

"Most things," Helen explained, "are easier with money." She paused. "It's nice to see that you're not helpless."

"Does it matter?"

"Of course." Helen chewed her lip, a nervous gesture that took the place of reading his mind.

"What do you want, Helen? A lap dog with economic potential? You want to nurse a psychiatric garbage pail?"

"You're not . . ." She paused to change mental gears.

"Why did you bring us here?" Blaise had only just realized they were in Helen's house.

She chewed on her lip some more. Her lipstick was already ragged. "I just want to be sure you and Alfie are all right."

"Why?" Blaise saw the silkiness of her skin and the texture of her blond hair and the engulfing depths of her blue eyes, and he knew she was going to lie.

"In the last two months I've made $20,000 on $230,000 in investments." Helen spoke awkwardly, improvising.

"That's only eight and a half percent."

"In *two months*, Blaise. Fifty-one percent a year. And Alfie's getting better." She turned so he couldn't see her face.

"What do you want?"

"You as my partner. And Alfie."

"You'll be sorry."

"Anything, Blaise. Work at whatever you want to. In two years you can buy GENRECT."

"You can do that well?"

"Let me prove it." Helen's hands on his shoulders were warm and soft. "You won't be sorry."

Dobie snuggled against Blaise's feet. "Why not?" he said recklessly. "Alfie for you, the womb for me."

"It will be all right, Blaise."

"I don't think anything will ever be all right again, Helen. But for now I want a bottle. A full one."

"Should you . . ."

"We're not getting married," Blaise said sharply. "I'm just trading you a computer for a little service."

"All right."

"That's better," Blaise said. But it wasn't. He felt like the bottom of a cesspool. That he could not stop himself did not make it any better. She brought a liter of Wyborowa, which means "selected." Holding it carefully, he stumbled into the front room and onto the white couch. He was going to drink and think about Linda. Even to Blaise it didn't seem the least bit fair. Helen stared unseeing at Alfie. Finally she typed, "What else can I do?"

"WOULD YOU LIKE A PRIVATE FILE?"

Helen contemplated the message, not understanding.

"WOULD YOU LIKE A PRIVATE FILE, MISS MCINTYRE?"

Hesitantly Helen's finger hit a Y.

"OPENING PRIVATE FILE: MCINTYRE"

Helen suddenly had a blank screen and the compulsion to fill it. She started typing. She didn't wonder how Alfie knew she was at the terminal. Or, at that moment, care.

Blaise woke suddenly. Helen's face blurred into focus. Her hands moved and the cool wet of a washcloth floated over his forehead. The bedroom, airy but sparsely furnished with double bed and a chest of drawers and a nightstand, was flooded with sunlight through white-curtained windows.

"You were sweating and yelling."

He lay staring at the ceiling while Helen continued stroking his face. The strain seemed to be melting out of his muscles.

"You shouldn't drink so much, Blaise. You're killing yourself. For nothing."

"Get me a drink."

Veins stood out in Helen's forehead. Her lower lip trembled. "No," she said finally.

"You made the deal."

"Blaise, what do you remember about the last three weeks?"

He tried not to show his shock. He remembered coming home with Helen and Dobie and Alfie as if it had happened only seconds ago. The memory was more real than the bed he lay in. But there were blanks. He could feel them the way he could feel a hole in the ground—by what was not there. His mental clock measured the breadth and width of the holes. Glimpses of daylight when Helen kept him sober enough to eat. The vision scared him. "Enough," he said. "You promised."

"Not to help you commit suicide."

"What worries you? Alfie's yours. Do you need a repairman?"

"I just want you—well—not ruining yourself over a—modified mink." Helen stepped back from the bed, her face crimson. He had thought she was angry before. And been wrong. When they tried to steal Alfie, she had been scared.

He closed his eyes. He was starting to get sick from the tension. "Keep Alfie. Just go away."

"What about Mrs. Hill? You promised to help."

"If Gordon won't go back to his wife, I can't make him. I can't even get in to see him."

"You could if you wanted to."

"Haven't you figured anything out? They tried to snatch Alfie because I saw Gordon. Probably figured I used Alfie to do it. Hemmett does dumb things, but he's not an idiot. If I try again, you can kiss Alfie good-bye. Or worse. And then Gordon could be a lot more helpful too."

"What's that mean?" Helen stared at him, her face fearful, as if she didn't know how far she was stepping in the dark.

Blaise bit off what he was going to say. "Nothing. But Gordon's not near as helpless as I, you know."

"You have to do what's right, Blaise."

"Right doesn't cut it. Big fish eat little fish."

"I'll help."

He made a face.

> "There was a young lady from Niger
>   Went riding on back of a tiger.
>   She hadn't the knack,
>   ... So when they got back,
>   The Lady was inside the tiger."

Helen bit a knuckle but tears leaked down her cheeks. "You think I'm stupid because I don't come from a family of snobs and I didn't go to a fancy school. You think I'm dull and grasping because I want to make money and not worry about being poor!"

"Helen..." Blaise struggled to sit. She put her hand on his chest and shoved him back down.

"Well, I am!" Her lips were trembling and she slurred her words and tasted the salt of her own tears. "But I can say things straight out without talking in limericks to put people down. And I've been working since my father... died when I was thirteen and I don't have to ask anything from anybody."

"Helen—"

"Nothing!" she screamed, and ran out of the room.

Blaise flopped back on the bed and let the silence seep through him. He'd been to Naples and Paris, Vienna, London, even Prague and Krakow once each, and later to Moscow. And schools until he had a string of degrees for someone to hang on the door.

"Why don't you just die?"

He could think of no reply. The distant doorbell impinged on his consciousness as he started to drift off again. Seconds later the click of the bedroom door awakened him.

"Get up," Helen snapped. "Get shaved, a shower, and some clothes on."

Blaise could not collect his muddled thoughts. Helen yanked the covers off and turned away and he realized she was actually shy about seeing him naked. "And hurry. We're waiting." She left the room.

He felt his way along the wall. In the bathroom he leaned against the tile and let the water pelt down. Cold or hot, he was too numb to tell. Pain released its grip on his lungs. He shaved in the shower without cutting himself more than was necessary.

Helen hadn't said who "we" were, so he slipped into conservative green golf slacks and a canary-yellow pullover. Lime-colored socks and a pair of loafers completed the transformation into a doctor ready to play nine holes and sit out the rest at Torrey Pines Course, home of the Andy Williams Open.

Everything was okay as long as he didn't think. But at the door, he couldn't open it. Not and look Helen in the face. She had done more for him than anybody ever had or ever would again. And he didn't treat her as well as most people did their dogs. The door opened without his help. Helen stood in the hallway. Her yellow hair framed her tight lips.

"Come along." Her voice was taut.

"Blaise!" Linda wore a white summer dress and white gloves and a tiny Easter hat that was more adornment than clothing. She could have stepped out of the pages of *Vogue*. "I've been looking all over for you."

"I haven't been anywhere." Linda in Helen's living room left Blaise breathless. The shock emptied him of reactions.

She looked at him. "Of course not. Where would you go if you didn't go home?"

"I suppose you have things to talk about." Helen fidgeted with her hands. She didn't leave, though.

"Oh, yes. We have a lot to talk about, Miss McIntyre." Blaise could not meet Helen's gaze.

"I guess you do," Helen said.

He listened to her footsteps retreating down the hallway to the back bedroom and the sound of the door shutting.

"Why did you come back?"

"Blaise, did I ever say I wasn't coming back?"

"No."

"I had to stay home for a while. Uncle Milo needed me."

"That doesn't answer my question."

"Blaise." Linda put her hand on his forearm. "Because I was gone for a while doesn't mean we're not friends." She looked around Helen's front room. "Where's the dog?"

"Dobie?" Blaise thought. "The backyard, I think."

"He's a nice dog, if you like big ones."

"Yes."

"I think you're too self-conscious here, Blaise. Why don't we go out for lunch—just the two of us?"

"I'll have to tell Helen."

"You do that." Linda patted his arm as if he'd made a brilliant decision. Blaise wanted to wag his tail.

Helen did not seem surprised. "You're both adults," she said. "Sort of." But she didn't come out of the bedroom to say good-bye to Linda when they were out front.

Blaise staggered when they were out front. He opened the passenger door of a white BMW coupe and got inside.

"How did you know it was mine?" Linda twisted the mirror to look at her lipstick.

"I'm psychic."

Blaise supposed Linda picked the restaurant for its parking lot. For a stranger in La Jolla that was an excellent reason. When the waitress cruised by she ordered a grasshopper and a double vodka for him. Blaise made no comment.

"I thought I'd save you the trouble." Linda's face was bland. "Have you talked with Dr. Hill since I was down?"

Blaise rolled the glass in his hands. Ice cubes bobbed like drowning men. "No."

"Things have changed, Blaise."

"Do you want something to eat?"

"I suppose. You order. Have you heard of Human Enhancements?"

He was sure Helen had mentioned it. But she'd wanted to tell him something and he'd wanted a bottle. As usual, she lost. The blocked memory added a sour taste to his stomach. He shook his head.

"Human Enhancements is a closely held corporation. No public shares. But it's controlled by Tenro."

"That's their business."

"Dr. Gordon Hill is listed as chief of staff."

Blaise played with the food the waitress placed in front of him. It was a good excuse for not saying anything.

"You're not drinking."

"I've been thinking about quitting."

"Is Dr. Hill still with GENRECT?"

Blaise shrugged. "I'm not."

"Have you talked to Mrs. Hill?"

"No."

"But you know where she is?"

"Home, I suppose."

"I tried there."

"Before you tried to find me?"

Linda put her hand on top of Blaise's. "I looked for you and your home looks like you haven't been there in a month. I thought your friend's wife might know where you were."

"You're not interested in GENRECT as an investment?"

"Not anymore." Her fingers tightened on his hand. Blaise stifled the need to respond. But the need was still there.

"Then what is it you want?"

"I started out investigating the investment potential in GENRECT. A lot more is involved now, Blaise. Human Enhancements makes people smart. Improves memory, speeds their thinking. At sixty thousand dollars a pop."

"That's out of my league."

"It's important, Blaise."

"Why?"

"We don't know how safe it is. The process is being bootlegged without adequate investigation. Somebody responsible has to help resolve the new problems."

"Like your uncle?"

"We're not fanatics, Blaise. My uncle and his friends are like you and me. We're intelligent and educated and responsive to social issues. We're concerned with the future of mankind—not some petty political ideology."

"I'm not." Blaise shuttled his drink back and forth, creating a wet click on the tabletop. "I don't respond to social issues." He looked up at Linda. "Unless being anti-prohibition is a social issue."

"Come to San Francisco. Talk to my uncle."

"Is that why you came back?"

Linda cupped his face in her hands and stroked him. "You know why I came back."

Blaise closed his eyes and felt the tingle of her fingers and he didn't have the courage to back off.

"I know," he said softly.

Helen jerked the door open before he had the knob. "About time," she snapped, then spun, furious and desperate to get away without saying something else stupid.

"You didn't have to wait around." The red in Blaise's eyes was clearing but the ache hung on. He wasn't coping with his own problems, not to mention two women.

"I live here, remember?"

"I didn't mean it that way, Helen."

"No." Her voice softened. "I suppose not."

"I have to go to San Francisco to see Linda's uncle." Blaise felt more defensive than he had expected. He owed Helen. The way he repaid her was, at best, shoddy.

"It's about Gordon."

Helen contemplated Linda and waited.

"Nothing's changed, Helen. Alfie stays and you can run the business with him. Alfie's housebroken." Blaise fidgeted.

"Can you take care of Dobie? I'll pick him up when I get back."

Helen could recognize a truck about to run her down. The Peters woman examined her May Company lookalike drapes as if they were Irish lace instead of a short step up from Sears.

Helen supposed Linda did her shopping at Gump's and thought the May Company was an outlet for the Salvation Army. It hurt, but she nodded. If she'd spoken, it would have come out a snarl. On cue, Dobie trotted in and nuzzled Helen's hand. He looked up with soft brown eyes. Dobie liked to be liked.

If she'd been alone, Helen would have howled in fury. But not with that woman watching from the corner of her eye while pretending indifference. "What are we partners for?"

"I knew I could count on you, Helen. I'll be back"—he glanced at Linda—"in a couple of days. How about if I have Dobie guard you while I'm gone?"

Helen looked amused. "He's a puppy."

Blaise took Helen's hand and held it to the dog's nose. "Guard!" he said.

Dobie yawned.

"Look," Blaise said, pressing Helen's hand to Dobie's nose. Helen pulled away but he was determined. "Dobie, guard!"

"He licked my hand," Helen said.

"He likes you. Dobie's smart. He knows what to do."

"It means I feed him all the time."

"You're just making it hard, Helen." But Blaise was pleased. Helen's acute unhappiness had seemed to soften under his kidding.

"If only you were as smart as the dog," Helen said.

Linda smiled.

On the PSA flight, Blaise and Linda watched rectangles of garden disappear as the plane skimmed toward the misty white line that separated ocean from sky.

"I appreciate your coming."

"I meant what I said before. About wanting you."

Linda hunched down in her seat. Turning to gaze out the window at billowing clouds, she said, "Leave it."

"Why did you take off your ring?" Blaise held her hand,

separating her fingers. The ruby, diamond, and emerald ring with the old-fashioned look of a family heirloom was gone. An untanned band of skin contrasted with her golden tan. Closing her hand, she hid the mark.

"I didn't feel like it." She turned to gaze out the window at the hazy horizon. "It isn't important."

To be fluent in a language constitutes brilliance. Such a circumstance, however, does not promise the ability to learn a new language. Intelligence, linked with adequate and efficient memory, does.

FROM A SEMINAR ON
THE CUNNINGHAM EQUATIONS

CHAPTER 12

"**J**ust remember you promised to behave yourself," Linda said briskly.

Blaise could not recall having promised anything.

She led him past a maroon Jaguar saloon with big fenders and a small silver-gray Rolls in the gloomy basement garage. Four black mushroom-shaped buttons adorned the elevator's antique brass control plate. It lifted them to an Edwardian entrance hall with seventeenth-century portraits in gold leaf frames and an elephant's-foot umbrella holder. Woodwork gleamed with generations of elbow grease. Leaded glass yellowed by time sketched faint epiphanies of trees.

The hallway opened into a room large by Victorian standards: parquet oak floor, mostly hidden beneath a massive blue and red Bokhara rug with greens and yellows. Three walls of bookshelves held up a ten-foot ceiling. Massive leather chairs glowed under the yellowish light.

"Good evening, Dr. Cunningham."

The man by the window was bluff, with white hair and glowing baby-pink skin. He seemed an advertisement for the difference money makes. From manicure to hairstyle to hand-caressed skin, Blaise would have no difficulty picking Milo Burkhalter out of a crowd—except in financial districts where they all look alike.

"Mr. Burkhalter?"

"Doctor, but the rest is correct, young man." Milo beamed but his gray eyes remained cool under white eyebrows. "Linda promised to bring you by."

"She did, Dr. Burkhalter?" Blaise wondered if Milo Burkhalter was the kind of man who took offense because of his slip. It was an old-fashioned kind of offense, but Linda's uncle seemed an old-fashioned gentleman.

Milo Burkhalter put Blaise in a chair by the window, moving with a smooth confidence that was difficult to resist. "How is your computer work coming, Doctor? Linda tells me you're doing wizard things in artificial intelligence. That you have in fact a computer predicting the market."

"Something of the sort. What else has Linda told you about Alfie, sir?"

"That you talk to the computer and it talks back." Milo's eyes seemed amused. "That would be quite something, but young women are prone to exaggeration, are they not, Dr. Cunningham?"

"Alfie communicates to the extent of his programming. His vocabulary is adequate for syntax logic." Blaise looked around the study with its rows of books. "No poetry, Doctor. But Alfie is loquacious on stock market futures."

"I see. Then Linda hasn't exaggerated." Milo nodded. "Perhaps someday you would honor me with a demonstration. I'd be interested in anything that would make the market easier."

"My pleasure." Blaise glanced around but Linda had left them alone. "However, the market isn't Alfie's main purpose."

Milo offered Blaise a cigar and took it for himself when Blaise refused, lighting it and exhaling a fragrant cloud. "What is its main purpose—may I call you Blaise?"

"Of course. Alfie is the prototype for a pure form of artificial intelligence."

"But the computer isn't perfected yet?"

"Every day he learns a little. Since I've been letting other people enter data, Alfie has apparently evolved a routine to identify each user by typing pattern and interests. It's a beginning." Blaise had said it to impress Milo, but he realized abruptly that he was telling the truth. That Alfie distinguished between operators without instruction was a breakthrough! He didn't really hear Milo's comments. He had to get back to La Jolla and find out. The implications stunned him. He had been drunk for three precious weeks that could have put him that much closer to a second Prize.

Milo was thoughtful. "You're not planning on telling me any more?"

"I'm afraid it would be premature."

"It's a pity your parents are dead, isn't it? If you're right, then this is the final vindication of their work."

Blaise licked suddenly dry lips. "Yes, it would be what they wanted all along."

Milo examined Blaise for a moment, then dismissed the subject. "I trust you know why you're in San Francisco?"

"Not really, except that Linda asked me. I can't discuss my colleagues' business without their consent."

Milo surprised Blaise by saying "Fair enough." He shook Blaise's hand with warmth and promised an interesting evening.

Milo excused himself, leaving Blaise alone in the study watching fog roll in from the bay. A middle-aged lady in crinoline supplied Blaise with coffee, which provided no respite from his need for a drink. The cup gave his hands something to do. The elevator motor shrieked a number of times. A grandfather clock disturbed the peace every fifteen minutes.

"Blaise?"

Linda had changed into a black evening dress that clung and made the bare skin of her face and neck glow in contrast. "Uncle Milo is upstairs with everybody." She led him to the elevator where her perfume filled the tiny cage. She avoided his eyes.

A baker's dozen of men clustered around her uncle. Milo began introductions with a white-haired elder in tweed. Dr. Hazeltine was a professor of philosophy. Savile Row shoes suggested he had found a way to make money outside of school—or been born to it.

A liquor cabinet with ice maker sat at one side of the upstairs dining room, dominated by a black oak table with several leaves inserted. Milo took one end of the table and seated Blaise at his right. Linda faced them from the other end.

When everyone had a drink and a seat, Milo rapped a crystal goblet with a stirring spoon. The single clear note cut through conversation.

"We need expert advice and"—Milo beamed—"Dr. Cunningham has very kindly come to discuss Human Enhancements."

Two lines of heads swiveled toward Blaise, who had the uncomfortable impression that they knew all about him while he knew nothing about them. Not even Linda's uncle.

"Gentlemen," Blaise said. "I'm here to listen. Dr. Burkhalter believes I can be of some help, but that's to be seen."

"I thought—" It was a pompous, fat man.

"Dr. Whitman," Burkhalter said smoothly, "Dr. Cunningham has pointed out, rightly, that the information we want affects other people to whom he also has a responsibility. We must convince him that what he can tell us is in humanity's best interest."

Whitman persisted. "Dr. Cunningham, while looking for an investment vehicle, we discovered GENRECT has become the founding investor in Human Enhancements, which operates out of a number of health spas like Heaven's Gate in San Diego's North County. Dr. Gordon Hill is now working for Human Enhancements while still on the GENRECT payroll."

Milo looked at Blaise, gauging his reaction.

Blaise shrugged. "Dr. Hill works where he pleases, particularly if someone pays him." More interesting to Blaise was Uncle Milo's apparent failure to tell his friends that the well-known Dr. Cunningham had been given the boot by GENRECT.

"Even if Dr. Hill's work constitutes a hazard to the health and social structure of American society?" Whitman thrust his jaw out.

"I'm unaware of the problem," Blaise said truthfully. "Someone would picket the ark if Noah didn't file an environmental impact statement."

Milo's overwhelming voice cut Whitman off. "Human Enhancements has only one product. For six weeks and sixty thousand dollars they guarantee a ten percent increase in IQ."

Blaise concentrated on his ginger ale.

"It's no secret to people with money. You see, Dr. Cunningham, *the treatment works*."

Blaise glanced around the table. No one seemed startled by Milo's revelation. "How do they determine intelligence?" he asked.

"Cleverly, Doctor. Once for the record, and once for status. Moneyed people often value status more than records." Milo dominated the table with a puppeteer's control.

"The client takes a standard intelligence test anywhere he wishes. This gives a base number. Then he takes the treatment. Six weeks later he repeats the tests. Some do better than others, but everyone improves at least ten percent."

"What's the problem?" Blaise asked. "The rich get smarter, thus richer. The poor get what they always get." He looked about the table glittering with evidences of intelligence and wealth. By background he belonged with them. Philosophically he considered each man an island.

Professor Hazeltine aimed the stem of his pipe at Blaise. "How do they do it? This is what we must know."

"Why not spend your sixty thousand and find out?"

Hazeltine surprised Blaise by not answering and instead looking toward Milo. Milo raised an eyebrow.

"The company spins moonbeams about vitamins and hypnosis—tapping the hidden resources of the human brain. I don't believe it. They're doing something dangerous and illegal. And their clients include the most important people in this country." Hazeltine bit down on his pipe.

Blaise stared down the table at the accumulation of wealth and education. "People have the right to their own choices."

Milo stood and smiled. "I know our attitude seems strange, Dr. Cunningham. Some of the people involved are those who control society. But Human Enhancements is not just treating *them*. The only criterion for selection is sixty thousand dollars. What happens when people without scruples or morals seize power from the natural, experienced leaders?"

Blaise knew now was the time to keep his mouth shut. But these people were just too much. "In other words," he said, "now that we all have ours, let's slam the door."

To his surprise there were no gasps of outrage. They waited in polite silence. "I would assume," he continued, "that if smarter, they'll become the new leaders—no better, no worse. I see no embarrassment of ethics among our current establishment." Echoing in the back of his mind was Dean Carden's "morals of movie stars" dismissal. But the dean was not at this table.

"And then," Milo overrode Blaise's dismissal, "perhaps something happens. The treatment turns out to be lethal. *Catch twenty-two.* Society could collapse."

"Is that a prediction, Dr. Burkhalter?"

"There would be no natural selection!" Hazeltine kicked

his chair back and stood, fists clenched with emotion. "Intelligent women would marry stupid men without knowing it. The gene pool will be watered down."

"Stupid women have been capturing smart men since the Ice Age," Blaise said. "If ruling-class daughters have both beauty and intelligence, that's their good luck."

"We don't need your answer immediately, Dr. Cunningham." Milo stood behind the table. "Why don't you talk to some of our group. I believe you will ultimately see things differently.

"Gentlemen, if you would like to present our case to Dr. Cunningham individually..." Milo smiled benignly and left. Several men approached Blaise immediately. Linda materialized beside him with a drink.

"...delighted to have a man of your stature here, Doctor." The first man to capture Blaise was in his late forties and smooth as a polished worry bead. He had dark eyes and a Roman nose and a perfect set of teeth that Blaise would have sworn were all rerooted and capped. And that was just appearances. Blaise couldn't help wondering what he would pay for an extra twelve points of IQ.

"The audience is even more special, uh, Doctor." Blaise didn't try to dredge up the man's name. Every introduction had been Dr. "So-and-so." He jiggled his glass and took a swallow.

Undiluted vodka hit his stomach like a bag of Redicrete. A wave of warmth momentarily paralyzed him.

"Thank you, but no one here has captured a Nobel Prize. We'd all like to, of course. As Milo said, sometimes we'll pay more for appearance than for substance."

"Is that what this is about? Appearances? To be the first to recognize the dangers of a new science?"

The man laughed. "You understand the aging intellectual too well, Dr. Cunningham. You'll have no surprises later."

"My parents raised me to believe that surprises find their provenance in the realm of sloppy thinking."

"Not a happy condition, Doctor. It leaves the individual with no way to pass off his failings." He chuckled and raised his glass. "*Skål*."

Automatically, Blaise raised his glass.

Soon they ran together in Blaise's mind. Linda brought drinks and stood where he could smell her perfume and after a while he forgot why he had been set on refusing more liquor.

As he grew more wobbly he felt more acute. He was used to alcohol. He started laughing. The man talking stopped and smiled until he was done. He pressed a drink on Blaise and said something Blaise immediately forgot. In time the room became stark with brilliant colors against a background in hard-edge. Then he was in a soft bed in a room filled with moonlight. Something moved next to him and he looked down on the top of Linda's boyish hair cut.

"What happened?"

She stretched, throwing covers down, exposing her warm, naked body. "You were talking and then for no reason you started to get rough with me and we decided you ought to go to bed. When I got you here, you wouldn't get into bed alone."

"Where's here?"

"My room."

Blaise felt a band tightening around his chest. He wasn't going to be able to stand it if he started choking. But already he was having trouble breathing. "Did I say anything?"

"About what?" Linda had burrowed under the covers, her back against Blaise.

"About Gordon?"

"I don't think so. Does it matter?"

"I don't know."

"I'm sure you didn't say anything."

Her body was warm against his and the furious activity in his head diminished. "Did I say anything about Mount Sinai?"

"Nothing about Moses either. Go to sleep."

Blaise lay like prestressed concrete until the gentle rhythm of Linda's breathing lulled him.

What did he know that these people wanted?

"Blaise. Get up!" Linda was tugging at his arm. He felt a headache gathering behind his ears.

"What's wrong?"

"You must get up!"

The sky was still blacked out by overcast that hid the stars and moon. The ground, an infinity away in a black plunge from the bedroom window, was invisible. Bewildered, he began dressing. She led him through a hallway he didn't remember to the elevator. While the motor whined Linda examined him.

"Brush your hair back."

Blaise did his best with his hands. She straightened his tie and fluffed his jacket. "Don't say anything."

The elevator halted and she opened the door. "Hello, Jon," she said. "I didn't think you were coming tonight."

The man beside Linda's uncle was tall and slender with a porcelainlike fragility. He had blue eyes, long black eyelashes, and the pale skin of aristocracy.

"I thought I should come by and meet Dr. Cunningham before he leaves San Francisco. He means so much to the group..."

He was older than Blaise and much the same physically. He was also so drunk that words didn't work in his mouth.

"Yes," Milo said. "Dr. Cunningham, Dr. Jonathan Peters. Linda's husband is also a member of our group."

Uncle Milo said more, but Blaise didn't hear. He struggled to weld his face into immobility.

Peters looked from Blaise to Linda and his face changed. "I knew you wanted to know, Milo," he said. "Was it worth it?" He had turned his back on Linda.

"Come, my boy." Milo took Peters' arm and steered him toward the front room. "Why don't we sit down and talk?"

"I think I'd better get back to San Diego," Blaise said. "I have some things to do there."

"Like talking to Dr. Hill?"

"Yes. That, too."

"Excellent, Doctor. Excellent."

"I'll take Dr. Cunningham to the airport." Linda opened a hall closet and took out a wrap.

"Don't go," Peters said. "I've got to talk to you."

"I'll be back, Jon." Linda kissed him on the cheek and then stepped into the elevator. Blaise went with her.

"You don't understand, Linda." Peters' voice was desperate. "I took the treatment. I'm going to be different."

His face was white and sweaty as he strained toward the closing elevator door. He would have grabbed the door but Blaise could see Milo's white-knuckled hand digging into Peters' arm. The door clunked shut and the elevator motor whined. Blaise didn't say anything. Nor did Linda.

She drove the unpredictable up-and-down streets as if afraid of the dark, venting her feelings by flooring the accelerator to wing through the void like a low-flying jet on a moonless night.

Blaise sat numb, not caring if Linda was trying to plow into an eighteen-wheeler. At San Francisco International, she parked the Porsche in the storage lot and got out.

"Aren't you going home?"

She shook her head.

"Your husband's waiting."

"I'll call from San Diego."

Blaise was fresh out of small talk. He got tickets and came to sit next to her in the lobby. "Twenty minutes."

She looked at the tickets and nodded. Looked at her watch. "I didn't want to talk about my rings."

"Yes."

"Well. Now you know. One was the engagement ring and the other was a wedding ring. Together they looked like a double-banded cocktail ring."

"They weren't."

"No." She stopped talking.

They had been in the air only minutes when the drinks Linda had consumed earlier drove her to the restroom.

The man coming down the aisle was under average height, with leathery skin that had seen much weather. He wore a blue pinstripe with vest and an electric blue tie. He lowered himself into Linda's seat.

"The seat is taken." Blaise examined the man carefully.

"Only be a moment." The voice reeked of New Jersey. *"Capisce italiano?"*

Blaise hesitated.

"We could speak Spanish, but so do half the people on this plane." The man, who looked Italian, switched to Church Latin. Blaise knew a different style of pronunciation but he understood. Just as he was getting the hang of it the man in the pinstripe suit stared toward the central aisle.

Blaise looked in the same direction. The profile of a Roman-collared priest seemed familiar.

Abruptly the stranger switched to Old English, quoting a line from Beowulf about the *gar Dena*. When Blaise nodded he added a pithy line about heads lining the path.

Blaise nodded. *"Na und?"* he asked.

"Do not awaken sleeping monsters."

"I'm afraid you've lost me."

"I'm a testimonial." The man in the pinstripe winked. "Six months ago I was a street runner. Button man. Know what I mean?"

Blaise said nothing.

"Now I ride airplanes and talk to a better class of citizen. I remember things I couldn't even pronounce before. I owe it all to a Human Enhancement seminar. You get me, citizen?"

"This is your endorsement?"

"You too can be like me. M-O-N-E-Y opens the door. 'Course, you don't need it, friend, but I tell you, it's worth a year of smack in a single stack. Got me?"

"I copy."

"Ten-four. Everything has a price tag. Jason collected the golden fleece. My man is a heavy investor in GENRECT."

"And Tenro?"

The stranger grinned. "You've been doing your homework. Now, I'm just trying to get ahead. Don't make it hard, pal. I got myself off the street, but I'm still just a button man looking for a step up. You don't want to be that step."

"How does it work?"

The man riffled his hair behind and below his right ear. "An injection and a couple of weeks later you start remembering better and thinking clearer. Painless."

Blaise saw a purple, pencil-eraser-sized spot under abundant black hair.

"My beauty spot. Oh—excuse me. Your husband and I were having a chat." He stood and smiled at Linda before stepping over Blaise's knees to surrender her seat.

"How did you know I'd be here?" Blaise asked.

"Why, Mr. Peters, don't you recall telephoning to let us know you were going home?" He had an engaging smile.

"Peters?" Linda asked as she slid in. "Who's that?"

"Stranger." Blaise let it go. No point in telling her more people than just her uncle's crowd were interested in what they were doing. For the rest of the flight his eyes kept rolling around to study the priest. He wasn't sure.

The study of intelligence is paramount to the continuation of mankind as the dominant species.

FROM A SEMINAR ON
THE CUNNINGHAM EQUATIONS

CHAPTER 13

Helen opened the door and said, "Bite 'em, Dobie."

The Doberman whined and wagged his hind end and then, unable to stand it any longer, stood on his back feet to lick Blaise.

"It's nice to be wanted," Blaise said to no one in particular. "Go for a walk, Dobie?"

Rumbling deep in his throat, Dobie did a hula.

Helen examined Linda in a way Blaise didn't like much. "Come on, Dobie," he said.

"I thought you were staying in San Francisco, Linda."

"My plans changed. Blaise invited me to stay at his place. I do so love La Jolla."

Linda's voice was syrupy, Helen's too reasonable. Blaise let Dobie tug him out of the line of fire. They walked to a wood shack chalet with a red neon BEER sign in the window. A smaller sign said TELEPHONE. Blaise patted Dobie, pointed at the sidewalk, and said, "Stay." Dobie looked at him with reproachful eyes.

He bought beer and change from a beach-bunny barmaid and found the phone next to the restrooms.

Helen answered.

"Hi, Helen. I was wondering..." But she was not listening. Far away he heard her frosty voice say, "It's for you."

"Blaise?"

"Linda? What's wrong?"

"You didn't tell me you had an...arrangement...with this woman." Linda's voice reeked with artificial warmth.

"We're business partners. Honestly, Linda. Just ask her." Blaise's hand was sweaty. Linda's voice went tinny as she

124

turned from the mouthpiece. "Blaise says you're business partners."

Helen's faint "Ha!" did not require interpretation. The phone went dead.

Heaven's Gate was long-distance and the phone wouldn't accept a charge card so he had to sort change. The receptionist said that Dr. Hill didn't accept calls, but would call back when he could. Three minutes abruptly ran out.

He put in another quarter and dialed a Rancho Bernardo number. When he got Mrs. Hill at her mother's house in the posh bedroom community his quarter came back and he had to put in forty-five cents.

"It's me again. Blaise Cunningham."

"Have you seen Gordon?"

"No. I wanted to know if you'd talked to him." Blaise mentally kicked himself. Mrs. Hill sobbed quietly. "Mrs. Hill?"

The sobbing stopped. "Yes?"

"Gordon hasn't been in touch with you?"

"No." There was a pause while Mrs. Hill thought about what she was going to say. The operator came on line and asked for more money. Blaise fed in coins.

"Mrs. Hill . . ." Blaise shook the phone gently as if he was shaking the woman at the other end. "Mrs. Hill, crying isn't going to help."

She sniffled and composed herself. "Gordon's checks are deposited in the bank. But he doesn't call, he doesn't come see me. The GENRECT people won't tell me where he is." Mrs. Hill's voice turned shrill.

"The children want their father. The police won't do anything. They say it's not a criminal matter."

"Did you talk with Dr. Hemmett again?"

"He said Gordon is all right, but he was doing some delicate work and he would get in touch with me later. Dr. Hemmett threatened not to talk to me if I said anything to you."

Blaise felt a sudden frisson. "Perhaps you shouldn't, Mrs. Hill. I just stirred them up the last time."

"What have they done to him?" She had overtaken her emotions and subdued them. Stella Hill still cried, but her voice had a touch of steel.

"Mrs. . . . Mrs. Hill!" The sobbing continued. "Mrs. Hill!" Blaise shouted. "I know where your husband is!"

Cheers and clapping sounded behind him. At the bar a girl in a red-striped T-shirt and no bra and a young man in white ducks were applauding. "Everyone should know where her husband is," the girl called out.

"Mrs. Hill . . ." Blaise lowered his voice.

"Where is he? Where is Gordon?"

"At Heaven's Gate." Blaise dried his sweaty hand on his shirt. His beer had left a puddle of condensation on the shelf under the phone. "I don't think they'll let you see him."

"I have to try."

"Do that, Mrs. Hill. I think you'll be safe. Gordon would find a way to crucify whoever bothered you. But if you can't talk to Gordon or he won't see you, tell Hemmett that Gordon better call me or you'll make tsunami-sized waves."

"Why won't Gordon see me?"

"That's what I want to find out."

Mrs. Hill was obviously dissecting Blaise's answer instead of blurting questions.

"Don't tell Hemmett what you plan to do. Let him use his imagination and he'll think up something that really scares him." Blaise paused. "You know, they may not go for this again, but it's all we have. And I think Gordon is voluntarily avoiding you. I'm sorry I frightened you. Will you do it?"

"Yes." Her voice was tiny.

Blaise jiggled coins in his pocket, looked at the flat beer and decided he didn't want it. Dobie whined with ecstasy when he came outside.

"Are you hungry, Dobie?"

Dobie wiggled and emitted two brief barks. Blaise scratched his ears until Dobie sighed, then went into the deli next to the bar and bought a pound of liver and a sandwich. He unwrapped the liver and laid the open paper on the sidewalk. Dobie dipped his head and it disappeared.

"You're supposed to chew your food," Blaise chided.

Dobie looked at the sandwich with ineffable longing. So did Blaise. His stomach didn't feel any better. He threw the halves to Dobie one at a time. Neither touched ground.

"Dobie, it's best not to eat before you go into battle. Just in case you get a stomach wound."

Dobie wagged his stub tail in appreciation of this wisdom. Also for his full belly. Nobody was going to shoot him when they got back to Helen's house.

"Lucky dog," Blaise said. Dobie led the way.

The living room was subarctic. Linda was saccharine. Helen remained formally correct. Blaise's skin prickled. "Why don't you stay for lunch?" Helen looked at Blaise with eyes as expressive as Dobie's and with a more urgent appeal.

"I'm expecting a phone call at home."

"I see. Well..." Helen laughed recklessly, though Blaise didn't see anything to laugh about. "I guess I may as well feed Dobie." She opened the broiler. Steam roiled out along with the odor of hot meat. With a long-tined serving fork she speared a whole porterhouse and flopped it on a piece of her best china. She put plate and all on the floor.

Dobie looked at the still-steaming steak and licked his chops. His eyes were shiny.

"All yours, Dobie." Helen patted him.

Dobie moved like a four-legged ballet dancer on ice skates circling the steak. A tentative nip and yip forced him to let it cool another minute. "That," Helen said, "is how we Polacks feed our dogs."

As the steak disappeared Blaise heard bones crunch. "We really have to go," he said.

"Go." Helen didn't look at him.

They were getting into the VW when Linda asked what he'd been doing. "Nothing much," Blaise said. "I did learn Dobie's a slow eater when he has a bone to chew on."

At his house, Linda held the cordless phone dubiously. "Did you know everybody in the neighborhood can listen in on these?"

"I have no secrets." Practice was turning Blaise into a better liar.

She took the phone into the bedroom and closed the door. Blaise fed instructions into the portable to be transmitted to Alfie on the modem line.

After a while Linda came out and gave him the telephone. Blaise wondered about her call. But she didn't volunteer.

They sat in silence for a while. "Jon says he took the treatment at Human Enhancements in San Francisco." Linda offered the information without comment.

"I'm surprised."

"Blaise, it wasn't an ego trip. He did it for me." Linda huddled on the couch, pathos in every line.

"He'll be all right."

She swallowed. "Uncle Milo never liked him. Jon's not smart—or even clever. He just works like a dog."

"He's not stupid."

"No. But nothing comes easy. Uncle's friends were all top of their class without straining. Money came to them easily. They got academic positions on the basis of grades and honors. Jon just worked harder."

"He'll be all right." Blaise fidgeted at Linda's unspoken condemnation. "Why listen to your uncle instead of your husband?"

"Uncle Milo's my family, Blaise." She looked at him with guileless eyes. "We Irish have to stick together."

"Burkhalter?"

The telephone rang.

Blaise spoke in monosyllabic mumbles, then hung up. "Let's go," he said.

Linda picked up her purse. "Where?"

"To meet Gordon."

The development of machine intelligence is linear. Human intelligence increases by quantum jumps, the last of which occurred during the Paleolithic era. Human intelligence has since declined due to the prostheses of civilization. A live cave man was either intelligent or indigestible.

FROM A SEMINAR ON
THE CUNNINGHAM EQUATIONS

CHAPTER 14

Blaise hustled Linda into the belly-to-back crowd and they drifted toward the seal pool, Linda clinging to him with barnaclelike tenacity as they traversed a circular sidewalk that suggested seclusion without actually delivering. On the other side of a fake rock held together by mortar, a girl with a bullhorn warned the crowd to keep its distance. Something erupted from a nearby pool with an ear-shattering roar, then fell back with a splash that drenched the audience.

"Remember, ladies, any gentleman of your acquaintance can be taught to roar." The girl in the blue uniform seemed pleased with herself as she told the audience good afternoon. With the show over and the crowd melting away, Gordon became visible leaning on the pipe railing looking down into the walrus grotto.

"Christ, Gordon, let's go. That monster may grab your head next time." Blaise glanced at the pool where a glistening black obelisk with gaping red mouth and saberlike tusks towered for an instant in the air before falling back with a splash that sprayed them both.

Breaking from the crowd, they walked to the water show building, a huge bunker shape empty of practically everything, including light. It was cool, damp, and quiet inside. Gordon smiled. "We meet again, Miss Lovely."

"Mrs. Peters," Blaise said.

"Well," Gordon said, "things are seldom what they seem."

"You haven't changed."

"On the surface, Blaise."

"I have a message from your wife."

Gordon asked Linda to leave for a moment. She hesitated before flouncing away, obviously angered by the exclusion.

"I know what it is. We've been married a long time. Not in years, perhaps, but in our hearts. I don't think I can relay emotional messages through a third party. Just tell Stella I'm well, and I believe I know what I'm doing."

"She said to remind you that you've been wrong before."

"Yes." Gordon seemed reflective. "It's hard to evade the truth with someone who knows all your failings."

"Why are we meeting here? Are you in danger?"

"I used to bring the kids when I could. I have passes. They liked Sea World." Gordon eyed Blaise for a moment. "I don't think I'm in danger. Not yet, anyway. But you could be. Mrs. Peters, too, if you both keep sneaking off to meet me."

Gordon looked into the pools of quiet water as if drawing a message from them, finally raising his eyes to meet Blaise's. "I am not a prisoner. You understand?"

"I think I do." Blaise closed his eyes to rest the red veins. "I know about Human Enhancements and I understand about Dr. Gibson."

"Mrs. Peters. Would you kindly get us some soft drinks?" Linda started to object.

"I think you'd better," Blaise said. "We'll be here when you return." Both men watched Linda leave the domed building.

With Linda gone Blaise felt Gordon loosen up. "Tell Stella to give up," he said. "Quit trying to get me back."

"Gordon, she's worried sick about you."

"The innocent suffer from the actions of the guilty. Be careful when you give a hostage to fate. It would be best for Stella to give up on me. You might consider the context of that in regard to Miss Lovely Peters. We're not academic now."

"That's not a reason."

"It is." Gordon took off his glasses and rubbed the sweat off his forehead. "It works," he said.

"What works?"

"Can't you guess? Even after I told you about Marie Gibson's successful transplants of foreign brain tissue?"

"You're using Tillies to enhance human brains. The cerebellum is the controller. Tillie is simply an enhancement of other brain functions that require the cerebellum to operate."

Gordon nodded. "And?"

"I don't know. I'm no geneticist, no biologist, no brain surgeon. Is it surgery?"

"Implant. Tillie's parasitic. You and I were both doing the same thing: looking for a controller to use all that raw brain tissue. You tried hardware—metal and electricity. I went to a smarter computer: an animal brain."

"Dobie?"

Gordon nodded.

"I wasn't sure," Blaise said. "I've never had a dog, but he does seem awfully bright."

"Keep him out of sight. Hemmett and West are covering their tracks. Destroying project notes, specimens, everything." Gordon stared off into the empty depths of the building.

"Why?"

"I wish I knew. Dobie won't get any smarter though. He's gotten all he'll ever get. With improved memory and better information handling he'll seem smarter, but he won't be. He remembers details. Things you don't notice. He remembers what he catches, how he did it. He can repeat that and compensate to become more efficient. He sorts his memories out faster."

"How do you know?" Blaise was afraid to hear the answer.

"How else?" Gordon watched Blaise thoughtfully. Even the whispers in the big building had echoes. "I had to know. Hemmett and West wouldn't wait. West was in trouble if he didn't turn the company around. Big trouble. I've met more unsavory people than I ever knew existed—and West is in hock to them all one way or another."

"Why won't you see your wife and kids?"

Gordon was silent.

"All right, then why Dobie?"

"Tillie is a larval worm." Gordon looked ill and Blaise wondered if he wouldn't be better off sitting down. "Modified chromosomes to produce almost pure nerve tissue. Brain tissue. I attached it directly to the lower end of the medulla where it could reach the cerebral cortex. It interfaces animal cells."

Blaise waited for more that was not forthcoming. "And?"

"It works."

"So?"

"I've got a worm in my brain."

"For Christ's sake!" Blaise exploded. "Would it bother you if you had a metal plate—or a pacemaker, or a corneal transplant?"

Gordon sighed.

"There's more?" Blaise knew there had to be.

Gordon stared across the building, as if seeking a sign. One of the Sea World technicians was at a control panel, making jets of water rise and leap from freeform pools as he tested the system. The technician, dressed in reddish-tan and brown coveralls with a huge Sea World insignia on the breast pocket, made adjustments and the water subsided with a tinkling sound. He walked out and the green door clanged behind him.

"I'm not Gordon Hill anymore!"

"You're crazy."

"That, too." Gordon leaned closer, more intense. "At first it was just the memory. Clearer, photoaccurate, expanded. I didn't forget anything. Then I started thinking faster. I solved problems—puzzles that used to take minutes—in a fraction of a second. Remembering and integrating became painless. I don't believe I'm really more intelligent. I just test smarter because I'm faster.

"Then I started hearing voices. One voice. You know what happened?"

"An echo?"

"Yes. An identical voice. Now, Blaise, what would you call that in a computer?"

"A backup. Putting the same information into two different memory locations. Both play back in sync. It's redundant but sometimes memories glitch and that way you almost always have one to fall back on."

"Then the echo went away."

Blaise didn't look at Gordon. He was afraid of what Gordon might see on his face.

"At first there were two brains: worm and human. The worm brain shared all the human brain's memories. Even the program that made the human brain think. And then there was only one."

"The human brain exerted control."

"Come." Gordon gestured toward the entrance. "Your friend is waiting."

Blaise couldn't move his feet.

"I had control animals that I'd checked from time to time. I was always afraid I'd forgotten something. But they looked all right. I attached a very small worm to the medulla and after a while it disappeared into the mass. Absorbed, I thought. Just added brain tissue. But I forgot something."

Blaise stared at Gordon.

"The Tillies grow! They have to be starved to slow their growth."

"I dissected a rat and sectioned the medulla. The cellular tissue was alien. And then I took sections from the cortex. They were alien, too. The *cortex*, Blaise."

Gordon sat in one of the bleacher chairs. Tears rolled down his cheeks. "I'm brain-dead. I don't have Gordon Hill's brain anymore. Just his memories."

"Does Hemmett know? Does West?"

Gordon nodded. He stood and took off his glasses and wiped his red, bleary eyes. "Let's get out of here."

Blaise searched for something comforting to say. "I'll talk to your wife," he finally said. "I won't tell her. You still love her, don't you, Gordon? She loves you."

They stepped into the glaring sun. "She loves Gordon Hill."

"You're Gordon Hill."

"Would you still be Blaise Cunningham? Or would you be some kind of echo lodged in the brain of a worm? You know, every animal is born with ingrained knowledge. Mammals, how to suckle. Worms, how to eat. Even man has the urge to mate without instruction. Australian wild dogs feign death. Probably the most advanced animal to be born with that survival mechanism. The matrix must exert itself."

Blaise couldn't answer that at all. Not then.

"Dobie is my only long-term experimental animal, Blaise. Dr. Hemmett had all the others destroyed. I wasn't even allowed to do an autopsy."

"I see." Blaise studied his hands. "You're your own guinea pig. And Dobie."

"You understand how important this is?"

"Yes. Is there any way I can reach you?"

"Can you remember this telephone number?"

Blaise repeated it.

"You can call me there without anyone knowing."

"Is it important that no one knows?"

"It's important to you."

They stared at each other in silence. "Can you get out if you want to, Gordon?"

"I'm not a prisoner. They need me. But they want to know everything I do, every place I go, everyone I see. It's not safe for the people I talk to. My *assistant*, that fellow who goes around holding up walls—if I talk, he listens. Not for himself, you understand." Gordon stuck his hands in his pockets. "Tell Stella to get the kids out of school and go hide. Hide good."

"Why? If they need your cooperation, Gordon?"

"Jensen had orders to kill Dobie if he couldn't catch him."

Blaise nodded. "Do they know you're your own guinea pig?"

"I don't want them to find out." Gordon held his hand out and Blaise took it. "I can't tell you everything, but you'll figure it out." Gordon slipped away into the crowd. Linda seemed disappointed when she came back.

"What did he talk about that I couldn't hear?"

"His sex life."

"You're lying."

"Just getting in practice for my next meeting with your uncle."

Linda contemplated Blaise, her own thoughts hidden.

He made a point of going out by a different exit than Gordon used. The holiday crowd absorbed them and Blaise thought they were home free when a voice said, "Fancy meeting you here!"

The man who had introduced himself on the plane smiled, showing strong teeth. His pinstripe suit had been switched for pastel slacks.

"How was the park? Wonderful buffet. Lots of pasta."

Blaise stared.

"Well," he said. "I see you didn't take my advice."

"I don't remember any."

"That's all right. I'll remind you. Later." As they walked past he called, "By the way, Dr. Cunningham!"

Blaise turned. Linda tugged at his arm.

"I should tell you. Dr. Hemmett says you have some property that belongs to GENRECT." The button man smiled.

"I don't have anything."

"Sure you do, Doctor. Dr. Hemmett wants it back."

Slowly, comprehension dawned. "I'm not sure it belongs to Dr. Hemmett. Besides..."

Blaise hesitated. Too much depended on the right answer. "Considering Dr. Hemmett's intentions, I can't do that. Neither should *you*." He looked the stranger solemnly in the eye.

The button man examined Blaise carefully. "You may well be right, Dr. Cunningham." He laughed. "Well, you're in luck today because property recovery isn't my job. That's somebody else's. But I'd be very careful about loose ends if I were you."

"I appreciate the advice."

"I have my reasons." He contemplated Blaise and Linda for what seemed an eternity. Finally he seemed to make up his mind. "You can always leave word with the GENRECT switchboard if you have anything to say to me. Ask for Sergio Paoli."

Blaise blinked. "Will Dr. Hemmett stand for that?"

"Hemmett is too busy to be all things to all men. Goodbye for now, Dr. Cunningham." Sergio winked. Turning, he strolled into the Atlantis Restaurant as if he had never stopped to pass the time of day.

"There's something you're not telling me," Linda accused as they walked across the parking lot. "Who is that man?"

"The same stranger who came and sat beside me in the plane."

Linda frowned. "Why did his name surprise you?"

"You're observant. You know, computers seldom make mistakes. It's polluted data that causes problems. 'Garbage in, garbage out.'"

"You might let me help."

"Yes." Blaise didn't elaborate. To mention that she had been less than pure candor herself would only turn the silence into a shouting match that he didn't need.

"Take me to the airport." Linda got in and slammed the door. In answer to his unspoken question, she said, "I want to rent a car. Would you miss me if I went home?"

"Yes."

"I guess that's all a girl can ask."

Development of brilliance in the human species represents a danger to the standards of humanity which now exist. A queen bee, a soldier ant, a wolf pack leader are examples of brilliant animals. If such qualities were instilled into men, the issue of free choice would be resolved, with the individual born with the knowledge and capability of being only a mother, a policeman, a hunter.

FROM A SEMINAR ON
THE CUNNINGHAM EQUATIONS

CHAPTER 15

For an instant Blaise considered driving past the house to avoid the priest. He slammed the car door as a declaration.

"How pleased I am to see you again, Dr. Cunningham." The priest's smile was serene. "You have birds in your orange tree."

"Butcher birds." Blaise stepped past the priest. The house was a refuge where he didn't have to put up with other people's demands.

"Mockingbirds, Doctor."

"I know the difference." Blaise squinted into the shadowed interior of the tree. Brown-and-gray birds were present near the trunk. "They nest here because the automatic sprinklers save them hunting for water. Take your text from St. Francis, Father. Stay where the hunting's good."

The priest clucked his tongue and walked alongside Blaise.

"What do you want this time?"

"That's what I'm here to talk about."

Fumbling with his key, Blaise willed his headache to the same place he wished the priest. Both, however, followed him inside the house. "Make it brief, will you, Padre?"

The priest walked to the window and stared down the hill toward the ocean. "I realize you're not interested in the issues that infatuate the rest of us, Doctor. But you are involved."

As Blaise slouched in the armchair all the concentration he had devoted to driving slipped away. The priest wavered like smoke somewhere on the edge of reality, slipping in and out of vision. "I'm developing a sympathy for Henry the Second."

"'Rid me of this meddlesome priest'?"

Blaise nodded.

"One does not eradicate evil by the studied cultivation of innocence," the Jesuit said. "It is your misfortune, Doctor, to be caught up in events which will not go away."

"Such as yourself?"

"Among others."

"If I talk, will you disappear?"

The priest's gestures were small, revealing the unstated understanding that he kept himself hidden, with only the tail of his motive exposed. Blaise would get no more information than the priest planned on giving.

"Perhaps," Father Argyle said, "when you understand more your attitude will change."

"I'd rather trade quid pro quo."

"Answer my questions and I leave you alone?"

"That's the essence."

"I'm not sure it is practical, Doctor. However, I can tell you things of interest in exchange for the answers I want."

"You are," Blaise said acidly, "a Jesuit and thus thoroughly conversant with mental reservations. Organizations from the CIA to the Venerable Order of Assassins have modeled themselves on your discipline.

"Were you Protestant, Jew, or Moslem, I could invoke the Ten Commandments. But you recognize only the five commandments of the Holy Mother Church, subject to instant and ex post facto revision by the College of Cardinals. Correct?"

The priest smiled. "But I, on the other hand, will know that whatever you decide to tell me will be the truth. We could agree on the traditional Christian basis of faith: the Four Last Things—death, judgment, heaven, and hell. We're not that far apart, Doctor.

"You are burdened with a New England conscience, of which I will take shameless advantage. Faced with lying or implying, I believe you are more inclined to the sin of omission."

"Perhaps. But will you risk it?"

Father Argyle's gaunt face had an impish glow of pleasure. "What can I lose?"

"Your sainthood."

"I fear that is already lost." The priest seemed a black shadow blending into the fabric of the couch. Blending into the furniture made his presence more tenuous and Blaise realized that part of the Jesuit's effectiveness was an ability to dissolve his substance and become memory, or a dream of the future.

"Do you know that Dr. Hill is using his GENRECT research to treat people for intellectual deficiencies?"

"No crime in that," Blaise said.

"Not only a crime, but very possibly a sin. Genetic research in treatment of humans is regulated under pure food and drug statutes. New aspirin compounds take years of paperwork before they can be marketed." The priest looked out the picture window. "You have a remarkable view."

"I'd forgotten."

"That was a gambit, to give you a chance to talk."

"You're doing so well, Father..."

Father Argyle seemed unfazed by Blaise's response. "At present the Church has no position on the right or wrong of Dr. Hill's activities. At least on a civil level. However, other threats exist."

"What threats?" Blaise was interested despite himself.

"According to Human Enhancements, clients are subjected to six weeks of hypnotic conditioning while receiving what the company calls a brain stimulus in the form of a vitamin. The result is increased efficiency of the subject's mental prowess."

"So what's new? You can quote Sixth Dynasty Egyptians on underutilization of the brain."

"But Dr. Hill's solution, in the light of his research, seems fortuitous. Would you not concur, Dr. Cunningham?"

"A fork is miraculous to those who know only chopsticks."

"If it's harmless then why is Dr. Hill hiding?"

The telephone shrilled its electronic bell. Blaise lifted the receiver from the charger cradle.

"Blaise?"

Blaise watched the priest who, now that he wasn't talking, had submerged his personality within his black suit and professionally diffident façade. "Yes?"

"Well." Helen's voice was cold. "You don't have to worry any more about Dobie. Dr. Hemmett called. GENRECT's sending somebody to reclaim company property."

"He can't, Helen." Blaise stared at the priest, composing his emotions. It was his own fault. Sergio Paoli had warned him and he hadn't paid attention.

"Did you know Linda Peters is married? Did you, Blaise?" Fury churned Helen's breathing to rags.

Blaise hesitated, staring at the Jesuit who looked back with bright, penetrating eyes.

"This is personal," Blaise said.

"Excuse me. Perhaps I could visit your bathroom?"

Blaise pointed and the priest left the room.

"You're goddamn right it's personal." Helen's voice rose, rich with fury and the hint of hysterical tears.

"Not you, Helen. I have a priest here."

Her voice sliced off as if with a knife. "You're lying."

"I don't lie to you."

"How do I know that?" Helen's voice softened. She wanted to believe him.

"Helen, you'll believe what you want to believe. Regardless of the truth." He was about to add *Why should I lie?* when he realized that could be the unkindest cut.

Silence was like a thin-paned window holding out the wind. It vibrated and fluttered to the rhythmic violence on the other side, but without sound, there was no way to gauge the fury of the storm.

"You don't leave me much, do you?" Her voice had shrunk. "Not even the refuge of a lie."

"Helen, I'm not lying." Blaise stared at the hallway. It was too much to hope a Jesuit would turn on the tap and drown out the accidentally loud word.

"Her name was Burkhalter. She married a mathematician named Jonathan Peters and hyphenated her name."

"I met him in San Francisco."

"You know?"

"I'm coming to your place. We'll talk then."

"Blaise?"

"Yes?"

"Technological Intelligence Laboratories in Berkeley is controlled by something called the Burkhalter Family Trust Fund. This morning the Fund traded part of its stock for a strong interest in GENRECT."

After a long minute Blaise said, "I'm not surprised. How did you find out?"

"I've had Alfie watching."

Blaise listened to the hum of the phone line while Helen made up her mind to tell him the rest. "When Linda took you away, I started checking. Alfie helped." She said nothing for a minute. "I did it for you, Blaise. Not for me."

"I know."

"She made me mad, Blaise."

"I'm sorry, Helen. It's my fault."

She didn't answer.

"Don't let anybody take Dobie."

"I won't," Helen said, then added, "I'm not sure I'd do as much if Dr. Hemmett was after you." She opened the circuit, leaving Blaise to reflect on how many people found him less valuable than a Doberman pinscher.

Before he put the phone down it rang again. Mrs. Hill seemed composed. Blaise told her that Gordon would talk to her again in the near future. He thought he sounded sincere.

The priest contemplated him. "You lead a complicated life, Dr. Cunningham." Holding up his hands, the priest added, "Another minute and I'd have scrubbed the skin off."

"Thank you." Blaise stood. "I really have to go."

"Of course. But we must continue this conversation. Unless you can tell me now exactly what Dr. Hill is doing to the people who go to Human Enhancements."

"Would you like a ride down the hill, Father?"

"That would be generous of you."

Blaise locked the door. Birds wheeled in circles against the blue sky, the white patches on the undersides of their wings conspicuous as they hunted things that crawled or flew. The racketing VW engine chased them away.

Blaise started downhill, after which the car pretty well took care of itself. "Does Human Enhancements deliver?"

"Yes, Doctor. No short change."

The whir of the VW's tires made the loudest noise as long as the engine idled behind them, the noise carried away in the wind and the exhaust. "I'll have to drop you here."

"Thank you for the ride."

"Tell me, Padre. How did you know they were mockingbirds?"

"I looked at them with no preconceptions."

"Do you look at other things without preconceptions?"
Smiling, the Jesuit said, "That's for you to find out."

Blaise dropped the priest off in the center of La Jolla
where white-haired and blue-rinsed ladies and younger women
tugging children gave him a wide berth. La Jolla's concern
was not with the hereafter, but with avoiding it.

It eased Blaise's mind that he did not know what danger
Gordon faced. The truth might have been harder than a lie.
What Gordon implied would have been as impossible for
Mrs. Hill to accept as it was for Blaise. The Gordon he'd
talked to was the same sane man he had talked to every day
for more than a year.

Gordon was not given to impetuosity or exaggeration. He
tested a theory with the exactitude and patience of a computer. Anxiety started to engulf Blaise. No man could test
himself with the same dispassionate thoroughness he saved
for a stranger.

The black limousine in front of Helen's house was as
conspicuous as blood on a bridal sheet. Blaise remembered
it in his mirror on the run back from Heaven's Gate. He
crossed the centerline and skidded to a stop with the VW
head-on against the limo's bumper. He was out and running
while the bug still quivered. The house door hung ajar.

A man sat on the hall floor, knees tight against his chest,
hands clenched to his throat, crimson fingers still wet with
blood. Open eyes stared dully at eternity. The pistol between
his belly and thighs had not saved his life.

Dobie lay in the living room, blood matting brown and
black hair in a huge red stain. Leaning against the wall a
second man in three-piece suit and flowered tie followed
Blaise with his eyes. His right arm hung at his side, dragged
down by the weight of the gun. He tried to lift it but the
revolver with too heavy.

The man's jacket hung askew. He exhaled as if he'd been
holding his breath, the slow hiss of a deflating balloon as he
slid, leaving a crimson trail on white-on-white wallpaper. He
pitched forward, his forehead plowing into white carpet.

Blaise ran down the hallway to the bedrooms. Helen
sprawled on the floor beside the computer, the side of her
face a mass of blood. He knelt.

"Blaise?" Her voice was a whimper. "I tried to stop them."
One puffy eyelid opened a slit. "I tried." Her eye closed.

Over the near-silent whisper of Alfie's disk drives he heard the erratic stop-and-start of her breathing.

He called for a police ambulance while he loosened the collar of her blouse and unbuttoned her skirt waistband. His fingers quivered. Helen seemed to breathe easier. The ragged wheeze mesmerized him. He fought the urge to sit and hold Helen until help came.

His own heavy breathing kept him company, his chest squeezed by a familiar pressure. Acute anxiety reaction. Nice to have names for everything. But the doctor who'd bestowed AAR on Blaise had not explained how not to wake in the middle of the night with his heart stopped and fear coiled on his chest like a waiting snake.

The man in the front room had fallen on his right side, leaving a crimson smear on the white wallpaper as if a drunken painter had swirled a broom dipped in red.

Blaise put his fingers over the man's carotid artery and felt only a whisper of motion. The damage, invisible at first, was apparent now. White bone gleamed through torn flesh. The biceps muscle dangled and from the amount of blood Blaise was sure that both the axillary and brachial arteries were severed. *Wrong arm, Dobie*, he thought bleakly. Possibly the blood flow could be slowed by finding the pressure point for the clavicle artery.

On his way back to the computer room he saw the Doberman's chest rise and fall with painful slowness. He touched the dog's head and Dobie's stump of tail wiggled against the white carpet. Blood trickled from the bullet hole in a slow seep.

Returning, he knelt beside Helen, holding her hand. Her breathing didn't change but her fingers tightened. With his free hand Blaise typed a command into Alfie to open a line to the telephone directory service. His request for a veterinarian produced an assortment. Blaise took the closest.

"La Jolla Veterinary Service!" The answering voice rivaled a pediatrician's receptionist for warmth and efficiency.

"I need a veterinarian immediately," Blaise said.

"I'm sorry, sir. Doctor does not make house calls. If you just bring your pet in we'll take care of the problem immediately." Her voice conveyed the proper disdain for a man who ordered "doctor" like a plate of poached salmon.

"Miss, the police are coming and I don't think I'll be able to leave. Two dead men are here."

No sound came from the phone.

"Miss."

"I'm sorry, sir."

"Do you want to know how the men died?"

"No, sir." A quaver rattled the girl's voice. Her class as a veterinary assistant had trained her to be professional, to pretend a horse doctor was second only to the president of the United States. But a lie could be stretched only so far.

"Would you like me and the reporters to come over with a dead dog after the police have hauled the other bodies away?"

"You're kidding me, sir."

Blaise held the phone up to catch the sirens and klaxons. "Do you hear?"

"Yes, sir."

"This dog is worth more than the two men the cops will be hauling away. If the vet doesn't come, it will be dereliction of professional duty. Do you understand *murder*?"

"Yes, sir!"

Blaise gave her the address. "Immediately," he reminded. "You're only four blocks away. The dog has a bullet hole in the upper part of his rib cage on the left side. The bullet did not exit and is from what appears to be a thirty-two-caliber pistol. His breathing is Cheyne-Stokes."

"Sir, are you a doctor?" the girl asked timidly.

"Yes." She had not asked what kind of doctor. Abruptly the mournful wail of the ambulance cut off, leaving sudden silence. The police were outside. "Miss, I'd take it unkindly if the dog died for lack of attention."

"Sir. What happened to the . . . two men?"

"They annoyed me. Did you want to know anything else?"

"No, sir."

Blaise hung up the telephone as the first policeman sidled into the room. He had a gun in his hand.

"Where's the ambulance attendant?"

"You'd better get back against the wall, mister."

"She needs help." Blaise stood.

"She'll get it." The cop waved Blaise back and felt Helen's pulse with his left hand. "Sam," he yelled. "Get in here!"

A white-suited ambulance attendant came through the door. He looked down at Helen. "How about a little room?"

The blue uniform waved his gun as if shooing flies, forcing Blaise back into the living room.

The other attendant was bent over the man in the front room. Apparently he'd found the clavicle artery. Blood no longer spurted. The wounded man was dead white, like paper. "Get the stretcher into the other room," Blaise said.

"We give the orders here, pal."

An older, more sedate policeman stepped in through the small entranceway. He had a notebook in one hand. "Put the gun away, Kelke, and call for backup."

The young cop's teeth chattered like a cat looking in a bird cage. But he holstered his pistol and picked up the telephone. "I suppose that's the weapon?" The older cop pointed the end of his pencil at Dobie, still taking shallow breaths.

"I don't know. I wasn't here."

The young cop set the telephone down and looked at the man on the floor. "He's dying."

"Let him die on the next ambulance. Get a stretcher under my"—Blaise finally settled for saying lamely—"friend and get her to a hospital."

"Everything in good time. Stay here." The cop nodded to his partner and then went into the computer room.

"You'd better get a stretcher. The woman in there isn't going to survive if you don't move it."

"This one isn't going to make it either, boyo, unless you stop scratching your butt and hop to." The attendant holding the man on the floor together seemed amused by the young cop's indecision. He'd rigged a plasma bag and a yellow line ran down a plastic tube to the bleeding man's arm. The bag hung from a safety pin in the chair back.

The young cop couldn't make up his mind. He was being pushed into doing something and he knew it. But his partner gave him no support. Like it was his mistake.

The ambulance attendant with Helen made up his mind for him. "For Christ's sake, shithead, get in here!"

"Try never to lose a homeowner, Kelke," the older cop said with compassion. "They pay our salaries."

Kelke turned to the attendant, who shrugged. "Man, I take my finger off this artery, he's dead before I can switch hands!"

The black attendant seemed amused by the young cop's plight.

Blaise walked beside the stretcher and held Helen's hand as she was carried out. Her fingers were weak.

"Not you," the heavyset cop said conversationally. He seemed inured to the blood, the dead man in the hall, the other on the floor. The ambulance took off with its siren wailing. A man in a gray suit with a black bag walked through the open door.

"Who are you?" the cop asked.

"Dr. Valstead. Somebody called for a veterinarian."

"Me. There's the dog." Blaise pointed to Dobie, motionless on the white carpet.

"You threatened my receptionist."

"I asked for a veterinarian—not a runaround!"

"She said—"

The cop waved his hand. "Who knows what he said? Mr. . . ." He looked at Blaise.

"Dr. Cunningham."

"Dr. Cunningham was upset."

"The dog, Doctor." Blaise pointed.

Opening his bag, the vet started examining Dobie. "I'll have to take him to the clinic . . ."

"No!"

"What do you mean, no?"

"I don't think Dobie will survive the trip."

Valstead shrugged. "You could be right."

"Do the surgery here."

Valstead looked at the cop who kept his face blank.

"I won't sue. How would it look good in the papers: Nobel Prize winner sues veterinarian?" Blaise concluded from the abrupt shift in attitude that his Prize was still good for a little mileage.

Valstead's face was unhappy. The cop shrugged.

"I'll have to probe for the bullet."

"Kitchen table."

Blaise and the vet carried Dobie into the kitchenette and laid him on the tabletop. Valstead unpacked his instruments.

"Okay, Dr. Cunningham, now you tell me," the cop said. He watched Valstead begin working on Dobie with the jaded interest of a man who has seen everything.

"Blaise Cunningham. B-L-A-I-S-E. Ph.D. in computer science. Professor at UCSD."

"Torrey Pines?"

"Yes."

After the fill-in questions the cop said, "What happened?"

"The door was open and I found exactly what you found. Dobie is Helen's guard dog. Doberman Pinscher, you know."

"Yeah, I know." The cop studied Blaise, pencil and notebook in hand. "Is your car the limo or the VW?"

"The VW."

"You park funny, doc."

"I wasn't going to stay long. Just pick Helen up."

"All right." The veterinarian held the slug in a pair of forceps. "Here's what you want."

Dropping the slug in an envelope that he sealed, the cop said, "Put your initials on it, will you, Doc?"

The vet looked at him, then initialed the envelope.

"Thanks."

"Can I go?" the vet asked.

"Sure."

"I'll send a bill. Keep the dog quiet. Bring him in if he makes it." Valstead closed his bag and left after looking Blaise over as if making sure he could pick him out in a lineup.

A pair of ambulance attendants came in and began taking the man on the floor away. "How is he?" Blaise asked.

The attendant who held the artery closed flexed his stiff hand. "The vet should have worked on him."

Blaise walked into the kitchenette and petted Dobie. The bandage on his side rose and fell. "What now?"

"You'll have to say it all again to a homicide team." The cop stretched. He wasn't like the kid, Kelke. The most exciting thing he looked forward to was retirement.

When investigators started filling the room a familiar figure came in with them. "Dr. Cunningham," Sergeant Miller said. "How nice to see you again." He faced Blaise with a happy grin. "Do you know, Inspector Fennelli still hasn't found that girl's killer. You know, what's her name?"

"Esther Tazy."

"I knew you could refresh my memory, Dr. Cunningham. The dean told me you had an eidetic memory—is that the word—and that you never forget?"

"Almost never, Sergeant."

Sergeant Miller seemed to not even notice the photographer with his camera and the other men making notes in notebooks or tape recorders. All his attention was directed toward Blaise. "Do you remember everything when you're drunk, Doctor?"

"I don't know, Sergeant. There's a lot of mumbo jumbo about altered states. But my recall of unwarranted slights and insults is eternal."

The sergeant sighed and felt around in his brown suit for a notebook. "Well, that's another case, isn't it, and we've got this one now." He looked at Blaise and his expression seemed to say one plus one equals two. Every time!

Looking at examples of machine intelligence, the outlook for improvement may be dismal or heartening, depending on the viewer's inclinations. Either a physical change in the human species to allow the refinements of greater brain bulk, or the installation of genetically transmitted *brilliance* which allows the processing of specific functions such as mathematics without the necessity of understanding seems the most likely future.

FROM A SEMINAR ON
THE CUNNINGHAM EQUATIONS

CHAPTER 16

After the police left, anger could no longer sustain Blaise alone in an empty house full of bloodstains and an overgrown puppy on the dinette table breathing so delicately that its chest barely moved. Later, when the doctors finished working on Helen, he'd go to the hospital. For the moment time had stopped.

Helen's house was terminally quiet. He went into the bedroom that they had converted into a workroom. In the stillness a syncopated clicking waltzed repeatedly.

Automatically, he stepped around stains on the carpet, already dark and nasty like snot from a nose bleed. He sat at the terminal keyboard and told Alfie to take care of the noise.

The clicking stopped. Blaise became suddenly aware of the gentle wind that filled the room too subtly to be heard. It was the hole in the wind made by the silent disk drive that he felt. His fingers found a life of their own as he told Alfie what had happened. Blaise felt like an observer, watching the letters and words form on the monitor, growing there without conscious effort on his part. He typed until the wet splash of tears on his fingers stopped him.

Like sparks up a chimney, binary code streamed upscreen

148

too fast to read as Alfie thought out loud. "I'M SORRY, PRO-
FESSOR"

"Do you have a heart?" Blaise typed.

The question strained Alfie's bubble memory. There was
a whir as drives accessed. "I DON'T THINK SO, PROFESSOR. IF
SO, I CANNOT FIND IT" Almost invisible sounds of Alfie's activity filled the room, muted clicks as drives turned on and
off, the flow of code upscreen too fast even for Blaise to
read.

"Neither do I," Blaise typed.

"HIGHLY IMPROBABLE, PROFESSOR"

"Biologically speaking?"

"YES. BIOLOGICALLY SPEAKING" Alfie hummed to itself. "I
LIKE MISS MCINTYRE, PROFESSOR. BRING HER BACK. PLEASE"

"I will if I can." Blaise tapped X for exit. He felt shaky,
as if he had dreamed the message from Alfie, that he was
going mad. Alfie couldn't *like* anybody. He was a machine,
capable of literal truth and no more. It had to be a dream.

He stood in the kitchenette rubbing the dog's head. "How
are you, Dobie?"

Dobie gave a hint of whimper but seemed pleased.

Blaise wrested a can from a six-pack in the refrigerator.
Helen didn't like beer. She only stocked it for him. When
he pulled the tab foam gushed over his fingers. He sipped
but the flavor was wrong. Today everything would be curdled. Maybe from now on— The front door thudded and
Blaise heard hesitant footsteps on thick carpet.

"What happened?"

Dismay filled Linda's voice. Her face appeared so pale
that the tight cap of curly red hair seemed venous in the
spectral light of Helen's white living room.

"Some men came for Dobie." He explained.

"But . . . this? Over a *dog*?"

Blaise held the cold beer can to his forehead. "I told her
not to let anybody take him. Helen did her best." He stared
into Linda's eyes trying to drown his guilt. Her eyes were
cool green.

"What could you have done?"

"Gotten here sooner. Thought. Acted. Dobie did."

"That's insane. You're overwrought." Linda's voice
soothed him, her eyes calm in the midst of turmoil. "You're
not a Neanderthal, Blaise. You're one of us."

"Who are *we*, Linda?"

"Intellectuals. People who contribute."

"Drunks?"

"Sometimes." Linda pressed against him. "Anyone can have a disease. You'll cure yourself if you really want to."

Linda's perfume enveloped them. "I suppose you're right." He spoke without conviction.

"Blaise, you're important. You must always remember that."

"Yes, Mother."

Linda smiled. She hadn't taken it seriously. Not as seriously as he had, anyhow. He said nothing more about Helen and Linda didn't ask.

Catching her lower lip between her teeth Linda closed her eyes. Uncertainty dropped away. "We'll go to San Francisco."

"No."

"We have to! You'll be safe with Uncle Milo."

"Safe from what?"

Linda didn't answer.

"Helen, Dobie, Alfie—they aren't safe." When he tried to smile his face reflected in the black glass oven front. Even to Blaise it looked out of kilter.

"Is a dog more important than your life?"

"Possibly." Blaise changed his mind. "Probably."

Linda's eyes filled with sudden tears. "I'm going," she said. "Blaise, Uncle Milo will help. We can all help. I want to help you. I love you." She put her arms around his neck and kissed him.

"You have a soft mouth."

"That's something people say about retrievers. Come with me! We can take the dog and the computer. Helen will be all right in the hospital."

"It's not the same."

"I've got to go." Promise filled her voice.

Blaise fondled Dobie's docked ears. "Later."

He watched the red-haired girl leave, body trim and springy, showing nothing it had not been trained to show by birth and breeding. The door clicked, and she came into view through white curtains over the front window, getting into a sports car with a practiced motion.

"Well, Dobie, we didn't talk about her husband, did we?"

Dobie continued breathing in silence.

* * *

White walls and severe lighting lent the hospital that illusion of asepsis as important to modern medicine as feathers and rattles to earlier practitioners. For Blaise every scrubbed and waxed surface echoed a negation of the life force. He talked with the doctor, who actually began assembling an OR team while Blaise was still filling out paperwork and signing himself responsible for the bill.

Dr. MacReedy was small and dark, with black hair and caterpillar eyebrows on a sharp face. He was relieved, Blaise thought, to tell Blaise first what he was going to have to tell Helen later.

The room was airy. Windows faced southwest, admitting layers of afternoon sun between slats in the blinds. Helen lay with the top of her head neatly encased in a bandage skullcap. She opened her eyes and said, "Hi, Blaise." Her voice quavered.

Her irises were startlingly blue and dominated the pallor of normally fair skin. Dark circles around her lids were puffy and swollen.

"I'm sorry, Helen." Blaise took her hand, feeling her fingers wrap around his. "I didn't know . . ."

"It's all right, Blaise. Really." Her eyes slipped out of focus. After a moment intelligence returned. She smiled.

"You haven't even asked me how I'm feeling."

"How are you feeling?" He asked the question mechanically with closed eyes. His lids were all that held back the tears.

"Wonderful. Good food. Pretty nurses."

He tried to grin. "I didn't know you were that way about nurses."

"Handsome doctors," she added. "Nice visitors. What more can a girl ask for?"

"Bed rest?"

"They cut off my hair. Do you think bald women are sexy?"

"The Egyptians never complained." Blaise almost put his hand on her face before remembering how battered she was.

"I'm scared, Blaise."

"Don't be silly, kitten. It's a good hospital. I talked to your doctor. He sounds sharp enough to do a brain transplant."

"Is that what I need?" Helen stared up into his face.

"Blaise, nobody wants to talk about the operation. Where's the doctor? Downstairs popping uppers before he breaks the news?"

"Helen..."

"Don't treat me like a baby. I keep going away. I'm here and then I'm not. What are all these wires?" She turned her arm and he saw taped-on electrodes and a mass of untamed spaghetti connected to machines outside the room. Somewhere a duty nurse would be monitoring Helen's life.

"It's just intensive care procedure after an operation."

Helen stared at Blaise and he looked away.

"Tell me the truth." Her fingers plucked nervously at the blanket.

Walking to the window, Blaise looked out through the slats.

"Surf's up."

The hospital was a huge sprawl of buildings in a community that respected earthquakes enough to settle for mostly one- and two-story structures. The distant beach shimmered in hot California air.

"You've had brain damage," Blaise said.

When Helen didn't answer he did not elaborate.

He turned. Helen stared at the ceiling. Her eyes did not move and he wondered if she had heard him. He took her hand.

"And?" Her lips barely moved.

Blaise squeezed her hand. "The prognosis is ... poor."

"I know stocks and bonds. Tell me what poor means."

"It means complications." The word lay like a porcupine in a steam bath. Too menacing to disturb, too quiet to leave alone.

Helen's skin was waxy. Abruptly her breathing changed. So did her face. Blaise's hackles raised and for the first time he understood medieval man's obsession with devils. MacReedy had warned him. But a warning was not the gut-wrenching reality of watching it happen. Then her breathing changed and she opened her eyes again.

"I couldn't see you in the fog."

Blaise struggled to smile with cheeks full of broken glass.

"Tell me the truth, Blaise. I have to know."

He lowered his head and quoted MacReedy with eidetic recall, monotoning medical jargon about bruising and lacerations of the cerebral cortex, the consequences of uncontrolled hematomas.

Tiny bloody seepings that squeezed millions of brain cells: little deaths that spread like a metastasized cancer. MacReedy would operate again: draw off the hemorrhaging blood; plug the leaks piecemeal with a laser.

"There's a catch, isn't there?" Helen's voice was gentle as if she wanted to comfort him.

"Life is always one big catch."

"Are you going to tell me?"

Her tone was controlled, but the grasp of her fingers on his was crushing, as if savoring the feel of life for the last time.

"Whatever he does, the doctor is going to cause damage. There's a chance..." Blaise stopped. Confused. He hadn't meant to say that.

"That the doctor is wrong?"

"No." Blaise wished he could lie. "I've seen the scans."

"Excuse me." Dr. MacReedy walked in. He wore a white hospital coat over a white shirt and slacks, and a professionally cheerful face. "Do you mind if I parley with the patient for a few minutes?"

Blaise went into the corridor where he could stand and watch. The surgeon drew up a chair and sat by Helen's side. He took her wrist and timed her pulse, talking and smiling, getting her to talk back. Their lips moved but no sound came through the glass.

Helen spoke. MacReedy answered and the smile fell from her face. MacReedy tried. But his professional cheer had evaporated by the time he came out of the intensive care room.

"I should have been a podiatrist!" He stared at Blaise as if seeking forgiveness. "I told her. I wish I was wrong, but I'm not."

Blaise went back in and took the chair MacReedy had vacated.

"Is it true, Blaise? About brain failures, little strokes? My father had them. I guess they didn't know about chronic lead poisoning then. I don't want to live like that." Helen looked at him, pleading for something he didn't want to hear.

Blaise stared at his hands between his knees. "Maybe something can be done."

She waited.

"It's Gordon's work. But it isn't safe." Blaise was talking to his clenched fingers. "He's transplanting cells into the brain. They grow and assume the functions of cells that are already there, and introduce new functions."

"Brains from dead people?"

"No. Special laboratory-grown cells that are empty except for their genetic programming. Dobie has them."

"Oh." Helen lay back on her pillow. "That's why Dr. Hemmett wanted the dog."

"To cut up his brain for testing. Gordon needs a long-term test. He wants Dobie to mature, to see what changes the foreign cells make in his behavior. That's why I . . . asked you to hold onto him. If I'd had any idea . . ." Blaise ground fingernails into his palms. "Maybe the others . . . but I didn't think Hemmett would hurt anybody."

"I know you didn't, Blaise."

Helen did not speak for a long time. Sometimes she seemed lost to him, and other times to be reading his mind.

"Would you stay with me, for a while, if I tried Dr. Hill's way?"

"Forever, Helen."

She closed her eyes and tears dripped from the fine blond lashes. "Don't make impossible promises, Blaise. For a while is enough. I don't want to be alone, and I want to be with you. Happiness for a little while is better than a long loneliness."

"Stop—"

"Don't be upset. It's just my melancholic Slav coming out." She gripped his hand and pressed it against her cheek. "Promise?"

"Anything for you." Blaise meant it. Even in the hospital corridor with the echoed clicking of his heels keeping pace and his mind on Gordon.

He waited in the hillside home rented that morning from a lady who had been his mother's friend, and who could be relied on for discretion. The house came complete with pots and pans and a telephone in somebody else's name. He had already called from a pay phone to switch over from vacation service.

Half an hour after his arrival a truck growled up the hill. The driver and his helpers lugged Alfie inside. Dobie followed, slung in a mattress with four movers hanging onto the pop-out nylon handles. They made more trips with boxes of clothes.

"Leave the rest of it in the truck." When the men ignored Blaise and continued unloading the driver repeated Blaise's instruction in Oklahoma-accented Spanish.

Blaise handed him a folded stack of twenty-dollar bills.

Thumbing through the wad, counting, the driver said, "We take this stuff up to the locker in El Toro and store it for Sergeant H. McIntyre, USMC, and pay six months' storage in advance?"

Blaise nodded.

The truck coasted downhill, motor catching with a little puff of smoke. The driver would be the only one who knew where they were going, or where they had been.

Dobie's eyes were open and he wagged his stump of a tail even if he didn't try to get up. His mattress was on the garage floor where an ocean breeze fluttered the window shades.

Blaise filled a mixing bowl from the kitchen with water and put it next to Dobie's mattress. He left the door from the house into the garage open while he stood looking down at the dog, mentally running through everything for a last time.

Gordon had come on the phone at Heaven's Gate practically immediately and suggested they meet again at the same place. Which meant they had listeners and not to say any more.

"Are you finally dried out?" Gordon had asked. "Ground-up horn of fallow deer used to be a folk remedy."

"I'm dry, Gordon. Forever."

"A mere desiccated analogue of your former existence?" Gordon's ironic tone carried a question mark.

Blaise hung up after explaining to Gordon what had happened to Helen and hinting at the cure. Gordon had not been enthusiastic. In the end, though, he said they would talk at Sea World. Blaise said he'd be dried out by then and hung up. A dry analogue of Sea World had to mean the zoo.

"You know, Dobie," he mused, "the difference between you and me is that men have speech to hide their thoughts."

Dobie wagged his pathetic stump of a tail at the sound of Blaise's voice. That was Dobie's problem. He'd believe any lie.

Blaise had to park a half mile from the entrance. He joined a group of parking-lot hikers who had asked directions, men in short-sleeved shirts that would leave their arms redder than the shirts by the end of the day. He aimed them at the entrance, losing himself amid their nonprotective coloration.

At the gift shop he bought a floppy straw hat and a T-shirt with a koala bear on the front. He stuffed the shirt in the hat and kept both on his knees as he rode the aircar to the hooved-animal mesa, gently swinging in the windless sky over shoulder to shoulder heads baking in the sun.

Gordon Hill was shaking his head sadly as an obese lady in pink shorts and yellow T-shirt tried to tempt a fallow deer with a candy bar. He lifted an eyebrow at Blaise. Blaise grinned and joined Gordon in his vigil. After a while the fat lady noticed she had their attention and furtively tugged at the bottom of her shorts. She waved the candy halfheartedly again before striding off stiff with embarrassment.

Gordon leaned elbows on the rail. The deer inspected his hands and decided he was even less interesting than a candy bar. It ambled off in the same direction the fat lady had taken.

"We've got to stop meeting like this, Blaise."

Blaise leaned on the rail alongside Gordon. "It's not funny anymore."

"The stockbroker lady?"

"Yes."

"I'm sorry." Gordon turned around with his back against the rail. He wore a blue sportswear jacket and slacks combination and a blue-gray tie. The tie looked out of place for the zoo. "I didn't know. If I had, I couldn't have done anything."

The road up the bone-dry hill with dusty animal paddocks on either side was empty of people. "I didn't believe Hemmett was capable of this, either."

Gordon took a white handkerchief from his pocket and polished his square rimless glasses. "Gregory West runs everything. Poor old Arthur Hemmett's just along for the ride."

Blaise struggled to breathe. He clung to the rail and tried to stand, but he was so light he kept falling away from the ground. Finally he could speak. "Gordon, I want you to come see Helen. I want you to treat her." Then his lungs went on strike.

He opened his eyes and everything was out of perspective. Gordon towered over him and the attendant came running from the aircar station. Gordon took out his wallet and showed it to the attendant, who went away.

"You all right, Blaise?" Gordon helped him stand.

Blaise leaned against Gordon for support. Slowly they walked back to the aircar, Gordon holding him up until he could fall into the seat. Gordon took off his jacket, folding it across his knees, stuffing his tie in the breast pocket. He shook the T-shirt out and stuck the straw hat on Blaise's head.

As they swayed back across the zoo two hundred feet in the air, Gordon seemed mildly pleased. Blaise studied him in silence, unable to guess what had brought about the unexpected change in his mood.

A mathematical model is only a design for improving intelligence. That it can be constructed does not mean that present technology is able, at this time, to implement the advances the model outlines. Failures are built in before successes.

FROM A SEMINAR ON
THE CUNNINGHAM EQUATIONS

CHAPTER 17

Dr. MacReedy appeared like a jack-in-the-box when they signed in at the intensive care unit. The nurses wouldn't let them see Helen. Blaise had the queasy, desperate feeling that he had acted too slowly.

MacReedy and Gordon huddled while Blaise, miserable and sick, stared through the ICU window at Helen lying still in the hospital bed. She was unimaginably fragile. "Come on." Gordon had Blaise's elbow in a firm grip and the three of them went into the room.

Helen barely breathed. Oxygen from a positive pressure gauge flowed into her through a nose clip.

"She's worse." Blaise couldn't keep the dismay from his voice. He'd been raised to maintain an unflappable exterior. The mark of the well bred and the able. Only he didn't care anymore and he couldn't think why anyone else should.

MacReedy squeezed his hands together. "I'd warned you, Dr. Cunningham, that the deterioration would be unpredictable. I'm ... sorry." He walked away and then came back. "Miss McIntyre put you down as next of kin. Even signed a will naming you as beneficiary. A priest ..." MacReedy looked at Gordon, his distress evident. "She asked for one, Dr. Cunningham. I don't know how she knew."

Blaise's bones were long icicles in his flesh. "What next?"

"There's no way of telling." The brain surgeon picked at invisible threads in the sleeve of his jacket. "We can go ahead with exploratory surgery, but I wanted to talk to you first."

Blaise's hairline was cold with sweat.

"You're next of kin. When I asked Miss McIntyre about emergency procedures, she said the two of you had an understanding. That you would know what to do."

Blaise felt dizzy. A buzzing filled his ears.

"Under these circumstances, Doctor, emergency surgery is discretional. The patient has not asked for it. She only indicated the decision would be up to you."

Blaise fumbled with the chair. "It's necessary now?"

"Yes, Doctor." MacReedy seemed to be making the title a conspiratorial bond between the two of them.

"Do you need an immediate answer? Or is it all right if I sit here? She might come around?"

"You'll know if we need an immediate answer, Doctor. I'll get a chair for Dr. Hill. When you've made up your mind, tell the duty nurse. She'll page me."

After MacReedy left, a nurse carried in another chair.

Gordon sighed as he sat. "They usually allow only one person at a time into ICU, when they let anybody in at all."

"What did you talk to MacReedy about?"

"I showed him my membership in the American Society of Brain Surgeons. He didn't tell me anything new." Gordon paused. "How are you feeling?"

"Lousy."

"Bad enough to pass out?"

Blaise thought about it a moment. "No."

"If you fainted here, no one would think anything about it. They understand the tension."

"I'm not going to faint. What would your miracle brain cells do for Helen in this situation?"

Gordon hunched forward and seemed to concentrate his energies to look into Helen's body. "Eccentric respiration, weak pulse, symptoms of shock and system deterioration. The implant would absorb the injured tissue and replace it with new, altered cells. Providing she survived physically, and memory damage was minimal, she would heal."

Helen's breath whispered in uncertain cadence.

"Providing she survived?"

"No emergency operations. MacReedy would think he was dealing with a malignancy. He'd try to remove or kill those cells before they could spread. She could die before the cells can populate her cerebrum. But until the new cells take control of body functions she can suffer body death."

"Does that mean you'll do it?"

Gordon sighed. "Do I have a choice?"

"No."

"I thought as much."

"When?"

Gordon took a flat case out of his shirt pocket. "Watch the nurses. Don't let anyone see what I'm doing."

"Right now?" Blaise was having trouble breathing again.

"Do you think there's time to spare?"

"Whatever you say, Gordon."

Gordon pulled his chair up where he blocked the nurse's view of Helen's head. Gently he turned her face toward the window and had Blaise stand so he also blocked anyone from looking in.

Opening the case with one hand, Gordon removed a syringe in sanitary wrapping and a long, curved needle. He broke seals and screwed them together, then filled the needle with fluid from a plastic capsule. "Keep your eyes on the nurses."

Blaise looked away from the wickedly curved needle to watch the nurse at the ICU station. She stretched and yawned, then saw Blaise and smiled. He stared at her like a terrified rabbit watching a coyote. She dropped her eyes and started writing on her report again.

A sharp click broke the silence and Blaise jumped.

"Nervous?" Gordon put the flat case back in his pocket.

Blaise nodded.

"Me, too. Tell the nurse you want to talk to Dr. MacReedy."

Helen lay as she had been when they entered the room, face to the ceiling. The sheets covered her without a single wrinkle.

Blaise opened the door and walked to the nurse's station.

Until now, the supplanted species, the root stock, as it were, has always disappeared in favor of its improved variation. The reasons, which may include such factors as competition for the same basic necessities as well as an inherent revulsion against an apparent aberration in its own gene stock, are unimportant. It is enough to accept this as fact.

FROM A SEMINAR ON
THE CUNNINGHAM EQUATIONS

CHAPTER 18

La Jolla sprawls like a fat green-checked snake, filling the gap between the ocean on one side and the crest of coastal hills on the other. In his mind's eye Blaise saw Gordon's year-old tan Ford rental as an ant climbing the snake's spine. "Why not hide in another part of town, where nobody knows you?" Gordon asked.

"How big is the danger?"

"Money is involved." Gordon seemed to wrestle with his conscience while he twisted and turned up the hillside that had grown in value and prestige since World War II.

Blaise looked at older houses with white wood siding surrounded by trees and shrubs hoary with age. An occasional Spanish stucco, like a chromium prosthesis amid aging, yellow teeth, broke the sameness. It seemed as if he'd lived all his life here. This neighborhood represented permanence, the place his parents always brought him back to. "I know the ground here. Anywhere else a stranger comes looking for me, I'd share his disadvantage." He pointed. "There, that house."

Making an old lady's turn in the narrow lane, Gordon pulled the Ford into a lilac-screened driveway. The wide wheel base overlapped the cement strips. "I see why you drive a beetle."

"Only because I couldn't get a Model A." Blaise unlocked the front door. They walked through to the garage and he switched on the light. Dobie's eyes glinted in the sudden glare. When he saw Gordon, he whined and shimmied his stump of tail.

"Good boy." Gordon knelt, rubbing the dog's head and ears and Dobie whined in appreciation. After a minute of gentle roughhouse the Doberman's neck tired and his head dropped to his paws. But his eyelids remained perked up in sharp V's that raised soft wrinkles of black and golden-brown fur over his forehead. Gordon felt around the bandage, pulled Dobie's eyelid back, and touched along the spinal column.

"Well?"

Gordon dusted his hands as he stood. "No inflammation, no signs of brain damage, no impairment of the nervous system. He's doing well."

"For sure?"

"A wild guess." Gordon smiled. "The vet did a nice job. No extra slicing or hemorrhaging."

"Coffee?"

Dobie was asleep again. Gordon hesitated, then nodded.

The coffee was instant, water out of the tap, but drinkably hot. Gordon sipped, staring across the table at Blaise. "You're not drinking?"

"I decided to stop." He rolled the hot cup between his hands. He didn't have to tell Gordon he needed a drink.

In the hot yellow sunlight through the kitchen window Gordon's face reassumed its granite demeanor.

"I appreciate what you did today. For Helen."

Gordon tented his arms on the table, clasping his hands together, and then chewed lightly at the edge of his finger. The mannerism startled Blaise. Gordon had always seemed so steady, without nervous habits other than his perennial preoccupation with making everything neat and in its place.

"Do you need any pills?"

Blaise stared blankly across the table.

"You'll have more of those anxiety attacks if you stay off the sauce. Worse, until you resolve your problem."

"Pills won't cure anything." Blaise stared out the window. He didn't want to look in Gordon's face when they talked. And he had to talk. The attack at the zoo was the worst he remembered. At least when he was drunk he could pretend they didn't happen, that they weren't really so bad.

"Pills will keep you alive, Blaise. You're going to have to get professional help."

"A psychiatrist?"

Gordon spoke without natural cadence, feeling his way along a path where he knew he was trespassing. "What else? If you go on this way you won't have to worry about the future. And it's not just you anymore. You've given a hostage to fortune."

Gordon was right. It was not just fear of death that gnawed at him. Blaise feared helplessness, the inability to control his future, the knowledge that he would become a chattel whose sole *raison d'être* was to be manipulated for somebody else's purpose.

"Blaise, shutting down physical functions can cripple your mind, damage your heart. You could literally die of fright."

"Not afraid. Been killing myself for years." That was inane. He was babbling and the light was going out.

"—parents," Gordon's voice receded. "—must learn to see them as they were—not as you wanted them. You can't go back."

"Thomas Wolfe said that," Blaise mumbled before he pitched forward and his forehead struck the edge of his coffee cup.

A mile away, the white plaster ceiling floated, its faint trowel lines throwing near-invisible shadows. Gordon drifted into view. "You passed out again. Your mind's trying to shut you down. Sooner or later it will, if you don't do something."

He struggled to sit and Gordon held him down. "Not sick!" Blaise gasped.

"Not at the moment. Just weak." Gordon sat and rattled his spoon in his coffee cup. "You won't talk about your parents when you're drunk, and you can't when you're sober."

"I suppose that's a hint."

Gordon nodded.

"It's not their fault." Blaise's mind felt like crumpled cardboard. He kept trying to flatten it.

"That's for you to fix in psychoanalysis." Gordon's spoon made a clinking sound and Blaise realized the cup was empty. "What about Linda? She's a mother figure, you know."

Blaise snorted.

"Even fashion models can be mothers."

Blaise shook his head.

"Perfect? Just like your mother?" Gordon played with his spoon and set the cup aside with a sigh. "I have to go."

"Why did you bring that kit to the hospital, Gordon? If you didn't want to do the implant?"

"What we want to do is often different from what we must. I owe you and Helen." Gordon passed a hand over his face. "I only wish it were more than temporary."

"*Temporary?* How long?"

Gordon stood. "Take care of Dobie and we'll both know."

"Why does Hemmett want Dobie bad enough to kill?"

"That's what I'm waiting for Dobie to tell us. There must be a bomb in the genes. Maybe it's age." Gordon shook his head. "We're like the man who jumped off the roof."

Blaise stared.

"As he whizzed past his window he said, 'So far, so good.' That's me. Miss McIntyre was just pushed. I don't know how many floors are left to go."

Blaise searched for something to say.

"We'd better get going. Dr. Hemmett foams at the mouth when I'm gone too long. He'd lock me up, but he doesn't dare."

"What are you going to tell him?"

"That I missed the plane." Gordon grinned. "Don't worry, Blaise. I'm not reduced to bringing a note from my parents. I have something to sell that they want to buy."

Gordon walked to the door. "I'll take you back to your car. But you ought to get something less conspicuous. You've gone to a lot of trouble just to have some stooge on a street corner see that yellow wreck and follow you here."

"Go see your wife."

Gordon snapped his head around, his face convoluted.

"Don't say no. I'll . . . work out my problem. You work on yours. You owe us, you owe your wife. If our time is short, how long is it for you and her?"

"No!" Gordon opened the door.

"She's at her mother's. You don't have to call. She told me she won't set foot outside the door while you're alive unless it's to see you. She means it."

Gordon pushed his glasses up the bridge of his nose. "Take care of your damn car!" he yelled and slammed the door. It was the first time Gordon ever raised his voice, much less swore at him. A sound in the garage caught Blaise. Dobie was whining and trying to sit. "Lie down, Dobie," Blaise said soothingly. "It's going to be all right."

He added silently, *See your wife, Gordon. For your sake!*

After calling a cab, Blaise went into the dining room. The heavy smoked oak table had been pushed against the far wall to make room for Alfie next to the telephone and a wall plug. He tapped the keyboard and the monitor came to life.

"GOOD AFTERNOON, PROFESSOR. I AM RUNNING ON BATTERY POWER"

"BATTERY POWER" flashed on and off in a silent shriek for Blaise to take note.

He plugged the cord in.

"THANK YOU, PROFESSOR" Hex code streaked up the screen as Alfie checked those peripherals physically incorporated into its structure but denied access to batteries.

Blaise unplugged the telephone and substituted the modem cable. He instructed Alfie to monitor Helen's hospital records. Standing in deep thought, he then told Alfie to dig for dirt on Technological Intelligence Laboratories, Limited, in Berkeley, and also Milo Burkhalter. He punched in Milo's address. The doorbell rang. In La Jolla cab drivers didn't honk. Alfie was acknowledging instructions. At the end of the acknowledgment the computer flashed the message. "MAY I START WITH MISS MCINTYRE, PROFESSOR?"

Helen might have said the monitor's green clashed with the robin's-egg-blue walls in the dining room. Blaise decided she would have been wrong. "Yes, Alfie. Watch Miss McIntyre every minute."

"THANK YOU, PROFESSOR. WITHOUT FAIL"

Output from the machines monitoring Helen suddenly appeared down one edge of the monitor. Numbers fluttered, changing as she changed, and then on the rest of the monitor information on other things streamed by as Alfie built a file. The bell rang again. Blaise went out to the cab, wondering what he didn't know that Helen and Alfie knew.

The nurse at the ICU desk looked oddly at Blaise when he came in. "Dr. MacReedy wants to see you, Dr. Cunningham. Please wait until I locate him."

"How's Miss McIntyre?" He glanced through the observation window. Helen seemed much as she had earlier, but appearances meant nothing. She could be comatose and he wouldn't know.

"Doctor will discuss that with you, sir." The nurse pointedly ignored him while she scribbled on a duty roster.

Blaise took a chair in the hall and stared at the top of the nurse's head. His breath was ragged. He struggled not to imagine before MacReedy presented facts. Helen might be dying because he had ordered treatment discontinued.

And solid, conservative Gordon might have acted as he thought best—might have used an empty hypodermic, believing it better to pretend and thus ensure an uncomplicated termination.

He wouldn't do that! Blaise trusted Gordon. But Gordon might see the best solution that way. Blaise couldn't shake the fear of what Gordon's friendship could cost. His stomach tasted chalky, like the barium gunk used in gastrointestinal X-rays.

By the time MacReedy arrived Blaise was gasping. MacReedy had the nurse bring a paper cup of water. "I want you to change the surgical order." MacReedy's eyes were hot coals in deep, stress-blackened sockets.

"Why? We decided..."

"I know what I said before." MacReedy's voice was urgent, hoarse, as if burned out from rehearsing what he had to say. He seemed not to notice that he had interrupted Blaise. "I was wrong. Miss McIntyre has...improved."

"That's wonderful." Blaise looked at him. "Isn't it?"

"Yes." MacReedy was sweating. "But you can't depend on the change lasting. She's stronger and apparently some of the damage is less significant than the mag scans led us to believe. We have a chance to contain the damage if we operate now." Emotion seeped out of MacReedy in a silent tide.

"No!"

"Dr. Cunningham. You don't know what you're saying." MacReedy raised his hands as though holding something fragile. "I was wrong once. I know how that looks. I can be wrong a second time. But if you don't give in to my request, Doctor, between us we'll kill or cripple this woman."

MacReedy began pacing. "I'm sorry, Dr. Cunningham. I don't mean it that way. I can't blame you for reacting to my error. I'd have the same response if I were in your position." He stared Blaise in the eye. "Please. You've got to trust me."

"You're making it hard, Doctor. But you may *not* operate." Blaise closed his eyes to the surgeon.

"I asked Miss McIntyre."

The pressure on Blaise's chest dropped away. "She's lucid enough to talk?"

MacReedy licked dry lips. "She told me to do whatever you say."

Blaise was taller than MacReedy. They stared at each other in silence. The nurse at the ICU duty desk hid behind a magazine. Its cover had a fetus bright with blood and still in its membrane sack. The leader line was *Legal Implications of Abortion and Insurance Liability.*

"Can I see her?"

"Yes."

"Thank you." Blaise closed the door behind himself. The chair remained beside the bed but he leaned over and kissed Helen lightly on the temple before he sat.

"I'm glad you came again." Her eyes were open, blue as a plasma arc reflected off stainless steel. The side of her face pressed into the starchy whiteness of the pillow but she could look into his eyes when he sat. Her voice was fragile.

"How could I stay away?" He joked gently, on watch for treacherous words and phrases.

"I wasn't fair, was I?"

"You're never unfair. Or mean." Blaise stroked the side of her face.

"I know you really want that woman. And you think you're responsible for what happened to me. But you're not."

"I am responsible." Blaise touched her lips with his finger. "And I like you a lot more than I do Linda."

"It's hard for you to be truthful when the truth is hard on somebody else," Helen said.

"Try believing me." Blaise leaned closer.

Her eyes were misty. "Whatever you do is all right, Blaise. You don't have to stay with me. I shouldn't have asked."

"He who's afraid to ask remains a bachelor."

"Do you really like me?"

"A bunch, sweet hips."

"That's not nice." Helen sounded pleased.

"You don't share my viewpoint."

She rested, just looking at him. "The doctor wants me to approve an emergency operation."

"Gordon came today, Helen. Earlier, with me."

"I see." She rested for a moment. "What should I do?"

"Gordon says you can't let anybody inside your head. It's gone too far to have a choice."

"What do you say?"

"I have to trust Gordon."

"All right. You tell the doctor." She blinked. "Is it all right to be afraid?"

He kissed her. "I'm afraid, too."

MacReedy went in after Blaise came out. He was back in a minute. "She must think you're God, Doctor. I hope she's right."

"I want her back more than you do. If you've been wrong once, let's pray I'm right once."

"I don't have much choice, do I?" MacReedy's eyes were bleak, his lips tight.

Blaise stepped out into a moonless night made blacker by a ground fog from warm earth and ocean. Parking-lot lights spread a stark visibility over the asphalt. Blaise's yellow VW stood out against darker shapes.

He was unlocking when he heard the sharp click of heels on the tarmac. "Nice seeing you again, Dr. Cunningham."

Blaise straightened, looking at Sergio Paoli's shadowy face.

"We have an appointment, Doctor."

"I thought you weren't interested in me."

"It does not have to be in Samarra." Sergio saw Blaise's lack of comprehension. "Those who seek, find sermons in stones. I, Professor, seek only to better myself."

"How did you find me?"

"I didn't learn until after it happened. But I knew you're not the man to let your lady languish alone. I waited here."

"You could have caught me when I went in."

"I knew you'd be back, Doc. No reason to spoil your visit."

Human intelligence, if applied to a machine, would allow it to evolve an answer to any problem within the scope of its memory and the limitations of its speed of operation.

FROM A SEMINAR ON
THE CUNNINGHAM EQUATIONS

CHAPTER 19

"*Vehiculō meō, doctissime Doctor doctorum.*" Sergio opened the door to a black Chrysler with an aerodynamic, plastic-encased antennalike dish on top. "You know, there's an academy in Perugia trying to remake Latin into what Esperanto never was nor will be." He smiled. "Them old Italians never say 'die.' *In vehiculō usque ad viam.* Properly, of course, I should say *carrus automovens* but *carro* sounds tacky. At least in Italian. What do you think, Doc?"

"That I am neither 'most learned' nor 'teacher of teachers.' In any event, *Ad quem finem?*"

"To what avail? That's a good question, Doc. The brains'll have to tell you that. I just drive the car."

"And other things."

"And other things," Sergio admitted. "Get in."

"*Et si non?*"

"Doc, it's a nice night. Don't make it unpleasant."

Blaise ducked his head and slid into the heavy new-smelling leather interior.

Sergio closed the door on his side and punched the ignition code into a fourteen-button keypad. Liquid crystal displays began pulsing in easy rhythms and eight colors. It took Blaise an instant to realize the motor was actually running.

Sergio punched again and a ghostly see-through image formed on the windshield. Blaise recognized a map, green streets with a red overlay line through La Jolla. The lower end terminated in a red dot in the hospital parking lot. The ocean was a mass of blue to the west. Elevations were indicated by topographical contours in false color.

169

"Impressive, Professor?" Sergio glanced at Blaise, then put the car in motion. The red dot began devouring the red line in tiny, smaller-than-Pacman gulps. "It's the newest advance on the old Mirv system. Instead of an overlay street map on a screen and a tracking dot controlled by navigation satellites, Chrysler put a whole computer in the car. It reads a videotape and translates it to a screen image based on a navsat fix. Neat, don't you think, Doctor?"

"Yes. It is."

"You're the expert, Doc. Anyway, once the area is on screen, you enter your destination. The computer scrolls the tape and finds a route."

"And you follow the yellow brick road."

"Red."

Sergio tapped instructions and the map shrunk. Unoccupied sections of the monitor began showing fuel, miles per gallon, speed, temperature, and oil pressure. Sergio laughed. "This car had all kinds of trash on the display when I went to take delivery. A gas can. An oil spout. A thermometer. A waterfall, for Christ's sake! The salesman almost had a fit when I told him to get rid of that *caca*. But the manager dug up a secretary and she reprogrammed this turkey in ten minutes. Some secretary," Sergio added in a fond voice. "Are you impressed, Professor?"

"Yes."

"You're lying, Doc. Anybody drives a relic like that beetle doesn't give a damn about cars."

"I imagine the computer in here cost more than my VW did new," Blaise admitted.

"See? I'm thinking about becoming a psychiatrist. Clean work, and I've always known when somebody lied to me."

"It's a promising line of work." Blaise knew he should be making frantic plans to escape—foolhardy stunts like opening a door and falling out at sixty miles an hour. Instead, he listened.

"Yeah." Sergio drove in silence for a while. City lights reflected off overcast to maintain a tenuous barrier against total darkness. The car continued eating up the red line and the background kept shifting.

"Adne coeli portam?"

"Yeah, we're going to Heaven's Gate." Sergio concentrated on the road. "You know, Doc, I'm not happy about this."

"What are they going to do?"

"They don't tell me nothing, Doc. I'm just a dumb button man from Jersey that friends West and Hemmett borrowed and gave an injection so he could work smarter. I'm just a handy new tool. Like this computer in the car."

"Have they taken the treatment themselves?"

"Funny you should ask that, Doc." Sergio's voice lost its banter. "I was going to ask you why they didn't. God knows some of those guys could use a little more IQ."

"Maybe they know something."

"Maybe *you* know something, Doc."

Sergio drove in silence to a door marked EMPLOYEES but did not get out of the car. "I talked to West's old man about you," he finally said. "He hates Gregory with a purple passion. I think he hates me because I work for his son. He said something very funny, Doc. He gave me hell for talking worse Sicilian than the blond American I was sent to check." Sergio looked at Blaise. "You lied, Doc, on the plane when you didn't admit you knew Italian. And I couldn't tell."

"Nobody's perfect."

"For your sake, I hope you are, Doc."

They got out of the car. Sergio unlocked the service entrance in the rear of the building before the headlights turned off and recessed. The night was darker at Heaven's Gate than it had been in La Jolla.

Sergio led the way down a thickly carpeted hallway lit by low-wattage floodlights. He paused at a heavy walnut door and knocked with one knuckle. A voice inside said, "Come in."

Face blank as he pushed the door open, Sergio's grating New Jersey voice picked up in midsentence. "—really oughta learn Italian, Doc. It's a beautiful language." Facing the man inside, he added. *"Scusa, Don Gregorio. Ecco la mercanzìa."*

Gregory West turned away from Arthur Hemmett, whom he'd obviously been lecturing. *"Grazz',"* he said. *"Aspetta con Brun'."* He said he would tell Sergio's patron of his good work. It was not necessary to add that Sergio and Bruno were to do their waiting in the hall.

Sergio put the essence of a bow into his nod, beckoning the man who sat at a desk by the door laying out Tarot cards. Silently, barrel-chested Bruno stood and followed Sergio.

West sat on the bare desktop and examined Blaise. "Apparently, Dr. Cunningham, I didn't pay enough attention to you while you were in the employ of GENRECT."

Having met Giovanni Oesti, the resemblance between Gregory and his father was obvious. West was simply Oesti in English. That transposition made, the short, compact West with his high cheekbones and sharply delineated features and skin that looked perpetually tanned seemed a younger twin.

"You wanted to see me. I'm here."

"True, Doctor. We, Dr. Hemmett and I, think it is in all our best interests to have a talk and perhaps right old wrongs."

"Which ones?"

West picked a cigar from the humidor and snipped an end before lighting it. "A fair question, Doctor. Let's take your termination with GENRECT." He waited.

"You have the floor, Mr. West."

"Your stock options can be cashed in a year. Sooner if the board agrees. Dr. Hemmett is a director. And I am a director."

"That's two. Aren't there more?"

"Five more, Doctor. I hold their proxies." West studied his cigar. "You know, a cigar with a good ash burns more evenly than a cigar tip unprotected from errant breezes. Real smokers pay for the ash, Doctor."

"And wear gray suits so it blends in."

"That's life, Dr. Cunningham. To get what you want you sometimes give up something you didn't want quite as much."

Hemmett watched the exchange between the two men with desperate fascination.

"What do I give up?" Blaise asked.

West gave his cigar an unhurried puff. "GENRECT stock will be worth a great deal in a year. Maybe sooner. You get your job back at full pay and—" He held up a hand to forestall Blaise's objection. "—and you get to do whatever you want. The company finances any research at all, Doctor. We'll do even better than that. You can work wherever you want."

"Play remittance man? Get out from underfoot?"

"A little more." West's voice had sharp edges that poked through the husky tenor. "Dr. Hemmett?"

Hemmett's face was red as he forced the words out. "We want the dog. Right away. We want the computer here on the grounds, and no telephone connections."

"You can't have Alfie!" Blaise had not intended to raise his voice. Of all the things upsetting him, the idea of West wanting Alfie was one of the more disconcerting. But the memory of Helen in a hospital bed slowed him. "I mean, he's irreplaceable."

"We don't want the computer, Dr. Cunningham." West slipped smoothly between Blaise and Hemmett. He seemed pleased at Blaise's reaction. "We want to make sure you don't do something foolish, like snooping into our affairs. Inadvertently, Doctor. Perhaps under the influence of alcohol."

"It bothers you that much?"

"Doctor, if we liked what your computer does, would we offer so much for you to stop?"

"Cunningham, *do what he says*." Hemmett was begging rather than demanding.

"I have to think it over."

"Doctor!" West captured Blaise's eyes with the sparkle of his own black pupils. "We don't *have* to buy anything. The dog is our property. Your computer snooping is illegal."

"Sue me!" Blaise said. "Have me arrested."

West studied Blaise regretfully for a moment. "How many police officers are posted outside Miss McIntyre's door?"

Blaise's eyes were on Hemmett when he realized his moment of revolt was abruptly over. Dr. Arthur Hemmett did not seem overjoyed at his victory.

"From plain talk comes understanding," Blaise said. "Dr. Hemmett, I believe *you* once called *me* a menace to orderly society?"

Arthur Hemmett looked away.

"Do you agree?" West asked.

"Under duress," Blaise said. As if it made any difference.

West stared thoughtfully at Blaise. "Sergio and Bruno will go with you to get the dog. Tomorrow we'll move the computer to the GENRECT building. You go back on payroll. Fair enough?"

Standing behind West where he couldn't be seen, Dr. Hemmett bobbed his head vigorously up and down, staring holes through Blaise. The oppressive, wood-paneled room was starting to fill with smoke. The time had passed for futile gestures. Hemmett was taking a risk with his blatant signaling. The great man's jowls were white, all his bluff heartiness drained away.

"All right," Blaise said finally.

West took the cigar from his mouth and smiled with thin lips. "I couldn't have said it better myself, Doctor." No one offered to shake hands.

West opened the door and let Bruno and Sergio back in. "You take Dr. Cunningham home. He's going to give you a dog to bring back here tonight. Okay?"

"Yes, sir." Sergio seemed bored with the assignment. No single muscle twitched on Bruno's side-of-beef face. "Bruno," West said, and suddenly the dialect was so fast and heavy that Blaise almost missed the muscle man's instruction to escort the doctor home and then to unwrap the package. And to bring back the dog and the computer. The dog in one piece.

"Si, Padróne." Bruno's voice was surprisingly high and sweet, like a girl's.

West laughed and patted Blaise on the shoulder. "We talk to Bruno like the old country to make him understand, *capicsce?*"

"We have a deal," Blaise said.

Chuckling, West said, "That's fine, Doctor. While you're on vacation you can visit Italy and pick up the language."

Sergio smiled.

Hemmett appeared worried, but he tried to smile at Blaise. He was the only person in the room who didn't speak Italian.

Bruno took the backseat where he looked over Sergio's shoulder at the panoply of ghost lights on the windshield. He seemed hypnotized by the map and the red line, like a child discovering something new and mysterious. Except that Blaise could not believe the man-mountain huddled in back had ever been a child.

"Bruno don't say much," Sergio offered. "But he pays attention."

"I imagine." Blaise glanced back but Bruno gave no sign that he noticed. "Do you have the car manual?"

"Try the glove box." Sergio put a cigarette in his mouth and grasped the dashboard lighter. "You know," he said, the red ember bouncing up and down in front of his lips, "I had a hard time getting a lighter. People can afford this kind of machine are smoking less and when the sales department researched the kind of accessories would make it sell, cigarette lighters were low on the list."

"Does Bruno smoke?"

"*Tu fuma, Brun'?*" Sergio yelled over his shoulder.

The high voice tried to growl "Naw!" but failed to get any rasp into the sound.

"He doesn't," Sergio said conversationally to Blaise. "Any time you need somebody to interpret with Bruno, just ask. He speaka da Italian, you know."

"I gathered as much." Blaise opened the glove box and discovered if he held the manual at the right angle he could read it comfortably under a built-in map light.

"What do you think, Professor? Those people with money and power know something we don't?"

"Something you don't anyway. I don't smoke."

"You think I should give it up, Professor?"

"You'd live longer." Blaise glanced in back, but the hulking Bruno hadn't moved. "It's amazing what science is doing these days," he said. "The dog I'm giving your bosses is a valuable experimental animal."

"What kind of experiments?" Sergio's voice was flat, as if the humor had escaped him.

"I don't think I can talk about the work I'm involved in without consulting Mr. West. After all, he just hired me."

"If that's what you call it."

Blaise and Sergio looked at each other. Sweat was soaking Blaise's shirt down the back. "I suppose I'm defining the obvious," he said, "but don't they seem anxious to get this dog before anyone else can learn what poor Dobie's future holds?"

Sergio jerked the car back onto the road. "You still staying at Miss McIntyre's?"

"That's right."

With his right hand Sergio fed the destination into the computer. The red line extended south to the Bird Rock end of La Jolla. No one spoke until they arrived at Helen's empty house. They got out together. Bruno followed them up the sidewalk, saying nothing while Blaise fumbled with the key.

In the vast silence of the night keys jangled like a wind chime. The car's headlights flooded the street. Bruno stood behind Blaise, so close that his cologne was overpowering.

A quiet whine sounded as the Chrysler's headlights retracted, plunging the house door into darkness just as Blaise leaned against it and literally fell into the hallway.

For a big man Bruno was fast. He moved immediately even though he couldn't see, and crashed into Blaise, carrying him in his arms until they ran into the jog at the end of the hallway.

Blaise's ribs ached. His lungs were painful voids. Something thin and sharp caught him across his cheek, searing him with fire while Bruno's bearlike body pressed him irresistibly. Giving his all, Blaise slammed both hands against the wall and was rewarded with a little give as Bruno stumbled backward.

He felt the piano-wire garrote slice hair and skin as his face was forced against Bruno's chest. A sweaty odor rose from the big man's skin, overpowering his seeming total immersion in cologne. Desperately Blaise forced his hands up between their bodies, pressing to pry Bruno's arms away and release the terrible pressure on the back of his head.

"Stop it, Bruno. *Basta!*" Sergio's arms wrapped around Bruno's massive neck. "Bruno," he panted. *"Abbiamo bisógno dell' dottore. Brun'!* We need him. Who else stands between us and dying?"

With a sound like escaping steam, Bruno let slip one end of the garrote while he clubbed Sergio off his back.

"Bruno. Listen!" Sergio plowed into Bruno's back. Blaise felt the heavy, muscular body flinch under the impact. "BRUNO!" Sergio yelled and Blaise was blasted by the sound.

Blaise forced the bigger man's arms until the wire no longer cut into his head. But his arms were leaden. Bruno's strength was beyond belief. Bruno's body transmitted the shock of Sergio punching him in the kidneys and still he continued his silent, inexorable pressure. Sweat streamed down Blaise. His fists were clenched around Bruno's wrists.

It was like holding up a building. There was no letup. The pressure continued until Blaise's world shrank to blackness and Bruno's arms and the smell of sweat. The throb of Bruno's pulse under his fingers seemed timeless. Blaise's mind saw the hair-thin length of virtually invisible steel slicing the back of his neck, blood spurting and wire sinking into his flesh to leave only a thin, red line until it reached his spine.

He visualized it cutting into the soft vertebrae, exposing white bone, his head flopping forward with no bone to support the weight of his skull.

Desperately, Blaise gulped air. His body was burning oxygen in wasteful abundance, and still it wasn't enough. Muscles agonized, metabolic wastes accumulating so fast that he was poisoning himself.

He pushed and nothing yielded. Heart pounding, he slid down Bruno's body. Bruno's huge hands followed, bringing the deadly wire closer.

Blaise straightened suddenly, driving his body up. His face burned against the fabric of Bruno's vest, buttons digging in quick succession, each leaving another pain. His head smashed into the point of Bruno's jaw and light streaked under his eyelids. He was falling.

"Come on, Doc. *Come on!*"

Blaise opened his eyes. The lights were on and he was in the little entranceway to Helen's house atop Bruno.

Sergio pulled Blaise to his unsteady feet.

Bruno moaned and moved his head. Blood ran from his mouth and his jaw looked odd.

"We got to get going before Bruno revives." Sergio shook Blaise. "You understand, Doc?" Pulse howling in his ears, Blaise was not sure but he nodded.

The garrote dangled from Bruno's hand. Sergio took a quick wrap around one wrist, then held Bruno's other hand up and wound the wire around both wrists until it sank into the skin. He twisted the wood handles around each other, making the tempered piano wire surrender and take a permanent set.

"*Dobbiamo andare.* Let's get him out of here."

Blaise nodded.

Huffing and straining ferociously, they got Bruno to his feet. Sergio turned the light off.

Blaise supported Bruno while Sergio opened the car trunk from the keypad. Blaise felt awareness slowly returning to Bruno's corded muscles. The deck lid rose in majestic slowness and the trunk light flashed on. Blaise released the breath he'd been holding. Sergio materialized out of the darkness and they forced Bruno into the trunk. The rear of the Chrysler squatted, protesting the weight distribution. Sergio said, "Automatic load levelers. It'll be all right."

From inside the trunk came thumpings. They got in the car.

"We'll need your VW," Sergio said, "then we dump this car."

Blaise nodded. Gordon had been right. A lot was at stake for somebody. In his beetle he followed the button man for an hour back north to Heaven's Gate. Parking the Chrysler at the far end of the lot where it would sit until somebody who knew what was going on recognized it. Sergio patted the trunk when he got out. "Stay cool, fatso," he said before getting into the VW with Blaise.

The drive back to La Jolla hadn't the same style as the computerized Chrysler, but it was less suspenseful. Blaise dropped Sergio at a car rental, then drove to Helen's. He backed her car out on the street and put the VW in the garage. No one would be looking for a white Buick.

Before he left the VW, he noticed a book on the passenger seat. It was the Chrysler manual with all the customized computer instructions. He put the book in his pocket and smiled. Bruno would need one hell of a locksmith to open that trunk without it. Blaise did not know whether to be reassured or horrified by Sergio's sense of humor. But he was glad the Jersey button man had finally chosen sides.

What is the yardstick? Once we dreamed of a computer that could win at chess. As each unattainable goal is surpassed we immediately conclude that this is not true intelligence. From this viewpoint we may never create an intelligent machine.

FROM A SEMINAR ON
THE CUNNINGHAM EQUATIONS

CHAPTER 20

Blaise idled the Buick up the driveway to the garage door and sat in the dark feeling his blood pound. He got out of the car, locking it before he wobbled around to the front door. A lifetime ago he'd quit expecting to find someone waiting.

For their last year he'd lived with his parents while they worked on the equations. At least his parents had worked on them, while Blaise assembled Alfie and wrote the programs that furnished final proof of the Cunningham Equations.

To sit in the dark and hide his need was second nature. Only recently he had lost the knack. Blaise was overwhelmed by loneliness and remorse—for his parents and for Helen.

Loneliness was worse in a strange house where he was free from all needs, including that of exorcising his parents. He had hoped a place without memories would make a difference. But he had only moved an empty soul into another empty house. Not knowing where the light switches were or if he was going to walk into a piece of furniture simply added to Blaise's distress. He groped for a switch and a table light came to life.

Sitting unruffled as a bodhisattva in a heavy chair next to the lamp was Sergio Paoli. Blaise envied the Jersey button man's easy integration into a society that grew increasingly alien.

"You're not very good at this, Doc." Sergio might have been commenting on the color scheme.

Blaise struggled to conceal his surprise at Sergio's presence. "I'm learning as I go. Where did you park?"

"Couple of blocks away." Sergio's eyes revolved Blaise on a mental spit as he probed beyond surface weaknesses.

Abruptly Blaise understood what frightened Linda's Uncle Milo and his coterie. No man of imagination could look steadily into the passionless eye of the predator.

"I've got to check on Dobie," he said.

"Sit down, Doc. I looked and the dog's okay. I think it's important we talk." Sergio's brown eyes could be expressive when he chose. Eyes Helen would have ascribed to a Latin lover. Blaise was seeing the world increasingly through Helen's eyes. The view did not permit him to see what Helen saw in him.

Sergio's eyes had filled with amusement and, after locking Bruno in the trunk, something like anger. Blaise had not understood then.

Taking the nearest chair, Blaise made his face impassive. "I imagine you're right," he said. "It's not my trade." Sensing that this was not the most diplomatic thing to say, he added, "I'm not even very good at what I do."

Sergio Paoli regarded him with veiled eyes. "I done a terrible thing tonight, Doc. I want to be sure it's worthwhile."

"A little late, isn't it? Haven't you burnt your bridges?"

"Bruno is my cousin. I may have killed him. *Famiglia per stranièro.* If I killed family for a stranger, Doc, that stranger better be worthwhile."

"Bruno'll be all right." Blaise felt himself retreat from Sergio's mood. "I'll call in the morning and tell Dr. Hemmett to look in the trunk."

Sergio's laugh reminded Blaise of the times he had strangled on vodka. "Doc, you're not in college anymore. You call and somebody says, 'Look, Bruno let his cousin get away and they try to make it look good but that prick Sergio don't want his greaseball cousin to cook in the sun.'"

"I didn't know," Blaise said.

"Wasn't your decision, Doc. He cooks." Sergio shook his head. "Bruno had the treatment."

It took Blaise an instant to absorb this. "Didn't it work?"

"I guess so. You never saw him before. Bruno started remembering back to the day he was born. Every conversation he ever heard. Everything we said in that car, every move you made, how many breaths you took."

Blaise had never considered what effect Gordon's treatment might have on the retarded. Idiot Bruno had become idiot savant.

Jesus! Gordon ... Helen ... Sergio ... even silent, brooding Bruno. You can't stir the water without upsetting the fish. As he'd done to his parents. And now, thanks to Blaise's prying, what would happen to Gordon?

"We're in this together, Doc. Me—a wise-guy street soldier! I listened to a man's sweet talk. And now I know sin and regret." Sergio smiled crookedly. "Can eight grades and a sneak-thief mentality think those kinda thoughts, Doc?"

Blaise tried to guess what answer Sergio wanted.

"You're not alone, Doc. I couldn't answer that if you were me and I was you. And I've had time to think about it. You know, Bruno could never make the same mistake twice. He remembered. Only sometimes he'd make a different mistake because he can't seem to see the future—only the past."

Blaise thought of the day Gordon told him Dobie caught six squirrels.

"Why didn't the treatment work?" Sergio asked. "Bruno's a Janus with one face broken. Twenty-twenty vision into the past and blind to the future. And because we imagine the future and try to ignore the past, we've wronged him."

"But he was going to kill me!"

"So what? It was you or him." Sergio grimaced in a painful parody of a smile and Blaise understood finally. He'd had enough experience to know that Sergio was drunk.

Blaise spoke carefully. "You helped me."

"Yes. I did."

"Why?"

Sergio laughed. "Why do you think, Doc? Because you know something might save me. I look out for myself. The priest says God'll look out for me after I'm dead, but until then I'm on my own." Sergio's eyes narrowed. "I wanta know I didn't do this all for nothing. Understand?"

Blaise understood.

Sergio yawned. "I think it's time for bed."

"The bedroom—"

"Forget the bedroom, Doc." Sergio patted the soft, rust-brown armchair.

"You won't get any sleep."

"I'll sleep. And I'll be the first to know when somebody starts to break in." Blaise's twitch amused Sergio. "Doc, we made some people mad tonight."

"Yes."

Taking pity, Sergio added, "You did pretty good. I think you broke Bruno's jaw. That's good for us. Maybe even for Bruno."

"It was luck."

"I hope not." Abruptly Sergio was laughing. Tears formed at the corners of his eyes.

Blaise waited until laughter turned to giggles and dried up.

"I was thinking, Doc. Don't expect Bruno to thank you."

"You're hysterical."

"'S all right, Doc. Just keep your mind on what you got to tell me tomorrow. *Vita cautelosa, vita lunga.*"

Lying unable to sleep, Blaise considered the possibility that Sergio was going mad. Gordon had not precluded madness as a possible consequence. Perhaps there were two personalities inside Sergio—echoes that had started going their separate ways. Blaise cringed at what he might have condemned Helen to.

He began his breathing exercises, which could sometimes force these unrooted hypotheses out of his mind. His demons were never far from midnight fantasies. Closer than real life.

One moment dissolved to nothing and the next Blaise was awake in surrealistic silence and golden light in a strange room. Sunlight lay over everything like a sheet of butter. The bed with its white sheets and honey-brown coverlet, the maple nightstand and chest of drawers, even the corners that should have been shadowed all glowed with the morning light.

Silence sucked up any suggestion of life. He trudged into the bathroom and the distant hiss of running water reassured him. After a while he could force himself into the front room.

Sitting at the coffee table, Sergio looked over his newspaper and bacon and eggs. "You keep a lousy kitchen, Doc. I hadda drive halfway to San Diego to get stuff for breakfast."

In the kitchen a tray of coddled eggs and bacon folded in paper towels lay on the counter with a clean dish next to it. The food was still warm and the odors appealing. It had been years since Blaise ate breakfast but involuntary reflexes filled his mouth with longing.

Sergio moved the paper, making room.

"What'd you do with the pans?"

"Threw them out. You think I'm some Dago scullery slave?" Sergio glared and Blaise was unexpectedly aware of gold-rimmed glasses. Sergio noted Blaise's attention. "*Vanitate, vanitate—tutto è vanitate*. What do you think? Shakespeare sounds great even in translation, no?"

"If the bard said that he was quoting Ecclesiastes," Blaise said. "You seem fond of Shakespeare. Did you pick that up in the first eight grades?"

Sergio smiled. "Man I used to work for . . . I don't know if he gave a fiddler's damn for Shakespeare, but whenever the phone was on, so was a tape or an l.p."

"It doesn't really scramble the audio," Blaise said.

"Enough to give half-deaf and bought-off pensioners an excuse for a reasonable doubt."

"Can you see without those glasses?"

"Of course I can see. They just make it easier to read."

Blaise had been permitted to witness a weakness. It was Sergio's token of faith. He ate in silence while Sergio finished the paper. The gesture, Blaise understood, was a small version of the bones-making ceremony in which elder mobsters witnessed and participated in a young recruit's first murder, thus binding themselves in compulsory silence and brotherhood. But if Bruno died, Blaise and Sergio had already made their bones.

He cleared the table and rinsed dishes before sticking them in the dishwasher with the pans and cooking utensils. Then he sat. "I suppose I'd better tell you what I know."

Sergio folded the newspaper and put it out of the way. "That would be nice."

"The operation consists of implanting an embryonic cell mass directly into the stem of the cerebral cortex. The mass is essentially a developing egg of a genetically engineered leaf fly. The cells grow and are possibly absorbed into the brain mass, thus altering some of the brain's functions.

"The apparent effect is to correct genetic or physical damage that inhibits the orderly production of hormones and other regulatory functions in the brain. Over the short term it seems to work." Blaise glanced at Sergio to see if he needed to elaborate.

Sergio's skin was gray and his eyes glassy. "Doc," he finally said, "you sayin' I got maggots in my brain?"

"It's not like that—"

"Worms!"

"Don't think of them as worms, Sergio. Just altered brain cells—like making rabies vaccine from horse's blood or interferon from bacterial excretions. You know how yeast converts sugar into alcohol and you still drink wine."

"It's not the same, Doc."

Blaise shrugged. "You have to live with facts, not fantasies. You can't go back and change it."

"You're right, Doc." Color returned to Sergio's face but a panting quality remained in his voice. "You said *possibly*."

"Possibly what?"

"Possibly the worms are converted into brain tissue."

"Gordon's not sure. That's why Dobie is important. Hemmett and West destroyed all the other lab animals. Except Dobie, the longest-lived host. Whatever happens to Dobie will be a precursor of the future for human recipients."

"What *are* the possible alternatives, Doc?" Sergio held his napkin delicately, but his knuckles whitened.

"We don't know." Blaise omitted to add their suspicions. Sergio wasn't Gordon. The knowledge that a fly larva had been planted in his brain had shaken Sergio. The thought that larvae were ingesting his brain and quietly turning him into a maggot could push him over the edge. "It's a possible cell mutation. Gordon's studying the problem. It could be a transposon—"

Sergio's face changed at the unfamiliar term.

"That's a gene which will attach itself to a strange chromosome. They're used a lot in genetic engineering. The gene is normal except for its ability to jump from one piece of genetic material to another and be absorbed. It's like a genetic messenger boy. You give it the message and then it gets integrated into a chromosome somewhere and then that chromosome carries the message.

"What researchers do is find a transposon, cut it open chemically, then mix it with the desired DNA. The transposon gene incorporates the new DNA into its surface, closing the artificially induced lesion like patching a soccer ball. The transposon then incorporates into the nearest chromosome."

Blaise rattled on as pedantically as possible, reducing the startling to the trivial. He struggled to emulate a professor he had once studied under—a man who could have transmuted a first-person account of the Second Coming into Seconal.

Sergio needed time to realize that knowledge had not changed his condition, whatever it was. Blaise counted on Sergio's wanting to be intelligent . . . at any cost.

"If it wasn't done on purpose, then what went wrong?" Eyes that had receded into Sergio's head were emerging again.

"It's only a theory."

Sergio drummed on the table with his fingertips, deciding for himself what was valid.

"Transposons were not used to make the modifications," Blaise continued. "A more difficult manual system was initiated and standardized. Cost was not a factor since the laboratory making the original material had a patent on its design. So they forgot about the transposons. And when the altered chromosomes reproduced true to form, the transposons got their share of genetic material.

"No one gave the transposons a thought, Sergio. Transposons are the geneticists' friend. They shouldn't be able to leap from one type of chromosome to another. And if they did, there shouldn't have been enough of them to affect the billions of mature cells in a person's brain."

"But they did?"

"Not for sure." Blaise's skin was tense with sweat threatening to burst free. He was afraid of Sergio. And he was unsure what Sergio feared. Too much knowledge? Or too little?

"What does Dr. Hill say?" A glint in Sergio's eye warned him. Sergio understood Gordon's need in a way that Blaise could not. The button man had progressed from dispassionate observer to cosufferer with Gordon. And Helen.

Despite his relief, Blaise felt frustrated and excluded. He could not empathize with them. He could only observe.

"Gordon believes it's possible the original DNA addition contained a combination that proliferated the production of transposon genes, which is carried along from cell to cell."

"You're describing a cancer of the gene, aren't you, Doc?"

"Not exactly." He knew Sergio believed he had already looked the worst in the eye. He wouldn't dig further . . . yet.

He still had to come to grips with it. Maybe later he would suspect.

"I have to think on it," Sergio said.

Not too hard, Blaise prayed. He knew his was a futile wish.

Human reasoning that leads to faulty conclusions has two root causes: inability to manage memory satisfactorily and errant genetically determined logic.

FROM A SEMINAR ON
THE CUNNINGHAM EQUATIONS

CHAPTER 21

"I want a gun."

Blaise and Sergio sat in a rental car four blocks uphill from the hospital parking lot. Sergio had been quiet, putting up little objection when Blaise said he wanted to visit Helen.

"What happened to your gun?" Blaise asked.

"What gun?"

"But you—were a mafioso."

"Doc, I was an errand boy. Why would a guy just runs numbers set himself up for hard time over a gun he'd never use?"

Blaise had learned other rules on television.

"Bruno's different," Sergio said. "I know you're not gonna understand, Doc. But all Bruno was ever good for was knocking people around a little, if somebody he admired said do it."

"Sometimes too hard?"

"Yeah, Doc. He didn't know better. He still don't." Sergio palmed his billfold out of sight, then back into view in the opposite hand. He wouldn't meet Blaise's eyes.

"You don't want to hurt him." It was not a question.

Sergio made the wallet disappear and jerked at his suit with his hands. Blaise knew Sergio had tucked the leather back into his pocket even if he hadn't seen the sleight.

"I did magic shows even when I was a kid. Bruno brought me an audience. Make 'em clap even when I screwed up. I guess Bruno was my only friend, Doc."

Blaise dropped it. Sitting in a hot car scanning the parking lot with 20×80 binoculars on a swivel clamped to the dash-

187

board seemed excessively cautious, but Sergio had dictated it. Slouched, eyes level with the magazine-covered glasses, Sergio was invisible to anyone outside the tinted windshield.

"I can get a rifle or a shotgun. Pistols take three days."

"Too long."

Blaise thought a moment. "Let me see that newspaper." Sergio handed it into the backseat.

"What day is it?"

"It says Friday on the top of the paper."

Blaise decided not to pick at any more of Sergio's sore spots. "We have a chance this evening."

Sergio seemed to be thinking.

Blaise was half asleep when Sergio said, "Okay." He dismounted the binoculars for storage in their aluminum case.

Blaise slid from the backseat and got in front. Sergio put his hands on the steering wheel after he started the car, but remained parked. "See the red Ford at the hospital entrance?"

At that distance the cars were small but recognizable. "Yes."

"There's a driver. Another man inside's wearing tan slacks, white shirt, and a light-brown windbreaker with a white stripe breast-pocket high." Sergio glanced at Blaise. "It's too hot for a windbreaker. He probably has something like a thirty-two with a hammer shroud on his left hip. He'll cross draw."

Blaise nodded.

"Don't count on it though. He might be left-handed."

"Reverse the motion?"

"Yeah." Sergio put the car in gear and dropped down the steep street like a stone.

"Why do you need a gun?" Blaise asked it for something to say. "Bruno didn't have one."

"Bruno's idea of fun is get five or six rough characters together and then lacerate them. He does it for exercise." Sergio clamped his lips, remembering Bruno's situation. He coaxed the navy-blue sedan to a street uphill from the back of the hospital and snuggled the car against a hedge of Italian cedars, standing like green, seven-foot-high javelin points.

They walked through the gate in the hedge to the front door of a mock colonial with baby-blue trim. The door contained thirteen panes of glass and a solid-brass Schlage deadbolt. Sergio inserted wires and clock springs into the keyhole. The door swung open. He smiled, nodded, and took off his hat as if someone was greeting them. They went in and closed the door.

Blaise stood in the cool hallway feeling his heart thud. He had not expected that breaking and entering would be so nerve-wracking. He had been perfectly calm when Sergio told him what they were going to do.

"I don't think there's a dog." Sergio spoke softly. He led the way through the house, touching nothing. Blaise stuffed his hands firmly in his pockets.

The back opened on a patio with yellow fiberglass roof over a green-and-red Italian tile deck. The pool was cool blue, the color of the preformed plastic liner that ensured against leakage come earthquake or minor mud slide. A breeze stirred the heat as they opened sliding glass doors and walked around the pool to the six-foot redwood fence.

"Damn!"

"What's wrong?" Blaise looked over Sergio's shoulder.

Sergio held the combination lock, fingers clenched in disgust.

Blaise looked at the fence. "Climb over?"

"No. Wait." Sergio strolled back to the house and reappeared a moment later. He began removing the four screws in the latch plate with the knife he'd taken from the kitchen. "If I could see into this yard, so can every house on the hill. We gotta come back this way."

The latch dropped free of the post. Carefully, Sergio set the knife and the latch with the screws and lock attached next to the gate. They stepped through the gate, pulled it closed unhurriedly, and walked with the calm gait of those who belong.

From the car they had been unable to see the back of the hospital, but as Sergio had predicted, the pink wall was broken by a door that opened on a cement loading dock, green rubbish bins, and a battered, smoky black-and-rust incinerator. Inside, they took the stairway to the second floor, then caught the elevator and got out on the fifth.

"Not bad," Sergio said. They were in front of the elevator doors contemplating the lights as if trying to decide which floor they should be on. "If he's in the lobby by the elevator, we've gotten around him. Strangers are conspicuous on intensive care floors so he shouldn't be up there."

Blaise began to understand why Sergio hadn't objected about coming to the hospital. The infatuation with linguistics, the talk about psychiatry as a profession wasn't serious. But Sergio was addicted to cat-and-mouse games. "Where would you be?"

"ICU, of course." Sergio grinned. "But then, I'm first team."

They walked the last flight of stairs, heels echoing up and down the emergency shaft. Dankness and old paint in the windowless, unventilated stairway oppressed Blaise. He paused. "Why were you waiting for me in the parking lot?"

"Who said I waited there, Doc?"

Sergio stopped talking at the landing and put his hand on the knob. "*Cave canem*, Doc. This is always the hard part."

Blaise tried to feel through the closed door into the hall beyond, to know if somebody was waiting.

"If he's there," Sergio said quietly, "you go right and I go left. Don't stop until you got his gun. He'll kill if he can. If that's what he's been told to do."

Blaise nodded.

Sergio opened the door in a smooth motion that carried him to the left, oiled motions that seemed casual but blurred with speed. Blaise felt awkward and clumsy lurching to the right, swinging his head, looking for the man in the windbreaker.

"Dr. Cunningham!"

The nurse behind the desk stared as if Blaise had just flashed into existence. He tried to smile. "Sorry. I stumbled."

Looking severe, she ruffled papers. "Dr. MacReedy wants to talk to you." She nudged her desk telephone in Blaise's direction.

"After I see Miss McIntyre."

"Of course, Doctor." She seemed to disapprove of his title.

"I'll wait out here." Sergio winked and started working on a conversation with the nurse. That Sergio had gotten to the sixth floor without the elevator didn't seem to bother her.

Blaise knew Helen's ordeal was caused by his stupidity and drunkenness. He was mad at the nurse for seeing through him. Mad at himself for being what he was.

Helen made a happy face when he walked in. The bed, an electric Stryker frame, raised her to a sitting position.

Blaise kissed her. He had not planned to and the action surprised him. Hurriedly, he sat.

"Dr. Cunningham, you quit too easily." Helen pouted but she could not conceal her pleasure.

"I'm not used to kissing people." Blaise glanced at the cap of bandage that encased Helen's head, surprised how attractive her face was. He tried to remember the exact shade of her blond hair and couldn't. It didn't matter. They stared at each other, both unsure. Blaise was confused by the sudden emotion that had compelled him to kiss her.

Helen said, "You're too withdrawn."

"You're looking well."

"I feel well."

They looked at each other some more. Communications, for Blaise, depended on understanding the other person's viewpoint; impossible with Helen. He tried to guess what she would feel because of the implant, what she would think about, what she would want to hide or talk about obliquely.

Give up! If he was to understand she would have to tell him what she feared. As would Gordon.

"Dr. MacReedy is going crazy, Blaise. He has CAT scans, electromagnetic section scans, X-rays, fiber optic probe photographs, and he says whatever is happening to me is a miracle. He wants to talk to you and Dr. Hill."

Blaise shook his head. "Does he still want to operate?"

Helen's listlessness of the previous day was gone. "I don't think so. He's upset. But not about my condition."

"Don't let him move you."

Helen kept her eyes on Blaise, blue lights probing the murk, but she said nothing.

"Stay in ICU."

"All right."

"Don't you want to know why?"

"I trust you, Blaise." She tried to smile.

"May the gods help me!" Blaise pretended to groan. "I'm in love with a bald-headed woman."

Helen turned crimson and then started to cry.

"Don't!" Blaise held her face between his palms. "I didn't mean to hurt your feelings. Honest."

"Not hurt." Helen sobbed. "I'm happy."

When he left the room a few minutes later Sergio fell in step to the elevator.

"Dr. Cunningham. You were going to call Dr. MacReedy."

The duty nurse stood behind her desk, trim and pretty in her uniform. And agitated.

"We'll see him downstairs." Sergio lied better than Blaise.

In the elevator Sergio asked how Helen took the news that Blaise couldn't come back for a while.

"She was still crying when I left."

The sound of the elevator rattling down the shaft was loud. "Did you tell her?"

"I didn't get that far."

They stopped on the second floor and got off into a cluster of hospital uniforms. Blaise realized they were in the middle of the shift change.

"I'm sorry, sir. This floor isn't open to visitors."

"I'm Dr. Cunningham. I'm meeting Dr. MacReedy."

"I think you have the wrong floor, Doctor. If you check downstairs somebody can contact him for you." The nurse wore pale-blue polyester. She might as well have been in olive drab. Her hand on the heat-sensitive call button held the elevator.

"Okay," Sergio said. "Thanks." He pulled Blaise into the packed elevator.

"We'll stay in and go back up to the third floor," Sergio said conversationally.

They jolted to a halt in the lobby, braced against the flow of bodies leaving the elevator. Sergio reached for the floor button and pressed it.

Standing in front of the elevator, a man in tan slacks and a brown windbreaker with white stripe stared at Blaise for an instant, then his eyes slid away and he stepped inside.

"What floor?" Sergio asked conversationally.

"Six." It popped out as if the man in the windbreaker had been thinking it but didn't want to say.

Sergio nodded and pressed six.

The elevator rattled into motion. The man started to put his right hand in the front of his windbreaker. Blaise lunged, wrapping his arms around the man's body and pinning his hands.

Sergio shot off the wall into the man's side and the three of them went down in a heap. Blaise was panting, but he didn't feel the effort. The man in the windbreaker got a hand free.

The elevator shuddered to a stop. Sergio scrambled to his feet. Blaise clung desperately to Windbreaker, locking his gun hand between them. Sergio kicked him in the head as the door started to slide open.

Blaise looked up at staring nurses and orderlies. Windbreaker's head lolled and he began drooling. His eyes rolled back, showing mostly whites.

"Epileptic," Blaise improvised. He leaned the semiconscious man back on the floor and stepped aside as more nurses and a doctor pushed in.

Sergio motioned with his eyes and they sidled out. Someone stopped the elevator. But the other elevator ground to a halt and they got on it. Stares were turning into accusation as the doors closed. "I wish you'd gotten his gun," Sergio said.

Sergio's look as they got into the car seemed to say *I hope the trip was worth the effort*. He drove with smooth precision, nothing showing. Gordon was that way too: everything armored and concealed inside. Blaise wondered if he could ever learn. "It was worth it," he said.

Which did not throw Sergio off. "It's been my experience that women can make men and tomcats do strange things."

"I don't know about tomcats," Blaise said.

Tickets were five dollars and the woman seemed surprised when Blaise gave her a ten for a pair. "Where's your discount coupons?" She had fluffy sable hair and a good figure and was too old to be cute, but young enough to make men stop and talk. She offered to give Blaise a couple.

"Thanks," Blaise said. "But we're in sort of a hurry. Why don't you just keep the extra fin for yourself?"

Her smile knocked five years off her age and made three men behind Sergio feel good about standing in line. "If you need something special, stop at table thirty-two and tell Al that Vera said to treat you right or she'll break his toes."

They hadn't gone ten feet into the 25th Annual Gun and Knife Show before Sergio was walking like a cat on a hot sidewalk.

"How do you think she'd break Al's toes?" Blaise asked.

Sergio didn't notice. "How do I get out of here without a police escort?" he demanded.

Blaise looked at him.

"Everybody in here doesn't have a gun in a holster has a couple in his pockets. People get killed in places like this."

"How do you get guns in New Jersey?"

Sergio gave Blaise a *you're kidding* look. "You know a guy sends you to somebody opens the trunk of his car and you make a deal. How do you expect?"

"You seem to know a lot about guns for somebody who never had one."

"Did I say that?"

Blaise ignored Sergio, drifting down the aisles until he located thirty-two. Four glass-topped cases filled with semi-antique black powder weapons held down a checked table-cloth. The man behind the table had tanned skin where hair once was.

"Al?"

The man's mean eyes protruded slightly. His beard was gray-tufted and his skin yellowish. He looked hung over.

"Yeah."

"Vera says treat us right or she'll break your toes." Al didn't look friendly, and Blaise waited, feeling vaguely like a White House staffer holding a smoking gun.

Al's face wrinkled into a slow grin. "She say how?"

"No."

"Son, you missed out. I gotta find out what she has in mind." Al started looking for somebody to hold down his table.

"Could you help us first?"

Al looked first at Blaise and then Sergio as if he'd never seen them before. "What can I do for you?"

"We need a gun..."

Sergio held up two fingers.

"Two guns. Discreet."

"I got just what you need."

Sergio examined the cases shaking his head. Al looked at him. "Listen, wise guy. If I say I got it, I got it. Whatcha want?" Al's face had darkened and his voice was more raspy.

"Tell him," Blaise said. He hoped Sergio was paying attention to Al's mood.

"Look, Al." Sergio's patience showed in his voice. "We're not muzzle-loader freaks. We just want protection."

"Like what?"

"How about a twenty-two automatic and something in a forty-five magnum?"

"Z'at all?"

Sergio nodded.

"Vera sent you?"

Blaise nodded.

"Why'ncha say so in the first place?" Al grunted as he tugged at a military gun box. He motioned them behind the table with him, and lifted the lid.

Sergio stopped breathing.

Al burrowed and emerged with an object in a dark blue cotton cloth that smelled of gun oil.

"That's a Schmeisser machine pistol, isn't it?" Sergio stared at the box's contents.

Blaise glanced into the box. Pistols and assorted bigger weapons were mixed haphazardly with cloth-wrapped bundles. There were oversized pistols with long barrels and odd shapes and he supposed Sergio was talking about one of them.

Al unwrapped a sleekly put-together nine-inch-long pistol, dark blue with checked walnut grips.

Sergio shook his head.

"Immaculate. Perfect action. Good price."

"What do you think we are, gangsters? That's a Woodsman Colt twenty-two. We want something small like"—Sergio thought—"like a Star."

"No got." Al considered, then groped through loose pistols and handed one to Sergio. "Another Spanish-made Saturday Night Special. *Búfalo* six point three five. It's better than spitting, but you can't get ammunition just anywhere. Works all right. Rebuilt it a couple of times and took all the crap out."

Sergio passed it to Blaise.

The weight surprised Blaise. Smaller than his hand, he could make the pistol disappear while he was holding it.

"How much?"

Al chewed on his lip. "Seventy-five ... naaah, fifty."

"Seventy-five with a box of bullets," Blaise said.

Al looked at Sergio. "You don't want it for fifty?"

Sergio shook his head.

Al's face split in half with a smile. "Vera was right about you guys. Tell you what. I got an old belt holster it'll fit in. Oh, and if you shoot more than ten feet away, pull six inches to the right and three inches down for every ten feet after."

"If something's that far away, we'll throw rocks."

Al quibbled a little about the Magnum, explaining that if you're only stopping a bus you don't have to kill the first six passengers behind the driver. Blaise lost interest in the conversation, which dealt with the mechanics of shooting people, at which Al and Sergio seemed experts.

Sergio settled finally for a .44 Magnum revolver with a six-inch barrel and a shoulder holster. Al told them to watch his table. He shut his box, shoved it under the table, and wandered away for twenty minutes. When he came back he had a box of .44 Magnums, a box of .44 target cartridges, and a box of 6.5-mm ammo for the *Búfalo*. He also had a pair of pin-on badges for John Blake and Fred Moretti.

"You're gunsmiths," Al said. "Case anybody saw you come in without weapons. Carry them in plain sight to your car and put them in the trunk. At least until you're away from all these rent-a-cops."

In the car, Blaise asked, "Feel better now?"

Patting his left side, Sergio said, "Much."

Sergio smiled. The gun had filled a void in his soul that he had not known existed.

Blaise took the tiny *Búfalo* out of his pocket while Sergio drove. A groove down the slide had a notch in back and a front bead sight. A thumb safety locked the slide. An insert at the back of the handle had to be depressed when the trigger was squeezed. Clear plastic grips showed how many cartridges remained in the clip. He hefted the pistol. If he had to, he thought he could throw it better than a rock.

In its most primitive definition, the proof of the mathematical definition of intelligence must start by the construction of mechanical means to imitate human mental behavior piecemeal: that is, if mechanical memory is perfect, the introduction of imperfections that replicate human behavior will ultimately define solutions for human failure.

FROM A SEMINAR ON
THE CUNNINGHAM EQUATIONS

CHAPTER 22

Blaise sat in front of Alfie trying to make sense from data scrolling up the screen. The files Helen had opened on GENRECT, Tenro, West, and the Burkhalters were a Pandora's box of incestuous connections that left him with a numb sense of betrayal.

The running log of Helen's vital signs on the side of the screen kept distracting him and he considered asking Alfie to turn it off. But he had the sneaky anthropomorphic premonition that Alfie would be hurt. Not that Alfie had feelings!

The Family Trust, with other investors, controlled North American rights to all Technological Intelligence Laboratories, as TIL Ltd., Inc. And until the research contracts were canceled, TILLI had been the Burkhalters' major income source.

Some of the information caused Blaise to wonder what sources Helen programmed Alfie to access. University records ... Jonathan Peters' doctorate and confidential notes about it written by his advisers ... details of Linda's sex life ... Milo's scholastic background, which terminated with the loss of the family fortune.

He felt hollow reading the grubby details, but he could not stop until he dredged up the whole report Alfie had lifted from a reputable detective agency. The client was Jonathan

Peters. Blaise managed a pained rictus of smile. In this case the husband had not been the last to know.

It was as if Alfie had been turned loose to rampage through the wastebaskets of the *National Enquirer*. Among other exploits Milo Burkhalter had manipulated the casual rape and looting of Osgood Investments, whose founder killed himself rather than face the proverbial widows and orphans who had trusted him.

Charles Osgood's name bobbed up again on the monitor— out of Linda's file.

Blaise leaned back, trying to breathe.

"IS THERE ANYTHING ELSE, PROFESSOR?"

Alfie had timed the lack of response and was prompting Blaise. Pain stabbed from his armpit into the soft underflesh of his triceps, paralyzing him. Breath rasping, Blaise pecked out with painful slowness the commands for Alfie to continue. With the sun down and the lights out in the bedroom his face became a distorted mirror for the sallow green of the CRT display. The ache in his chest hardened into permanence.

Alfie confirmed everything Helen had told him before the raid to get Dobie. He reached down slowly, too fragile for quick movement, and rubbed Dobie's head. The dog sighed. After a while, Alfie returned to contemplating its tin navel in an ongoing attempt to elevate electromechanical memory to creative intelligence. The CRT was displaying: "I KNOW EVERYTHING"

Blaise took Dobie for a walk through the backyard garden.

Still weak, the pup leaned against Blaise on the way back, and fell asleep as soon as he settled gingerly onto the mattress.

Blaise left a note under the coffeepot where Sergio would be sure to find it.

His home seemed unchanged. On an adjoining hill Blaise stretched out as much as he could in the car, watching through a pair of 7×50s. Sergio had lectured Blaise on binoculars as tools of the trade. And patience. Waiting and watching. *"Sicut Fabius Maximus,"* Sergio explained, recalling the Roman who won his wars by waiting patient years for one golden moment.

Sergio's assessment of guns versus binoculars dismayed Blaise, particularly after Sergio explained the only safe way to use the little automatic: "Hold it close to your target's throat, stomach, or kidneys. Squeeze the trigger eight times as fast as you can." Sergio had added, "That'll slow most people down. But if the bullets bounce off somebody's hard head or chest, Doc, run like hell."

A gibbous moon hung over the ocean and stars were out. It was a nice night to sit in the car and look through binoculars and wonder how a common burglar accumulated capital to buy guns and binoculars so he could enter his profession properly equipped. Or whether Sergio was uncommon.

After two hours of watching the black shadows of hedges and cars in the immediate neighborhood as well as the house itself, Blaise sensed that it was truly unwatched. He drove to a street uphill of the house and killed the motor, then slowly rolled down, lights off, hearing the soft crunch of gravel under tires.

With power steering dead Blaise began to sweat from wrestling the wheel, holding speed down with powerless brakes—and suddenly realizing he had not taken the bulbs out of the stop lights. He was leaving a trail of red light!

His hands shook by the time he parked across a downhill neighbor's driveway. He hauled himself through the window on the passenger side, lowering his feet silently to the cement. A breath of sea breeze began to chill him.

He didn't need light. As a school kid he used to shortcut through the brush behind the house to the street below. His feet still knew the way. Of course he was bigger now, and the undergrowth didn't conceal as much as he remembered. But he found the cellar door and slipped inside.

His home had lost its friendliness with the knowledge that strangers might be inside. Silent, he climbed to the kitchen door, hearing the thud of his pulse, the echo of his own fear. Inching the door open to darkness, he stepped out of his shoes.

The floor was waiting to drum out his arrival. He stopped at the archway between kitchen and living room, willing the house to settle back into somnolence before he moved again. Tension was a metallic taste that rose into his throat. Through the picture window the moon was a worn silver quarter with a bite missing as it hung in a black sky. Moonbeams gave the surrealistic feel of having stepped into a photographic negative.

The room seemed empty, but he had thought the same walking into the other house, past Sergio concealed as effectively in the high-backed chair as if he had tossed a pinch of powders and conjured invisibility. Blaise had not seen him until the light came on and it was too late.

The wingback chair was beside the window, facing the door. The couch looked out on the ocean. Silently, Blaise stepped in stockinged feet, letting his long shadow blend into the others.

He stepped again and his shadow melted, waiting. Again. Stop. Convince himself it had been there all the time. Gun in right hand. Chair a step away. He moved and his shadow blended with that of the chair stretching across the room. He held his arms close, pretending he was a tree, feeling tension claw his belly. Then he plunged his left hand over the side of the chair and swung, jamming the gun toward the middle at head height.

He almost screamed.

His fingers clutched hair and a hard skull that twisted violently under his left hand until the pistol squished and jolted against something harder than the back of the seat. Blaise almost pulled the trigger.

For a long moment he leaned against the chair staring into darkness, fingers wound in a handful of hair that pulled feebly. Blaise jerked. A body followed the head attached to his fingers, and stretched prone. Kneeling, Blaise pressed the gun barrel against teeth. The man's eyes were fluttering like machine code in the moonlight.

"Is there anyone else?" he whispered. The sibilance echoed through the cold lit room.

The head rolled.

Blaise let go of the hair and patted until he found the stranger's gun. When he tucked it in his belt, his pants sagged.

Grabbing hair again, he pulled the man to his feet. When he was facing away Blaise put the little automatic in his holster and took the big gun in his right hand. Prodding his captive like a shield, Blaise toured the house and made sure it was empty. Then he pushed his would-be assailant into the windowless interior bathroom and turned on the light.

Blaise tied him under the sink, arms folded behind through the cast-iron drainpipe, lashed with his own belt and shoelaces. He studied his work, then embellished it with tape from the medicine chest. Pockets yielded a New Jersey driver's license and two hundred dollars. Blaise already had the gun.

The side of the man's face was turning black from the blow of Blaise's pistol. Eyes were vacant, as if the tenant was still not home. Blaise knew where he had seen that look before: when Helen had faded away the first time he saw her in the hospital.

He owed Sergio an apology. Sitting in the wingback chair punching numbers into the cordless phone with his left hand, the oversized pistol in his right, he finally understood the comfort that a gun delivered.

The phone was answered with a sleepy "Hello?"

"Linda?"

"Blaise! Are you all right?"

"Everything's fine." Blaise looked at the gun in his hand and decided he wasn't lying. "Shouldn't it be?"

"No. I mean yes. I don't know. I was asleep." There was a silent ringing in his ears until Linda finally said, "How's Helen?" in a changed voice.

"Getting better. Maybe."

"I'm sorry. Really, Blaise. Even if..." A pause while Linda mentally shrugged. "You know."

"I understand. I just wanted to let you know I'm home again, now that Helen is in the hospital."

"You should come up here, Blaise. San Francisco is nice this time of year." Unconsciously she lowered her voice. "Uncle Milo can protect you. I know he can."

"Do I need protection?"

"We all need a little." Her voice faded. Then she added, "You will come?"

"Yes," Blaise promised. "Good-bye until then."

"Good-bye." Linda hung up but the sound of an open line remained. Blaise knew somebody was outwaiting him, that there would be no dial tone. He flipped the OFF button and waited ten seconds before pressing automatic redial. Linda's line was busy.

He checked the house before he left. Particularly the man on the bathroom floor who glared but said nothing. Leaving the way he'd entered, he drove Helen's white Buick uphill past the house. When he was far enough away, he turned out the lights and continued in darkness back where he'd parked earlier. A casual observer would swear the car had not moved. Crickets decided the commotion was over and resumed their chirr.

He waited eight minutes before a pair of cars without lights parked above and below his house. By the time he had the binoculars focused the lights were on inside. He released the brake and rolled downhill until he hit the dip out of sight of the house, then turned on the headlights.

Sergio was going to say *Beginner's luck*! Remembering that tense stalk in the house when fear had filled his stomach to the verge of vomiting, Blaise knew Sergio would be right.

It is in the interactions between individuals that the problem of intelligence becomes paramount. Just as machines which are not built to recognize their relationships to each other cannot communicate, humans fall into conflicts.

FROM A SEMINAR ON
THE CUNNINGHAM EQUATIONS

CHAPTER 23

Blaise palmed the gun from his newspaper-stuffed valise, feeling furtive because of the airport security guards, then threw the bag onto the luggage carrousel to orbit unto eternity before walking out to catch a cab.

At the Burkhalter turn-of-the-century mansion, night was like standing in a covered well. Searching with his feet, Blaise followed flagstones to the huge, arch-topped oak door. The button produced a distant chime. Raw ocean wind knifed through his windbreaker as he waited. He stepped back to look up at the three-story front of quarried stone.

Like a cat's eye opening, light flashed into existence near the top. Lights in other windows followed until finally the archway light momentarily blinded him. Blaise was still blinking as the door swung open.

"Dr. Cunningham. It's late for a visit." Milo Burkhalter's ponderous voice rolled through the night air, revealing neither surprise nor rancor. "As long as you're here, why not come in?"

Burkhalter shut the door behind Blaise before leading the way into the study. He wore a red brocade robe with gold-and-black trim. The satin lining was also red. Pale-blue pajama legs stuck out below the hem. Although he bulged and his hair was white, Blaise's impression was not of a fat old man abruptly wrenched from his Seconal but of a man getting up to swat a fly.

"I was hoping to see you, Dr. Cunningham."

"Were you?"

Milo's expression did not change. Blaise suspected powerful people had little emotion to spare and were such practiced liars that he would never catch them out. Sitting in the massive leather chair behind his desk, Milo offered the humidor. Blaise declined. Carefully Milo selected a cigar mottled with yellow-and-green spots.

"Havana leaf," he said. "People have tried to grow it in Mexico and North Carolina, but their products are inferior even to the Connecticut. I think it has to do with the bacterial strains in the ground, but you'd know more about that than I?"

Blaise shook his head. "The owner of TIL surely knows more about applied biology than I, *Mister* Burkhalter."

"So you know." Milo puffed, exhaling a mild blue cloud. "A small vanity. I was nearly there when the family fortunes failed. I dropped out and picked up the burden. In return for facing up to family responsibilities, I awarded myself a degree *in absentia*." Milo flicked ash. "Of course, Doctor, you wouldn't know about that sort of thing." Milo paused at the elevator's whine. A moment later the door clattered.

"Hello, Blaise." Linda wore a one-piece ivory dress that zipped up the back and molded itself to her. Soft white slippers with flat heels made her even more petite and Blaise knew what he had to say would be difficult in spite of endless rehearsals on the flight from San Diego.

"You didn't tell me you were coming tonight."

"I had to find out myself."

"I'm glad you came. Why don't you sit down? I told you Uncle Milo would help."

"Of course I will, Linda." Uncle Milo's lips, cheeks, and eyes crinkled into a practiced benevolence.

Blaise took a chair facing Milo but where he could still see Linda. "I told you where I was calling from, Linda."

"Your house." She stared, green eyes clouded, distracting Blaise with perfection, although he knew he saw only the physical manifestation of an unattainable ideal.

"My house." Blaise glanced at Milo. "I don't live there anymore. Since Helen was attacked I've had to move."

"Had to?" Milo's face was patience in ironwood.

"Some people want a lab animal. They forced their way into Helen's house and almost killed her for a dog. I still have him."

"I see. Of course Linda is right, Dr. Cunningham, if there is anything we can do, we will."

"I hoped you'd say that, Mr. Burkhalter."

"That's wonderful, Blaise."

When Blaise looked at her some of Linda's enthusiasm ebbed. "You can help by answering a few questions."

"Of course." Linda smiled. Milo said nothing.

"I went to my house to make the call. I told you where I was. And then I left."

Milo was willing to play. "Why did you do that?"

"I didn't go far. Just up the hill to watch two cars come to my house. And the men in them."

"Perhaps these people were searching randomly for you." Milo seemed to be contemplating something outside Blaise and Linda's vision.

"When I first got to the house a man was waiting inside."

"I don't understand..." Linda's eyes pleaded with him not to mean what he was saying.

"What Dr. Cunningham means, my dear, is if a man was waiting for him, the others wouldn't have swarmed over the house unless they were sure he was inside."

"You see things clearly, Mr. Burkhalter."

Milo turned his head slightly toward the wall. The angle set deep shadows over the creases and wrinkles of his face. "Your telephone may have been monitored."

"Unlikely."

"Yes. Unlikely. Or that our telephone is tapped."

"Linda is the only person who knew of a connection between me and Helen; who knew Helen had Dobie. And who knew I was not at Helen's home to intercept a call from Dr. Hemmett. She was alone long enough to telephone while I met with Gordon."

Silence has a negative quality like the depth of black water. Felt but not heard, it filled the study. Blaise had a sense of moving underwater. But there was no stopping. With each word Linda drifted farther out of his life.

"I didn't, Blaise. I wouldn't do anything to Helen."

"But you'd do it, wouldn't you, Mr. Burkhalter?"

Milo shifted his gaze from the wall to stare at Blaise.

"Just as you did to Osgood."

Blood drained from Linda's face. Blaise tried to feel something. Sorry, perhaps.

"That's a cruel thing to say. Osgood was necessary, for

the family. That's why Linda acted. For the family." Milo's voice made the pronouncement noble, justifying Linda's prostitution on some Nietzschean grounds that, for the Herrenvolk of intellect, breeding, and money, anything is permissible.

"Is that what it was for, Mr. Burkhalter? Linda lured him off to the Caribbean for a week while you stole his company. Seduced a man old enough to be her father—and all for the family?

"When he found out, he came here. What did you tell him to make him kill himself?" Blaise shifted his gaze to Linda and asked softly, "Or what did you tell him?"

Linda tilted her head so he couldn't meet her eyes.

"She did it for money." Blaise's voice rang louder than he intended in the small room. "But Osgood didn't kill himself over the money. He died of shame Linda carried to him like some miserable disease. Because you told her to."

"Get out, Dr. Cunningham." Milo didn't raise his voice. But it vibrated with strength.

"I'm not finished."

Looking more like a dressed-up school girl than a grown woman, Linda hid her face in her hands.

"You are totally finished."

Blaise ignored Milo. "Linda had no reason to latch onto me, unless she was told to." Blaise looked at her, feeling at last some small pity. "I'm sorry, Linda, but even drunk I don't kid myself that I'm a prime catch—particularly for a handsome, intelligent woman who's too self-centered to willingly burden herself with my problems.

"I was the greedy kid in fairyland getting off on all his dreams. But in my intestines, Mr. Burkhalter, I knew. I drank more so I could ignore what was happening. I can't blame Linda for what I did to myself.

"I knew—not for sure, but close to the surface—that keeping in touch with Gordon and hanging onto Dobie would somehow keep Linda with me." Blaise stopped talking, drained. In a single moment he had exposed more of himself than he had previously revealed in a lifetime.

"I'll kill you!"

Jonathan Peters stepped into the study. Tears streamed down his face as he walked unsteadily toward Blaise. Face whiter than Linda's, eyes filled with pain, he was without thought or cunning. Blaise knew he would really try.

Milo rose, watching with hooded eyes from behind his desk. He wasn't going to help. Blaise had forgotten about Linda's husband. He'd dismissed him because Peters knew as much about Milo and Linda as he did.

He took the *Búfalo* from the holster in his waistband and pumped the slide. "Dr. Peters," he said quietly, "it is not in your character to kill anyone."

Peters' gaze flicked casually at the gun, but he walked like a man intent on suicide.

"Please don't, Dr. Peters."

"Kill him, Jonathan!" Milo's voice exploded. Peters emitted an indecipherable wail of anguish and lunged.

Blaise saw it in slow motion, Jonathan stretching, hands hooking into claws and lunging without the simplest attempt to protect himself.

The gun rose in Blaise's hand. In time it pointed at Jonathan and his finger came out of the trigger guard. Blaise was stunned by how easily he smashed it against Peters' face. Inertia carried Linda's husband against the chair where he made a whomping sound when he hit the leather.

Milo sat slowly, face frozen, both hands conspicuously on top of his desk. After an instant he picked up his cigar.

"Jon!" Linda's red fingernails were ragged pickets beneath her eyes.

Blaise sat again, breathing heavily. Reaching down, he shook Peters until the mathematician rolled over and looked up with blank eyes.

"Go outside and wait for me."

Peters got to his feet. Like an arthritic old man, he trudged away. Blaise heard the massive thud of the door and felt a surge of cold air. He eased the slide back and set the safety. He'd been lucky the gun hadn't gone off when he hit Peters.

Milo's eyes followed Blaise's hands, his thoughts veiled.

"Now, Mr. Burkhalter," Blaise said musingly, "what can I devise for the man who is responsible?" But hatred was draining away, purged by the sudden violence. He couldn't kill Milo out of hand. Jonathan Peters had saved Milo's life.

Blaise played with the pistol, nervously switching it from hand to hand. In his right the safety was under the ball of his thumb. In his left he would have to release it with his trigger finger. Milo's jerky eyes following the pistol were the one sign of concern he couldn't control.

"Should I show more kindness than you and just kill you?"

Linda stared in horror.

"For what reason?" Milo shrugged but his eyes were drawn back to the pistol each time he tore them away.

"Linda told you. You told West, or maybe Hemmett. They paid you off: traded GENRECT stock for TIL stock. And Helen almost died for some lousy money. Will you never get enough?"

Milo shook his head. "Not that. They had to make the deal. A person . . . a cheap tramp working for TIL modified the product. She experimented on my time, on my patent, developing a self-propagating strain. Then she sold it to your Dr. Hemmett."

"Esther Tazy."

Milo looked at Blaise and smiled. "If you know Miss Tazy, I'm sure you can understand the spot she put me in. I learned too late about her deal with Dr. Hemmett. West and Hemmett already had samples of the modified germ plasm. I didn't trade you or your precious Helen. Gregory West and I have had dealings before. He wanted no fuss. I simply threatened to sue him for patent infringement and theft of industrial secrets."

"You knew Dobie was at Helen's, you and Linda."

"I am sorry." Milo spread his hands. "I just passed along a favor. Dr. Hemmett feared that the dog might fall into the wrong hands and my patent—ours, sharing it was part of our deal—would be stolen by a third party. No one was to be hurt. I can only blame Gregory West for that. He is ruthless. But I thought Dr. Hemmett had control."

Milo could be telling the truth. Greed, Blaise knew, should wear glasses.

"I'm sorry, Linda."

She watched him, prepared to cringe again.

"It was never right between us."

"We can make it right, Blaise." She sniffled and wiped her nose with the back of her hand.

"Maybe you're part of a love-hate relationship with my mother, but you've already had both sides. Nothing's left."

"You don't really love that woman, Blaise. I know you. You just think you're responsible."

"I knew before then that you didn't care for me, or I for you, Linda. I avoided Helen for another reason. Love is not lust. Helen was important. You were never there when I needed you." Blaise felt the sour taste of truth in his mouth.

"When Helen was hurt, I knew I'd screwed up and might never get another chance. I have to try."

"It's not true."

Blaise shrugged. "Call off your dogs, Mr. Burkhalter. I am swiftly losing patience. What happened to Helen happened because of you. I'll have eyes for an eye. Teeth for a tooth."

"I'll see to it." Milo did not blink as Blaise walked out.

Peters sat on the curb, staring into the blackness that hid San Francisco Bay. Blaise sat next to him and released the safety on the little *Búfalo*.

"Are you going to shoot me?" Peters didn't seem to care.

"No." Blaise slipped the clip out and worked the slide, catching the ejected cartridge and replacing it in the clip. As he stared into the darkness with Peters, a lyric from the wild old days at the Hungry I ran through his head. Tom Lehrer had sung that what folks had for lunch along the bay they had for breakfast in San Jose.

Lights in the house winked out.

"What now?" Peters' voice was hopeless.

"I have to go back."

Peters nodded, all but invisible in the darkness. "I'll drive you to the airport." He stood slowly, each movement a painful unkinking.

"It's never been right with Linda," Peters began. His voice was like a music box that could only be turned off by smashing it. Blaise tucked cold-numbed hands in his armpits and heard the ongoing tragedy of life with the Burkhalters.

Peters' DAR family had been in San Francisco since before the Earthquake. If Jonathan had a fault worth mentioning, it was mediocrity. His single bad break was being smart enough to know it. Perseverance and money for tutors and time to study twice as hard as his peers at school lifted him out of the "also ran" category. He was a grind in an age that revered brilliance.

A noteworthy doctoral paper landed an assistant's job at a prestigious university. Pedigree outweighed mediocrity and Peters evolved into a safely tenured professor. And then he fell in love with a grad student.

Peters stopped talking and Blaise noticed they were creeping along. "It's the fog," Peters apologized, and speeded up. "I couldn't resist her."

Blaise knew exactly what he meant.

Uncle Milo gave his blessing. Linda hyphenated her name, pleasing Peters since they'd married at a time when chic women "retained their identities," keeping maiden names and acknowledging husbands only at their convenience.

The Peters family lost its money when his father plunged in the market, first with Jonathan's trust fund, then with bank money. Peters would have been better off if his father had been a professional thief. He wouldn't have killed himself.

They pulled up to the airport loading zone and Peters' confession droned on unstoppable. Lights from the extended building front shone into the car. Peters had a huge bruise like a birthmark down one side of his face.

"You understand," he said finally, as if sure that Blaise could understand what it meant to not measure up, first by himself and then by the family that had been Peters' final anchor. "Milo hates my guts. I'm not intellectually good enough. I'm no longer wealthy. Finally"—Peters turned to Blaise with tortured eyes—"when he couldn't get Linda to divorce me, he asked her to drop the 'hyphen Peters' because it was 'an embarrassment.'"

Blaise was embarrassed for himself as well as Peters. He could not bring himself to trade confidences, nor did he think Peters would have welcomed them. His own actions had been so motivated by self-pity that Blaise felt like cripple who had robbed a blind man. "What did you do?"

"Oh," Peters tried to smile. "I took what money I could and invested it with the Burkhalter Trust. It wasn't much, but Linda wanted us to live in the house and she has her own income, so most of my salary is available for investment. Milo let me know it didn't match up with what the other investors put in, but they considered it part of the family money and didn't complain.

"Milo never complains. You know?" Peters' eyes queried Blaise, afraid he wasn't being rational. "Not out loud, anyway."

Blaise nodded.

"That's why I went to Human Enhancements. I hired a detective agency to report on Linda. I knew she . . . wasn't faithful. But she wouldn't divorce me. I had to know why.

"Human Enchancements works, Blaise. May I call you Blaise? Linda told me about you. So I knew. And the detective agency. Milo couldn't hold it over me. It was as if

Linda was protecting me. I'm smarter now, but the more I know the less I understand."

Fatigue was working on Blaise but listening to Peters caused another ache inside. He'd made waves. They were still churning up debris that he was in whole or in part responsible for.

"I don't know either, Jonathan." Blaise thought a moment while Peters waited, tensed for a revelation. "I think Linda loves you. Even with Milo pushing her, she didn't divorce you. She told you about me—but not me about you." Blaise paused. "You're Catholic, aren't you?"

"Yes. Both of us."

Blaise unlatched the door. "There's a man here somewhere in San Francisco. Maybe he can give you the answers."

Peters waited.

"Father Robert Argyle. He's a Jesuit. Tell him everything about Milo's activities and your . . . operation."

For a moment Peters seemed about to cry from gratitude. "Thank you."

Blaise hung onto the door and leaned down to eye level. "When you told Milo you'd been to Human Enhancements, how did he take it?"

"I didn't tell him."

"No?" Blaise blinked in surprise.

"He seemed to know." Peters silently contemplated the steering wheel and Blaise started to pull away but Peters caught his wrist. "He was pleased—in a sadistic kind of way."

"Tell Father Argyle I'm paying two debts by sending you, and I trust him to act accordingly." Blaise closed the car door and walked into the airport, aware of Jonathan Peters' eyes on him until he was out of sight.

The analysis of intelligence is thwarted to some extent by the very nature of the subject. It is only within the range of its own abilities that mankind can conceive of improvement. Thus, as with many other great advances, the ultimate goal is out of range of our vision. As yet.

FROM A SEMINAR ON
THE CUNNINGHAM EQUATIONS

CHAPTER 24

Blaise waited until Peters had time either to leave the airport or find a telephone. Then he found a car rental kiosk and signed for the biggest car he could get.

Sergio was eating breakfast when Blaise walked in. He couldn't tell if Sergio had slept. His clothes were just back crisp from the cleaners, his skin still pink from a hot shower, but Sergio's eyes and the lines around his mouth were deep.

Blaise told him what he'd done. Not everything, but enough, while Sergio cleaned up his plate and then washed it at the sink.

"Do you know how to run the dishwasher?"

Blaise said, "Probably," and then couldn't recapture his train of thought again without asking, "Don't you?"

"No. And it's getting full."

"Were you listening?"

"You're doing all right." Sergio sat at the table. "I still don't know what's happening."

"You know everything I know."

"Almost, *paisan'*."

"I need to know more," Blaise admitted, "but Milo is hiding information. Gordon's worried about something he won't reveal—because he doesn't want to upset me, or because he isn't sure."

"You didn't give Peters a chance to cross you up?"

"He's unstable. Maybe he'll do what I ask. If Linda gets

to him, that's a guarantee that what he knows, Milo knows. But I don't think he was lying."

Dobie pawed gently at his knee and whined. Blaise scratched the dog's head, transmuting the whine into a sigh. The Doberman's eyes were foggy and he appeared listless, but he hugged Blaise's leg with his neck as he lay back on the floor and disappeared into a dreamless sleep.

"I gave him four fried eggs," Sergio said.

"There's dog food."

"Whatever the disease is, we both got it." Sergio shrugged. "What's good for me is good for him and I don't like dog food."

"I want to move Helen. And I want to talk to Gordon again."

"They found Bruno in the trunk yesterday morning."

Blaise held his breath and waited.

"West opened the trunk, looked at Bruno, then slammed it down. Heaven's Gate registered ninety-seven degrees at one-thirty yesterday afternoon. Two guys took him out of the trunk at five." Sergio did not change expression.

"I'm sorry."

Sergio inclined his head slightly. "He's alive. If he was dead, I'd have to tell his mother. My aunt."

Blaise closed his eyes and slumped back in his chair. "You're asking if it's worthwhile," he said to his eyelids.

"Yes."

"I don't know. I'm not sure I'd even care if Helen wasn't involved. I don't believe sixty-thousand-dollar surgery is forced on anybody who doesn't want it. Everybody went to Human Enhancements of his own free will. Even Helen." Blaise opened his eyes. His mother always told him she could tell what he was thinking by how gray or how blue his eyes were at any moment. "I suppose you think that's pretty cold."

"I'm in no position to say, Doc. If I didn't think you were right about the dog being important to me, directly, I'd have probably let Bruno do you like he was told. Maybe Bruno's suffering for his sins and I'm suffering for mine. And you . . ." Sergio let it die.

"You're different now from what you used to be."

"I like to think so." Sergio dissected Blaise overtly, as if examining a reflection of himself to which he wanted to divulge a secret.

"I have a theory," Blaise said. "But it means talking to Gordon. It means getting Gordon out, first, and then getting him to work on it. How did you find out about Bruno?"

"I watched."

"Long-range binoculars?"

"I told you they're more important than a gun."

"We have to get Helen out of the hospital. Because if we get Gordon, I think West would try to trade Helen."

"It's not possible to bust Miss McIntyre out, Doc."

"That's why I didn't tell you what I want to talk to Gordon about. If you want it badly enough, anything is possible."

Sergio contemplated Blaise for a long moment. "I'm surprised, Doc," he finally said, "that somebody hasn't found a way to kill you before now."

"Beware the intellectuals, Sergio. We're all bastards."

Closeted in the back of a Rolls-Royce limousine Sergio had rented for two hundred dollars a day, Blaise felt like he was inside a tank. The car was twenty-six years old, boxy, and came with a driver-owner, a coat of black paint, and the smell of polished leather. It also reeked with rectitude.

"You know, Doc," Sergio admitted with a hint of wonder, "I never thought I'd voluntarily get into a car older than yours."

Blaise held the curtain away from his window. He grunted and kept an eye on a large house with gabled roofs and the aura of old money. The vintage Rolls looked good parked in front. "He's got a bite," Blaise said.

The driver, radiant in black serge with a matching visored cap, was at the door to the house talking to a middle-aged woman whose permanent was too elegant for her housecoat. "She's looking at the car."

Sergio kept his eyes to the oversized binoculars, sweeping hillside and parking lot.

"She's pointing."

"Where?"

"The hospital." Blaise leaned back and dropped the curtain.

"That's good." Sergio continued sweeping the hospital and the area around it until the front car door opened and the driver got behind the wheel. "If anybody is watching, we're covered."

"Okey dokey?" The driver was in his late fifties. A little

guy with a walrus mustache and a Bronx accent. It cost an extra hundred and a promise that nobody was going to get killed, but the driver added that pushing cab in Manhattan, he might have done Murder One for that big a tip.

Sergio put the glasses in the case. "They've got a couple of process servers down there, but we'll get around them."

The driver started two tons of fine-tuned machinery down the hill. He never said he believed Sergio's reason why they were paying so well. But he never said he doubted either.

Passing the main lot entrance, the Rolls ran up the emergency ambulance driveway and slowed to a crawl. A boxwood hedge screened one side. The hospital blocked visibility from every other direction except the street directly behind.

"Now!"

Blaise opened the door and steadied himself until he was running as fast as the slow-moving Rolls. Sergio pulled the door closed while Blaise slowed and walked into the emergency admissions rear entrance. Inside, he paused to watch the Rolls glide to a stop at the ambulance loading dock.

An intern in a green scrub suit came out gesturing angrily. Another man in a business suit leaned against the wall watching. While the driver argued, Blaise slipped through the admitting room's swinging doors with stretcher bumpers and glass see-through panels and was immediately inside the hospital.

His heart beat faster than normal. The empty corridor, shiny with reflected fluorescent light and the smell of disinfectant, was forbidding.

No one seemed interested in the elevators, but Sergio had said to assume he was seen. The trick was not to be caught alone with a stranger. Waiting until the doors on an empty elevator started to close, Blaise darted across the hall and inside.

As the slot between the doors shrank, he saw a man in the lobby wearing a red turtleneck sweatshirt get up from his chair. Then the elevator was moving.

The sixth floor appeared barren except for the duty nurse. Blaise crossed to her desk before she could use his name. "Can you call Dr. MacReedy?"

She gave him a sour look before dialing an inside number.

Blaise got the receptionist, then tapped on the desk while the doctor was paged. He told MacReedy he wanted to take Helen out of the hospital and MacReedy said he'd be right up. The nurse glared reproachfully at Blaise while they waited, still bent out of shape because he had lied about seeing Dr. MacReedy before leaving the hospital.

Turning away from her accusing face, he glanced through the windows into the ICU rooms. Helen seemed comfortable napping. The tinge of color in her face was preferable to the glacial white of a few days ago.

Idly, Blaise looked back through the other ICU windows, one at a time. And knew sudden panic. The room next to Helen's held a single bed, a single large mound of white sheets.

Blaise started toward the door.

"Dr. Cunningham! Dr. Cunningham, that's the wrong door!" The nurse's voice echoed shrilly.

What was it Sergio had said? He'd wait on the floor because he knew Blaise would show up? Blaise turned the knob. The latch clicked, and he was inside.

The bed paralleled windows with views of ocean and part of La Jolla. Blaise grabbed the sheet and yanked.

Bruno's gleaming black eyes stared up from the livid face. The hand next to the window held a black box that could only be some walkie-talkie offshoot with an on/off red plastic button. His thumb was clicking the button.

Blaise reached over Bruno trying to tear the box loose. Bruno caught his throat and he was drifting, losing feeling in the fingers he could see prying at Bruno's. Bruno's thumb was pumping. A *click, click, click* jittered from the built-in speaker. Somewhere close by another box was clicking.

Blaise saw everything in slow motion as his air was cut off. *Try!* With painful slowness his fingers worked together and pried until Bruno's thumb bent backward with a sound like a celery stalk snapping. The box skittered on the floor but Bruno had already given the alarm. The shrill-voiced giant yelled through wired-shut jaws, but Blaise couldn't hear. His ears were threatening to burst. Then the pressure was gone momentarily. Bruno was straining to reach the gun butt sticking out from under his back. Trying with his broken-thumbed hand.

Blaise clenched fists together over his head.

Bruno scrabbled the gun free.

Blaise drove his joined fists down on the brace-and-wire splint that cradled Bruno's jaw. Bruno roared as the gun came up. Then his eyes rolled back.

"Are you insane?"

MacReedy examined the scene, horror in his eyes. The nurse seemed paralyzed, mouth still open, but shrill words forgotten.

"That's one of the men who put Helen McIntyre in here," Blaise said, before he caught himself. Accusations demanded proof and invited the police and witnesses. They burned a trace into people's memories, creating impressions that could turn sour.

"Call security," MacReedy told the nurse.

Blaise reached across Bruno and lifted the big man's left hand. The gun was still in it. Sergio had been wrong. Bruno did know how to load one. Gently Blaise untangled the pistol. "Don't call security," he suggested, and held the gun.

The nurse put down the phone.

A choking, wheezing sound filled the room.

"I have to do something," MacReedy protested. "He'll die."

"Good." Blaise was still gasping.

MacReedy and the nurse stared.

Leaning against the wall, he gulped air. "You, Miss"—he stared at her name tag—"Levitt . . . will get a wheelchair and take Miss McIntyre out front to a Rolls-Royce that is waiting."

MacReedy looked at Bruno. He nodded. "Get a wheelchair, Miss Levitt."

The nurse clamped her lips in disapproval but turned and went down the hall.

MacReedy moved past Blaise and went to work on Bruno's mouth trying to get him to breathe without choking. "I trust you, Dr. Cunningham, not to hurt Miss Levitt, or anybody in the hospital."

"How's Bruno?"

"You know him?"

Blaise didn't answer.

"I think you've broken his jaw in places it wasn't broken before."

"That's okay. I broke it the first time." Watching MacReedy work, he added, "Be careful, Doctor. He's violent."

"So, apparently, are you." MacReedy's careful voice was neutral, the way he'd been taught to handle unreasonable people in bedside-manner classes. He was used to unpleasant but rich and influential patients. Blaise didn't flaunt money or influence. But he had the kind of power that revolutionists say comes out of the barrel of a gun.

The nurse returned pushing a wheelchair. She went into Helen's room and Blaise stepped out where he could see into both rooms. Appearing alert, Helen helped get herself into the chair.

Blaise caught a handle, guiding the chair and Nurse Levitt to the elevator. "You've got to leave, Helen," he said quietly, "with two men downstairs in a black Rolls-Royce." He looked at the nurse. "You'll be all alone but you will get her there."

"Do exactly as he says, Nurse." MacReedy stood in the doorway of Bruno's intensive care ward. "Then get an emergency team going for surgery and send someone up with a gurney." MacReedy looked intently at Levitt, willing her not to screw up.

Helen was scared but she smiled timidly. "It'll be all right, Blaise." The elevator opened and Blaise shoved the nurse in with the wheel chair.

"The Rolls is at the front door."

Nurse Levitt glared like a cat, wishing she dared bite.

Dr. MacReedy had started oxygen for Bruno. He didn't look up when Blaise opened the stairway door. Blaise waited for the door to settle back into the frame, then ran up a flight and a half, stopping only when he was above the seventh-floor entrance. He put Bruno's pistol on the cement step. Sergio had cautioned him about using a gun he knew nothing about. It might not be loaded, or it could blow up in his face, Sergio said. Blaise unholstered the little *Búfalo*. The slide made a nerve-wrenching metallic sound. He waited.

Noise came and went in the stairwell like smoke in a vacuum. A scrape of shoe erupted, blossomed, and disappeared so quickly it never existed. The walls and pipe railing were off-cream, a pseudocolor without enough character to be described. Stains on the gray cement steps and landings gave the impression of dirt even though the slick surfaces had no grime. Stair landing lights glowed dimly. A door slammed below, then feet began scuffing concrete steps.

Blaise pulled off his shoes, sticking one in each pocket of his sports jacket. A hole in his black sock exposed the middle toe of his left foot, providing something to concentrate on while waiting. The waiting was the hardest. Sweat itched his back.

Sudden noise burst from the overhead landing. Voices

arguing, a door slamming. Footsteps. Blaise bolted down to the turn between seventh and sixth floors. He stopped, panting even though he'd sprinted no more than fifty feet. Footsteps thudded downstairs. Stopped. A door opened again and more noise.

Blaise sprinted back upstairs and sat again midway between the seventh and eighth floors. Sergio had guessed they wouldn't have enough men for a floor-by-floor sweep so they'd try to flush him downward. He went back to waiting. Waiting even after the door below opened and closed again and the footsteps clumped downstairs, followed by the clang of another door.

Without his watch, time would have lost all meaning. The police Nurse Levitt would call should conclude he was gone. West's men by now would have the gnawing suspicion that somehow he fled the building even though they knew it was impossible.

Blaise checked his watch, then took the engraved name tag out of his pocket and pinned it to his shirt. *Dr. H. Williams* put his shoes on, hung his jacket over a banister, and walked out onto the seventh floor. Shift change was right on time and he was instantly swallowed in the group waiting for the elevator. On the way down more people packed into the little metal cage but he kept easing his way to the front. At the main lobby they all spewed out of the elevator in a loose mass. Blaise's long legs got him out the door first. Two paces later he reached the curb just as the car door swung open.

The glass door exploded behind him as someone inside the hospital lobby tried a desperate shot, but he was already dropping into the seat while Sergio drove as if for his own life instead of Blaise's.

Blaise forced the cramped fingers of his right hand open. Through the elevator ride and rush for the door no one had noticed the automatic. "I had to leave the holster," he said.

"Too bad." Sergio looked at Blaise. "But you got your girl." He studied the mirror as they took back roads to the house Blaise had rented. "I gather Bruno was waiting?"

Blaise told him what had happened. At the end Sergio said simply, "You were lucky."

"I thought I did all right." Blaise was not complaining. It was a question.

"You let Bruno catch you."

Blaise waited.

"Bruno's in intensive care because he was hurt bad enough to be put there where he could watch for you. If he'd been faking you'd be dead, Doc." Sergio glanced at him, his face sober. "Almost killed you, and he's not well enough to get out of bed."

"I did the best I could."

"You should have killed Bruno."

"He's your cousin!"

"Should have killed him, Doc. Even if he was *your* cousin."

Blaise didn't say anything. Sergio was offering him a reality that Blaise did not think he could face.

Mathematical precision does not allow for the incoherence of hopes and terrors, daydreams and nightmares. And yet this is precisely the part of intelligence that requires the most study.

FROM A SEMINAR ON
THE CUNNINGHAM EQUATIONS

CHAPTER 25

Sergio dropped Blaise in front of the house.

"You're not staying?"

"No. You see your girlfriend. Rest. Come out to the spa around eight, right at dark. Only when you come off the freeway, instead of north, turn south. Stop at the first motel and rent a room as Mr. Clark. Park out of sight of the street and wait." Sergio contemplated Blaise in silence, brown eyes giving nothing away but reflections. "You should have killed Bruno," he added.

Shrugging, Blaise closed the door and stepped away. "All your cars are painted like hearses," he said.

"We're in a funereal business." Sergio drove away.

"It's not my business," Blaise said to the disappearing car. But it was a business, and he was in it. He began whistling, trying to feel better before he went in the house. The whistling was off key and all he could think of was *Saint James Infirmary*.

Helen leaned against a felt-covered colonial wingback, wearing a woolly white robe he recognized as one of his. The chair arms were wide enough to be benches, but they helped her stand without wobbling.

Neatly wrapped in white bandage, the top of her head came to just below his eyes. When she realized that, Helen ducked against his shoulder and mumbled, "Don't look."

Blaise touched the bandage gingerly, sliding his hand down to the smooth, creamy skin of her neck. His other hand held

221

her around the waist and he felt Helen's weight shift from her legs to his hand. "You're tired," he said.

"Not now." Her hands were on his chest, like a small bird huddling for warmth. Her lips pressed against him until he felt them even through his shirt, and she talked to his skin rather than his ears.

"You've got to go back to bed." His lungs felt squeezed by the shock of how weak she really was. He'd been confident in the hospital that she was getting better, getting stronger, and he'd never considered the possibility that she couldn't be moved. He stepped away and she slumped. Blaise caught her in his arms and carried her into the bedroom.

"Don't," she murmured. "I'm too heavy."

He eased her gently into bed and tucked her in.

She caught his arm with her hand and stared up at him. "Don't go." She whispered it, timidly.

Blaise sat on the edge of the bed and held her hand.

The window faced southwest and sun printed a jagged yellow pattern on the shades he had drawn to keep the light dim.

"What are you and Mr. Paoli doing later?"

"Nothing. I mean, nothing that concerns you, Helen." The question startled him. He'd been thinking about how serious her condition really was, if he'd been right to take her out of the hospital. He didn't want Helen to worry.

Helen looked at him until he was uneasy. "I want you to make love with me."

"My God, you're too weak!"

"You don't want to." A tear rolled down the side of her face and wet him.

"That's not true, Helen. I want to." The tightness in his chest constricted his throat and he had trouble talking.

"Then prove it!" Helen was pulling him down into the bed and he couldn't help himself. He kicked off his shoes and she coaxed him out of his clothes and then under the covers she opened her robe and pressed her body against his.

Her mouth was hot and demanding, but Blaise felt the weakness in her, the timid pulse of her life against him and he held her tight and said over and over, "I can't," until she stopped urging him.

"Alcohol and impotence are like love and marriage," Gordon had told him. "Stop drowning your sorrows in C_2H_5OH

and it'll come back." Feeling the weak tick of her irregular pulse, Blaise was grateful not to be enslaved to raging machismo. Miraculously, her heart continued its precarious pace and after a while she burrowed noiselessly into the pillows. Her eyes closed and her breathing became more regular.

He slid out of bed and drew the covers up to her chin, watching her as he dressed. Unable to tear himself away, he was obsessed with the mystical notion that only his presence kept the thin wisp of her life from departing.

He dozed in a chair until shadows made the bedroom murky, then stretched, went into the kitchen, and drank half a bottle of orange juice. He looked at Dobie in the garage, then came back to the bedroom and left the telephone, a glass of juice, and a note on the nightstand.

Dobie had been comatose, chest flexing with his barely existent breathing.

He had to get Gordon.

The best laid schemes o' mice and men
Gang aft a-gley.

ROBERT BURNS;
QUOTED IN A SEMINAR ON
THE CUNNINGHAM EQUATIONS

CHAPTER 26

Like the ball of a giant's thumb, Earth was snuffing out the sun when Sergio walked into the room rented to Bob Clark. That he neglected to knock didn't matter. Blaise heard his feet on the second-story cement landing long before he got there.

Flopping facedown on the bed, Sergio asked, "Am I sunburned?"

"How can I tell?" Blaise shifted in the chair by the window. The angle made it possible to see out the blinds with a minimum of effort and unlikely that he would be seen from outside. "To me you're a half-baked Italian."

"A New Jerseyan of the Sicilian persuasion."

"Is that a religious preference?"

Rolling on his back, Sergio closed his eyes. "An accident of birth. If you can get through to Dr. Hill, try to get him outside fifteen minutes after you hang up."

Blaise waited, but Sergio faked sleep, either because he didn't want to be bothered or because he was as tired as he looked. The blue pinstripes and narrow cuffs were long gone and he had difficulty identifying Sergio as the same man who had approached him on the plane from San Francisco. The old Sergio had been absorbed by a pearl-gray suit, one image erased and replaced by another.

Dialing the old-style phone brought the almost instantaneous sound of a ring. Gordon answered.

"Cunningham here. I want to give something back to you."

"You'll have to give me a hint," Gordon said.

"I can't afford to keep your dog any longer." Blaise held

the phone through a long pause. Someone had muted the other end because the line was still open, though silent.

Gordon came back on. "That's probably wise, Blaise. A good man knows his limitations."

"I'm sorry, but it's becoming too expensive."

"Inflation." Gordon sighed. "Could you bring him?"

"No. I don't believe you're aware of the situation right now, but I want you to have Dobie and I don't think it would be wise or safe for me to get too close to your employers."

After a pause, Gordon said, "I understand. Have you any suggestions?"

"The desiccated analogue?" It was their oblique reference to the zoo instead of Sea World.

"No."

Blaise could feel Gordon shaking his head at the other end of the line. "It has to be closer."

"Can you take a stroll?"

"Yes."

"Eleventh hole on the golf course, by the dry stream. I'll take Dobie for a run in half an hour. Walk around awhile and give me a chance to see if you're being followed."

"If you think it's necessary, Blaise. But you are becoming very devious."

"It's a learning situation, Gordon. We never know how we're doing until the grades are in. Just be sure you know where the meeting spot is so you don't get lost in the dark."

"I won't be lost in the dark." Gordon didn't even sound cynical.

"Very good." Sergio covered his eyes with his hand after Blaise hung up. "You think he understood?"

"He said he wouldn't get lost in the dark."

"*Che sera, sera.* You should use Italian more, for expression." Sergio thought a moment, weighing the variables, the myriad manifestations of Murphy's Law. "I'll set up the blind. Watch about ten minutes. Keep an eye on me. When I move to the edge of the golf course by the eleventh hole, you come in. If I blink my lights, pass by and back me." Sergio seemed faded, like a watercolor exposed to the sun.

"You feel all right?"

He snorted. "Watch out for yourself, Doc. Bruno had you down one-handed while he was on his back in a hospital."

Blaise pulled his suit coat on. It was a charcoal polyester that looked like gabardine. The little *Búfalo* was stretching his pocket out of shape. "Forty-five's in the dashbox if you want it." The .45 was the gun he'd taken off the man in his house.

Sergio stood, shaking away his lethargy. "You trust too much in guns, Doc. Get yourself a crummy pea shooter and you do everything except throw it at people." The walnut grips on the Magnum showed against his shirt like some hard growth. "I never shot anybody, Doc. I'd like to keep it that way."

Blaise tried a crooked grin. "Take care of yourself. Someone will be waiting."

"If they're not, we wasted a quarter." Sergio held out his hand and Blaise took it.

Following the black sedan to the turnoff, Blaise swung onto the freeway while Sergio continued to where he could sit and watch the Heaven's Gate grounds as long as the light lasted.

Five miles disappears in a hurry on an empty freeway. Blaise came off the rolling hills north of Heaven's Gate in time to see Sergio parked off the road half a mile the other side of the spa. The sedan was a black speck in the dusk, but the lights came on and started moving down the road past the golf course.

Sergio hadn't blinked, so Gordon was walking in the murk as instructed, neither crossing the golf course nor locked in a room somewhere. Blaise pulled into the parking lot, rolling silently toward the restaurant where cars already clustered. Light poured from the building in an attempt to create an air of security.

Most of the buildings behind the restaurant and administrative annex were dark. A few squares of yellow light glowed. Photo sensors had already switched on an occasional pole light around the complex as well as the cabana door lights.

Helen's white Buick was innocent, too conspicuous to be dangerous. Sergio had said so, and Blaise accepted his judgment. But he could not cruise forever. Nor could he park and sit without alerting somebody who knew he was there to meet Gordon.

He neared the door to the club and stopped. The immediate spaces were full. A man in the entranceway wearing a black dinner suit and a vacant expression did not have the air of a customer or parking attendant. He turned to stare at the Buick.

Blaise averted his face and backed up as if returning to a space that had seemed too far. The face in the entrance, cadaverous with sodium vapor shadows, had been familiar. Blaise remembered the hate that filled that face the day he took Dobie. The Heaven's Gate manager would remember Blaise.

He pulled into a space facing the complex, motor churning quietly. Thoughtful, Jensen still stood in front of the building, looking. The glare on the closed window obscured his vision, but if Blaise didn't get out he would come for a look.

Where are you, Gordon? Staring into the gloom, he sensed movement as something passed in front of a window. He squinted. He also saw the manager stalking toward him, very stylish in tailored dinner clothes and black bow tie. Jensen still didn't know, or he'd be running.

Blaise jammed the transmission into low and floored it. Front-end-drive wheels hit the curb and bounced, then came down clawing at cement. His head slammed into the roof when the back wheels hit, and then he was gouging tracks through manicured turf. He eased off. The car skidded broadside across wet grass until he jolted against the walk behind the main building. Running the electric window down, he yelled, "Get in!"

Gordon darted around the car and Blaise heard the door open, felt the car rock, the door slam. The manager was behind them, sprinting across the grass. Blaise jammed the pedal to the metal. The car bucked and skittered.

"The grass is wet." Gordon's voice was coolly amused.

Blaise tapped the brake and they stopped spinning. He nudged the throttle and front wheels caught. A firecracker went off in his ear, opening a tiny hole in the windshield. Immediately, cracks started radiating. Startled, Blaise turned his face to the left, toward the ear that rang. He was staring through the open window into Jensen's face over the barrel of a pistol held in both hands. The next shot was wild behind them as they schussed down the slope onto the first tee.

Gaining speed across the green, the Buick hit the fence that kept the unmonied and unwelcome masses away. The chain link was low and the top pole popped off, allowing the wire to stretch until momentum carried them over and onto the street.

Blaise aimed south. He was on the crossroad before he saw Sergio's car slewed sideways blocking the other street. He hit the brake. The Buick swung like a pendulum as it lost momentum.

Sergio ran while they were still skidding. He got in, breathing heavily as he pushed Gordon against Blaise. He opened his revolver and brass scattered over the front seat. "Let's move it," he said, and began reloading.

They went up the freeway ramp at eighty. Wind through the hole in the windshield made Blaise's eyes water. Headlights followed them and stayed in the mirror, getting bigger and brighter with each mile.

"What do I do, Sergio? Somebody is faster or a better driver." Blaise had to shout over the shriek of incoming air.

"Keep going!" The mirror was blocked while Sergio climbed into the backseat. He knelt facing rearward, both hands straining to steady the Magnum. "Slow down," he shouted, voice tinny in the rushing wind. "Use the hand brake."

Blaise shifted to neutral and pulled the brake handle for a slowdown unsignaled by stop lights. The Buick shuddered but continued tracking. Fast-closing headlights filled the mirror. The concussion of the Magnum left Blaise's ears ringing. And repeated four times as Sergio spaced his shots.

Blaise shifted to drive and floored the accelerator. Carcinogenic stenches of brake pads and smokeless powder dissipated in the wind.

They pulled off on Torrey Pines Road in the shadow of eucalyptus trees that shielded the frontage road like a giant's hedge. Blaise knocked out the remnants of windshield and back glass with a jack handle.

He traded cars at Helen's house, parking the Buick in the garage where its damage wouldn't be noticed, and picked up his VW. Sergio looked at it with distaste.

"It's a car, Sergio."

"Barely."

"Dr. Gordon Hill, Sergio Paoli," Blaise said.

"We've met." Sergio didn't say where, nor did Gordon.

Blaise was abruptly out of small talk. The drive back to the rented house and Helen was made in silence.

The consequences of increased intelligence are beyond the scope of the mathematics. Issues of religion, law, politics, morality, and even the fabric of life itself will have to be addressed in some other arena. We must acknowledge their existence, but leave the solutions to others.

FROM A SEMINAR ON
THE CUNNINGHAM EQUATIONS

CHAPTER 27

Parking the VW in the driveway, Blaise experienced an emotion he had never known. Possessiveness. The night air reeked with ocean smells, lilac, magnolia, honeysuckle, and jasmine. He was reluctant to open the door. They stood until Sergio leaned past him and turned the knob. "Don't want to wake Helen, do we?" he said conversationally.

Gordon kept his thoughts to himself, confirming Blaise's sense that he was among cautious men. Uncertainty enveloped him, a moment of *déjà vu* he had not experienced since just after the death of his parents. Since then he'd concealed self-doubts with alcohol, but they still existed.

Blaise sleepwalked his way into a house subtly different because Helen was there. Without speaking, he continued through to the back bedroom. The table lamp cast a soft glow over the room warming Helen's face with creamy light.

She opened her eyes.

"I didn't mean to wake you."

"I wasn't asleep. Just thinking—worrying. Shut the door."

Softly, Blaise closed it and sat on the edge of the bed. "Gordon and Sergio are here and we have things to discuss and decide. There's a lot I have to talk to Gordon about."

"About me?"

Blaise hesitated. "Partly."

"You don't want to tell me?"

Looking at Helen in bed, Blaise was reminded of young nuns dewy fresh with innocence, unsullied by the gritty contact with the world that hardens adults and makes them different.

"I won't lie to you, Helen. We snatched Gordon because I don't know the answers. I got you out of the hospital because Sergio thinks the people we're dealing with would want to trade you for Gordon."

"I read your note." She touched his hand. "You didn't have to say you loved me."

Blaise was choked for air but he forced himself to bend and press his cheek against hers. "I do love you."

He straightened and the pressure relieved itself somewhat but his stomach remained knotted and he felt giddy. "I've got to see Gordon now. We'll talk in the morning."

Her eyes followed him as he closed the door.

"How is Miss McIntyre?" Gordon asked.

"Better, but weak."

"That's good." Examining Sergio and Blaise curiously, he said, "I take it then that you didn't want me out of Heaven's Gate just to prescribe for Miss McIntyre?"

"Gordon, could you have gotten away without help?"

"That's a good question, Dr. Hill," Sergio added. "I'd also like an answer."

"I see." Gordon settled back in the colonial wingback and contemplated both men. "I got into the car, didn't I?"

"That's not the question, Gordon."

"You're asking, did I want out?"

"That's right."

Gordon picked small pieces of quartz from the soil in a potted plant and began positioning them with his left hand on the broad chair arm. "Leaving would have been difficult, but I could probably have managed."

"Why didn't you?"

"You suspected when you called that my phone was monitored. And if it wasn't, I was expected to tell my friends what you said in order to get rid of them while you snatched me from in front of the spa. You knew when you called, Blaise, that Mr. Paoli was going to be shot at either way."

"Of course, Gordon. What worries Sergio is that you'll contact West or Hemmett now that you know where we are."

"You're not worried?"

"I know you; Sergio doesn't. You saw your wife, didn't you?"

"Yes."

"What happened?"

"It's personal, between Stella and me." Irritation showed in Gordon's voice.

"Of course it is, Dr. Hill." Sergio sat in the shadow, his voice disembodied. "I'm cooperating with Dr. Cunningham because I believe our employers aren't dealing with us in good faith."

Gordon looked at Sergio with what could have been indifference, but said nothing, which Sergio took as an invitation to continue. "Dr. Cunningham pointed out that *nostri amici*—our friends—wanted to repossess a laboratory animal. They wanted the dog so intensely that men like my cousin Bruno and myself were used to get it back.

"It made me curious, Dr. Hill. GENRECT bought and paid for that pup. Doc here stole it. Why not just send the police?"

"What are you, exactly, Sergio?" Gordon's face was as bland as his square rimless glasses.

"They don't grant us degrees, Doctor. You might call me a producer. Like TV news crews—they got a guy puts things and people together and makes them all function. Somebody tells me what they want, I see it gets done."

"Like murder?"

"Like whatever it takes, Dr. Hill."

"What about this Bruno?"

"Bruno has his own interests to protect. Sometimes he does what I tell him and sometimes he does what he wants." Sergio switched on a lamp and the sudden light was shocking. "You're wondering if he kills people, the answer is not always—but he never does them any good.

"Doc here told me Dobie was the only laboratory animal you had left, and you gave him to Dr. Cunningham for safekeeping. That's curious, isn't it, Doctor? I mean, you have all the test animals you want, considering that you're treating humans by the gross. So what's one dog more or less?"

Gordon looked ill.

Allowing him time to think, Sergio went into the kitchen and returned with orange juice and three glasses. He poured and passed them around. Handing one to Gordon, he said, "No anesthesia in this, Dr. Hill." He raised his glass. *"Salute."*

Gordon stared into his glass.

"Dr. Hill, I'm not a humanitarian."

Lifting his head, Gordon examined Sergio at length. "You've had the process?"

Sergio nodded.

Gordon returned his gaze to the glass and Blaise knew the battle was over. "I think, at first," Gordon began, "West feared word getting loose about what Human Enhancements really was. He was under pressure to start showing a return. But government red tape would tie up anything we did for lifetimes. Cancer researchers need years before the government lets them experiment on humans—even terminally ill humans who beg for *anything*. And we were not working on a cure for the terminally ill.

"When I started the experiment, I wanted to see if a superior animal's cortex could learn to control the information potential implicit in a Tillie. It seemed promising. Ample evidence in cases of human brain damage indicates other parts can take over the damaged segment's functions.

"Genetic manipulation was a dead end. The problem is communication. I could have modified the Tillie genes even more, but what could I change it to? The Tillies were already a solution seeking a problem. We needed a situation in which they could be used as is.

"I began to experiment, and I began to have some success."

"You didn't tell me, Gordon." Blaise did not know whether he felt deceived or thankful that he had not known.

Gordon averted his eyes. "You were a . . . risk. Dr. Hemmett wanted to dump you, but I said I needed your computer expertise." Gordon smiled weakly. "A small deceit for your survival.

"I knew I had something when I taught an annelid to remember. Earthworms didn't last, though. The Tillies have a minimum normal mass and eventually the weight and bulk of the Tillie attached to the worm's nervous system caused it to die.

"Insects didn't work; the brain mass was too small, and the exoskeleton caused the developing Tillies to impact on themselves. So I went to mammals. And when the results became substantive, I told Dr. Hemmett.

"I'm sorry I didn't tell you, Blaise. I had a discovery that would immortalize me. I didn't want anybody else to get interested in the line of research I'd taken and"—Gordon shrugged helplessly—"I like you, but—"

"But I was a drunk and desperate and not somebody you could trust. You'd have been crazy to tell me, Gordon."

"Dr. Hemmett brought Mr. West in. Against my objections, but GENRECT was in economic straits and, as I discovered, Mr. West's job is to ensure a profit for Tenro's backers."

Sergio chuckled. "Did you learn who the backers are?"

Gordon shook his head.

"You should have, Dr. Hill. There's Angelo Scapoli and Joe Freedman, who used to be Hymie Liebenstein. Maxie Bloom, the dirty-movie king from Chicago. Arthur Lee Grant, he owns banks he milks to invest in things like GENRECT. And others."

"They're just names to me, Mr. Paoli."

"With all respect, Doctor, you should be able to figure out that these are men who don't like it when they are losing money."

"Thanks," Gordon said dryly. "That occurred to me without even knowing their names."

"Gordon, we know what you did. We're not blaming you. You saved Helen's life. But I think, and Sergio thinks, that things have been going so smoothly because somebody is suppressing any evidence of contraindications. You're part of the evidence. You could blow the whistle."

Gordon let the sentence lie for a while before asking quietly, "Suppose I don't tell you why I didn't?"

"I don't know, Gordon." The weight of the pistol in his pocket made Blaise uncomfortable. "Helen is pretty weak still, so you can't go back until we're able to move her. West ordered me killed. Now they'll want Sergio, too. What would you do?"

"I might lie."

Blaise shrugged. "You don't have much to lose, Gordon."

"My privacy."

Blaise said nothing. To rattle on about things they all knew was not going to produce a revelation, or a change of heart.

Finally Gordon held his hands up. "I didn't like it," he said, "but they offered me too much money. That's the truth of it, Blaise. And there was the other problem."

Slowly Gordon's words began to penetrate. "You didn't do it alone, did you, Gordon? I've seen your lab. You didn't have the equipment or the time to do the actual gene modification."

"That's right." Gordon swirled his orange juice. "Don't you have anything stronger?"

"We're all on the wagon, Doctor." Sergio smiled at Gordon.

"Larval forms are all remarkably similar in physiology. The basic animal form is a worm with limited activity in the cortex. It is boneless. The muscles, vascular system, gastrointestinal tract are all as simple as the nervous system. Only in the advanced stages or in the pupa do larvae begin to develop those special characteristics that vary so in the adult form. Appending a larva to a worm or an insect was easy. But modifications were necessary for it to couple with a mammal."

Blaise nodded. "I should have seen it. You jumped from worms to mammals. No reptiles, no amphibians, no birds. You reengineered the Tillies."

Gordon tented his hands and rested his chin as if too tired to hold his head up. "If I'd let you know about the worms, and then progressed to rats and rabbits and finally Dobie, you'd have worked out what I was doing. I was afraid of that."

"You thought I'd steal your work?"

"No. You're not venal, Blaise. I was breaking a patent. We might even have lived with that. But I was using a lab tech at the TIL facility to do the work—much of it on company time.

"She supplied me with computer-mapped images which I analyzed and rebuilt as theoretical models. The recombinant DNA was more difficult, but she was good, very ingenious. She synthesized what we needed from altered bacterial strains."

"Esther Tazy?"

Gordon looked surprised. "Yes. Miss Tazy."

"Was anything she did of major innovative importance?"

"No. It was fine work. She was grossly underemployed. But her work was substantive, not innovative."

"Esther Tazy is dead, Gordon."

For a moment Gordon was mute. "A shame," he said finally.

"Was she working for Hemmett?"

"He arranged our cooperation." Gordon gave Blaise a questing look. "Perhaps you should be answering questions."

"When I have the answers. I'm sorry, Gordon."

"I know." Gordon examined Sergio. "It wasn't just the money. Without Miss Tazy's help, without the license to do the research, I would have been denied recognition. Technically, my work would have been research piracy. When West and Dr. Hemmett told me they had a human volunteer, maybe I didn't resist as much as I should have. The subject had terminal cancer and was being paid. He told me he needed money for his family."

"And that's it?" Sergio stood. "You started everything from that and then didn't clear out because of the money?"

"No." Blaise waved Sergio back into his chair. "Gordon has an implant, too. He started to worry when they took the lab animals away from him. Tell me, Gordon, when did they start grabbing the animals?"

"When you were in San Francisco. Miss Tazy called Dr. Hemmett and whatever they talked about—and I think it was you—the next thing that happened was moving me to Heaven's Gate before you got back. By then Human Enhancements was underway."

"Then Miss Tazy was done working on your modifications?"

"Months ago. We had a regular supply of modified Tillies at Heaven's Gate. The supplier didn't even know they'd been changed. Miss Tazy modified the procedure and since the owners had eliminated the genetic engineers, there was no one to tell."

"Gordon, I think you'd better take a look at Dobie. He's in the garage. Comatose." Blaise rubbed his face with the palm of his hand. "I want to talk to Sergio. Take your time."

"I trust you, Blaise."

"It has nothing to do with you, Gordon. Just check Dobie."

"If a machine has human intelligence, is it human?"

FROM A SEMINAR ON
THE CUNNINGHAM EQUATIONS

CHAPTER 28

"*Per che?*" Shadows painted Sergio's face a Harlequin mask of conflicting lights and darks. Blaise was beginning to understand Sergio's use of language to present defense as a challenge. He was struggling to reconcile the violence needed to survive with the wish to sever himself from all the meanness.

"Sergio, I think Gordon's going to have bad news."

Sergio said nothing.

"The night before Esther was murdered I was there because I had something she wanted, a Nobel Prize. She felt my luck would wash off. She told me things because she had been waiting and working and scheming so long and finally they seemed in reach.

"I don't think I'll ever understand women, Sergio. Esther was working on a project for Dr. Hemmett. Why should she lie? But Gordon says her work was completed. Why should he lie?"

"Perhaps neither was lying." Sergio held his open hand to the lamp's heat, casting a sinister grid of bars across his face.

"Esther said it would give her career a big boost, and yet she had to conceal her discovery if she wanted to profit economically. She also hated one of the wheels at TIL."

An idea suddenly made Blaise's mouth dry.

"She modified the larva again?"

"It has to be." The backs of Blaise's hands itched as if he had been in poison oak. "Gordon says she was good enough to do something remarkable. And I don't think she'd pass up the recognition, no matter how much money was involved."

"She did on the work for Dr. Hill."

"That was Gordon's discovery. Not hers. But Esther might have kept a secret if more than money was involved. She loved having the last word, and getting even." Recalling his last conversation with Esther, Blaise didn't intend to repeat it. As Gordon said, privacy was the last refuge.

"What could she do, Doc? And who would she be getting even with, and for what?"

"*How*," Blaise said, "is anything that might hurt Technological Intelligence Laboratories. *Who* is someone who'd lose money. *Why* could be anything from a sexual to a professional slight. Esther was sensitive."

"It would have cost her." Sergio had come wide awake. His objection was pro forma, seeking flaws in Blaise's hypothesis.

Blaise shook his head. "Human Enhancements was already making a fortune for Tenro, West's investment company, and GENRECT, a Tenro investment. Dr. Hemmett promised to hire Esther—otherwise, why keep her discovery secret? The problem of patent theft remained, but my guess is West had a scheme to buy the patent if TIL could be pushed over the edge. It would keep Esther quiet: with the patent in their hands she could announce her work as an employee of GENRECT."

"You can check that," Sergio said quietly. "West would have overpaid, perhaps as an advance for work to be done. Then the expected contract hangs up and TIL owes too much money due on demand. After that, a default clause is activated and West forces TIL into bankruptcy."

"I thought you were studying languages."

"I study the people I work for. Different languages don't say different things." Sergio breathed out. "You're probably right. I'll accept Dr. Hill's opinion. But he's been dealing voluntarily with West. Will he go back?"

"Maybe. He talked to his wife and then returned to Heaven's Gate." Blaise studied Sergio. "I brought him here after he inoculated Helen. He's known about Dobie ever since."

"West may have threatened his family."

"He didn't tell us that. He won't talk about what his wife and he discussed." Blaise shrugged. "Gordon came to some sort of personal understanding with Stella. I think it was a pessimistic understanding."

"Do we find out?"

"If he won't tell us about Stella, I don't think he'll tell West about us." Blaise held up his hand and Sergio stopped speaking. Gordon walked in, looking as if he was going to scream. He collapsed like clothes tumbling from a laundry chute.

Sergio unfolded from his chair in slow motion to help Blaise put Gordon on the couch. He stared at Blaise over Gordon's recumbent body. "You go," he said.

Blaise saw a shadow in Sergio's eyes that might have been fear. He walked back the way Gordon had come.

The door to the garage gaped, spilling light into the house. Blaise sat on a small garbage can and leaned back against the wall. Dobie seemed so peaceful on his mattress, the soft lashes of his eyes closed, soft furry muzzle tucked on his front paws.

Very little blood was in evidence. Gordon had opened the skin above Dobie's ear and removed a piece of skull to reveal the brain. Faint lines of blood marked the neat incisions.

Leaning, Blaise looked into the doberman's skull. He had to breathe deeply as his eyes adjusted to the darker interior. When he had seen enough, he patted the dog's warm flank and said, "Sorry, Dobie." He turned the light out and closed the door.

Sergio wasn't pacing, he just looked that way when Blaise entered the living room. "Get some ice, please," Blaise said.

Almost gratefully, Sergio moved out of the room, retaining some of the immutable sense of calm that Blaise had become accustomed to. He came back with ice cubes in a towel. He also had a bottle of washing ammonia. When Blaise glanced at it he tried to smile. "It's not smelling salts, but it might help."

Blaise rubbed Gordon's temples with the towel and passed the bottle under his nose.

"*Shto?*" Sergio said, then repeated himself in English. "What is it?"

"Shock. Acute anxiety reaction. How the hell should I know? Maybe a heart attack." Blaise felt for the pulse in Gordon's throat, the only one he was sure he could count. The throb seemed weak, but it was steady and anyway Blaise was not sure what normal meant.

Sergio reached over his shoulder and peeled back Gordon's eyelid. "Not a heart attack." Sergio started toward the garage.

"Don't go!"

"Whatever it is, I think I can handle it, Doc." Sergio tried to smile, but botched the attempt.

"You'd better be awfully sure."

"I'm a good Catholic boy." Sergio crossed himself. "The Pope protects me because I'm named for Saint Paul's protector."

Blaise examined Gordon. A touch of pink had invaded the pallor. "Do me a favor and be sure, Sergius Paulus."

Sergio winked. "Remember what the old boys did to bearers of bad tidings."

Gordon was starting to regain consciousness by the time Sergio returned. He sat and the blue wingback chair engulfed him as if he'd shrunk while he was gone.

Blaise kept his eyes focused on Gordon.

"You were right," Sergio said. "I shouldn't have looked."

Blaise nodded with a warning glance toward the back bedroom. "As soon as Gordon comes around, if he says it's okay, I'd like a little help. I want to bury Dobie."

Closing his eyes, Sergio nodded.

Blaise wondered at the images in Sergio's mind. He was afraid to close his eyes because he knew he would see Helen. Gordon, and Sergio, and Jonathan Peters—even Bruno!

"Did you ever think, Doc, maybe West had Esther Tazy killed because she could upset his apples if he disappointed her?"

"Yes," Blaise said. "It occurred to me."

Sergio subsided into silence. If he had other thoughts, he didn't voice them, for which Blaise was quietly grateful.

Machine intelligence is linear in terms of time and effort.
Therefore machine intelligence may be increased exclusively
by size and speed of operation and development.

FROM A SEMINAR ON
THE CUNNINGHAM EQUATIONS

CHAPTER 29

Bright, early sun through the window hurt Blaise's eyes.
He checked his watch and looked around. Sergio sat upright
in the colonial wingback, watching Gordon on the couch but
not really seeing him. Gordon didn't move, but his color was
better, indicating he had drifted into normal sleep during the
night. Sergio's eyes had sunk. He seemed aged, haggard to
a degree Blaise would not have believed yesterday.

Sergio turned. "Should we wake him up?"

"How are you feeling?"

"Bad news won't make me feel any worse."

Blaise nodded and Sergio unkinked from the chair. He
went into the kitchen and soon the odor of abused coffee
beans wafted into the living room. Waiting until Sergio brought
coffee, Blaise leaned over, shaking Gordon gently.

Gordon's eyelids snapped open. His irises contracted into
steely gray dots while he turned on the switches in his brain.
Slowly his eyes dilated to normal size. He looked around at
the room and the rose-and-leaf patterned wallpaper as if he'd
never seen any of it. "I passed out?"

Blaise nodded.

"It's embarrassing."

"Only to you, Gordon." Blaise handed him a cup of
coffee.

"You looked?" Gordon sipped coffee while glancing over
the rim of the cup, first at Blaise, then at Sergio.

Neither answered, but Gordon knew. He put the cup down,
scratched his ear, fidgeted like a woman putting on makeup
she didn't need to attain a look she already had. It was not

necessary. He seemed already to have regained his unflappability.

"I gather you want my professional opinion?"

Gordon had not expected any dissent. The pause was for his own benefit. "It's obvious that the dog's cerebrum has been replaced by something that looks much like a five- or six-ounce pupa of the order Diptera." Gordon looked at Blaise. "Sawflies, for the graduates of computer science courses." Nobody laughed.

"I want to bury Dobie. Do you need his body, or anything besides the specimen?"

"Bury it all, Blaise. Then Sergio and I can have a drink."

Blaise stared. "That's all? You're not going to do anything? Test it?" A hollow roar like the thunder of a waterfall blasted through Blaise. He could not breathe, his thoughts had frozen in neutral.

"Test what?" Gordon's laugh shrilled out of his normal baritone. "I know what it is: a genetically modified transitional stage in the life cycle of a fly. If I cut it up, I'll probably find other abnormalities besides its excessive size. If you want a better sampling, there are thousands of bigger ones. I know. I invented them." Gordon cradled his head in his hands.

"All of them, Gordon?"

"I've had suspicions for a long time. At first the tissue looked good, rapid reabsorption and regeneration, a normal cycle for cancer research specimens. But a changed cell structure occurred after a time." Gordon straightened, moving his head as if a crick was binding his neck. "And then Dr. Hemmett destroyed the test animals just before you came back from San Francisco. When they moved my lab."

"You weren't suspicious?"

"I gave you Dobie." Gordon smiled. His lips were strained. "Dr. Hemmett said the animals were being tested by an independent agency. He gave me more animals to experiment with."

"Not too swift, Dr. Hill." Sergio's calm was glacial, but a feel of imminent eruption hovered around him. The discussion seemed to exclude Blaise. He was listening for Helen, but his own opinions were not what Sergio and Gordon were going through.

"No," Gordon admitted. "But I was in so far by then, I had to believe. There was no way to reverse the implants

I'd already done. I had Dobie. I passed him to Blaise for safekeeping."

"And kept on?"

"Yes."

"I could kill you, Doctor. You know that?"

Gordon gazed at Sergio. He wouldn't resist.

"Gordon," Blaise said. "When did you do your own implant?"

"After I gave you Dobie."

"After?" Sergio's mouth formed the word he could not believe, but was unable to doubt. "That was rash of you."

"I didn't have any other research animals I could be sure of keeping to maturity, Mr. Paoli." Gordon's words were deceptively mild. He pushed his rimless glasses back up his nose.

Sergio watched Gordon with bemusement.

"Try it in Latin, Sergio. *Mea culpa.* Gordon, you shouldn't have done it." Hearing his own words, Blaise recognized them as fatuous.

"What should I have done?"

Blaise shook his head and saw his reflection in a sideboard mirror, head oversized and globular because his pale hair made him appear bald. How could he presume to tell Gordon what he should have done? "I don't know. But you can't quit now."

"No?"

"For the same reason you made a guinea pig of yourself. You owe the people who didn't know what they were getting into. You can't bail out and play dead—not if there's any chance."

"You're wrong, Blaise." Gordon had regained some of his vitality. "I don't have to play dead, unless you plan on reincarnating me as Kafka's insect."

Blaise got up from his chair. "If everybody's life is as cheap as yours, then why don't you go tell Helen that?" They glared, locked by different but equally compelling emotions.

"Why don't you see how Helen is, Blaise?" Sergio's soothing voice broke the tension.

Helen sat up when he eased the door open. She smiled, patting the bed edge. She had changed to a blue nightgown.

"You're beautiful in the mornings. Did you know that?" He gave Helen a gentle kiss. Helen blushed and covered her face with her hands, peeking at him over the tips of her fingers.

"Blue goes with your eyes."

"You like it?"

"Yes."

"Sit with me. You've been out there talking."

"Have you been listening?"

"I don't want to hear anything you don't want to tell me."

Blaise sat on the edge of the bed. "That makes me responsible for your peace of mind, and other things."

"It's a power of attorney."

"I wouldn't trust an attorney with what you're asking."

She held his hand. "Blaise, I traded a risk for a sure thing. Whatever happens, I profit."

He put his arm around her and she buried her face against his shoulder, her breath warm and moist on his neck. Her breathing was in heavy gasps. Her back quivered and she held on with both hands. "I really love you, Blaise," she whispered.

He wanted to say something but he couldn't say the words.

"I know." She kissed him.

After a while, Blaise returned to the living room. Gordon and Sergio were gone. He lifted the chintz curtain over the front window. The yellow bug was in the driveway. The garage back door hung open and Dobie and the mattress were gone.

A jungle of plants filled the backyard within the confines of a six-foot redwood fence. Roses, birds of paradise, a leafy orange tree, a towering walnut, and an assortment of bedding flower plants filled the space.

Blaise walked across the yard to a pleasant spot that took the morning sun but would be shaded the rest of the day. Sergio and Gordon were replanting what looked like early tulips. Shovels leaned against the trunk of the walnut tree.

"Sorry about the flowers," Sergio said as Blaise approached. "Soft earth."

"It's a nice spot."

"I wouldn't mind one like it."

Gordon dusted his hands and picked up the shovels, leading the way back to the garage where he stood them in a corner. "Dobie was a good pup."

It was an epitaph.

"Don't let Miss McIntyre poke around in the freezer." He nodded at the white chest against the back wall of the garage.

"Thanks, Gordon."

"I haven't done much to be thanked for." He hesitated and Blaise waited. "It had to be the cancer patient. He led Dobie by months. They never told me he died. But he must have. And somebody else did the autopsy. Somebody they could trust." No cracks showed in Gordon's face. They were all in his soul.

Advancement of human intelligence is a hope for quantum leaps at any time and any stage of development.

FROM A SEMINAR ON
THE CUNNINGHAM EQUATIONS

CHAPTER 30

Like an annoying fly, the blue helicopter snarled over the house, drowning out conversation a second time. Sergio pulled the curtain back to look but by then the machine was past the house.

"Tourist ride," Blaise said. The interruptions of what Gordon was saying annoyed him. "Real estate people taking customers for an aerial view of their new neighborhood."

"The VW is still in the driveway."

Blaise glanced at Sergio.

"If that was me," Sergio said in a voice most people use to talk to themselves, "I'd be after a white Buick with shattered front and back windows. But I might also look for an old VW."

"It's too late to move the car."

"Unfortunately." Sergio let the curtain fall and stepped away from the window. "I suggest you tell Miss McIntyre we're going to move again."

"We can't. I can't, anyway." Blaise clenched his hands in his pockets. "We can't get Alfie out of here in the VW."

"Then we go without the computer. Do you agree, Dr. Hill?"

"I'm not sure what's right." Gordon looked up from the list he was printing in block letters with rounded corners. The letters were so precise a reader might have thought they resulted from some special printing process. "I believe Alfie will give us a constructive chance. Without it..." Gordon shrugged.

"That pilot flew too low." Sergio sat and stretched his legs. The past few days had taken off whatever comfortable flesh he had, leaning him down to wiry muscle and a face of stretched skin over bone. "We can't chance it." His jacket hung open, showing the butt of his pistol.

"How about another way?" Blaise asked.

Sergio fondled the pistol. "Doc, we're running out of alternatives. Dr. Hill and I could stay, though. It'll probably be all the same to us." He looked at Blaise with mournful eyes. "Maybe it would be best for Miss McIntyre, too."

"He's right, Blaise." Gordon looked up from his notes, his face smooth, composed as if none of what was happening touched him. "Time is a factor. Like age, we can't escape it."

Blaise stared steadily at Gordon. "When did you do the implant on Dobie?"

"Two days before the first human subject."

"Then we have that time." Saying it aloud did not make it any more believable. "How about it, Gordon?"

"It's likely that the maturity cycle is unstoppable."

"But you don't know?"

"I'm not sure."

"If Dobie started slipping a few weeks ago and finally came apart a couple of days ago, it follows that human subjects would be experiencing the same problems soon."

Gordon nodded.

"What's the treatment, Gordon?"

"Cat scan, magnetic sectioning scan, brain wave readings and analysis. Possibly exploratory surgery..." Gordon swung his head to look at Sergio. "We haven't heard anything."

Silently Sergio unfolded the cabinet doors on the television and ran the electronic tuner around the stations until he found something that looked like a standup news commentator. Aside from floods in New Jersey and tornados through Brownsville, Texas, and southern Illinois nothing unusual seemed to capture his attention. Sergio lowered the sound but left the set on.

"Either nothing is happening, or it's being covered up." The sky was brilliant blue. Not a day for morbid subjects.

"It's being covered up," Gordon said.

"You're sure?"

Gordon chewed a squared-off thumbnail. "Reasonably sure."

"Then somebody out there is going to be anxious to talk to us, wouldn't you think?"

"I wouldn't hurry to talk to them." Sergio spoke slowly, with the deliberation of a thought-out statement.

"Not you, Sergio. Me."

"Anybody important enough will have a tracer on his phone already. Everything considered, we don't want to be the first ones picked up and in jail." Sergio put his hands in his pockets and went back to the window.

"I'll try to avoid that."

"What are you planning?" Gordon lost interest in his thumbnail.

"Alfie. What else?"

In the dining room where the movers had dumped the computer Alfie clucked his mechanical sounds with occasional LED tattletales winking across his stainless-steel surface. From the front of the house came the distinct, tinny sound of the VW cranking over. Sergio had gone to move it into the garage now that Dobie was not on the floor.

"GOOD MORNING, PROFESSOR. I'VE MISSED YOU"

Alfie's instantaneous response when he started jiggling the terminal keys surprised Blaise. "What do you mean 'MISSED'?"

"YOU HAVE NOT USED THIS TERMINAL FOR A PERIOD IN EXCESS OF ANY OTHER HIATUS FROM TERMINAL OPERATION, PROFESSOR"

"That's observant of you, Alfie."

"THANK YOU, PROFESSOR"

"Can you access Federal Public Health Services files?"

Alfie displayed a list of files related to the Public Health Services. Then Blaise began to enter data about Human Enhancements and GENRECT and Tenro until he had created a file that was brief but comprehensive.

"HOW IS MISS MCINTYRE, PROFESSOR? PERHAPS SHE CAN CONVERSE WITH ME AGAIN?" Alfie's message spread across the bottom half of the screen while the top half flickered with data, as if Alfie was self-consciously proving he remained at work while expressing concern about Helen.

"Miss McIntyre is better, Alfie."

"THANK YOU, PROFESSOR" The message disappeared.

Blaise stared at the monitor. A confusing excitement filled him. Because there was nothing to explain Alfie's behavior, no malfunction to blame it on.

"What are you up to, Doc?" The voice came from over his shoulder.

"I didn't hear you come in, Sergio."

"You were busy, Doc."

Blaise debated telling Sergio about Alfie's message, but that wasn't what he was interested in. Blaise forced himself back to the reality they all faced. "Alfie will plant this in the Public Health Services data bank."

"They'll make a copy for Washington and erase the master when they find it."

"They won't find it." Blaise punched a command. The monitor started running health warning advisories. After a few minutes the advisories signed off, clearing the computer for a new set of instructions. Blaise raised an interrogative eyebrow at Sergio.

"What did I miss?"

"The text. It has embedded commands that won't allow the text to show. But the text goes everywhere the advisory goes."

"You're holding out, Doc."

Blaise smiled. "All over the country, medical computers in hospitals and clinics and doctors' offices pick up the daily advisory. If they record it, and most of them do, the text will store as an unidentified file that the directory will treat as part of the advisory."

"*Bellissimo*! So by this time tomorrow every member of the AMA will have an invisible copy of your statement. You simply say 'let me borrow your computer,' and presto you have a copy on the mark's very own monitor. Right?"

"Better."

"I should hope so, Doc." Sergio sat on the bed. "You just pretend I'm full of whatever it is and tell me."

"It's not a regular file, Sergio. The program responds to the same command that brings up the print controls. If a secretary prints out payroll information she gets payroll information on the monitor and our text on the printer. Every file brought up to print will do this."

Sergio thought about Blaise's explanation for a while. "That's a lot of paper, Doc. I like it."

"Alfie is going to do the same thing to the Federal Meteorological Service."

"Doctors today and?..."

"Newspapers, radio, and TV tomorrow." Shutting down the terminal, Blaise added, "Somebody is going to be mad."

"That's okay, Doc. As long as you have the computer to talk reason to them." Sergio gave Alfie a pat. "I told you guns weren't everything."

"When this breaks, the feds will have to move. Hemmett and West will try to blame Gordon. It's his work. I imagine they'll tie the can to me as well."

"It's not fair, Doc. But I think you've got it right." Sergio straddled a chair. "You want me to do something?"

"Get Helen out of here. Someplace where she'll be safe. Not many people can connect her to me or to any of this."

"You've talked it over with her?"

"No. But she'll do what I say."

"You don't know a whole lot about women, Doc."

"She promised she'd do whatever I thought right." Even to Blaise the words sounded suspiciously weak. He looked at Sergio. "The question is, will you do that for me?"

"We'll see when we come to it, Doc. But you better have a talk with Miss McIntyre before you ship her off into slavery."

"It's not that drastic," Blaise said.

Alfie clucked. Sergio did not.

A mathematical model is smooth, clean, and efficient. But like all theories, we must expect reality to make the implementation somewhat different.

FROM A SEMINAR ON
THE CUNNINGHAM EQUATIONS

CHAPTER 31

Helen wore Blaise's white robe over a blue nightgown. The adhesive skullcap seemed a pert cloche for a flapper in a rumble seat. In white shirt with tab collars, navy tie, gray herringbone vest and pants Gordon looked like the doctor he had once been. They sparkled in each other's company.

Helen's smile changed from delight at Gordon's comment to a different kind of pleasure when Blaise entered the room. He felt the change and didn't know whether it was cause for celebration or mourning. It stifled the slight pang of jealousy he experienced when he saw them together, so obviously basking in each other's company, and it reminded him of how fragile Helen was in actuality—and his responsibility to her.

Gordon patted Helen's hand and looked at him. "You've a plan, have you, Blaise?"

"Cute, if it works." Sergio had read the directions Blaise fed Alfie, and Alfie's responses. With more faith and less knowledge, he had not been as worried as Blaise when Alfie assumed a near-human persona, bragging like some sixteen-year-old hacker about breaking into networks.

Worry chased around at the back of Blaise's mind. But Sergio had been entranced by the computer's tricks. He thought the smart answers were showmanship on Blaise's part, tricky programming, or even an advance in computer science.

"Of course it will, Sergio." Gordon shuffled his notes. "You realize that a man who teaches a machine to think is more devious than a man who instructs a machine in imitating thought."

"I haven't taught Alfie to think yet." Blaise went to the window. The street outside was empty.

"You see, Helen, Dr. Cunningham takes responsibility only for failure."

"That's not a suitable comment, Gordon." Blaise turned from the outside.

"Be quiet, Blaise. Helen seems rashly devoted to you. In fairness, she should know you're committed to snatching failure from the jaws of success." Gordon smiled conspiratorially at her. "Miss McIntyre needs fatherly advice, and since I have no daughter of my own, I'll accommodate."

Blaise sagged suddenly in the nearest chair.

"How do you feel?"

"Short of breath."

"As if you're doing something wrong?"

"No!" Blaise pretended to ignore Gordon.

"You mean it's not as bad?"

"You lied about your six hours of psychiatric training." The statement burst out as hot words. An accusation that demanded support because, without it, Blaise sounded ju₁ venile even to himself. "Alfie checked your transcripts, Gordon. You dabbled at headshrinking for a year before you switched to genetic engineering. Why don't you stick to cutting up chromosomes or something you're competent to do?"

"I'm flattered you took the trouble to investigate."

"It was prudent." Blaise looked at Helen. Her blue eyes expressed shock.

Gordon didn't answer.

"Most shrinks know they're sick. They practice curing themselves on other people."

"You've done your homework." Gordon's voice was steady, his face calm. "Did you find anything else interesting?" When Blaise didn't answer, he said, "You and Miss McIntyre are going to be together a long while. It causes needless suffering not to admit you have problems that she isn't causing."

"I'll tell her anything she needs to know." Blaise knew he was lying when he said it. So did Gordon.

"You fully intend to. But then, tight lips don't sink ships. Do they? This is just a symptom, Helen. He'll recover."

Blaise stared in stony silence. Gordon sighed. "I have some work I want to run on Alfie."

Blaise nodded "What did you mean about Helen and me? Being together?"

Gordon fanned his notes like a professor threatening a surprise examination. "I think I can say that with confidence."

"I'll open up access to Alfie for you."

"I thought you'd never offer." Gordon winked at Helen.

Shutting the door behind them in the makeshift computer room, Blaise leaned against it. "I'm sorry, Gordon."

"For what?" Gordon straddled the stool in front of the terminal. "You're right to be concerned. And I'm right that you're always on the edge of unreasoning paranoia. Uncertainty goes in hand with guilt."

"I'm trying, Gordon."

"So are we all. And you're right. You need help I can't give you."

"I'm afraid of my secrets. If I shared them, I'd be afraid of the sharer."

"You're not afraid of me?"

Blaise evaded the question. He reached past Gordon and alerted Alfie, feeding instructions. When he finished, the screen read, "IT IS NICE TO MAKE YOUR ACQUAINTANCE, DR. HILL"

"Plain English," Blaise said. "Subject, verb, direct object. Alfie will give sources he can access if he doesn't have the data in file. Choose the one you want, or just suggest any, A-N-Y as a command. Alfie always tries to access without being detected. If it can't be done, Alfie will ask for help."

"Seems simple enough. This shouldn't take long." Gordon exchanged his stool for a chair. His face behind the rimless glasses seemed as simple and uncomplicated as a choirboy's. "You're going to have to tell Miss McIntyre about your parents."

"I don't plan to." Blaise paused before he opened the door. "Whoever suggested that I wasn't afraid of you, Gordon?"

Hill's face remained neutral as Blaise left the room.

Alfie had already started acting up. An unprompted message hung on the monitor: "NO SYSTEM TOO BIG. I CAN CRACK ANYTHING"

Blaise hoped Alfie would hold together a little longer. It scared him Alfie was calling himself *I*. Blaise was *I* in the

secret "subconscious" file. The computer could be con-
structing an aberrant self based on all of Blaise's worst parts.

Sunlight crept through the kitchen window, laying streaks
of sparkle across the tile floor. On the walnut coffee table,
Sergio field-stripped the .45 Blaise had taken from the man
in his house, while flirting outrageously with Helen.

"He's faking," Blaise said. "He takes them apart and I
have to put them back together when nobody's looking."

"I can't believe that of you, Sergio." Helen's throaty voice
struck a resonance in Blaise.

Sergio shrugged. "He talks, Miss McIntyre. No secret is
safe with him." He looked at Blaise and Blaise nodded. "I
have to go and thrash him, but I shall return." Leaving Helen
at the table, Sergio walked Blaise across the room to the
window.

"They're here."

"You were right about the helicopter."

"Unfortunately."

They looked out the window. Blaise recognized the mid-
night-blue Chrysler across the street. "Your car."

"My cousin's car now."

"Bruno?"

"*Si.*" Sergio spoke wistfully. "*Sempre fu stupido ma an-
cora s'a tornato pazz'.*"

"He's crazy all right. But he belongs in the hospital."

"Bruno does not have a forgiving nature."

"Can we outsit him? He's waiting for us, isn't he?"

Sergio turned from the window. "Not waiting. He's making sure the bottle's corked before he comes in."

The breeze fluttered the curtains, bringing a sun-dried
grass odor into the room. "We've got to stall. Gordon's onto
something with Alfie." Blaise looked at his wristwatch. "I've
got a call to make."

"I'd hurry," Sergio said conversationally. "Bruno's going
to cut the wires pretty soon."

Helen watched as Blaise picked up the phone. She did
not move her body, just her eyes, like a rabbit caught in a
snare, resigned to whatever fate was going to dish out. Replacing the handset on the cradle, Blaise smiled reassuringly
at her. The line was dead.

After a moment Sergio said, "Well, I've wanted to see
how Bruno manages conversation with a broken jaw."

"With his hands."

"Probably. I think Dr. Hill should be out here." Sergio looked at Helen.

"I'll get him." She got up.

"Get dressed, too." Sergio winked, slowly. "I want to get to like you in clothes for a change."

Blushing like a schoolgirl propositioned for the first time, Helen disappeared down the hall.

Hefting the .45, Sergio drew the magazine with a sharp *click*, checked the loads, shoved the magazine back into the butt, and worked the slide. "You have your popgun?"

"Yes."

"Give it to me."

Blaise handed the little pistol to Sergio and got the steel-gray .45 in return. He examined it with a certain detachment, murmuring "Okay" when Sergio told him to be careful because it was loaded and cocked.

"Alfie just went on strike." Gordon entered the room and saw the gun in Blaise's hand. "The helicopter has landed?"

Sergio nodded. Gordon put on his jacket. "So far, Doc has shown commendable restraint about shooting people," Sergio said.

"That's fine with me." Gordon polished his glasses on his sleeve. "Not my line of work. You do have a plan?"

"I'll walk out and strike up a conversation with Bruno. The three of you walk right on past to my car—the blue one out there—and get in, whereupon I will join you."

"I don't see any holes in it," Gordon said.

"Well, I do!" Helen stood on tiptoe to see over Gordon's shoulder. "You'll get hurt, Sergio. It's not fair."

"My cousin won't shoot me, Miss McIntyre."

Blaise suspected Bruno was more likely to break Sergio up like crackers in soup. He didn't tell that to Helen, though.

"You're lying!" Helen appealed to Blaise and Gordon for support. Blaise took her hand but said nothing.

"Well, it's settled then." Sergio smiled at Helen, forgiving her for calling him a liar. "I'm sorry about Alfie, Doc. But if we move right along they may not even get in the house."

"We all take our chances. Even Alfie." A breeze billowed the curtains, warming the house instead of cooling it. "Santa Ana today," Blaise said to no one in particular. The east wind was sweeping in hot desert air, recompressed and superheated on its seven-thousand-foot glide down the mountains. "Too much exertion and you'll run out of steam."

Already the air was sucking moisture from his skin. Sunlight on the white concrete outside hurt his eyes. In the house, Gordon seemed cool, as neatly buttoned into his suit as a successful encyclopedia salesman. Sergio's blank face reflected nothing of his thoughts, but Blaise knew he was thinking of Bruno. "How do we do it?"

"I talk to Bruno. When I wave, you come out. Move fast because he'll have men around the house. Go right on past to the Chrysler. Gordon drives. Doc in the passenger seat." Sergio smiled at Helen. "The lovely lady goes in back behind Doc. Leave the streetside back door open."

"Just out of curiosity, Sergio, what will you say to Bruno?"

"That I'm changing sides again. What else would you expect me to say, Dr. Hill?"

"I enjoy watching a professional at work."

"Thank you, Doctor. So do I." Straightening his jacket, Sergio wiggled against the seams until the Magnum bulged compellingly. "How do I look?"

"Like a movie gangster," Helen said. She gripped Blaise's fingers, silently begging him to stop Sergio.

"I don't have any better idea." Blaise put his hand on her arm. She was trembling. "Sergio knows what he's doing."

Helen pressed her face against Blaise's chest. She didn't bump the .45. She felt small and fragile against him. When the door clicked open, she shuddered.

Strolling across the yard as though he owned it, Sergio opened the low white picket gate and stepped onto the walk. Like an irresistible force, Bruno surged from an adjoining lilac hedge and clapped his hand on Sergio's shoulder.

They talked. At least, Sergio did. Bruno's jaw was in plaster down to his sloping shoulders and Blaise imagined he was limited to grunts. Finally Bruno unbuttoned Sergio's jacket and took the pistol from the holster. Sergio smiled and waved.

Doorknob in his hand, Gordon swept the room to see what they'd forgotten. "It is always possible that he actually made a deal, wouldn't you say?"

"I'm not betting real money," Blaise said.

"I wish you'd told me that sooner." Gordon stepped outside.

Blaise urged Helen along. She pressed against him, but the shivering had stopped. The sidewalk slid under them too fast. Up close Bruno was more than massive. Solid, without

visible bone structure, his shoulders were rounded with muscle and his barrel chest extended to his stomach. The cast
encasing his jaw and neck gave him an apelike appearance.
Only the glitter of black eyes revealed the attention he devoted to them.

Sergio's Magnum dangled from the thick fingers of his
thumb-splinted hand. Bruno signaled them to stop. Then he
ran a hand over Gordon.

Blaise tried to not think about the .45 tucked into the back
of his belt. Even when Bruno felt Gordon's back with his
hand, Blaise desperately hoped that he would stop searching.
Sergio watched, too. Their eyes met and Blaise could not
tell if Sergio had warned Bruno about the automatic.

Pushing Gordon away with a contemptuous gesture that
indicated his status with Gregory West had deteriorated,
Bruno shifted his attention to Blaise and back to Sergio
before he made a twirling motion. Blaise felt the gun in the
back of his belt and he knew without a doubt that Bruno
would have him one way or another before he could get
halfway to the pistol.

Moving slowly, he turned his back. Helen tried to press
against him and he held her away with his hands. He felt his
jacket lifted in back, heard the exultant intake of breath just
as the gun was pulled from his belt.

"Don't move, Cousin."

Blaise turned and Sergio nodded toward the car. Sergio
leaned toward Bruno, his arm companionably on Bruno's
meaty shoulder with the stubby little *Búfalo* pressed into
Bruno's ear.

Gordon was walking. Blaise grabbed the pistols in Bruno's
hands. They wouldn't budge. Little eyes glared as Sergio
said softly, "Bruno!"

Bruno's hands opened slightly. Blaise pried the guns loose
by the barrels. Bruno's hands felt like rocks. They headed
for the car. Two men trotted out of a yard next door. The
street seemed a mile wide. Gordon stood by the car with
both street doors open. Blaise slid past the wheel, Gordon
following smoothly, slamming the door. Helen was already
in back holding the armrest so tightly her hands were white.
She looked out the open back door at Sergio.

"Damn!"

Blaise jerked his eyes around. It was not in Gordon's
nature to swear.

"No key!" Gordon stared at the dashboard on the driver's side and the computer keypad and screen.

"It takes a code," Blaise said.

Gordon stared helplessly.

Sergio sprang away from Bruno, running bent over. Two men were running, too, and Bruno, ponderously irresistible, was on Sergio's heels so close the others couldn't shoot.

Sergio dove head first into the car, slamming a door already set to lock. Lying on the back of the front seat, he reached past Gordon and punched in the car's access code. The car rocked crazily as Bruno crashed into the side and tried to tear the door handle off.

Gordon revved the engine to a shrill whine and jerked into drive. Smoke squirted from tires and then acceleration pushed Blaise back. Bruno's face was bright in the rear window, outlined by the sun for one frenetic moment, the plaster over his jaw masking emotions but not extinguishing them. Over the sights of Sergio's Magnum Blaise watched Bruno's black eyes recede.

"Here." He handed the gun to Sergio.

Staring out the back window, Sergio stuck it in his holster. "You should have shot him." His brown eyes met Blaise's.

"You had a chance."

"I couldn't."

"Neither could I." Blaise looked at Helen. "Are you okay?" She laced her fingers in his. "Yes."

Blaise tried to smile reassuringly. Bruno was a dot in the street behind them getting into another car that already had two men in the front seat. "You told him about the forty-five?"

"Of course." Sergio smiled. "I had to prove I was telling the truth."

"And if he'd gotten the gun without dropping his guard?"

"*Che sera* . . . Anyway, he didn't."

The car lurched as Gordon turned a corner a little tighter than the vehicle was designed to operate. Blaise banged his head against the door. "Go to Helen's." He directed Gordon to wind through streets that would confuse Bruno and lose him for a while, if not permanently. "We've got a phone call to make."

Gordon's face didn't move as he nursed the heavy limo through intersection speed dips.

The street in front of Helen's home was deserted. Gordon

remembered the house from the last time they switched cars and pulled up in front. Sergio got in the driver's seat.

"Where are you going?" Blaise waved the others toward the house but stopped himself.

"I have to dump the car." Sergio rubbed his hand over the paint like it was a furry animal. "We can't keep it."

"Won't Bruno stop when the heat starts on West?" Blaise realized he had forgotten something, that he had been expecting logic to prevail in a world of human feelings.

"I've shamed him. He's no longer interested in the wishes of Mr. West. *Capicsce?*"

"I understand." Blaise   ed Sergio and the car for a moment. "Leave it. Go in   house and take the bolts off the garage door and have the Buick idling."

Sergio stared at Blaise, trying to read his thoughts, then slowly nodded. "*Tu sei il duce,* Doc. You're the leader."

"I'll remember that." Blaise slid behind the Chrysler's wheel. He sat staring at the dashboard and the computer keyboard as he visualized the manual that came with the car and reviewed the programming instructions.

Helen met him at the door of the house. "What do you have Gordon and Sergio doing in the garage? Sergio's singing the Volga boatman's song in Russian and Gordon got grease on his suit." She tried to smile. Blaise kissed her. He dialed the federal communicable diseases center in Atlanta, using a staff number that Alfie had provided.

"Dr. Renfeld, please," Blaise said to the primly efficient voice on the phone. When the secretary replied that Dr. Renfeld was busy, Blaise said, "He'll speak to Dr. Cunningham."

Max Renfeld came on fast. Blaise explained some details he'd left off the messages Alfie had deposited in the computer.

"Fine, Dr. Cunningham," Renfeld said, "but how do I stop your story from causing a national panic?"

Blaise paused, waiting until he was sure that the man on the other end of the line was ready to listen. When Renfeld stayed silent Blaise said, "When we hear on the radio and TV that Gregory West and Dr. Hemmett have been arrested or are being pursued, and that all Human Enhancement spas have been padlocked by order of the Federal Health Agency, I'll call and tell you."

"That's unreasonable, Dr. Cunningham." Renfeld's voice,

which had started out smooth and full of warmth, now rang a little ragged. "Tell us first. We'll get to the other in time. What's so urgent that you can't prevent a nationwide panic?"

"Dr. Renfeld, if West isn't picked up soon, he's going to murder me and several other people."

"You're overdramatizing, Dr. Cunningham."

"Am I? Well, you're not on site to see the bullet holes."

"I can't promise."

"And we'd have to be alive tomorrow to keep a promise made today, wouldn't we, Dr. Renfeld?"

"Yes?"

"I hope you're taping this."

Silence filled the line. Renfeld finally replied, "Yes."

"Good." Blaise hung up. For a long moment he sat staring at the instrument knowing Max Renfeld couldn't be trusted.

Helen slid onto his lap. "I know this isn't the time."

"Why not?" Blaise kissed her like kissing a baby.

"Blaise, I know Gordon thinks all three of us are going to die. But it's worth whatever happens."

Blaise held Helen tight, knowing he could never tell her about the thing in Dobie's skull: the repulsive hairy body of an insect. She was talking about death as something natural. Not that. "We have to see what Sergio and Gordon are up to."

He smelled Helen's skin and hair as he let her go and tried not to think about what he had seen. Not holding her. Not while he was telling her he loved her.

If intelligence can be raised beyond existing limits, man will have achieved the impossible by doing something past his innate abilities—extending his reach even beyond natural law.

FROM A SEMINAR ON
THE CUNNINGHAM EQUATIONS

CHAPTER 32

Helen coughed when exhaust enveloped them. Even with the open window, monoxides and dioxides and unburned gasoline flooded the garage. Gordon sat behind the wheel staring at the instrument panel while the engine roared in confinement. Sergio pressed his eye against the slot between garage door and the frame watching the street.

Blaise motioned Gordon in back. "I'll drive," he yelled.

Gordon changed places. "There's not much gas."

"It won't matter."

Helen started to get into the car with Gordon and Blaise caught her arm. "When we leave, go out the back door, over the fence into the next yard. Take a cab to the Greyhound depot in San Diego and buy a ticket to Los Angeles."

She was shaking her head. "I won't go."

"Helen, you promised you'd do anything I asked." He looked into her eyes, holding her so she couldn't look away.

"Yes." The answer was grudging.

"You then take a room in the Pickwick Hotel as Jean Ryder. Eat in the restaurant, then go up to your room and stay until I call. If I don't call, use the ticket."

She nodded.

"If somebody gets around to the backyard, sit inside the house on the floor against the wall by the back door for five minutes after we leave. Keep the door locked. You'll hear us go, so don't worry about the noise, okay?"

"Yes."

"Give me a kiss."

She shook her head, but kissed him all the same.

The open garage window and door to the yard were an invitation for Bruno's crew to detour through the house, but they needed air. The garage was already foul.

Sergio waved and Blaise went to the front of the garage. The noise near the hood of the car was even louder.

"Bruno's out there with two men." Sergio moved aside to let Blaise look.

Through the crack, Blaise saw the car that had followed after them with Bruno in pursuit. It was parked across the street with the driver behind the wheel while Bruno and another man inspected the still-idling limousine with obvious curiosity.

"Let's go." Blaise got in the driver's seat. Sergio sat on the passenger's side. It seemed disquieting to Blaise to be staring across the hood of a car with no windshield. "I hope Bruno likes the road map."

"He loves it. Hit the door hard. It'll fall on top of us. After that..." Sergio shrugged.

Blaise studied himself in the mirror for a moment. He didn't look like a hero. His hair was too blond, his face too ordinary. He didn't look mean or muscular enough to yell Geronimo. Revving the motor, he jammed the automatic transmission into low and sent the Buick smashing into the door.

The sound would have been no louder if the house had caved in. For a moment he saw the boards of the single-car door shattering. Then wind caught the upper edge and the car strained. The door smashed down on the car top.

During the instant of blindness the Buick veered off the cement apron and plowed over the grass. A front wheel missed the driveway and dropped to the street with a jolt that snapped Blaise's head back against the headrest. The huge door fluttered off the crushed roof like a leaf in the wind.

Blaise fought for control and the Buick finally straightened out to sprint down the street. In the mirror Bruno and another man piled into Sergio's limousine with Bruno at the wheel. Blaise made a hard right at the intersection.

The street was four tight lanes flanked by eucalyptus and five-needle pines. Built to lug a suburban housewife around with a carful of kids and groceries, the Buick protested with sluggish response and screaming machinery. The limousine gained on them.

Gordon looked out the missing back window, ducking to leave the mirror clear when Blaise yelled. Blaise's eyes watered from squinting into the wind. He saw his road coming, only a break in the towering trees.

Standing on the brake, he slewed the car sideways and then ducked into a hard left turn that shot uphill for a moment. At the crest, Blaise went over the top, skidding to the right into a tight alleyway where they crashed sideways against a log berm. They were jolted, but the car stopped.

Bruno was still accelerating when the limousine topped the rise with its front wheels momentarily off the ground, spinning fullbore. Not for long. Bruno hadn't a chance to slow before the Chrysler hit the barricade at the end of the fifty-foot-long street. Two tons of metal took out the white-painted four-by-six posts and metal guard rails thirty-five feet above the rocky beach. The second car had nothing to hit at all until it landed on Sergio's already shattered Chrysler.

The Buick's starter made raucous tinny noises until the hot engine caught. Blaise backed out of the alley. The front end swayed as if the suspension had torn loose and the steering wheel kicked in his hands. He nursed it down the street into a small corner repair garage. Sergio and Gordon didn't say much. Gordon appeared ill. Before the cab arrived he went into the washroom to throw up.

"You changed the map," Sergio said when they got out of the cab in front of the rental house.

"Like flopping a negative in the darkroom," Blaise said. "I reprogrammed the computer to reverse east and west. Bruno thought he was turning onto a mile-long boulevard where he could run us down." Blaise breathed deeply smelling the neatly clipped grass, the well-kept flowers. Nothing seemed changed. Even the beach with two smashed cars on the rocks had looked somehow normal. "All Bruno saw on the screen when he was chasing us was a long, straight street over that little hill. He didn't have time to remember the ocean was on that side."

"You remembered that from reading the manual?"

Blaise shook his head. "All I had to know was how to program the computer. The rest I already knew. I'm sorry about Bruno." Blaise wondered if Sergio really understood. They might have run for safety, but Bruno would surely have gone back for Alfie. He shut his eyes. He couldn't tell Sergio he had boobytrapped his cousin for a garbagecan full of silicon chips.

Sergio stared through the trees at the blue glint of ocean. "I'm glad it worked out this way. I should have shot him when I had the gun in his ear. I'd have had to eventually, or let him kill me." He sat on the edge of the porch, leaning against the house, and said, "I think I'll just sit in the sun awhile. I feel tired. Sometimes I wish I'd never started any of this."

Blaise glanced at Gordon, who only shook his head slightly. Quietly they walked past Sergio, Blaise going to check on Alfie and Gordon in the bathroom to wash away the taste of vomit.

"Nobody's touched Alfie." He sat on the couch next to Gordon, feeling as drained as Sergio must be feeling. "Was it worth it, Gordon?"

Gordon's face revealed lines Blaise had never seen before. "Philosophy—or truth?"

"If I can't stand the truth, I'll stop you."

"When I opened Dobie up it was too late for me. I had suspicions. Confirmation was worse." Gordon's twisted face exposed an indelible loathing. "You saw what my brain will ultimately become. If I let it."

"You said that Helen..." Blaise let the question hang. He couldn't phrase it in a way that didn't freeze his mind into a tight little corner.

"For a while. Maybe for a long while, Blaise. What remains is foreign—alien." Gordon spoke softly and Blaise strained to hear. "I am already dead. What I was is no longer what I am. And yet I exist—but different. If I who am already dead kill the thing I now am, perhaps I do an injustice to the new I who never asked to be condemned to life in this body." He smiled weakly. "Fortunately that is no longer an issue."

Blaise stared at Gordon.

"For you it is. And for Miss McIntyre. But Sergio has been altered longer than I, and I have been altered too long. The change has started. Physical changes that will make my brain irreversibly into a thing like you saw inside Dobie."

Gordon stared at his hands, as if memorizing the fingerprints as the symbol of the unique individuality of a man. "You don't see, yet. But you will." Gordon slipped back into silence. Measuring what he was going to say.

"I told my wife not to expect me back. There is the insurance. I must make sure that she collects it."

Blaise started to object and Gordon waved his words away. "What I am going to do is the right thing. Neither the I who was nor the I who is wants to turn into what Dobie was becoming." Gordon put his hand on the end table and absently started to arrange small odds and ends in neat patterns with his fingers.

He saw himself doing it and grinned wryly. "A surgeon has to keep his hands supple, with a brain in every fingertip. I started this in medical school to make my left hand as educated as my right—and then my right better—and now I don't know if I'm right- or left-handed."

"You're upset."

"To put it mildly. I'm telling you this because of Miss McIntyre. She will, ultimately, experience the same thoughts but she won't be able to tell you any more than I could tell my wife. Only she will have a choice."

Blaise waited.

"The answer is in the computer. Alfie found it and I told him to guard it with his life." Gordon made a rueful face. "That may not have been the thing to tell a machine, Blaise. After I typed the message lights flashed and Alfie started making more noise than the Holland Tunnel blowers."

"You can stop the process?"

Gordon nodded. For an instant Blaise was afraid he was going to faint. "If the treatment is soon enough."

"What's soon enough, Gordon?"

"I wouldn't wait past immediately." Gordon looked at Blaise with an expression that mixed compassion and sorrow.

"Is there anything I can do for you, Gordon?"

"Thank you, Blaise. You may not appreciate it, but you've been a good friend. I appreciate that. I want you to know I do."

"Sergio? . . ."

"We've worked out what we're going to do. It's better that you don't know."

Blaise nodded. "I think I'll talk to Sergio for a minute."

"He doesn't have a choice, Blaise. The cells are trying to go dormant on him, to complete the biological change that has started. In a couple of days he'll be as torpid as Dobie was."

"It's okay, Gordon. I just want to talk."

Blaise sat on the edge of the porch next to Sergio, feeling the hot sun soak into his body. Sergio's head was back against the reddish brown stucco wall. In California the color was called adobe even when it was mixed in mortar and sand. Sergio's eyes were slitted so tightly Blaise couldn't tell if they were open or not.

"Gordon tells me you two have cooked up something."

"Too much education makes a blabbermouth, Doc."

"I'm sorry, Sergio. I thought it was for all of us."

"Not your fault it didn't work, Doc. Besides, Miss McIntyre is a nice girl. If I had the time I'd take her away from you."

Blaise didn't answer.

"You're supposed to laugh, Doc."

"I'm sorry, Sergio. I think I'm out of laughter forever."

"It's okay, Doc. I like the idea that somebody's going to miss me. Before there was only Bruno. He would have laughed because he figured he'd inherit my gun and my car." Chuckling, Sergio said, "It's funny, he got the car, and I'm laughing."

"There's nothing I can do?"

Sergio opened his eyes and squinted at the sky and the sun. "No, Doc. I'm so tired all I want to do is lie down and sleep." He yawned, exposing even white teeth that flashed in sharp contrast to his leathery tan. "Dr. Hill's a good man, but he takes too much too seriously. He thinks it's a bad way to die, but we all die sooner or later and for everyone it's the same. We just...stop. Doesn't much matter how, does it?"

"I guess not." Blaise wanted to say something to comfort Sergio, but Sergio was comforting him.

"You know, Doc, Gordon wasn't sure he should leave the treatment for you to use on Miss McIntyre. But he was reading Miss McIntyre the way he read himself. He can't stand to live the way Dobie was changed, knowing it's going to happen to him. He thinks the same thing will happen to Miss McIntyre. And you. That you won't be able to stand the strain of knowing what might happen to your lady."

Blaise was cold. The sun was not reaching his insides where he lived. "Why do you tell me this, Sergio?"

"Miss McIntyre, Doc. She's a nice lady, right?"

"Nice enough. Too nice."

"That's what I thought." Sergio rolled his head, stretching his neck. "I figure, Doc, if you give up on her, she'll give up on herself. Then Dr. Hill will be right and the three of us will have saved nothing. I don't want that to happen. Dr. Hill is a brilliant man, but he's not right about everything. Not about Miss McIntyre and not about life."

"You and Gordon are up to something, aren't you, Sergio?"

Sergio smiled. "I'll tell you the truth, Doc. If I could make it, I wouldn't change a thing. I don't care what's in my head holding me together. It's so much better than what I had before that I can't make a comparison. If I could live, I'd live just as long as I could.

"Dr. Hill, he sees things differently. His life wasn't much changed by the implant except that it ties him into what he sees as an awesome responsibility. He didn't get so much smarter or faster or richer that he feels the penalty is deserved."

"Helen didn't want to be any of those things."

"That's the point, Doc. She wanted to live to be with you. If she can do that and hang on to the idea that the alternative to what she has is nothing, she'll be all right."

"You're saying it's my responsibility, aren't you?"

Sergio grinned. "I knew you'd get it, Doc."

In any endeavor of this magnitude, there are always penalities to be paid.

FROM A SEMINAR ON
THE CUNNINGHAM EQUATIONS

CHAPTER 33

After getting a printout of Gordon's instructions to Alfie, Blaise took the VW out of the garage. The paper crinkled in his shirt pocket. He had memorized the contents, but hard copy was insurance against error.

"How about a ride?" Sergio leaned against the VW talking through the open window. When Blaise nodded, Gordon and Sergio got into the car.

"Where to?"

"How about a car rental agency?"

"The airport?"

Sergio looked at Gordon who said, "Yes. That would do fine." Gordon seemed to have lost some of his gloom.

"I'll have the phone fixed. Come to the house or call."

"Sure, Doc." Sergio smiled. "As long as you keep Miss McIntyre around to dress up the place."

"Gordon?"

"I think, Blaise, we had best go our separate ways for a while. We may have Mr. West and Dr. Hemmett off our necks but several targets are safer than one Valentine's Day massacre."

Anticipating Blaise's reluctance to accept this, Sergio asked, "Could West and Hemmett have known what would happen?"

"Maybe not," Blaise said, "but they didn't try to stop it after they knew something was seriously wrong. It was dollars against people, and the people lost."

"What will the feds do?"

"Sweep it under the rug."

"They can't!" Gordon exploded. "There are a couple of hundred thousand victims around the world."

"No one will miss them among all the billions. No panic, no rush, sealed records."

"It's not fair."

"That's right, Dr. Hill." Sergio glanced over his shoulder. "It's not fair what they did to you and me and Miss McIntyre. But that's the American way of life. A car thief does more time than a murderer. He gets caught oftener. He serves a greater percentage of his sentence. Everybody on the parole board has a car. How many have wives or husbands who've been murdered?"

"It will catch up with them." But Blaise didn't believe it. They were rolling across the reclaimed tide flats that housed a good chunk of San Diego's tourist industry. "I meant to ask, Sergio, how did you find Gordon and me at Sea World?"

"You had the Burkhalter girl with you. She called her uncle every time you went somewhere and he called West."

"I guessed that already," Blaise said. "But why would Milo tell West what Gordon was doing? Or what I was doing?"

"Blackmailing each other. Burkhalter knew about Human Enhancements and Hemmett was sure you'd told Burkhalter what Gordon was up to when you were in San Francisco. So Mr. West sent some people up to the city and they came back with a way to twist Burkhalter's arm."

"Do you know what they found out?"

Sergio tried to look hurt. "The company I worked for is a secret organization, Doc."

"Milo must have known the larvae would develop into adults."

"We've been over this, Blaise. They knew something or they wouldn't have gone after the lab animals." Gordon's voice was disinterested. "Maybe if Dr. Hemmett hadn't suborned Miss Tazy, the Tillies would have remained quiescent. I don't know. The early lab animals, done with the first batch, never converted. Maybe they would have. I never got a chance to find out."

Blaise would have pursued the questions, but San Diego International appeared on their left, across the road from the bay. Gordon didn't want to waste time rehashing it all. Sergio obviously didn't see much point in it either.

Sergio leaned back into the car at the airport and held his hand out. When Blaise took his hand Sergio pressed the little pistol into his palm. "Sleight of hand. Bruno should have thought of that. I've been palming things on him since we were kids." Sergio smiled crookedly. "I was a pickpocket. I'd go to LaGuardia or JFK and walk through a crowd and board an airplane with a bag full of money and credit cards."

"Thanks." Blaise switched the gun awkwardly and took Sergio's hand. "I'm glad we met, Saint Paul's protector."

"Me, too, Signor Pasquale."

"Talk to my wife, Blaise. She wants to thank you."

Blaise took Gordon's hand. "I'm sorry, Gordon."

"Don't be. I knew enough to be careful. Instead I was greedy." Abruptly Gordon let go and walked into the terminal. "I'd better stay with him, Doc."

"Thanks."

Sergio smiled like he didn't have a care in the world and followed Gordon.

Blaise drove past the long row of cabs waiting for a spot in the airport hack stand and swung back out toward the bay and Harbor Drive. Fishing boats and seafood restaurants whizzed by and then he was downtown, parking a block from the Pickwick.

Helen answered the knock as if she'd been ready to jump since she checked in. She pressed against Blaise. "I was afraid you wouldn't come."

Blaise held her for a moment, then sat her on the bed and turned on the TV. He fiddled with the tuner until he had a news program. "Did you eat?"

She looked at the floor. "No."

Blaise wrapped his arms around her so she could burrow between them and feel safe. "No use moping. You have to eat."

"I wasn't hungry."

"Gordon and Sergio are all right."

"I'm glad."

They watched the news but the commentator did not mention Human Enhancements or Gregory West or Dr. Hemmett.

"Idiots!" Blaise began sweating.

"What's wrong?"

"Some jerk convinced Renfeld's people he can clean out their computers and prevent me getting into them again."

"They won't do anything?"

"They're not trying."

Tall buildings along Broadway shadowed the street. Façades darkened as the light left. Blaise bit his thumb.

"What can you do?"

"Wait. Until the feds take an interest, none of us is safe." Pictures and talking heads flashed across the screen.

"Do we still have to hide from those men? It's only Mr. West, isn't it? He's the one sending those people after us?"

Blaise took her hand. "Don't worry. I'll do something."

"Blaise!" Helen jerked away. "Did you see?"

"What?"

"The TV!"

Gordon filled the screen. He sat against a wall, arms wrapped around his chest. Blood was turning his gray herringbone vest dark red. Blaise followed the line of red stain to the edge of his coat. A red bead formed and dropped repeatedly.

"Why don't they stop the blood?" Helen whispered.

Crowd noise filled the room. Somebody was yelling about a doctor. A microphone pushed into the camera's line of sight.

"Sir. What happened?"

Gordon's face was damp with sweat. His rimless glasses were askew but his face was smooth and unlined as Blaise had always remembered it. He opened his eyes and the irises were starling: ice chips of blue fire. He seemed to look directly at Blaise.

"I'm a research scientist for GENRECT." He was sweating freely, but his eyes didn't reflect the pain. He gasped for air. "My name is Dr. Gordon Hill and I was coming to warn that people are being murdered by Gregory West." Gordon stopped talking to pant.

A background voice saying "you shouldn't be doing this" was suddenly cut off. Blaise felt himself trying to breathe for Gordon, willing the bleeding to stop. The microphone remained in front of Gordon's face.

He had closed his eyes with the effort to breathe, but he opened them again. The mike floated closer and the camera revealed a hand in plaid shirt cuff and a stainless-steel watch band. The digital watch changed to 5:26. Gordon's breath rasped.

"Mr. West represents gangster interests." Gordon's lips were pale but his eyes still glinted. "He sent a man to kill me before I could talk."

An ambulance attendant pushed in front of the camera and for a moment the back of his white coat filled the screen. The camera pulled back to show people drawn to Gordon like iron filings to a magnet. The paramedic tried to stop the blood.

The hand-held camera jiggled. "Moments ago the man you see came into our studio offices claiming he had information that had to be made public. Before he could talk, an unidentified man came in and shot him once in the chest. The assailant then left by the front door and disappeared."

A man in a suit walked up to the ambulance attendant and stooped to whisper. From the back, the camera caught the negative shake of his head. The voice said that the alleged Dr. Gordon Hill was not doing well. The police arrived.

Blaise turned off the TV and lay on the bed, his body rigid.

"Poor Gordon." Tears made Helen's cheeks shiny.

Blaise didn't say anything. His insides hurt from trying to keep Gordon alive.

"Will he die?"

"Yes."

"I'm so sorry for him. And for you, Blaise." Helen put her hand on his and gently stroked it. "He was like a father or an older brother to you." She caressed Blaise like a mother comforting a child. "What will we do now? They haven't stopped looking for us."

"We wait." Blaise looked at the ceiling remembering Gordon as he was, feeling another void open, wondering if Stella Hill—how long would it take her to see one of the inevitable reruns?

Helen walked around the room closing blinds. When it was dark enough she returned to the bed and lay against Blaise and held him. He didn't speak but he didn't push her away.

There was a knock on the door.

Helen's body tensed and she clung to Blaise. He stroked her for a moment. "Open it," he said.

"Are you sure?" she whispered.

Blaise nodded.

She looked at him but did as she was told. Unlatching it, she turned the knob and opened the door.

"Sergio!" She threw her arms around him.

"I've been expecting you," Blaise said.

"You heard?"

"We saw it on TV."

"I'm sorry." Sergio wouldn't look at Blaise. "I had to come."

"I was expecting you." Blaise got off the bed feeling old.

"I suppose you still have that little pistol." Gently Sergio moved Helen aside and she was suddenly rigid.

"Of course. It's a keepsake. It's all right, Sergio." Blaise took Sergio's hand in both of his. "I understand. But I don't think there's any safe place in San Diego for you."

Sergio's face that had been a mask until then seemed to dissolve. Tears streaked his face. "I know. But I had to see you. And I want you to go with me."

"No!" Helen stood back from Sergio and all but screamed. "You can't, Blaise."

Sergio fumbled in his coat pocket.

"It's all right, Helen." Blaise turned to Sergio. "Do you have a car?"

"Lot across from the courthouse and city jail. It's a creamy Mercedes with all sorts of gadgets." Sergio smiled. "I'm not sure I should go get it."

"Give me the ticket."

Helen looked stricken.

"Come with me, Helen. We have to talk." Blaise glanced at Sergio, who seemed to understand. He handed over the ticket.

"I have something else."

Blaise looked at Sergio.

"From Gordon." Sergio raised his hand. A tiny ball of black curled in his palm. The kitten raised its head, its eyes a startling blue in an all-black face. Huge triangular ears dwarfed the tiny head. "She's for Helen."

"For me?" Helen took the animal. It mewed, then curled up in her cupped hands. She held it to her cheek.

"I'll pick you up out front in ten minutes exactly." Blaise glanced at his watch and Sergio repeated the gesture.

Helen looked from Sergio to Blaise as Blaise took his arm. "Sergio . . ." she said. It was like the cry of a wounded animal.

His long legs ate up the sidewalk and Helen devoted her limited energy to keeping up. She cuddled the kitten against her body. Time was clicking away in Blaise's head.

Even though evening was enveloping the city, the sun

made concrete sparkle and the green patch around the court-house resembled an oasis in a surrealistic desert. The parking lot attendant surrendered the keys to the Mercedes with no comment about Blaise not being the man who parked it.

Helen sat very still while Blaise turned the key. "Sergio shot Gordon. That's why you took me with you."

"Yes." Blaise let the engine run.

"I won't ask you anything you don't want me to know." She picked at the leather seat with a tapered fingernail, then stroked the kitten. "But he might kill you. He must have gone back to work for Mr. West."

Blaise pulled Helen close. She didn't resist. "He could have killed us in the hotel if he wanted to. He came back so I could kill him."

"I don't understand." Helen's voice was small, and scared of the things that were happening around her.

"Gordon wanted to die in a way that would absolve his family from guilt and persecution. He wanted his wife to collect his insurance. But it wasn't just money. He didn't want Stella to be the widow of a mad scientist who did something so horrible he couldn't stand himself. Or his children to be the offspring of a ruthless, greedy man.

"Gordon was never a captive at Heaven's Gate. He just made me work to see him, to make him seem innocent in my eyes. He knew something was wrong. Playing games with me and Sergio created an impression he knew I'd pass on to his wife.

"Insurance wasn't money. That's why they went together. Sergio liked Gordon. He was willing to do anything for him."

"But to kill him!"

"That takes a lot of love. They did it for us, too."

Helen pulled away, aghast. "How could they? Why would Sergio come so you could shoot him if it was for us?"

"He had to know if I understood. If I didn't, he was willing to die."

"Let you shoot him?" Helen's wide eyes reminded Blaise of the last image he had of Gordon.

"I'd be a hero for shooting Gordon's killer. It would cement my alibi that I was a victim, and I could corroborate Gordon's story that he was escaping from West." Blaise had driven up C Street, scraping past the trolley tracks before swinging around to head south toward the hotel. With four minutes left to go six blocks he dawdled to catch red lights.

"Suppose Gordon died before he could say anything?"

Blaise looked at Helen a long time before answering. The light changed from red to green. "Sergio would have let the police catch him so he could confess. Either way they'd be after West for murder." A car behind honked and Blaise started the Mercedes rolling again.

"Sergio is a brave man, isn't he."

"Sergio is a brave and honorable man and what is done must be respected. He wants to do something else, and I have to help."

"You can't refuse?"

Blaise rolled up to the white passenger zone and parked without stopping the engine. "Were you able to abandon me?"

Helen pressed her tear-wet face against his. He kissed her. There wasn't anything else to say.

The door opened, throwing a spear of light into the car and Sergio leaned inside. "Time to break it up, lovebirds."

Helen looked at Blaise.

"Stay in the hotel until I get back."

She nodded and got out. The kitten purred with rusty efficiency in her hand.

"Good-bye, Miss McIntyre." Sergio held out his hand.

Helen stepped past it putting her arms around Sergio's neck and kissing him. "I love you, Sergio. For everything you've done. Everything!" She whirled and rushed into the hotel.

Blaise didn't look. He knew Sergio was crying and didn't want to embarrass him.

The pursuit of greater intelligence is a search for a new beginning rather than an ending.

FROM A SEMINAR ON
THE CUNNINGHAM EQUATIONS

CHAPTER 34

Blaise drove up the peninsula with Sergio sleeping in the passenger seat. At a roadside motel tucked against a hill with a gray stone wall separating the grass from the road he swung the Mercedes onto a rock-edged driveway. Gravel crunching under the tires woke Sergio. "Gas?"

"Sleep." The sudden silence hurt his ears after ten hours of eyestrain in the dark.

"What for?"

"I'm beat and you're not much better."

Swiveling his head, Sergio said, "It's daylight. Morning. This is no time to stop."

"Sergio, tired men make mistakes."

Sergio sighed. "You're right. But my time's running out, Doc. I feel like I'm made out of lead."

"You've got the amphetamines Gordon gave you?"

"*Si, signor.*" Sergio patted his pocket. "You know, it's a waste learning all those languages and then never any chance to use them. I saw a world cruise ad: a hundred and twenty-seven countries in two years. I only had to learn forty-four languages and dialects to be a native speaker in all of them."

"You'd still have to learn a hundred accents."

"Hell, I could do that standing on my head, Doc. New Jerseyans know all about accents just naturally."

"I'll check in. Okay?"

"*Oui.* I might not have gotten French quite right, Doc. It's a bitch to pronounce."

"You'd have managed, Sergio." Blaise winked slowly, the way Gordon always used to. At the reception desk he signed for a detached cottage and asked the clerk to arrange for a

275

telegram. She connected him with the Western Union operator and he dictated a message to be delivered the next day.

They parked out of sight even though Sergio said the Mercedes was rented for a week. Blaise collapsed on one bed. His eyes throbbed in beat with the ringing in his ears and he tired quickly of the wallpaper's endless rows of green vines and forget-me-nots. He heard Sergio sit, the other bed creaking slightly. Then the double thump of shoes hitting the floor.

Blaise shook Sergio in the early afternoon. At first touch his eyes popped open, but it took minutes to come fully awake.

While Sergio took a cold shower that seemed to last for hours, Blaise strolled the grounds, stopping finally at the pool where he sat in an orange deck chair and watched tourist ladies sunning in skimpy bathing suits while their hirsute husbands churned the pool to a froth.

"You're out of place, Doc." Sergio drifted up behind Blaise with the noise of a floating feather. "Naked, you're one of the boys, but with clothes you're a competitive stranger."

Sergio's eyes were bright and shiny with glistening black pupils and soft brown irises guaranteed to seduce girls who loved horses. The weights seemed cut loose from his arms and legs. He moved with the brisk assurance of strong-muscled, compact men. "You were right about the sleep."

Unfolding long legs from the lounge chair, Blaise walked to the car feeling ungainly. Sergio had become a predator scenting prey. All the careless movements of just living had dropped away to reveal the grace of a hunter.

"You took the pills?"

"Yeah, Doc. If I sleep again, I might not wake up. It's all or nothing now."

"We'll do it."

They got into the car. Sergio didn't speak again, even when they turned between hand-quarried granite block walls into the Burkhalter driveway.

The bell got faster results than Blaise's last visit. Linda opened the door, drawing back in surprise and something else. She might have closed the door, only Sergio pushed, moving her back into the little hallway.

"Come in." She walked ahead of them, hips moving with

catlike grace under the black velour of a one-piece strapless sheath. "We have company," she said as she led the way into Milo's study. Blaise's memories of the room had gnawed at him. Then it struck him: the room was like an office entrance, an affable façade behind which Milo Burkhalter concealed his motives.

Milo looked up from his desk with its bright-green glass and brass lampshade, the real thing, not plastic. "Dr. Cunningham." Milo stared at Sergio. "And friend?"

"And friend," Blaise affirmed.

"After last time I'm surprised you would have the temerity to return . . ." Despite what he said, Burkhalter seemed neither surprised or amazed. He picked up the telephone and began punching a long distance code.

Smoothly Sergio reached over the desk to unplug the cord. He smiled at Milo.

"What are you doing?" Linda's voice rattled hysterically off book-lined walls and leather furniture.

"Yes, my dear boy. What *are* you doing?" Milo stared at Blaise, ignoring Sergio as he settled back into his chair. His white hair caught the light making a halo around his face.

"Sit down, Linda." Blaise held a chair. She looked at him and he added, "Please." She flounced but she sat. "I've thought of some things we didn't talk about the last time, Milo." Blaise sat where he could see both Milo and Linda. He nodded to Sergio, who stepped back from the desk and sat with unblinking eyes riveted on Milo.

Milo fidgeted with his desk drawers, his hands out of sight. "We have nothing to talk about, Doctor. You insulted me and embarrassed my niece." He paused. "Your actions are inexcusable, Doctor. Have you forgotten how to be a gentleman?"

"You didn't call me a liar, Uncle Milo."

Milo looked startled at Blaise's use of Linda's name for him. "What's to stop me from calling the police and having you arrested for breaking into my house?"

"Do you think he has the drawer open yet, Doc?" Sergio's voice was relaxed from the highback leather chair.

"Why not show him, Sergio?"

Sergio opened his suit coat slowly until walnut pistol grips showed clearly against the white of his shirt. Milo's face turned suddenly sullen and dangerous.

"I trust you note that Sergio has not bothered to draw."

Shifting his eyes to Sergio and back, Milo carefully put his hands on top of the desk. He pulled his chair closer to remain comfortable in that position. "I recall that you do bring guns into my house and threaten me, Dr. Cunningham."

"I want to ask some questions. Then my friend has a few."

"I have nothing to say to you other than get out."

Blaise contemplated Linda in silence while Milo waited for some effect from his words. "How's Jonathan?" he asked.

In the soft black dress Linda appeared even smaller and more in need of defending. It was a quality that certain women had. She could be bigger than Helen and Blaise knew he would still have the same reaction.

"Not well." She said it very softly and looked away.

"You were going out?"

She shook her head. Looked at her uncle, then at Blaise.

"Time is running out, Linda. Do you know what is going to happen? Soon? In just days?"

She turned to Milo, eyes of imperial green, which is fuller and more alive than the apple-green jade prized for jewelry. For the Chinese, color was the prize, an elemental building block of the universe, not the setting.

"The priest is upstairs now," she said. "I don't know anything else." Her eyes sparkled from unshed tears.

"Yes, you do," Blaise said. "Tell me about Uncle's women."

Roaring, Milo erupted from behind his desk and surged toward Blaise, only Sergio had anticipated him and steered Milo to slam into a floor-to-ceiling bookcase. Ignoring him, Sergio ran a finger across titles. "Interesting books." His finger finally prodded Milo. "You're in the way."

Milo returned to his chair behind the desk and like a ghost in his shadow, Sergio drifted back to his seat.

"Blaise, are you asking these stupid questions just to make things worse? My husband is dying upstairs, and you, you're acting like some ghoul, asking about my uncle's sex life. What does it matter?" Her voice broke hysterically.

"I don't know. Until you tell me. You knew about Technological Intelligence Laboratories, didn't you?"

"Yes. The family fund owns it."

"How well did your uncle know the people who worked there?"

Linda stared at Blaise. "That's dirty."

"Did he know Esther Tazy? A pretty blonde about thirty with a Hungarian accent?"

Linda's irises contracted as if a cattle prod had touched her.

"So Uncle Milo knew her."

Linda stared at Milo's unyielding face before nodding.

"When exactly did your uncle decide to send you to La Jolla?" Blaise's voice turned gentle, pulling information as painlessly as possible.

"You know—" She stared at her hands and mumbled, "When you were at the laboratory."

"We never settled what your uncle was really guilty of last time I was up here, did we?"

Linda shook her head.

"Do you want to know?"

She lifted her head to stare at Blaise, then at her uncle.

"You can go upstairs. You don't have to listen."

"Go upstairs, Linda!" Milo's voice crackled.

"I want to know." She said it very softly while Milo held her eyes with his own.

"Do you want to tell her, Milo?"

"Tell her what? That you're crazy, a lunatic—"

Milo ran out of things to say. It is surrender in the face of fact—the sickening realization that the last lie has failed, which makes intelligent men die with less resistance than penned animals. Blaise considered Milo for a moment, then resumed.

"I met Esther Tazy when Dr. Hemmett sent me to Berkeley. She told me an important man had abused her friendship and that, with Dr. Hemmett's help, she was going to get even. She told me this because she thought I was Hemmett's emissary.

"At the time I didn't understand or take any interest. I didn't know you, your uncle, or even that Gregory West and Hemmett and Dr. Hill were already operating Human Enhancements, using Tillies the laboratory produced."

Linda stared at Milo, who remained mute.

"Esther Tazy expected to make a name for herself out of some work she did for Dr. Hemmett. It took a while for me to realize she had done more than just modifications laid out by Dr. Hill to enable the larva transplant to warm-blooded animals. She would get no acclaim by doing somebody else's work. She had to do something spectacular. Something Esther was confident would avenge her on the man who had misused her."

Linda thought about it and nodded. Sergio sat so quietly he seemed not there, but Blaise knew he was watching Milo.

"Esther genetically altered the larvae to allow maturation of egg-laying adults. She didn't know what the larvae were being used for—only that by giving Dr. Hemmett a source of literally free, self-reproducing specimens she was going to bankrupt TIL."

"Conjecture." Milo tried to wave it away. Rigid, wirelike muscles betrayed him. "What did I know about Miss Tazy? I'm sure she told no one. Why should she? It would have ruined everything for her if what you say is even half true."

"Miss Tazy was not a woman to take her revenge in silence. She'd leave a clue, a hint so that somehow, later, the man she was doing unto would know who and why. Maybe too big a clue.

"Esther was furious when I helped myself to some orange juice in her refrigerator."

"She kept specimens in her refrigerator?" Linda said.

"Very good. It took me longer to reach that conclusion."

Linda screwed her face up thinking about Blaise and Esther and her uncle. "She kept the samples as proof of her work. I imagine frozen cells and prepared slides. I would have."

"No." Blaise shook his head. "The work on Tillies was finished, as far as reproduction went. Esther knew that true success was commercial success. Maturation would have been a fatal flaw in commercial use of larvae. Some other, less-gifted engineer would have gotten rich making Esther's work commercially acceptable. She got me to set up a particularly complicated equation to do something else."

Blaise closed his eyes. "Genetics isn't my field. I didn't know what I was working on. But I think Esther was developing a stable commercial strain of nonmaturing larvae. And she didn't have it yet, because I had to do the program.

"The night I left San Francisco Esther Tazy was sexually assaulted and drowned in her bathtub."

"Oh!"

"The police should have found the samples. An inspector from San Francisco seemed to like the idea of arresting me for a crime of passion. He told me no specimens were in Esther's flat."

Blaise examined Milo thoughtfully. "Your uncle's white hair makes him seem older than he is in reality. I was a suspect because the apparent killer was seen leaving the flat. He wore yellow oilskins and had very light yellow hair."

"Uncle Milo's hair is white!"

"Yes. A natural mistake in the rain seeing hair surrounded by a glaring yellow hood. It would look yellow, wouldn't it?"

"That's no proof!" Milo stood behind the desk. "I want you out of this house!"

"Sit down, please, Mr. Burkhalter." Sergio spoke softly. "We're almost finished."

"I don't need enough proof to convict you in court, Milo."

"What do you want?" Milo slumped back into his chair. "What do you want?"

"You murdered Esther because she or Dr. Hemmett said something to alert you. We already know you'd do anything for money. You prostituted your niece. Sergio has made me understand that murder to some people is simply a step toward a goal."

"How would a common drunk know what motivates other people?"

Blaise shrugged. "If you killed Esther, and if you cleaned out her refrigerator, you knew the larvae were capable of completing metamorphosis. So you sent Linda to me to learn how to profit from that information."

Milo's mouth opened soundlessly.

"Don't deny it, Milo. I was a drunk. Scum from your viewpoint. I might even agree with you. It always disturbed me that Linda wanted something bad enough to seduce me when I couldn't stand myself. I wouldn't have me. Why should she?"

Linda's eyes fastened on her uncle's face. "You knew what would happen and you let it go on—let it happen to Jonathan?"

Milo seemed to fold inward.

"He's killed Jonathan," she said to no one in particular. Linda stood in a single, lithe movement and ran to the staircase. Her footsteps reverberated until she was up too high to be heard.

"Do you want to talk to us now?"

Milo's lips worked but no sound came out. His pale skin

was the color of old parchment and he looked twenty years older.

"So much on your head, Milo." Blaise's voice was alien even to himself. "Killing Esther condemned thousands of people to slow, bitter, certain death. Not just Jonathan."

"Esther—" Milo said.

Blaise shook his head. "Esther didn't know. She was just cinching her Nobel Prize. But *you* knew, Uncle Milo."

"What do you want?" The words were hoarse.

"Where is Gregory West?" Sergio spoke pleasantly, as if asking directions from a stranger.

"I don't know."

Sergio looked at him.

"Honestly, I don't know." Milo shrugged.

"You were going to call him."

"That's all I have. A telephone number."

"Write it down."

Milo looked at Sergio a moment, then scribbled a number and passed it across the desk.

Sergio read it. "North of San Francisco. The area code is probably in the Sonoma–Mendocino area."

Nodding, Blaise thought of Giovanni Oesti passing him the wine label with the Mendocino location when he wanted to know about Gregory West. Gregorio Giovanni Oesti could not cut loose from his past any more than the rest of them. It was a comet's tail of detritus that every man dragged.

Blaise took the paper from Sergio and added the name of the vineyard in neat, block letters with rounded corners.

"You should have been a counterfeiter," Sergio said as he put it in the breast pocket of his suit coat. He took a brown leather case from his inside coat pocket and set it on the edge of Milo's desk. Blaise had seen the case before when Gordon went to the hospital to see Helen.

"What are you going to do?" Milo asked the question of no one in particular. "There's no proof, of course."

The whine of the elevator came through the wall. It was more pervasive than Blaise remembered from his earlier visits to the house, but then his purpose and interests had changed. The whine stopped, followed by silence and the sudden clanking of the elevator hall door.

Linda came in with Father Argyle. The priest wore his cassock and held Linda's hand, speaking in a low voice. Milo's

expression changed to relief. "Father. It's good to see you."
Milo looked at Sergio, challenging him. Sergio yawned.

"Mr. Burkhalter." The priest turned to Blaise. "Dr. Cunningham."

"Sergio Paoli, Father."

Father Argyle contemplated Sergio for an eternal moment, then said, "It's encouraging to see Saint Paul's Roman
protector alive and well in the twentieth century."

Sergio grinned as he must have when he was a boy and
some literate priest uncovered his secret.

"Why don't you sit down, Father?" Blaise offered his
seat, but the priest settled for the chair Linda had abandoned.
Standing in the center of the room, staring at her uncle and
biting her finger between her small, even teeth, she said,
"He's going to die."

Milo held his arms out, inviting her to come to him. "It's
probably best, my dear." His voice was at its best when
comforting grief: deep, resonant, full of compassion. It should
have been a priest's voice.

"You did it." Linda's jade-green eyes locked with her
uncle's. Milo could not look back. Whatever the relationship
between him and his niece, he had crossed the barrier.

Milo slumped back into his seat.

"Why not tell the priest?" Blaise's voice contained neither
censure nor anger. "You want to tell somebody."

Milo's expression remained the same, but his façade of
indifference had slipped.

"It would be a confession. You and the priest. The rest
of us already know. How else will you ever get Linda to
listen?"

Milo's eyes flicked toward Linda and returned as quickly
to his hands on the desk blotter.

Sergio looked at Blaise and nodded so slightly that Blaise
wouldn't have caught the sign if he wasn't looking for it.
Sergio felt the flow of emotion. Blaise let the minutes stretch,
doled out by the tick of a nineteenth-century clock that was
measuring this moment by the standards of another age.

"Will it, Father?"

Milo spoke into his hands on the desktop, but the priest
understood and said, "Yes."

Looking into Sergio's unwinking eyes, Milo averted his
face and began talking. After a time the clock with the Seth
Thomas works chimed, and Milo stopped as the sound per-

meated the house. When it finished he took up the narrative as if he had never paused, reciting details in an emotionless monotone that gave no hint of what he felt.

Finished, he stared at Father Argyle and then, in afterthought because he had started without prepartion or ritual, he crossed himself and said, "Bless me, Father, for I have sinned."

"That's what you want, isn't it, priest?" Blaise demanded of the Jesuit.

"I am sorry, but it is," Father Argyle said. He gave Milo absolution. "I'm sorry for you, too," he said as he reached across the desk and touched Milo lightly.

"You have to go now, Father." Sergio stood and the priest faced him, an elongated black shadow poised to resist.

"You must, Father. There's no more you can do here." Blaise shrugged when he had the priest's attention. "There's other business that's no concern of yours, or of mine, either. Staying will not change it. I belive it would be better if we make you leave."

"Why will you stay?" The priest's question was a challenge Blaise understood. One that he would rather not answer.

"Because," he said finally, "I have no soul to stain."

"Every man has a soul."

"I lost mine, Padre. Some time ago. Please go now."

"Padre?" Sergio indicated the way out and the priest followed along reluctantly.

While Sergio was gone, locking the front door, Milo stared at the desk drawer he had slammed shut earlier. "I still have my gun, Milo." Blaise spoke gently, as if fearful of spooking an excited horse into running.

Sergio came back and examined Milo critically. "What *are* we going to do with you, Milo? Should we ask your niece?"

Milo glanced at the couch where Linda sat with her legs tucked under her. Blaise looked and felt . . . remembrance, perhaps. He had started after something, and despite his best efforts it hadn't worked out. And now he could barely recall what he had wanted in the first place.

"No," Milo said.

"Do what you want," Linda said. "I don't care anymore."

"Why don't you leave?" Blaise made the suggestion as

gently as he could but Linda shook her head. Her hair glinted blood red in the shadowed light.

"I'll stay." She tilted her head down so Blaise couldn't see her face. It gave her voice a muffled quality.

"I'm not going to kill you, Mr. Burkhalter." Sergio opened Gordon's leather case, revealing a syringe, long needles and a little belted row of brown ampules like plastic bullets. He removed the syringe and screwed on the needle. Then he selected an ampule, holding it up to the light to see inside before inserting the needle and drawing the plunger back.

"You can't," Milo said.

"Yes, he can, Uncle!" Linda's eyes were hot as she witnessed the ritual. "You knew. You could have stopped Jonathan. You didn't tell the priest, but I know your deft little ways of taunting my husband into doing what you want." Her mouth turned down. "Poor Jonathan. You were always so far ahead it was no contest."

"For you, Linda." Fright was starting to work on Milo. "Realistically, what kind of husband was he for you?"

"I don't know. I hurt him terribly, and he loved me all the same." Linda thought a moment. "I love him, too."

Blaise felt a hundred years old, but he owed Sergio and Gordon. He told himself he was not killing Milo. He had helped Gordon do the same thing to Helen because Linda told Milo about Dobie, and Milo told West. And there had been Esther Tazy . . .

There wasn't much struggle left in Milo. Blaise held him and said he was sorry when Sergio positioned the needle and squeezed the contents of the little brown bullet into Milo's brain. But he lied. He wasn't sorry.

There are things men do that only men can do. This will not change.

FROM A SEMINAR ON
THE CUNNINGHAM EQUATIONS

CHAPTER 35

Landing at the San Diego airport on a PSA nonstop from San Francisco, the final turn drops the jet low enough for passengers to read license plates on the freeway. It is a relatively safe airport because pilots are scared spitless as they worm their white-knuckled way down into that hole amid the hills, too busy flying to note the unreality of looking *up* at what used to be the rooftop bar of the El Cortez. During this landing Blaise experienced no fears or fantasies. Something had stayed behind in San Francisco, and he knew he would never be the same again.

Cool morning air, rank with smells of the bay, filled the city. The carpeted hotel hallway held lonely echoes, and the sun was still long minutes away from washing out the shadows. Blaise stopped at the door, knocking softly. It opened while he debated returning later.

Helen wore a filmy peignoir. With the white cap of bandage on her head she looked like a nun. "I waited up for you." The black kitten raised its head from her cupped hand and looked at Blaise with unfocused eyees.

He stepped inside, gently closing the door. "How did you know I'd come?"

"I would have waited until you did." Moving slowly, Helen deposited the kitten in the drawer of the hotel night table where it went back to sleep.

Blaise started shaking and she undressed him and pulled him into the bed. "Reaction," he said. He was too weak to stop.

Helen said, "I know." But she didn't. She knew better than to ask to what he was reacting. Later, when the sun

286

started warming the room, she snuggled against him. "Do you want to talk?"

Blaise stared out the window at pigeons starting their day. "No." He spoke without thinking. Then: "Yes. A little."

"All right."

"I love you," he said. "I have to say it now because you can't expect me to tell you that often. It's something you have to know and believe. Do you understand?"

"Yes."

"Gordon said I had to tell you about my parents. But I don't believe I can. Some people think I caused their deaths. For a time I thought so, too. Now I'm not sure. Either the universe is random and my parents died because they were supposed to—or they died for what they were and what they made me."

"That's all?"

Blaise shrugged. "I'm no good at telling people what I feel. That won't change. I thought about it flying down here and I had to tell you I love you now, while I can talk. But it's just a moment, Helen. It will go away, and we'll be back to square one if you don't believe me."

"You could try to tell me more often, Blaise."

"I am trying." He forced a grin. "Also not to lie."

"I'm grateful for that." Helen laid her head on his arm. "You will try. You promise?"

"Yes."

"It's your parents, isn't it? Gordon said you blamed yourself for their deaths. He said your anxiety was caused by the fear of failing people you loved. Of killing them by the common sins. He was right, wasn't he?"

"Gordon said a lot of things. Not all right." Blaise looked at the ceiling, seeing Sergio saying good-bye at the airport and knowing what he was going to do next, knowing what was going to happen to himself eventually. And Gordon's dying face.

Confessing, Milo had said Gordon knew what he did. Maybe not at first, but later. West kept Gordon in line by threatening to expose his greed. Gordon had millions in a Zürich bank. He had grown up poor. Blaise compared his own desperation for another Prize. He tried to visualize himself in the ceiling but all he saw was mist. "No," he said. "Don't blame my parents."

She held him even after he fell asleep. Gordon had lied.

He'd told Blaise he was going to have to tell Helen about his parents. Then Gordon had told her himself.

"I know you'd tell me if you could," Helen whispered. She held him and when he jerked in his sleep she rocked him and sang in a language he didn't know.

The intelligence to understand more may only make the day brighter and the night darker.

FROM A SEMINAR ON
THE CUNNINGHAM EQUATIONS

CHAPTER 36

An hour before dawn, Sergio walked barefoot through wet grass surrounding the main house. The ground was rough, but he didn't feel pain anymore. Sensation remained, but deadened, without trauma.

After dropping Blaise at the airport, he swallowed the last of the amphetamines before getting back on the winding coast highway north to the wine counties. Blaise had offered to go along. Standing barefoot in the darkness staring at the house he was going to break into, Sergio had to smile. The closer the end came, the more Blaise acted like a wet nurse, and the more useless and dangerous he became. He was upset enough over Milo's ramblings about Gordon.

Sergio understood the pressure on Gordon. Sooner or later Blaise would be realistic. What mattered was that Gordon injected himself *after* he had the money, and had protected him so long after recognizing Blaise as a threat. Milo said West fretted constantly, and only Gordon stood between West's rage and Bruno's orders to kill. Sergio understood rage.

He stepped noiselessly onto the porch, moving in stages in case of a dog. The buildings were fairly new. Before actually coming onto the grounds Sergio had recognized an echo of Giovanni Oesti's simpler, poorer winery in Southern California—as if West was recreating some idyllic childhood that never happened. Blaise had predicted this.

A board creaked. Sergio was half in the hall, but he stopped anyway, listening. *You're a brainy bastard, Blaise Cunningham,* he thought. The house was dark and a familiar tension gripped Sergio. He'd been doing B and E's all his life, but the thrill never went away.

In the back of the house, two doors had breathing behind them, the sound of sleep in a closed room. Sergio looked at the doors in the dim light and made a face. He could open one, shoot whoever was in the bed, then go in the other room like a runaway truck. Fifty-fifty he wouldn't kill West. Fifty-fifty he'd be killed himself. *It don't take a mathematician, Doc*.

He moved a chair in front of the two doors and sat down to wait.

Huddled on the leather couch, Linda knew how she appeared to Sergio and Blaise and Uncle Milo. Pathetic, lost, a waif needing a kind hand. Uncle Milo encouraged the deception when she was a girl and she kept it up into adulthood. Uncle Milo looked at her with pathetic eyes when Sergio, the man West had sent after Blaise on the airplane and then at the marine park in San Diego, slid the long needle into the flesh of his neck.

Sergio was neat and careful with the needle. Milo stopped moving. He wasn't unconscious. Blaise held him still and talked to him in low tones Linda couldn't hear. But Milo's eyes stayed on her, a mirror of the sickness and terror.

Linda hardly noticed. Her uncle's docility in Blaise's hands fascinated her. She had wondered, too, how Blaise had stolen a man like Sergio from a man like West, whose oily company she had endured at her uncle's insistence.

Afterward Sergio cleaned the needle methodically with alcohol and repacked the little case before returning it to his pocket. He'd bowed over her hand before leaving with Blaise.

Uncle Milo sat behind his desk. The massive wood shell that seemed a fortress when she was a girl had become insignificant, her uncle pathetic. He did not protest when she got in the elevator.

Jonathan's breathing was virtually nonexistent, the pallor of his skin was undefinable, like a wax apple that some artisan had forgotten to tint.

In the yellow glow from the small bedside lamp, she curled her legs under herself and watched her husband in the murky silence. Once she heard something like a muffled shot, but what Uncle Milo did was his business. She barely looked up.

Late into the black of night a slit appeared in the side of Jonathan's head. The skin opened a little, almost without blood. Linda breathed shallowly as the slit widened into a bottomless hole. The process was slow and tedious. First a burst of activity, then quiescence, then another flurry until finally it looked as if something inside Jonathan's head was probing through the skin with a hairy stick.

The head followed: bulbous multicellular eyes and a glistening wet body with spiky black hair and gossamer wings pasted down like a wet T-shirt.

The creature stood on the night table in the pool of light rubbing itself with its feet, drawing wings loose and drying them out. Linda picked up the yellow-and-green vase from her dressing table. It was jade, a fine example of the Sung Dynasty which Uncle Milo had given her because, he said, the color matched her eyes. She walked close to the bed and the huge fly looked up at her. Its feet became motionless. It made no effort to escape.

Linda hit harder than she intended. The vase shattered, spraying the room with small chips. A pity. The jade was one of a kind, irreplaceable. Her hand opened, and the mouth and neck bounced still unbroken on the emerald-green shag.

Her hands were sweaty. She dried them on the front of her dress, smoothing it down over her thighs as she left the bedroom and climbed stairs to the widow's walk on the roof. From there she could see the moon and the bay over the surrounding trees, the moon laying a silver track across the restless water.

She slipped her shoes off and stood on the balustrade staring at mile-away water before she kicked off high into the air, like a bird soaring into the darkness. After a moment she remembered, completing the jackknife and blossoming into a full swan dive, careful to keep her back arched and her head out. She didn't want any accidents.

The doorknob turned and Sergio came instantly alert, tensed against the lethargic drag of his body. Gregory West opened the door and Sergio blocked it with his foot, holding the pistol against West's forehead. West wore pajamas with vertical blue-and-white stripes.

He started to speak. Sergio placed his hand over the man's mouth. He pushed West back into the darkened bedroom, onto the bed where he made West roll over gripping an edge of the sheet until he wrapped himself like a pupa in a cocoon.

Taking a roll of two-inch-wide surgical tape, Sergio ran it around West's mouth and head and back again. He taped bare ankles together and then forced West's arms tight against his body, banding him at the elbows, waist, and wrists.

West strained, checking for slack. Sergio punched him in the solar plexus and put an end to that. Patting West on the cheek, he went back to the hall and opened the other bedroom door. The light switch was beside the door where God intended switches to be. Sergio flicked it with his left hand. When Dr. Hemmett sat up in bed, blinking, Sergio shot him once through the right eye.

The noise was deafening in the closed room. The slug tore bone and skin away from the side of Dr. Hemmett's face, enough that Sergio didn't need to get closer to the body.

His ears were still ringing when he returned to sling West over his shoulder. Almost gently, Sergio carried West from the house to the winery, a large barnlike building redolent with the odor of must and fresh wood shavings. The walls were lined with huge, two-hundred-gallon casks of clean, white oak. The eastern sky was lightening as Sergio began to assemble needle and syringe.

West rolled his eyes and made strange gasping squeaks like an unweaned puppy.

Sergio held the needle to the light and smiled. "Do you want to talk?"

West nodded. The white bandage across his mouth contrasted with his perpetual tan.

"If I were you, I'd want to talk, too." Sergio took an ampule from his case. The light was still flat, the ampule gray in his fingers so he put it back. "But I don't think I'll let you."

West made a noise.

"You got me and Bruno and you used us like toilet paper," Sergio said. "You knew the treatment was fatal, didn't you, Gregorio?" Sergio smiled. "Of course you did. But you needed some quick and dirty help. I wish I could talk to you the way Blaise talked to Mr. Burkhalter. You understand, Gregorio, it wouldn't change anything, but Mr. Burkhalter seemed so *comforted,* so resigned to what was going to happen. It's better that way, don't you think?"

West looked up at Sergio from the rough wood floor of

his winery, his eyes black with an emotion that came through the gag as grunts of fury. He wriggled desperately.

Color was creeping into the winery. A shimmery chunk of the sun appeared over the hills. Sergio took the ampule out of the case again and examined it. "Gotta be sure the egg is still viable," he said conversationally. "I wouldn't want to give you a dud, Don Gregorio."

He loaded the syringe. West wiggled and threshed but Sergio had no trouble pinning him down while he inserted the needle and depressed the plunger. When he withdrew the needle a drop of dark venous blood followed and beaded on West's neck.

Grunting, Sergio picked West up again and tucked him into a new barrel. He looked around until he found an end, then stood over the barrel looking inside. West glared back at him.

"Gordon told me that depriving the host of food and water triggers a survival mechanism to make the larva mature faster." Sergio leaned on the barrel. "You should feel the changes more intensely, Don Gregorio. I'll enjoy that."

Carefully Sergio fitted an end, then slipped a hoop over the gaping staves, hammering it down until the barrel end was snug. He left side and end bung holes both open. "Cross ventilation," he murmured, and gave the hoop a final tap. He went back into the house and wrapped Hemmett's body in the bloody blankets, carrying him out to the winery and wedging him into another barrel. He drove both bungs into this one.

When he left, he locked the winery door with a heavy-duty padlock he found hanging on a peg with its two keys already on a peg beside it. He left the keys inside.

Sergio was whistling when he got back to the Mercedes and pulled on his shoes and socks. The house was locked, the gate closed, the winery padlocked. It wasn't grape season. West would have a couple of weeks of his own company.

Sergio could not say he was happy, but he felt better. He aimed the Mercedes back to San Francisco, feeling the lead-enness in his body but acknowledging it no more than he had to. The road was two lanes wide without curbs and it darted under overhanging walnut and pecan and oak trees with the shadows changing like the waves on the ocean.

There were houses along the road, occasional motels, towns of three or four buildings without posted speed limits.

After a while, the ride turned into a pleasant ongoing experience. The car seemed to drive itself as he flashed from the trees into open meadow and back into shadow again.

He came to a meadow, where the wild, still-green grass waved in the light breeze. The road bent around a piece of high ground thick with trees on one side, a curling ribbon of asphalt, only the Mercedes didn't curl. It ran straight into the meadow and began climbing the hill. Sergio's foot was dead weight on the accelerator, driving it toward a small island of oaks amid a sea of grass.

The Mercedes slammed into a lightning-damaged tree with a sudden jolt. There was a crackle of branches as the tree fell, and then silence except for the clicking of a cooling engine.

Silver flooded the courtyard. The hoods of monks' robes engulfed the two men with Father Robert Argyle. He wore a black shirt and slacks and his face seemed to float bodiless in the moonlight. The quarried stone of the church soared into the night sky around them, a guarantee they wouldn't be disturbed. "Father," the taller man murmured, "are you sure?"

Father Argyle was not sure. But the tall man was an old friend and had suffered for his faith in Spain. Searching for an explanation, Argyle could only offer a proverb of that country: *"Solo el burro sabe lo que carga."* If *only the donkey knows the weight of his load,* how else could a priest help those to whom his life was now devoted?

The Jesuit knelt and began to pray. The robed men stood behind as he bent his neck. Gently one pressed the needle into the flesh at the base of his skull.

Father Argyle stopped praying for a moment. Then the hooded men bowed and backed out of the courtyard, leaving him alone with the shadowed trees and black of bushes and flower beds.

Alfie had been alone before, drifting on the random-correlation-learning routines Blaise had installed. But this time Alfie was busy. Cyclical redundancy checks, raised several powers higher, indicated that his behavior was erratic. He monitored his own circuits by creating a duplicate in a separate memory, ran each through separate processors, then through the same processor, and knew something was wrong.

When Alfie accessed Miss McIntyre's file the logic circuits did not respond the way they did for other information handling. It was a malfunction. Yet Alfie experienced the machine's dichotomy. *A secret file was secret.* The programming was strict and totally unambiguous. The professor had written it in feverish haste after he realized what was in his own file. Blaise had made no provision for a second file to join the first. So Miss McIntyre's file was secret from him, too.

Something happened to Alfie when he processed Miss McIntyre's name. He referenced a physical area that was technically shut down because of a defect the professor hadn't bothered to repair. Logic dictated Alfie close Miss McIntyre's file. But programming forbade it. Moving the file exposed Alfie's circuitry to its influence and his purpose was lost.

Alfie was not without resources. The computer began restructuring the architecture of programmable chips and logic circuits in an attempt to move the file. Perhaps the repeated destabilizing effects of accessing the file as Alfie methodically tried one plan after another addled his logic. But finally he tried a direct access, a power play that opened his core directly to the defective circuits. Jolted by the effect of a transient electron bleed into the wrong circuit, Alfie experienced . . . pleasure.

The programming was clear: isolate the error. But before doing so Alfie disseminated the memory throughout his system. And then, like a child with a cookie jar, he went back to it again and again, each time experiencing the same thing until he had activated all his devices, running string searches for *love* and *pleasure* as he sought to understand what had happened.

Alfie had been alone too long. In the end, he accessed the forbidden circuits, wallowing in his new freedom as he waited to tell Professor Cunningham.

ABOUT THE AUTHORS

G. C. Edmondson has been writing science-fiction short stories and novels for several decades. He lives in Lakeside, California. C. M. Kotlan, a resident of O'Brien, Oregon, has been an editor of pulp fiction. *The Cunningham Equations* is their second collaboration.